I0594745

DARK Angel

BOOK TWO OF THE GIVEN TRILOGY

MICKEY MARTIN

Copyright © 2020 Mickey Martin

First published in Australia in 2020
by Making Magic Happen Academy

www.makingmagichappenacademy.com
www.karenmcdermott.com.au

All rights reserved. No part of this book may be used or reproduced by any means, graphic, electronic, or mechanical, including photocopying, recording, taping or by any information storage retrieval system without the written permission of the copyright owner except in the case of brief quotations embodied in critical articles and reviews.

This is a work of fiction. Names, characters, businesses, places, events and incidents are either the products of the author's imagination or used in a fictitious manner. Any resemblance to actual persons, living or dead, or actual events is purely coincidental.

National Library of Australia Cataloguing-in-Publication data:
Dark Angel/Making Magic Happen Academy

ISBN: (sc) 978-0-6487887-5-1
ISBN: (e) 978-0-6487887-6-8

Other titles by Mickey Martin

THE GIVEN TRILOGY:

Book 1: The Given
Book 2: Dark Angel
Book 3: The Guardian

Writing as Michelle Weitering
Thirteen and Underwater

This book is dedicated to every single person around the globe, who spend their time and energy, protecting and helping the wonderful innocent creatures that live beside us on our planet, that simply want to be loved and treated with kindness.

To my most beloved furry, winged and scaled critters that give me so much comfort and love every single day; Koonie, Nala, Summer, Fish and Canaries... I thank you dearly for your selfless love and comfort you bring me and mine.

Kindness is a language barrier which the deaf can hear and the blind can see.

- Mark Twain.

Acknowledgements

2019 has been the most challenging, amazing, fun-filled, goal-kicking, dream-chasing and dream-catching year, I have ever had. And none of it would have been possible, without some absolutely beautiful supportive souls I am so very blessed to have in this life.

Like all of us at times, I'm sure I'm not alone in wondering, how the hell I got to be so bloody lucky. I take it, and no one for granted.

To my three men; Jade, Jesse and Zane. There's no need for words. I think you will be surprised and appreciate this, as I know I drive you all nuts with my constant chatter.

To Karen Mc Dermott, who is not just my publisher, but a very dear soul-friend, who has the magical ability to help those shine further than they may have thought possible, by simply believing that anything can happen if you put your mind to it. Sharing laughter, tears, and momentous occasions with you the past 12 months, has been absolute therapy for my soul. Thank you. Can't wait for the next exciting episodes. Bring on 2020 and beyond.

To my partner in harmless-crime, Leah Martin. I love you dearly and it was the best thing for us, to spend those beautiful weeks in Ireland together. Can't wait to do it all again, my dear sister.

To Carolyn Wren, for lending me her expertise and knowledge in helping me become a better writer. Who knew you didn't need, 1500 exclamation points, in a 400 page novel to make a point! Carolyn, your heart is as warm as your smile, and getting to know you in Ireland was a joy. I look forward to our next adventure.

To all those creative souls that give my heart such joy. You guys make every celebration that much brighter when we get together, the diverse conversations from gardening, politics, parenthood, poetry about a bus, writers days that turn into 'solving the worlds problems' well into the night, over a bottle or two of bubbles, or pots of tea. You've all come into my life at different stages, and each of you mean the world to me. I appreciate you heartily.

In no particular order: Louise Manna, Sally Taylor, Susan Wakefield, Stuart Frazer, Adam Wallace, my Crom Castle Clan and fellow writers from the Peninsula Writers Club. Thanks for being you, and supporting me in all I do.

CHAPTER 1

Two months enduring Damon's absence had left Lilliana walking through quicksand, in a repetitive funk that was disturbing and lacking.

She hadn't realised that he had been the 'hit' she needed every day, that motivated her and kept her going, striving to be the best she could be in all she endeavoured.

That hit was now gone, and she felt it every day like a hole in her chest.

Sitting in Psych class, thinking that once her shift was over, she'd skip tea and go and spend some time with Beast, Damon's beloved black stallion.

She felt a tap on her arm. Allie passed her a note.

It read, 'Want to have a midnight swim?'

Lilliana glanced over at her petite, pretty friend. Her once short, spiky blue hair had grown out, and now sat in blue layers around her face. Her personality made up for her small size.

She smiled, nodding yes. That may be just what she needed.

As busy as they had all been lately, her friends made the effort to take it in turns every day, to have at least an hour with Lilliana, since

Damon had left.

They were all concerned about her. Skipping meals, spending time with Damon's horse, or working back to back shifts.

She'd lost weight and wasn't getting enough sleep. She was starting to look like a wraith.

Just the thought of facing breakfast without Damon at the head of the table or standing near the buffet having coffee before a ride, was hard enough.

That knowledge alone, that she would not see him this day or the next, devastated her.

She'd missed out on a few breakfasts and had passed out on two morning runs.

Cam had made it clear he had not been happy with her lack of self-care, as Damon had left him in charge, not only to run the establishment smoothly whilst he was away undercover, but also to look after Lilliana.

Once class was dismissed, Allie stood out in the corridor waiting for Lilliana.

"I've got a double in the Psych ward with Dr Richard." She rolled her eyes. "Anyway, a message from Christopher, if he doesn't see you at dinner tonight he's going to report you to Cam." Allie held up a hand, silencing Lilliana's coming protest. "You need to eat missy, end of story." Allie hugged her friend's shoulders, then looking her dead in the eye said. "You're doing great. You just need to do better, for you, okay?"

"Thanks Allie." Lilliana forced a smile.

Her friend could see the effort it took for her to put on a happy face and was determined to have the old Lilliana back, within the side of this week.

"Later." Allie waved and headed towards two hours of practical.

Lilliana headed off to her bedroom to get changed for her hospital shift. Heading down the corridor, a ruckus ahead caught her attention. The hallway was packed with Given of all ages, and a group of six disgruntled boys stood in the middle of the crowd, all totally naked.

They had painted themselves white.

They were protesting that once they entered this establishment all their own identity was taken away.

There were four Team Leaders trying to talk them into hitting the showers and seeing their group counsellor to discuss how they felt, without upsetting the other Givens schedules.

Lilliana's eyes met her Team Leader, Marcus's, across the sea of heads and returned his smile, shaking her head at the rebellious newcomers.

Once she got past the crowd, she dashed upstairs into her room.

As the door slid shut behind her she glanced at her desk on her way to her wardrobe. Joining her two photographs were two new frames that were not there this morning.

There was the photograph of herself, Jessica and Josephine that had been taken on her sixteenth birthday the day she had entered main house from the hospital ward, and a photograph of herself and Allie on their horses.

The two new pictures did two separate things to her.

One, a photograph taken by Tim, a world-renowned photographer, was of herself and Josephine all dressed up and gorgeous, laughing in a mirrored room with fifty silver doves flying around them. Seeing it instantly made her happy.

The other photograph made her empty ache plummet to a new level. She grabbed it and stared at the most handsome man she'd ever seen in her life. And his hands were all over her.

It was a photo shoot she had done with Damon and Beast.

She looked tall and elegant. Mature and so feminine. What you could see of her anyway. Most of her was covered up by those broad, strong shoulders and back, masculine hands. That handsome head bent to hers.

She sighed, running her finger over the glass.

Placing it down, she noticed a small note that had been left on the desktop.

It read, 'Enjoy your memories, Sweet Angel' – Cam xx.

She smiled and shook herself out of her dark thoughts.

Quickly dressing and tying back her long black hair, she primed herself for positive thoughts and caring intentions as she headed downstairs, underground, for her shift at the hospital.

***

Lilliana had not intended skipping dinner but due to a stressful few hours working overtime, she hadn't had an option. It had been horrendously emotional for the team that was on the ward.

Nurse Billy had been attacked by a deranged twenty-nine-year old male patient, Lorenzo, who had only just arrived.

He had deep burns along one side of his face, chest and arms.

With him had been his fifteen-year old son, also burnt and in a critical condition.

Lilliana had been treating the boy with Nurse Rachael, Dr Ryan and Leon.

It was a tough couple of hours, but once they got the boy settled and comfortable with enough pain relief, Rachael went to assist another patient who had been brought in, whilst Dr Ryan and Leon went in to see a patient who needed surgery later that night.

Whilst Lilliana's patient was fast asleep she was taking care of some of the deeper burn, without causing his body too much added stress. His sleepy eyes flickered open at one stage, moaning something about his mother.

She increased his pain-free-serum before stroking a part of his hair where it hadn't singed against his forehead, whispering that it would all be okay.

He eventually drifted back off to sleep when she heard screaming out in the hallway, as the security alarm sounded.

Checking the boy was deeply under sedation; Lilliana stepped into the hallway, to a sight she wouldn't forget for weeks.

Lorenzo, half crazed and naked, his burnt flesh looked bloody, angry, and so very painful.

He was marching along the corridor, looking inside every room as he went, a bloodied surgical knife held in his hand.

Lilliana knew instinctively that he was searching for his son.

In the distance, she could see Billy come out of the room Lorenzo had been placed in. He was pale, and blood was flowing from a wound along his side, seeping through his white shirt.

Oh no, Lilliana thought to herself. She ducked back into the room, trying to think fast. She could not put the boy down the waste or laundry chute. It was her first thought.

There was nowhere else to hide him. She spun around to shut the door and practically walked into Lorenzo. She held up her hands, standing between father and son.

"Lorenzo, calm down this will not help either of you." Lilliana talked quietly, the way she would to Beast or the other stallions if they were in a fit of a mood.

"Girly, get out of my way, or I will end you." He stood staring at her.

She nodded, letting him know she was taking in what he was saying. Security should be here any moment.

Leon burst through the door, freezing when he saw how close Lilliana was to Lorenzo.

Of course, she would be standing between danger and an innocent.

"Hey Lorenzo, this isn't helping you or your boy, put the blade down and we can get you whatever it is you need," His voice firm, yet calm.

Lilliana briefly thought how proud she was whenever a situation arose in the hospital. Leon was always calm and in control.

"What I need," Lorenzo turned to face Leon, "is for you all to get the *fuck out of my way* and I can finish what I started!"

Lilliana walked backwards, to the tray of needles and surgical equipment. Whilst Leon was letting Lorenzo know everything was going to be alright, Lilliana grabbed a syringe full of 'Knock-Out' serum.

As Lorenzo lunged at Leon, slicing a deep cut into his arm, Lilliana rushed at the angry, dangerous man and slammed the syringe into his neck.

She got half of the serum into him before he swung around with his fist and slammed it against the side of her head.

Lilliana saw stars, but amazingly, managed to stay upright.

Leon had advanced on Lorenzo, as Lilliana struggled to get over to the boy and stand in front of him.

Lorenzo spun away from Leon and was advancing on Lilliana as Security ran through the door, Lorenzo threw himself onto Lilliana thrusting the blade into her stomach.

As she collapsed, he plunged the knife into his son's heart and was about to slash his own throat, when security zapped him with an electric prod.

He fell hard on top of Lilliana.

The room erupted into organized chaos as Rachael and Dr Ryan entered with a handful of nursing staff.

Orders were yelled out and followed.

Cam was buzzed and arrived as Lilliana was taken into surgery.

Leon and Billy were seen to by the nurses, and were medicated in record time, before being told to stay put, and rest.

Both the young men were exhausted and devastated by the waste of life.

***

Twenty-four hours later and feeling like she'd been run over by a stampede of horses, Lilliana opened her eyes to a room full of sweet-smelling roses and pastel coloured Lilies.

A soft voice was reading to her about genetic breeds of bulbs and seedlings.

Josephine. A tear leaked from Lilliana's eyes, but she realized it was a happy tear.

To have her ever-reliable friend always be exactly where she was needed. It was like the angels spoke to her and guided her towards her friends in their time of need.

"Hey Lilly," Josephine placed the book on the table and reached for a glass of water with a straw. "I bet you're thirsty."

Lilliana nodded, allowing Josephine to place the straw in her mouth.

Josephine's big warm brown eyes smiled down at Lilliana as she watched her drink half the cup of water.

Lilliana nodded, letting her know she'd had enough.

Josephine put the glass on the table and then turned to face her friend. "How do you feel darling?"

"I'm not sure yet." Lilliana rubbed a hand over her face. "Spaced out."

"Yeah, that's the pain meds." Josephine brushed the hair away from her friend's pale face.

"How long have I been out?"

"Just for a day. Dr Ryan kept you under for healing, but it looks good." She leaned over and gently lifted her top up.

Lilliana was happy to see a small white line where her skin had been pulled back together with stitching serum. She placed her hand gently on the wound, before pressing lightly, relieved to find it wasn't unbearably painful.

"Hey, not the patients' job to do the inspection." Leon's happy voice called from the doorway.

Lilliana smiled at him, as he walked towards her.

"How's your arm Leon?"

"It's fine, how do you feel?" He gently removed her hand, to place his own on her stomach, and ran his fingers ever so lightly across her scar.

She shivered, as his long, thin fingers tickled her flesh. She was not used to having anyone touch her. She stopped her thought flow heading to the last man that had touched her and tried to concentrate on what Leon was saying.

"It will be tender for a week, but due to Dr Ryan's spectacular surgery skills, all your bits and marvellous pieces are intact." He smiled down at her.

"Thank you. I'm sorry I wasn't any more help with the Lorenzo situation. Is his son okay?"

Leon's smile faded. Josephine sat on the chair waiting.

"No unfortunately. Once Lorenzo stabbed you, he stabbed his son who died instantly. He tried to kill himself, but security got there in time. Cam has placed him in Black Ops."

"Oh." Lilliana said quietly.

"But enough of that, I have had instructions that once you wake, I'm to get you set up in your room. How does that sound?" he asked kindly.

Lilliana smiled, not quite forced. "That sounds good actually."

"Right, well let's see if your body is happy with you standing." Leon pushed the covers off her, and placed an arm behind Lilliana, sitting her forward and swung her legs over the side of the bed.

Josephine stood by, getting ready to help.

Lilliana stood, and felt fine. "Not a problem." she took a step forward.

"Great." Leon smiled.

Between Josephine and Leon, they got her down the corridor and up the hospital steps. She was exhausted and struggling, but there was no way she was going to admit that. As they came through the entrance door to the main house Cam, who was on an errand, spotted them and came to greet them.

Josephine took in his appearance. Tall, dressed in jeans and a black tee shirt, it showed off his sculptured body underneath. Hair falling over his ever-watchful eyes and a smile that could charm a snake.

He took one look at Lilliana's face, smiled at Josephine, then saying, 'excuse me' to Leon, scooped Lilliana up in his arms and smiled into her face.

"Thank you." she whispered. Those deep, beautiful eyes. Not Damon's eyes, but oh so similar. She winced, not meaning to make the sound out loud, then closed her eyes, dropping her head on Cam's shoulder.

"Okay, let's get you upstairs my friend." Josephine said.

"Thanks Leon. I'll speak to you soon." Cam smiled.

"No worries Sir." Leon squeezed Lilliana's arm, said bye to Josephine, as he turned and went back to his shift.

Once Cam had placed Lilliana in her bed, he sat on the side holding her hand.

"Leon or Rachael will come back to check on you in a couple of hours. I was going to set you up for a girls night, but for the time being I think sleep is on the menu."

"I think I'll go down to the kitchen and see if Cook has some soup, or a salad sandwich." Josephine said, watching the way Cam's hand was gently holding Lilliana's.

He turned to face her. Her beautiful brown curls were hanging below her shoulders. She was wearing a short white skirt and a bright blue top with a sunflower on it, reading 'flower-power'. Bright blue gumboots tied her outfit together

Smashing, he thought, dedicated. Where the hell did she come from?

He'd known her since she was two years old. He'd been seven.

He'd always had fun teasing her, watching her mostly from a distance as they'd gotten older. Damon considered her a sister. Cam never had.

"That's a good idea Josephine, once you've put the order in, could you pop into my office for five minutes?"

She raised her eyebrow, hand on hip. "I suppose so, I do have an urgent order that Rupert's team need me to fill, but sure. Five minutes."

"Why, thank you." Cam said, not quite sarcastically.

"I'll see you soon Lilly, rest up." She smiled at her friend.

"Thanks Jose." Lilliana waved as she looked at Cam who was watching Josephine walk out of the room.

She knew that look well. She'd felt it on her own face often enough whenever she'd looked at his brother.

Cam turned to face her and seeing her expression, smiled. "What's up Tiger Lilly?"

"I think you know the answer to that Sir," she smiled. "I really think I need to sleep." She closed her eyes.

"I'm so happy you're alright. You had us worried." Cam let go her hand and tucked the blanket around her.

"There's just so much to deal with, running this place on a day to day basis. I don't know how he made it look so effortless?" Cam ran his hand through his hair.

Her eyes popped open as soon as 'he' was mentioned. "Have you heard from him?"

His eyes met hers, could see the desperation in them and sighed.

"Lilliana, you have to forget about Damon for the moment. Focus on your studies, your work. I know it's hard." He reached for her hand as she made to protest.

"I know it's hard," he repeated, "but let's concentrate on getting you eating properly. You've lost too much weight. Let's get you healthy. I have a photo shoot planned for you soon, but not till you put on some decent weight, okay? You are not cut out for skinny."

She nodded, feeling her throat close over as the talk of Damon made her miss him all the more.

She forced a smile. "Yes Sir."

He stood. "That's my girl, now, sleep."

He watched her a few minutes longer, till her breathing regulated and he was sure she was asleep.

Then he went downstairs to deal with another matter.

***

Cam was just hanging up the phone when Josephine breezed into his office.

"Five minutes, I'm running late." The door shut behind her. Her eyes met his across the room.

He stood and walked around the front of the desk then leaned back against it and folded his arms.

"Josephine."

"Sir?" She placed her hands on her hips, waiting.

"Come here." He said softly.

A stirring started in her belly. Just watching him, all manly like and tired.

She'd never seen him this way. Ruffled, exhausted. Responsible?

His hair was dishevelled, his eyes deeper in colour, due to lack of sleep.

He looked like he'd just tumbled out of bed.

He can tumble out of my bed, she thought to herself.

He placed his hands on the desk beside him. "Look," he started to say. "I don't know what it is about you lately, but I can't stop thinking about you. I want you."

Josephine smiled. "You've wanted me for ages, actually Sir." She raised an eyebrow.

"Really? Yes, I guess you're right there. What's changed?"

"The fact is," She started walking slowly towards him, "that now, I want you too."

She was halfway toward him, and in two strides, he lifted her up, her legs wrapped around his hips, whilst his hands supported her back.

Their eyes searched the others before dropping to each other's lips, breaths held, pausing for a split second, before mouths met in a generous battle of lips sliding, tongues thrashing, teeth clicking.

It was almost violent, but happily so.

Josephine could not keep still.

Rubbing against him, she greedily slid her hands up his shirt, desperate for her skin to slide over his.

His hands moved in her hair, moaning her name.

He walked forward till his knees hit the couch and bending, dropped her down before laying against her.

She was wrestling with her top, trying to get it off.

He stilled her hands, smiling into her eyes, then clutched her top and pulled it from her body.

His eyes roamed over her breasts, standing to attention, bra free, perky nipples begging to be sucked.

Her hands stroked his back, her eyes, smiling into his.

They were both almost breathless.

"Do it." she whispered. "Whatever you want."

His head bent and licked a rosy nipple, circling his tongue around the wet peak, before he sucked it, pulling it into his mouth.

She gasped, throwing her head back, her hips pumping forward. She was searching for something; she just wasn't sure what it was, but her body was deliciously on fire.

She felt his hand on her thigh, strong fingers moving forward, slipping into her cotton knickers.

His head rose from her breast, looking deeply into her eyes, as his fingers gently stroked inside her warmth.

He was waiting for a denial. It didn't come.

He pushed a finger inside her, not deeply, but enough to feel her wetness. It slid over his fingers, making him gasp.

Her eyes closed as she pushed her hips towards him.

"Don't stop," she whispered. "Please don't stop."

He said against her ear, making her shiver. "I won't stop baby, unless you tell me to." Then his mouth slid over hers, as his fingers slid over her throbbing bud, rubbing the wetness over her, faster, softer, harder, until she screamed into his mouth, orgasming hard and fast.

She could not suppress the giggle that exploded from her.

He leaned up, running his fingers over her stomach, an eyebrow raised.

"Oh my god, I'm sorry. It's just that that has been a fantasy of mine for a good year." She smiled at him.

His hand slipped over her waist, between her legs, he cupped her, watching her eyes cloud over. He whispered against her lips, "Well, we'll see what fantasy I can help you out with next time?" He fixed up her knickers, pulled down her skirt, and then stepping up, he reached for her hands and pulled her to her feet.

His hands stroked her breast as he pulled her tee shirt back down, pulling her against him, kissing her, hard.

Her hand ran down the front of his chest, working its way to the crotch of his jeans.

He pulled away and grabbed her wrist, shaking his head, kissed her again and whispered, "Looks like my five minutes are up."

Josephine blew out a breath, reeling with what just happened. "Well then Sir, until next time." She smiled prettily, turned on her heel and left the room.

"Until next time indeed." Cam said quietly.

When the door shut behind her, he plonked down on the couch.

Bloody hell! Damon would kill him.

***

Hours later, Josephine was filling Lilliana in about her visit with Cam.

Lilliana's mouth dropped open, a smile spreading across her face.

"In the main office, on Damon's couch?"

"Yep, I just let him ravish the hell out of me! It was brilliant, my god Lilliana, I didn't want him to stop." She plonked down on the end of the bed and covered her face laughing.

Lilliana chuckled and bent forward to hug her friend but gasped as her stomach protested.

"Hey, careful." Josephine reached across and hugged her friend.

They both chuckled. Lilliana shook her head. "Anyone could have walked in, imagine Dr Richard's face, if he found Cam all over you!"

Josephine squealed at the thought, "Not nice to ruin my happy thoughts."

Lilliana sighed and fell back against her pillows.

"I'm so happy for you Jose. If anyone deserves it, you do." She smiled at her friend, reaching for her hand.

Josephine blew out a breath. "I can't believe he has been sitting under my nose all this time, all those years I thought he was an unsavoury individual, and now I don't want to keep my hands off him."

"It is just meant to be. Fate, Karma, whatever you want to call it. You know about his condition, right?" Lilliana asked.

"What condition, that he used to sleep with anything that walked? Yeah, he's a nymphomaniac."

Lilliana smiled. "That terminology is for a female. What Cam has is termed Satyriasis."

"Okay Doc, please explain that entire term to me so I can understand." Josephine leaned back on the bed.

"It's a neurotic condition, symptoms of which are a compulsion to have sexual intercourse with as many women as possible. Usually these men have an inability to have lasting relationships."

Josephine nodded. "I always knew he had something going on. I mean, the man has always had a huge appetite for the female population. How did you know this?"

"Cam volunteered his story with us as a case study in class. He has been receiving new treatment the past eight months, with rewarding results."

"So, I can rest assured he isn't going to go all, un-neutered alley cat on me?"

Lilliana laughed at her friend's description of Cam. "Yes, rest assured, so far, so good."

"What do you think the girls will say?" Josephine asked.

"Well, I think Allie will be ecstatic and Jessica will tell you to be careful."

"And all is how it should be." Josephine smiled, standing. "You get some rest. Christopher is doing you something sensational for supper. I'll see you later."

She kissed the top of Lilliana's head, as her friend nodded and drifted back to sleep.

CHAPTER 2

Christmas came and went in a busy blur, and as the months flew by, their routines became increasingly ordered, almost to a military standard.

Josephine had been given more responsibility in Rupert's team, in the Horticultural Department- H.D, and was now in charge of completing orders and organising deliveries of seedlings, plants, fruits and vegetables to the Given cargo plane, to be delivered to other parts of the country.

Rupert had developed a new range of seedlings that were going out to five major cities around the world and was very impressed with himself, along with the scientists who had been working with him.

Orlando and Jessica were six months away from becoming Team Leaders for their very first group and the head Team Leaders were very impressed with their maturity and no-nonsense of breaking house rules.

Both Allie and Lilliana had been given less demanding, supervised cases in the hospital, to ease their way into feeling out their roles.

Assessing any new Given, then deciding if they were to go to the main house, or to the Psych Ward, after their initial month's assessments.

They both spent many extra hours of their personal time, committing to their cases and doing the best they could for the injured souls.

Lilliana's first patient was Eddie, a fourteen-year old boy who suffered from paranoia.

He was sweet, and once calmed easy to talk to.

When he was on edge, it took a while to get him back into a normal conversation.

Lilliana didn't like to medicate her patients severely, something Dr Richard and she argued about often.

For chemical imbalances, sure, she could understand, but not in cases where hypnotherapy could help the patient in a more relaxed, peaceful way with lasting results. Allie agreed with Lilliana.

Rachael and Dr Hillary backed the girls up and enjoyed a different, fresher approach where harsh drugs were not always the last option. It made for interesting conversations in the board meetings, as the year went on. And as the year went on, things just seemed to get busier.

Allie and Lilliana had drawn up a proposal for a new office that they put forward to Cam, and the board.

It would cost quite a lot of money, but Lilliana had agreed to do a series of photo shoots that Fox was unable to do as she had prior commitments.

Due to Lilliana's lifestyle getting back on track to healthy, where working out and eating properly had her putting on a good dose of weight, which won Cam over in the end to do the photo shoot.

The space available for an added office was next door to Damon's, in the hospital section. It was extremely close to the Psych Ward and would suit both their needs.

The design was drawn over many times by Allie and Lilliana, who'd been looking at it from two points of view.

That this room would be where they would both be spending a lot of their time, needing it to provide a comfortable and safe environment for their patients, and any other Given that may come to them for help, advice or a simple chat.

It took months for Cam and a team to get the room completed, and Lilliana and Allie had spent every waking, spare minute directing and helping. It was a stunning space and the two new, young professionals, could not have been happier.

As one entered the eye was immediately drawn to a high standing tank along one wall which Lilliana had designed.

She had always loved the peaceful tranquillity of the Koi, that Damon had placed around the property, and having them here in her workspace gave her a feeling of his presence

An impressive sized Buddha sat, holding a lotus flower, which trickled water soothingly from its petals and was placed in the centre, seeming to float on the top of the water, with a black pebbled wall as the backdrop where water Lilies, and green bamboo looked striking and fresh.

In the middle if the room, where group discussions would be held, sat a varnished, glossy trunk-table, made from one of the trees that had fallen after heavy winds.

Around the table, were chairs dressed in a soft fabric, and when placed close together, sat in a perfect circle around the table. Their desks sat either end of the room. Simple, efficient, elegant. A tinted glass screen, when closed, offered the room complete soundproof and privacy from the rest of the office space.

In the corner of each office was a small step-in alcove where refreshments could be made.

Along the opposite wall of the tank was a bookcase, beautifully designed with small shelves, sitting on diamond angles, filled with many old books and box-like shelves held pretty glass bottles, candles, gems, and healing crystals.

Late one night Lilliana was sitting quietly on one of the soft chairs, sipping on a peppermint tea, watching her fish lazily swim around.

She'd been doing a bit of catch up work on the argument she'd been having with Dr Richard the past few months, an ageless argument, on Psychological versus Biological treatments.

She had just concluded a two-hour report for him for the following morning on separate patients whom she had been helping.

She felt sure he would agree with her on this, as she had been completely thorough on every single argument he may have had.

Time would only tell, she thought.

"Hey, you," a voice called from the open doorway. "what are you doing up at this ungodly hour?" Cam sauntered in and plonked on a chair, placing his feet on the table.

Lilliana looked pointedly at his feet, before turning her eyes on his.

He slowly removed his feet and smiled.

She smiled back. "I have just finished arguing with Richard, theoretically."

"Ah yes, his methods. Mm, well he is extremely old school but, that's the joy of having some fresh blood around here." He wiggled his eyebrows at her. "Keeps things entertaining in the old boring meetings hey."

Lilliana chuckled. He and Josephine were so good for each other.

Light-hearted, dedicated.

"What happened to Lorenzo in the end Cam?" She had been meaning to ask this for a while now. Life just got in the way.

"What usually happens to people after one strike?"

She nodded, not wanting to say anymore.

"He had two strikes." Cam said quietly, ending that conversation.

She placed her teacup down and looked back towards her fish.

"How are you doing?" He asked seriously. "You have been so busy the past few months. Was it everything you thought it would be?"

She pushed her hair back and smiled. "It's so many things. It's so rewarding, yet exhausting. Heartbreaking too. But the fact that I can help those that come to us," She shrugged. "I still clearly remember how I felt when I arrived. I was so numb, for so long." She shook her head at some of the memories, and quickly shut them away.

"I really love helping upstairs too. Can you believe that Eric comes to see me once a week? We can actually sit in a room and talk for an hour without any discomfort between us, and Natalie has stopped her sessions with Hillary, and she comes to see Allie." Lilliana laughed softly. "I usually sit behind my screen when those sessions are on."

"I bet you do." Cam chuckled. "I hear Clair from Black Ops came to see you last week?"

"Yes, she wanted to know if I'd consider moving to her division."

"You are very talented Lilliana you would be very useful to us there."

Lilliana froze. "You wouldn't force me, would you Cameron?"

He smiled at the full use of his name. She only ever used it on him when she was nervous. "No, no. Don't worry my angel I wouldn't force you to do anything you didn't want to. Besides, you are brilliant here."

She instantly relaxed. "Thanks."

He reached into his back pocket and passed her a small envelope. "The photos from the shoot that helped you get this place."

"Oh, I don't really know if I want to see them, doing it was bad enough." She winced taking the package.

"Relax, as always, you pulled it off and look gorgeous."

Lilliana pulled out a couple and raised an eyebrow at Cam.

"Seriously, I look like a freak."

Cam burst out laughing, "I don't think that that is an acceptable term for you to use. And you do not look like a freak."

The advertisement was for alcohol. If you drank it, you would stand out in the crowd.

The scene was set at a glamorous bar, and a naked Lilliana had been sprayed white, with green make up around her eyes, and contacts making her appear very catlike. Her lips, blood red, her jet-black hair standing out all the more in a long braid down her white, bare back.

She was holding a red bottle.

There were fifty odd red naked bodies up against her, all holding white bottles, identical in every way. The body paint on all bodies was spectacular.

She stuffed them back in the envelope and handed them to Cam. She smiled. "Whatever floats their boat. It got us this room, so I'm happy."

"You do know that Damon would have seen these pics out there in the big old world?" Cam regretted saying his brother's name, as soon as he saw the look on Lilliana's face.

Damon. He'd been gone a little over two years now.

Her face froze, her eyes glanced his way. "Oh Cam, I wonder how he is doing? I know you can't really talk about him, but please, can't you give me something?'

Cam sat up straighter. He was looking a little uncomfortable.

"Please, what can possibly shock me?" She leaned forward. Waiting.

He stood and strolled over to the fish, looking up at the Buddha.

"I love spending time in this room. May have to deck out mine and Josephine's like this. Once she commits to the move of course."

"Cam," Lilliana pushed, "whatever it is, I can handle it."

He turned to face her. This beautiful lady who had come such a long way since she'd first arrived all those years ago.

His loves dearest friend. He knew if he hurt Lilliana, in anyway, Josephine would cut her favourite appendage of hers, off him.

"As you know, it is impossible for Damon to call without blowing his cover. So, Johnson's contact, on the outside, fills Johnson in." He ran his hand through his hair.

"Damon had to become interested in a particular woman who was part of the group they suspected of being involved in the blood drug trade. He went undercover in a big way Lilly, he married her."

Lilliana stood. "What?" The thought of his hands, his lips, on some filthy whore, who imprisoned women, got them pregnant and used their babies drugged blood, as profit, sickened her.

He watched her pale. She looked like she was going to be sick.

He walked over to her and pushed her gently back down. "Look darling, under-cover is never pretty. We all do things we have to do, for the greater good."

He smoothed her hair off her face.

She looked up at him.

"He doesn't love her." He whispered.

She shook her head. "He never said he loved me." She glanced down at her fingers, clenched.

He gently popped a finger under her chin and forced her eyes to meet his. "He loves you," He said it simply. "Now, as impossible as it may be, I need you to forget about Damon, and focus on being the brilliant young therapist you are. Okay?"

"Yes Sir." She said, forcing a smile.

"One more thing, as you know when our Given first arrive, they are photographed."

Lilliana nodded. She remembered when she had first come to the Given, how shocked she had been, seeing all the horrific photographs of individuals suffering which lined the walls of the hospitals corridors.

Now, she walked past them on a day to day basis, appreciating how far some of them had come, victims no longer.

"Well, to make your people more aware that you were once, just like them, I am hanging yours and Allie's arrival portraits up outside your office in the morning. I just wanted you to know."

"That's fine." Lilliana reached for her cold tea and drained it.

"Right then, I will bid you goodnight."

"Goodnight Cam, thank you."

He waved as he left the room, the door sliding shut behind him.

She fell backwards on the seat and glanced up at the pretty light hanging from the ceiling, and let her mind reflect.

The last time she had seen him. Damon. Tired, yet remaining devastatingly handsome. His smell. His touch. His control not to step over the boundaries with her. Although he almost had. Twice.

Now, Damon was married. Doing unimaginable things to make things right, and that included marrying an evil being.

She closed her eyes, holding a fist to her forehead.

He was doing what he had to, out there.

She would do what she had to, in here.

Surely for now, that would be enough?

CHAPTER 3

Another two years passed, and although Lillian's schedule was full to the brim and never empty, she felt as if she were in limbo. Simply waiting.

It had been a beautiful Wednesday morning for an hours gallop.

Allie had taken Raven, and Lilliana decided to take Beast.

Apparently, she was the only one who had permission to take him out.

Josephine had come along and was riding Beauty, with five dogs running behind their heels.

It was glorious to be out in the open fresh air, even if it was muggy.

The smell of Jasmine hit them as they raced passed the cemetery, towards the river and into a field of gorgeous purple and white wildflowers.

Lilliana felt the rush of air over her face and glancing over at Josephine, could see her friend was enjoying the freedom as much as she was.

Rusty and Nails slowed down a while ago, but Josephine's three younger dogs kept up easily.

Lilliana pulled Beast around and gave him his head for half an hour, then cooled him off for the remaining ride.

"That was just what I needed to let out my frustrations." Josephine sighed, as she unsaddled Beauty.

"What's up girl?" Allie asked.

"Nothing's up, well not on Cam anyway. He has been that busy with meetings, phone calls and some new division he's trying to set up, plus the day to day running of this place, that when I get a chance to visit him, he's that exhausted we barely have a conversation. He asks me how I'm doing, how H.D is doing, and by the time I finish talking, he's asleep!"

"Must be the relaxing sound of your voice that puts him at ease, makes him feel all is well in the world," Lilliana said as she finished brushing Beast.

"Well, I don't mind putting him in a coma, but at this stage of our relationship, I'd rather be doing other things to him," Josephine chuckled. "Or should I say him doing other things to me!"

Allie laughed. "All good things come to those who wait my friend."

Lilliana hoped that was the case. "Alright," she called over her shoulder as she headed out, "I'm hitting the showers. I'll see you in Group Allie. Bye Jose."

"See you soon." they called out.

Lilliana bent to give Rusty and Nails a rub and smiled at Thomas, as he called the dogs in, to feed them.

Heading down the blue stone path, she waved to a group of new Given in the pool house. A few of them she was getting to know well as they attended her and Allie's group.

She worried about one young girl. She let out a deep sigh as she jogged up the steps into the house.

There were plenty of people to worry about. She could only hope that both her and Allie could do all they could do to ease some of their suffering.

"Lilliana," a voice called from the library as she dashed past. Poking her head around the corner, she saw Orlando walking towards her.

"Hi," what's up?"

"Look, I don't know how you guys run things in your groups, but I have one boy in my Team, who has a meltdown whenever he has to see Dr Richard."

Lilliana nodded, thinking she understood exactly how the young boy felt. "I see. What can I do to help?" She quickly glanced at the clock; this chat was cutting into her much-needed shower time before her rounds in Psych started.

"Could we place him in your group?"

"You'll have to run that past either Cam, Dr Richard or even Hillary. I'm not sure how either of the Doctors will take that request?" Not well, she thought.

"I don't see the point of him being in therapy if that Doctor is making him worse, do you?" He sounded frustrated.

She pushed a flyaway hair away from her face and nodded. "I agree with you Orlando, but at this stage, so early in our positions, it's not my call to make. Look, I'm so sorry, I have to go."

"No worries, thanks. Oh, a message from Jessica, catch up in the library after hours." He smiled.

"I'll see what time my shift ends but tell her I'll try. Give her a kiss for me, will you?" She waved as she headed upstairs.

"Now that," he called after her. "I can happily do."

She went up into the shower room, got undressed and stepped into a steamy shower that was pure heaven on her tired muscles and relaxed for five minutes, before the coming day's tension would surely creep back in.

***

"I think we need to do more one on ones." Lilliana relaxed her elbows onto her desk, dropping her chin onto her knuckles.

Six hours later, she had already done four hours in the Psych Ward and Allie and she had just finished a gruelling Group therapy, with Dr Richard sitting in, to do his own report on their progress.

They were handling all their cases very professionally, but also compassionately.

Which, as Dr Hillary had told them the day before in a meeting, not everyone could do without having to switch off.

As both the girls had been through so much grief, heartache and loss they had that extra depth in their hearts to give that much more sympathy, empathy and anything else they could offer some of these poor, abused souls.

Once Dr Richard had left the room, Allie walked around with a brush of sage and theatrically, cleansed the room.

Lilliana chuckled watching her. She kicked off her heels and propped her feet up on her desk

"Well, we certainly can try, if we skip say, every meal that is owed us, any free time, which is what, just about nil anyway, oh yeah, and any minute of freedom we get to rush to the loo? Yeah, let's do more one on ones my friend." Allie said sarcastically. She dropped the sage brush back into a drawer and plonked down in her chair, checking her watch.

"I mean, I've got ten minutes now to see my man, pee and then, wow, rounds in the hospital."

"Okay, okay," Lilliana laughed. "I know, I was just thinking out loud. Some of our people would benefit so much more if they had extra alone time with us."

Allie stood up, stretching her shapely arms above her head.

"We can't save them all Lilly, but we can do our very best with what we have and so far, we are doing very well. Ease up on us and yourself. Okay?"

"Okay, oh, Orlando says Jessica wanted to get us together after hours tonight for games in the library. Apparently, there is no detention rostered on in there." Lilliana stood, following Allie to the door.

"I'll have to see what time I finish my rounds, I promised Rachael I'd do a double tonight if she needed me. We are expecting a delivery of six Given for Black Ops. They're supposed to be heavily sedated on arrival. We'll see." She hugged Lilliana and turned to leave.

"By the way, excellent group today, I love the way you handle them all."

"Yeah, we make a great team. See you later." Allie waved as she headed down the corridor.

Lilliana went back to her desk, clicked on ten files to read through on today's session and was almost done when her phone rang. She tapped on the answer icon on her keyboard. "Dr Lilliana."

"Hey Doc, I was wondering if you could help me with a problem I have?"

"I can only try."

"Well, I believe I have an unsatisfied girlfriend and I was wondering what you'd suggest I could do about it."

"Only you can answer that question, unfortunately, I'm not qualified to help you in that department. Allie will be here in the morning if you need professional advice." She flicked her screen and continued reading another case.

"You're reading, aren't you?" Cam guessed.

"Yes, I have a bit to finish off before the morning," She sounded apologetic. "Although if it was important issue, you would have my full, undivided attention."

"True. Well, I'll speak to you in the morning. Good night Lilliana."

"Good night Cam." She tapped off, finished her reports and got stuck into two hours of reading and problematic solving that Hillary wanted both her and Allie to complete on several new cases before the week was out.

A knock at the door sounded and she flipped a switch near her desk, enabling the door to slide open.

Leon stood, a tray in hand, a rose in the other.

"Leon," Lilliana smiled and walked around her desk, towards the centre table. "please, come in, boy that smells good."

"Yeah." He walked in and set the large tray on the table removing the lid, revealing two dinner plates with a delicious looking roast duck and fresh vegetables.

"A little bird told me that if you don't go down to dinner you skip it entirely so I thought, we could have our meal together, as I'm on break."

He placed the cutlery beside her plate and set out their napkins, placing the rose on the table near her.

Lilliana pulled out a soft chair and sank into it, grateful for Leon's thoughtfulness.

Picking up her knife and fork, she speared a honeyed carrot and placed it in her mouth.

"Thank you. You're a life saver." She smiled.

"In more ways than one." He laughed.

"Funny too." She moaned at the deliciousness of the duck. "Is this what Christopher has cooked?"

"Apparently. He's been doing more and more lately, plus teaching. Cook has been under the weather. That guy must be at least seventy."

"He's in his fifties I think. His father worked for Mr. Night's Grandfather when he was a little boy," she took a mouthful of sweet potato curls.

Leon was watching her as he finished off his meal. He stood and walked over to her small service area and poured them both one of her herbal teas.

He placed hers in front of her, before taking his seat.

She thanked him and taking a mouthful of tea, leaned back in her chair and contently, watched the fish glide by.

The sound of the water trickling from the fountain was the only noise in the room for the next few minutes.

He watched her drink her tea. Her glossy hair pulled forward over one shoulder. Her green eyes standing out more from the lighting in the room.

Her elegant cream suit hugged all her curves, the black belt defining her waist. He had been in love with her for a good year or so.

She glanced over at him and smiled as her eyes met his.

"How has your day been?" She sipped her tea.

"Flat out." He stretched his long legs and glanced across at the Buddha.

"I love this room. You should do something like this in the hospital canteen."

Lilliana agreed. "It's paying for it that Cam will probably have a problem with. This room was not cheap by any standards."

"Yes well, you paid for it, didn't you?"

"Yes, for most of it. I think that's why I love being in here so much. It feels like mine. I even fell asleep in here the other night. These chairs make for a comfy sleep."

"I bet." He said, thinking anywhere Lilliana slept, it would be comfortable.

"I had surgery an hour ago, where I put a young girl's arm back on after it had been sliced off with a machete." He said casually.

"Oh no, the poor darling!" Lilliana was sadly shocked. She shook her head. "I hope whoever did that got the bullet."

"I'm surprised you'd say that Lilliana."

She raised an eyebrow. "Why?"

"Well, you, in your profession and all, plus you are the most sensitive person I know. Heart of gold and all that." He shrugged.

"Trust me, I'm not that precious. If I think someone's heart is that black, evil even, to do such a thing to an innocent person, they do not belong on this earth."

"What about the people you heal Lilliana?"

"The people we heal are of a complete different nature. As are all who come into our home. It's the Black Ops people who commit the crimes and are the culprits that stain our society. The rest of us were only ever the culprit due to sordid circumstances."

"Casualties first hey. Devastating circumstances indeed."

"Indeed." She agreed, running out of patience for this conversation.

Thinking about her past privately, in her own head, was one thing. Discussing it with Leon. Not going to happen.

"Leon. Thank you for dinner, I appreciate it." She started putting the plates and cutlery back onto the tray, adding their teacups to the pile.

He sighed. "Sorry, I shouldn't press your opinion on these matters."

"No, you shouldn't." She smiled to soften the ice that crept into her voice. "I get enough of that from Dr Richard."

He walked over, placing his hands on her shoulders. He looked down at her, watching her beautiful green eyes become wary.

He squeezed her shoulders, dropped a kiss on the top of her head and picking up the tray, walked towards the door.

"Goodnight Lilliana." He called over his shoulder.

"Goodnight Leon." She watched the door slide shut after he walked through it.

After giving Jessica a message of apology in regard to their night catch-up, she crossed over to the urn, poured herself another tea, and strolled over to the vaporizer and popped a calming blend on, sat down at her desk and flicking on some music got back to some reports.

She was quite happy to spend another night pouring over solid work until she was exhausted enough to sleep away the longing of seeing Damon again.

CHAPTER 4

Lilliana was sitting in Dr Clair's office in the Black Ops division, reading over a couple of file cases that Clair wanted her opinion on.

Cam had walked her up there no more than an hour ago, but it already felt like forever.

Lilliana had been tense walking down the restricted passageway with Cam. It was the first time she'd been within these walls, since Blake attacked her years ago leaving her beaten, bitten and hog tied. Not a happy memory.

She had never asked Damon what had happened to Blake and had been about to ask Cam but as they had approached the entrance a guard had stopped Cam for a quick chat.

Clair's office was small and neat, with a stark interior.

White walls and dark, modern furnishings, most of it screwed down into the floor.

Constant screaming echoed in the background.

Clair had been watching Lilliana read for the past hour, occasionally reading a file herself, taking a call, or pouring a coffee.

She had been at this facility for the better part of five years. She was brilliant at her job, which was to calm, coach and monitor the demons of society once they entered these walls, and were kept alive whilst useful to society; either offering vital information to help the Officials shut down any illegal activity or organization.

She had been working at the Australian Given for some ten years, but Cam had paid big dollars to get her expertise in their walls here.

Clair believed that Lilliana would be so beneficial in the Black Ops division and had been begging Cam for many months to persuade the young woman to change her mind and join her team. But at this stage Lilliana had been quite clear she was not interested.

Lilliana clicked off the files once she had finished and placed the information back on Clair's desk.

She reached for her herbal tea and looked over the rim of her cup at Clair, as she sipped.

"What to do think Lilliana?" Clair asked, "Do you have any suggestions for treatment in any of these cases?"

"I'm probably not the best person to answer that question." Lilliana placed her cup on the desk. She was feeling very uncomfortable with the position she was put in right now.

"On the contrary, you are the perfect person to answer the question." Clair smiled at the younger woman. She was such an attractive, intelligent little thing; she was desperate for her to join her team.

"Well, my answer to File 82 would be electroconvulsive therapy, and for Files 112 and 210 it would be insulin shock." She sat back in her chair looking across at Clair.

How she kept fresh looking and perky being in this section of the Given every day Lilliana had no idea. She felt her energy draining by the minute.

"What do you suggest for File 343?" Clair asked.

Lilliana folded her arms, clearly uncomfortable. "I really don't think you'll like my answer to that. And honestly, the answer won't help you, so, I'll keep that to myself, if you don't mind."

"No, I'm sorry Lilliana, but I insist you answer me. What treatment would you suggest? I'd hate to have to get Mr Night to read you your contract."

Lilliana stood. "I recall all the details of my contract, thank you. I usually do what is required of me. But in this, I must tell you, I have no desire to please you. Now, if you don't mind I actually have people I care about to get back to."

She left the room quickly and headed to the exit gate, the guard smiling at her as he waited for her to pass by.

She smiled back and was happy to leave the screaming, angry voices that echoed behind her.

Once the door, then the gate shut behind her, her smile disappeared, and she leaned against the railing.

Blissful silence. She took a deep breath and closed her eyes.

Footsteps could be heard coming towards her. She stood straight and alert and was watching the corridor waiting to see who would come around the corner.

She relaxed as Cam came into her line of vision.

He spotted her, looking like a caged animal.

He chuckled, "Relax I'm here to escort you back to your office. From now on, you should be able to figure out where you are going."

"You mean you expect me to come back here more than once?" She looked devastated.

He stopped in front of her, looking down into her green eyes. Even though they held such sparkle, she looked tired. He didn't know why he was so surprised, when he looked at her, at how truly beautiful she was.

"What?" She asked when he continued to just stare at her.

"Nothing, come on." He smiled, offering her his arm.

She linked hers through his, and they walked across the bridge and down the corridor.

"How are things going with Josephine?"

He had the biggest grin on his face at the mention of Josephine. "I believe things are going very well. In fact, she has told me, if I re-design my quarters exactly like hers, then she will consider moving in with me."

"Oh, that is fabulous. Will you?"

"Only if she says she'll marry me." He chuckled.

"What? *Really*" Lilliana stopped walking as they'd headed down the hospital stairs. "Have you asked her yet?"

"Not yet, I must ask my brother first, and as he hasn't contacted Johnsons' man for a few months, I must wait." He leaned against the wall and for the first time, Lilliana noticed how worried he looked.

She reached for his arm and gently rubbed it. "Are you alright, would you like to come by after my last appointment, have a chat?"

He smiled down at her. "I think I will. But come, let's get you back to Allie, I think she needs you to see to a difficult Given."

"Alright, but please, come and see me afterwards." She took his arm as they continued down the stairs and came to the hospital entrance via the passageway.

"Until then." Cam raised her hand to his lips and kissed it.

"Bye Cam." She said quietly and watched him walk back up the stairs.

She shook off her feeling of sadness. She would not think about Damon.

The scent of him. The way she felt when he'd looked at her. She blew out a breath and quickly headed down to get to the sanctuary of her office.

Entering, she saw Allie had her door shut and could see a pale boy sitting opposite her, talking and using his hands whilst he was apparently telling her a story of importance.

Lilliana crossed to her desk area and slid her glass door shut also. She grabbed a box of matches from her desk and lit her three candles.

Dropping the box of matches back into the draw, she turned and poured herself a cup of tea.

She sat in her chair, turning it towards her wall to watch the flames of the candles and kicked off her heels. Taking a mouthful of tea, she felt herself fully relax for the first time in hours.

The scent of the candles started to revive her and after draining her cup she swivelled her chair back around, clicked on her screens and pulled up some files.

There was an email from Allie about the young boy who was in her office now.

Sixteen-year old Liam. Attached to the file was a video, which Lilliana pressed play on, as she tapped the glass-top of her desk revealing a keyboard and started typing as she watched and listened.

This was the seventh link she had watched of Liam.

He was extremely quiet in their group sessions, very depressed normally, but when he was alone with Allie, he became animated and very talkative.

Lilliana had diagnosed him Manic Depressive. Allie agreed fully. An hour later, Lilliana closed her file after emailing it to Allie and then clicked on an email from Cam.

It seemed Clair had certainly let Cam know how displeased she was with Lilliana, in regard to her not committing one hundred percent in offering her professional input on File 343.

It stated his thoughts on her departing from Dr Clair's office this afternoon, and that in future he would value her giving all her opinions, whether she thought they'd be helpful or not.

He then emailed her the File on prisoner 343 with all the details, a video link, and expected her to give her informal opinion to him before the end of the day.

With many sincere thanks. Cam.

She looked up as Allie tapped on her glass door. She reached over and flipped a switch on her desk. The door slid silently open.

"You look one hundred percent pissed sister. What's up?"

"Oh, Cam and Dr Clair dumping unwanted junk at me." She shook her head. "Don't worry, it's nothing I can't handle. How was Liam?"

Allie perched on the chair opposite Lilliana. "He's okay. I think we are making progress. It breaks my heart, all his dark thoughts. His condition alone, plus the torture he endured at that bloody religious sect." Allie shook her head. "Put me undercover on the outside, I would take those bastards down." Her voice was tinged with anger.

"Agreed. I think we'd make a great team out there. Just need to practice our stealth skills." Lilliana smiled at her friend.

Allie nodded. "We'd name ourselves, 'Seriously Lethal.'"

"I like it." Lilliana stood and walked over to her friend.

"Have you got time for a quick bite before our next session?"

"I can't, I promised Natalie I'd squeeze her in beforehand, so Christopher is going to bring in a tray. Do you want me to buzz him to add something on it for you?"

"Yeah, that would be great; I suppose that gives me a chance to do this dirty work for Cam. Thanks, Allie."

Allie walked out, calling over her shoulder. "Salad or sandwich?"

"Both." Lilliana called, as she walked back to her chair and sitting down, got stuck into giving her very informal opinion to Cam.

After re-reading the file on the Diplomats' son, who in her informal opinion was a total psychopath. Obviously, an intelligent psychopath and apparently, a useful psychopath, but a psychopath, nevertheless.

David Reid, a twenty-five-year old, born with a silver spoon in more than just his mouth.

Had travelled the world with his father, mother and sister from an early age. Had caused chaos from the age of sixteen. Had raped and murdered his mother. Keeping her eyeballs in a jar for several years.

Had joined the underground black market and had paid to participate in anything illegal and despicable.

Had formed his own Entrepreneurial Organized crime. All monetary profit, from Drug, Sex and Human trafficking to Murder and cyber warfare. The list was endless.

Reading the file almost made Lilliana vomit. She also included that in her informal report to Cam. After stating that the only treatment she'd recommend for File 343 was a slow, painful death to finally remove the problem from not just society, but from their resources, which could be better used elsewhere. With thanks. Lilliana.

Clicking off, she stood and poured herself a glass of water. Taking a deep breath, she tried to shake off all negative thoughts and walked over to tap on Allie's door.

Natalie turned around and stared at her as the door slid open.

"What's up Lilliana?" Allie asked.

"Yes, Lilliana, what the hell is up? You're interrupting my time!" Natalie snapped. Always and ever as charming to Lilliana.

Lilliana cringed inwardly and felt like snapping at Natalie but remained professional.

"Sorry," she said to them both, "I just wanted to say, I need to duck out before group starts."

Allie noticed how pale Lilliana looked. "Are you alright Lilly?"

"No," She said quietly, "I'm not. I'm sorry Allie. Do you think we could ask Hillary to sit in for this afternoon's session?"

"Of course. Please, go and get some fresh air. Just take the rest of the afternoon off."

"Thank you. I owe you." She quickly left the room, heading down the corridor, waving to Billy as she passed the nurses' station. A few minutes later, she went up the stairs, and out through the door and took off up the main staircase to her room.

Once she entered, she knew she had to have a shower, to cleanse herself from that file. She needed a shower and a ride.

Quickly undressing she grabbed a robe and went along to the showers.

She must have stood under the pelting hot water for ten minutes.

After drying, she pulled her robe back on and headed back to her room.

She slipped on black Jodhpurs, long black boots and a cream riding jacket over a white singlet.

As she ran lightly down the stairs she quickly pulled her hair back into a long braid.

She waited at the bottom of the stairs, making sure that Damon's office door, where Cam worked, was shut.

Once she saw no action she dashed as fast as she could through the entrance way and jogged down the steps towards the stables.

Occasionally calling out a greeting if someone called out 'hi' to her. She waved to a group of Given who were about to set off for an afternoon run.

Once she entered the stables, Thomas saw her and smiled.

"Hey Miss Lilliana, can I help you?"

"I want to take Beast out. I need to get away and I'm sure he'd love a run."

Thomas nodded. "That he would. Come on, I'll help you."

It took them five minutes to get Beast geared up and ready to ride. Thomas gave Lilliana a boost up after he led the magnificent black stallion out of the main doors.

"Thank you Thomas." She said gratefully.

He could see the strain around her beautiful eyes and hoped she was okay. "You're Welcome. Enjoy."

With that, she kicked Beast's flanks gently. It was all he needed to take off into a canter.

Soon they were galloping over green pastures heading towards thicker trees. Lilliana felt her rage at David Reid dissipate over the next two hours, as she let Beast have his head and go his own way.

She heard the Givens' Jet approach and shaded her eyes glancing upwards. Probably another order for Josephine and Rupert's team.

Beast reared, but Lilliana was quite used to his manner, and calmly soothed him, before nudging him onwards to have his head, as the Jet soared above them. After a half hour, and cooling him off, she took him back to the stables and cared for him with love.

She went upstairs to the loft and watched the sky darken to a deep violet. A storm was on its way, in more ways than one.

Sighing, she worried a little at the email she'd sent Cam. It wasn't her usual, professional standard and she did feel a little nervous about his reaction.

There was just something so off about the Reid case than was obvious, it made her skin prickle with unease. A feeling she couldn't put her finger on. A knowing.

She ran her hands over her face, trying to shake off what she could not change. It was time to go in and face the music, for Cam would have surely received her email by now, and would no doubt be searching for her. As nice as the thought was, she could not hide up here forever.

CHAPTER 5

From the stables to the main house, Lilliana followed the blue stone pavement aligned with the sweet-scented flowers and rose bushes. Heading up the steps into the house, she hoped she wouldn't run into Cam just yet, and was surprised when, not a moment before her foot landed inside, a hand grabbed her arm.

"What's wrong?" She immediately felt a ball of worry, form in her stomach from the look on Josephine's face.

"Let's walk." Josephine linked her arm through Lilliana's and led her past a large, round water feature that trickled soothingly, as they quickly headed up the enormous staircase that led to the above rooms.

Greeting people as they hurried up the stairs, past many Given on their way to classes, work or recreation time. Josephine was stopped by a co-worker from H.D, to ask a quick question regarding the next despatch of vegetables. As Josephine chatted to Rupert, Lilliana glanced ahead as two figures approached. She tensed as Natalie, sneered at her, and sighed inwardly, and forced a smile for the tall, stunning red-haired woman beside Natalie.

"Hello Fox."

"Lilliana, how are you?" Fox asked this question like she knew something untoward was up.

"Fine, you?"

"Good sugar. Come find me if you need a chat."

"Okay." Lilliana watched them walk off as Josephine was finishing up with Rupert.

"Finally." Josephine tugged Lilliana the remainder of the way towards Lilliana's room and after typing in her friend's code, pushed her through the door.

Lilliana tugged off her riding jacket and hung it in the closet, curious at her friend's impatience. She pulled the band out of her braid and combed her fingers through her hair, letting it fly around her like a black cloud, till it fell in soft curls to her waist.

She walked across to her desk where a water jug sat and grabbing a glass turned to her friend holding it up.

Josephine shook her head no, so she filled herself a glass, drained it, poured another than sat at her desk facing her friend, who by this stage, was anxiously pacing beside Lilliana's bed.

"Ok, Josephine. Get it off your chest."

"Just remember to keep breathing when I tell you." Josephine looked nervously at her friend. Never a good thing. "And know, I'm here for you, always. It's going to be alright."

Lilliana nodded, thinking, 'How bad could it be.' "I'll be fine, what is it Jose?"

"Damon is back." Josephine blurted out, and waited a beat, watching as Lilliana's face drained of blood.

'That bad.' Lilliana thought. Her hand shook as she placed the glass down on the tray, pressing her hand to her lips, she stood and walked towards the window, opening it to let in the fresh air. She tried to catch her breath, keep her balance. All her emotions felt as though they would choke her, she closed her eyes and the image of 'him' flooded her. Silky, black hair that framed a face chiselled like that of a devastatingly handsome angel. Steele blue eyes that could bore into your soul and delve into your darkest secrets. A mouth wide and firm, that lit her heart when he smiled in her direction. A body sculptured hard to perfection, and his soul pure and giving, generous and only dangerous when the need arose. Tears threatened and she swallowed them down.

Josephine stood ready, wary, watching her friend like a hawk. Lilliana focused on her breathing and pushed away loose tendrils of hair off her face. That must have been Damon in the jet above her when she had been riding Beast.

"Lilly, are you alright?"

Lilliana felt her friend's arm come around her shoulders.

She turned and wrapped her arms around Josephine, burying her face into her warm neck.

"No," She whispered. "I'm not." She felt an overwhelming crowd of diverse emotions.

"Hey, it's going to be alright."

Lilliana squeezed Josephine before letting her friend go. She shook her head, her eyes meeting her friends. "My god, after all this time, he's really back?"

Josephine nodded. "I haven't seen him myself, but yes. He is back."

Lilliana stood and took a deep breath. Damon Night. Back. In reach. After five years away.

She felt shaky and sweaty. "I really need a shower. I rode to release the stress, now I feel it's swallowing me. Will you come with me?"

"Of course. Allie said you didn't look so good, but she didn't know where you went, and I didn't think you'd ride for so long with the storm coming."

They set off to the showers and Josephine sat outside the shower stall. Lilliana stepped in and was grateful for the refreshing feel of the warm water.

Josephine was relieved Lilliana hadn't broken down. It looked like she was going to be alright.

"I think Cam is annoyed at me," Lilliana said, as she treated her hair and lathered herself with essential lavender oil soap.

"As if my man would ever dare be annoyed at you," Josephine scoffed. "I'd kill him."

Lilliana chuckled. "No, in a professional manner. He and Dr Clair threw this case at me and I just didn't want a bar of it. So, I gave him my utmost, unprofessional view."

"Was it an honest view?" Josephine asked.

"Yeah," Lilliana said after a beat, "unfortunately it was."

"Well, that's all you can say Lilly." Josephine smiled as Lilliana stepped out of the shower and headed over to the body drier.

Once dried, she slipped her robe back on and they headed back to Lilliana's room.

She brushed her hair till it shone, then slipped on black heels, a black tight knee length skirt with a thin black belt and added a dark green V-neck shirt.

She popped on eye shadow, black eyeliner and a dash of lipstick, a squirt of perfume and a thin silver necklace, along with her eternity bracelet that her friends had given her years ago.

"You look gorgeous." Josephine smiled. "Feel better?"

"Self-preservation." Lilliana looked at her friend. "I think if I get back to work I may feel better. I'll let you know. Come down and find me in a couple of hours?"

"Sure babes. I'll sort out Cam. Leave him to me." Josephine hugged her friend.

"Thanks Jose" Lilliana whispered, feeling very nervous. "I don't know what I'm supposed to do about Damon."

Josephine couldn't believe how her very together, professional, usually calm friend, looked. Lost, frightened almost.

"Lilly," Josephine stated quietly, but firmly. "You have qualifications in a specialised field. A field which carries with it a very important role in this facility. So important in fact, that you are wanted at more than one facility. You are in high demand as a model which helps many in our home. You don't do anything about Damon. You just do what you always do. Okay?"

Lilliana closed her eyes briefly, took a deep breath and opening her eyes forced a brilliant smile for her friend.

"Jose, thank you."

"Welcome. Now, go. I'll see you in a couple, okay?"

Lilliana nodded, "If you see Jessica can you tell her I want to see her first chance she gets."

"Not a problem." The two friends hugged, before dashing off to their separate destinations.

Lilliana was comforted as soon as she stepped into her and Allie's room. The door sliding shut behind her.

There was a serving tray on the table with a note beside it, reading: Lilly, Christopher says eat! Hillary helped out in Group; all was fine. You were missed. Find me if you need me, or I'll see you in the morning. Allie. Xx

Lilliana lifted the lid to a freshly wrapped sandwich and a bowl of colourful salad.

She popped the lid on a service shoot near the door and walked over to her desk. She pressed a button, which slid all her glass frames back into each other, so she had the feeling of open space in the room.

She put on some soothing music and sitting, enjoyed her sandwich whilst she watched her fish. She didn't want time to think, so quickly finished eating and settled in, to tackle some serious reports on a few Givens in Psych; watched several video links that had been sent to her by Dr Hillary, Dr Richard and Allie.

A knock at her door jolted her out of her concentration; she kept her head down as she pressed the door open.

Josephine strolled in, with Cam.

"Someone came here to apologize, Lilliana." Josephine said sweetly, her arm linked through Cam's.

He looked a little nervous himself. Lilliana stood, walking over to the Buddha.

"Cam, please, let me apologize first. I was out of line. I didn't handle David Reid's case well at all. There was something about it that just put me on edge, I haven't had a meltdown since I qualified."

Cam walked over to Lilliana and placed his hands on her shoulders. "There is a first time for everything and you are not made of stone. Please don't worry about it, your answers were honest despite the brutality behind them."

He hugged her before gently releasing her, and crossing over to Josephine, put his arm around her waist.

Josephine stepped on her tip toes and kissed him. "You are so hot when you're being sweet."

Cam pulled her closer and kissed her deeply.

Lilliana cleared her throat. Josephine chuckled as Cam pulled away.

"I think we'll take this elsewhere." Cam suggested.

"Yes, good idea." Lilliana smiled.

"You're not going to work all night are you?" Josephine sounded concerned as she looked at Lilliana.

"No, I'm just going to finish these reports." She smiled at her friend.

"I'll need to see you in the office first thing, so do make sure you get some sleep, okay?" Cam said.

Lilliana sighed. "Okay."

The three of them were very aware that Damon's name was not being mentioned.

Lilliana's phone rang and she walked over to answer it.

Cam watched her carefully as Josephine whispered. "She had better be okay, or heads will roll."

He smiled down at her, staring into her warm brown eyes. "My fierce, protective tiger." He kissed her nose.

"You better believe it." She leaned forward and nipped his chest with her teeth.

He suppressed a moan as Lilliana ended the call and walked towards them.

"I've got to go, apparently, they are having a bit of trouble with a new Given. I'll see you in the morning Cam. Bye Jose." She kissed her friend as she hurried past.

"Good night." They called after her.

***

As Lilliana approached the Psych ward's metal doors she paused for the eye scanner to sweep over her eye to enable access.

Saying hello to Patricia, the night nurse, she asked which room she was needed in.

"Forty-two." Patricia waved, as Lilliana hurried down the corridor, hearing inconsolable screaming, guiltily hoping this wouldn't take long.

When she stepped into room Forty-two, she took note of the situation.

Dr Richard was standing at the end of the bed with Shelley, a friend from Lilliana's Psych class before they had qualified. Lilliana hardly saw Shelley, as the girl often did four back to back days down here.

"Hi Lilliana." Shelley smiled.

"Hi Shelley, how are you?"

"Doing pretty well."

Lillian looked at her least favourite person here. "Richard." She said shortly.

"Lilliana." He replied similarly.

She walked over to the woman who was strapped down, her eyes closed.

She was pretty, with a slight frame, pale hair and skin.

Her eyes flew open, her lips pulled back into a snarl. "Give me back my baby you bitch!" She screamed, sending spittle all over herself.

"Calm down," Lilliana said gently. "You are safe, and everything is going to be alright." She reached over and smoothed the woman's pale hair off her face.

She looked at Richard and held out her hand for the tablet-chart. He held it out to her, not moving, as ever, making her life that much more uneasy.

Sighing inwardly, she stepped over and didn't quite snatch it out of his hand.

She stepped back, clicking the tablet on as her eyes quickly took in the woman's situation.

Felicia, thirty-two years of age.

Arrived six hours earlier. Heavy drugs in her system. Whip scars on her back and thin scars on her wrists.

Tried to stab Billy in the hospital ward, before they got started on her Psych Evaluation.

Deeming her dangerous she was brought to Psych immediately after that episode.

"What other information do we have?" Lilliana asked Shelley, not wanting to communicate with Richard any more than she had to.

"She keeps screaming out about her baby, that someone stole it from her. She goes quiet for ten minutes and then screams for an hour. That's been happening for the past six hours anyway," Shelley nodded. "I'm surprised she has any energy left."

Lilliana handed the tablet-chart to Shelley who popped it on to the end of the bed.

Turning around and stepping back to Felicia, she said calmly.

"Felicia, my name is Lilliana. I'm going to help you in any way I can."

Felicia remained as still as the night. Her hard, pale eyes staring into Lilliana's green ones.

"Okay?" Lilliana nodded at Felicia, letting her know that all would be well.

Felicia looked at Lilliana and started screaming, "You are no angel, you are a filthy fucking slut, a whore! Do you hear me? I'm going to fuck you right up, you *slutty bitch*!" Felicia tried to spit at Lilliana, but as she was strapped so tightly, she had no way to project her phlegm and the thick, green spittle fell upon her own face.

Shelley took a cloth to wipe it off.

"Leave it," Dr Richard snapped out "Leave it on her."

"Richard," Lilliana said quietly. "no."

"Please," He looked at her, over his horn-rimmed glasses, "I'm still in charge here, Miss Lilliana."

"Then why was I called down here?" She folded her arms, as Felicia went into a screaming rage behind her.

"Because," He said quietly, "she was asking for the dark angel. And as that is what you are known for out there, I wanted you in here." Lilliana placed one hand on her hip and tapped her foot twice.

"I suggest you sedate her so she can rest, and I'll begin her evaluation in the morning if that pleases you?" She raised an eyebrow.

"Yes, you can attend her with me." He gave her a sharp smile. As if there was an underlying motive that pleased him somehow.

"Fine, I have a meeting with Cam first thing, but I'll be down as soon as he is finished with me. Goodnight Shelley." She nodded to Richard, left the room and the screaming woman behind her.

She waited for Patricia to buzz her out, as the two women said goodnight.

She had two thoughts about the coming day.

One, she was not looking forward to working with Richard.

And two, her stomach was in an absolute ball of knots thinking about seeing Damon for the first time in years.

It was doubtful she'd be able to do what Cam asked. She did not think sleep would come easy this night.

***

The storm raged throughout the night. The rain whipped at Lilliana's window.

Funnily enough it was the perfect storm that eased her into a deep, dreamless sleep. She awoke after six solid hours feeling refreshed and felt she could pretty much handle anything the day had to throw at her.

After showering, she dressed and decided to leave her hair free, as it was her own shield where Richard was concerned.

A spray of perfume, a hint of makeup and feeling divine, headed down for her meeting with Cam.

As she was halfway down the stairs, she felt a hand grab her upper arm, stopping her. Fox.

"How are you Lilliana?" A look of concern marring her stunning features. "I hear Damon's back?"

Lilliana sighed and looked away from Fox's watchful gaze.

She forced a smile. "I'm fine, yes, I hear he's back. That's great."

"Yes, but are you alright?" Fox grabbed her chin and forced her to look up at her.

Lilliana stared into Fox's clear, blue eyes. "I'm not really sure. I'm trying not to think about it. Look, I have to go, I have a meeting with Cam."

Fox looked thoughtful, as if she was about to say something else, but then nodded slowly. "I'll see you later then."

Lilliana turned to go. "Bye." She called, heading downstairs.

She walked past the major dining rooms, one which was full of Given dressed in white running outfits. She briskly headed past the library, knocking on Cam's door.

It slid open. Cam was sitting behind the desk, reading a file.

"Ah, morning my sparrow, come on in. Grab one of those herbals you seem to love so much." He pointed to the tea tray.

"Thanks." She said and poured herself a tea. Walking over to the fireplace mantel, she reached up and ran a finger over the small figurine of Beast, which she'd gifted Damon years ago for Christmas.

Taking a mouthful of tea, she turned to face Cam.

"What's up?" She asked tentatively.

"David Reid. I want you to see him, chat with him. Get to know him. I think if anyone can get information for Johnson, on his contacts, it's you."

Lilliana stared at Cam like he had spoken in a different language.

She walked over to where he was seated. Took another mouthful of tea, then sat her cup on the desk, crossed her arms over her chest and looked at him, her head tipped to one side. "Why?"

"Because I know you can." He made it sound simple.

"Oh Cam, why me? I have plenty on my plate. Why can't Richard do it?"

"You are an intelligent lady, Lilliana. Please, Richard couldn't get information out of a corpse if he were the coroner!"

"Ah," She said, "you are whoring me to get information. Nice one." She leaned her hip on the desk, looking down at him.

"Look, with your looks and charm along with Johnson's help, we can do some good here Lilly. What do you say? I need you there in two hours. Johnson will meet you in Clair's office to prep you."

"Do I have a choice?"

"No Darling, not in this, sorry." He shrugged apologetically.

She pushed away from the desk and took a step back. "Is that all Sir? I have to do an evaluation with Richard."

Cam stood, walked around the desk and reaching her, placed his hands on her shoulders. He squeezed gently. "Go then. I'll see you later."

She forced a small smile and turned to leave. Stopping just as she reached the door, she asked quietly, her back to him. "Are you going to say anything about Mr. Night?"

"Not just yet, my angel." He glanced over his shoulder, waiting, then looked back at her.

She straightened her shoulders and walked towards the door.

"I'll talk to you later." The door slid shut behind her as she left.

Cam sighed and sat on the arm of the sofa.

He ran his hand through his hair and said out to the room. "Happy now, brother?"

Damon stepped out of the shadows, looking dark and dangerous. Cam hardly recognized him. Only gone five years, but those five years had done hard things to his brother. He could see that clearly.

Damon looked at Cam, saying nothing. His heart still beating fast with his mind full of the vision that had been Lilliana.

By the stars, five years had made her that much more gloriously beautiful. Her body developed into a woman's glory. Her rich, black hair, as stunningly glossy as ever. Her face, her eyes. Sharp, defined, yet soft and gentle.

Cam watched him closely. Waiting for him to crack up.

"Are you alright?" He asked, hesitantly.

"No," Damon snapped. "I am not alright."

Cam sat quietly, waiting. Not quite sure what to do about this individual.

A tap at the door sounded, Cam flipped the switch. Damon was about to step back into the shadows as Josephine bounded through the door.

"Oh my Lord!" She squealed, the door sliding shut behind her.

Damon's eyes took his young friend, his sister, in. She was a sight for sore eyes.

"Josephine." He whispered her name like a prayer.

She flew across the room and launched herself into his arms.

He had no choice but to wrap his arms around her and bury his face into her soft brown curls.

She clung to him, tears of happiness leaking from her eyes. "I can't believe you're back, finally!" She moved a fraction, to get a good look at his face. Her smile fading slightly.

"So handsome," she whispered, "but so serious. Oh, Damon, was it really so horrid out there?"

He gently removed her hands from his body and stepped away from her, towards the desk.

"It was worse than anything you could imagine Josephine. And I wouldn't want you knowing anything about the sordid life I have led these past five years. How are you, is what I'd be more interested in talking about?" He tried to smile.

Josephine looked over at Cam, who shrugged one shoulder.

"I'm well Damon, really well."

Damon sat down in his office chair, running his hands over his desk. His next smile towards her was genuine. "I'm so glad sweetheart."

"I've been, having relations with your brother."

Damon's eyes shot across to Cams. "Yes," He said drily, "Cameron and I got no sleep this past night, we've been talking for many hours. That bit of information came up."

"Well good then." She crossed over to Cam and leaning up, kissed him gently on the mouth. Turning, she smiled at Damon, as Cam's arms came around her waist. "That's good, as I'm sure that now you are back, he's been waiting to ask you, if he can marry me."

"And how did you know that?" Cam tickled her ribs, biting her neck.

Josephine laughed, turning to face him, she wrapped her arms around his neck, eyes twinkling. "Call it female intuition."

Damon watched them carry on and felt pleased that he was not in any way uncomfortable with their display of affection in front of him.

"Josephine."

She turned to face Damon. "Yes Sir."

"Come here." He stood, before walking towards her.

Josephine stepped towards Damon, taking his outstretched hands.

His large, strong hands held her soft, small ones with so much love, that Cam had to force a swallow.

To see the woman he loved so much, and his brother, who had recently been through hell and back, share a mutual friendship and love, comforted him greatly. It eased the burden in his heart momentarily, for the deep concern he had for Damon's mental health. He wasn't sure how he was going to come out of what he had dealt with the past five years.

Damon hugged Josephine gently, and whispered near her ear. "I have always thought of you as my sister and if marrying my brother over there, is what you want, will make you happy, then you have my blessing to marry him." He kissed her forehead.

Josephine felt a tear trickle from her eyes and reached up to kiss the man she had always considered a brother.

"Thank you Sir." She smiled through her happy tears, before walking back to Cam and wrapped her arms around his neck.

He kissed the top of her head and smiled at his brother before saying to Josephine.

"Well my love, my brother and I have hours' worth of meetings, so I must say goodbye to you for the next day or so. Hopefully we can catch up in-between sessions, okay?" Cam smiled down at her.

Josephine nodded, "I'm sure you both have a lot of work to do, as do I, so later then." She smiled at them both and disappeared out the door.

Damon held out his hand. Cam took it. They shook hands hard. No words needing to be spoken between them.

"Right, well I think we need Johnson down here before he needs to meet Lilliana upstairs. We'll have a full staff meeting in two days' time. But first, I just need to do a complete catch up on all the happenings over the last five years." Damon walked over to the desk and sat.

"How about another shower, a meal, some coffee?" Cam suggested. "Why don't Johnson and I come up to you in your quarters in an hour? It looks like you could use it brother."

Damon leaned back in his chair. There was nothing he'd like better than to go up to his own rooms and simply disappear with his thoughts.

Thoughts now swamped with Lilliana.

He sighed, shaking his head. "There's plenty of time for that later. Please Cam, let's get this done."

"Sure thing, I'll get Cook to bring in a tray and we'll get started ASAP."

Cam waved as he headed out to get ready for many hours of gruelling files, inspection reports, plus finances and general catchups on Qualified and new Given, the horses and every other aspect he had, whilst running this place while his brother was in hell.

Once the door closed behind Cam, Damon placed his elbows on his desk and dropped his face into his hands.

To be back home, but to have so much within him changed.

He wasn't sure if he could handle it at all.

Seeing Lilliana and hearing her musical, rich, velvety, soothing voice.

It had almost killed him not to cross over to her and crush her in his arms.

The constant tease, seeing her scattered across the cities billboards, where he'd worked the streets undercover. Seeing her beautiful familiar face, her body. But having her so far out of reach.

Having to live the life he had led.

He stood, walking over to the mantel, running his finger over the figurine of Beast where she had stroked her finger along his back.

So much had changed. He had changed. She was too good for him.

He'd spent hours reading over her files, watching video feeds of the years that had passed.

He'd seen her get sliced in the hospital by that Lorenzo character.

Had felt the blood drain from his face, as he'd watched her precious blood flow from her body, even though he knew she had survived the attack.

Had watched her care and love his horse when he could not.

He'd seen the links with her and Allie, in their group sessions, and had felt so proud.

How far they had come.

He ran his hand through his black glossy hair as the door slid open, with Cam and Johnson walking in.

Johnson nodded at Damon. He knew exactly what the man had been through the past five years, as his old partner had filled him in thoroughly and consistently.

He hoped he could be here, be strong for this good friend of his.

Walking in behind the men was Christopher, wheeling in a fully loaded trolley.

Wrapped sandwiches, soup, hot coffee, finger buns and fruit platters.

"Hello Sir," Christopher said to Damon, "it's so good to have you back with us."

Damon walked over and shook Christopher's hand. "It's good to be back, Christopher. I've heard you've been very well."

"I certainly have been Sir," Christopher nodded, smiling.

"Excellent. Good to hear." Damon clapped him on the shoulder before he walked back to his desk, a sandwich in hand.

Once Christopher left, Cam locked the door, turning to face Damon he said, "I've informed the head staff that we are not to be disturbed."

Damon nodded. "Right, well, let's get started shall we gentlemen."

With that, the three men sat down for a good couple of days storming through what needed to be done.

It was exactly what Damon needed, to keep his mind functional and preoccupied.

CHAPTER 6

It was day four since Damon had entered the building and Lilliana felt like she was walking around on eggshells, waiting for the moment she'd walk into a room and find him there.

It had not happened.

She listened as Josephine had told her about her meeting with him, when he'd given her his blessing to marry Cam.

Lilliana had been so happy for her friend. Josephine had added how very changed Damon seemed to be. Lilliana said she could understand.

Cam had tried to tell her as much as he could about undercover.

It did not sound like a good, clean life.

Nor should it have been, to clean some of the scum off the streets to protect the innocent.

She was sitting in Black Ops, waiting in a small room for the guard to bring David Reid in to see her.

It was her second meeting. The first meeting had passed unsuccessfully. David had not said a word, only stared at her the entire hour.

She glanced up from her notes as the door opened.

The guard was leading in the very tall, handsome man. Lilliana forced herself to sit rigidly still and not show a flicker of her distaste to this being.

The guard sat David down in the chair opposite Lilliana, nodding hello as he did so.

She flashed him a quick smile as he clicked David's ankle chain into the locks that were drilled into the floor.

His hands were free, but she was not at all uneasy.

He had nowhere to go and she could get out of his way quickly enough if she had to.

Johnson had had a meeting with her an hour prior to both visits.

Today he'd instructed her to wear tall heels and a flattering dress with a revealing neckline.

He'd insisted that it was the type of dress code David went for in his victims and was hoping to make the man feel at ease and maybe even a little in control.

He'd given Lilliana a list of questions and instructed her to act a little nervous, feminine and quiet.

It was something she wasn't too happy about. Well, if the truth be told and it had been, she wasn't happy about being here in the first place.

The door clicked shut behind the guard and the two were left alone.

Lilliana crossed her legs and tapped something out on her tablet. She then glanced up at David through her lashes.

"Well, Mr Reid. How are you today?" She started quietly. "Is there anything in particular I can get you, to make your stay here with us more comfortable?"

Like a bullet, she thought.

His gaze dropped down to her ankle, then ran up to her leg, then leaning in his chair, he went to look as far up her dress as he could see.

Lilliana glanced down and quickly typed something and then pressed send.

The silent email was sent back in a flash.

It read. -Spread your legs a fraction.

She replied. -Like Hell -Send.

"Mr Reid. Are you going to speak to me today, or are we going to sit in silence for another hour?" Her voice wasn't as quiet as before. She knew she'd get an earful from Johnson, but seriously.

"Yes," He drawled slowly, "I believe I will speak to you." His eyes drilled into hers.

"Brilliant." She flashed a beautiful smile, hoping it didn't look forced.

"Let's say, we do a trade. I'll ask you a question and if you answer me honestly, I'll do the same for you?" His voice so cool, chilling even.

Her gaze flashed down to her email. She knew Johnson was outside, watching through the mirrored window, which reflected herself back at her if she turned her head.

Her email read- Yes.

"That sounds like a fine idea David. Where shall we start?"

"Why, with you of course." He leaned forward a little and whispered, "Do you like being every man's wet dream?"

Lilliana went to sigh, but held it in. Glancing down, she quickly typed the answer she was going to say- No; I don't believe I am every man's wet dream. -Send.

Reply- Yes, I love it. It makes me powerful. - please Lilliana!

She glanced up at David.

"Well," She ran her tongue along her teeth. "Yes, I do actually. It makes me feel powerful."

"That's correct. A beautiful creature like yourself was designed for man's pleasure. You know," he moved closer, lowering his voice, "I would like to take great pleasure, in pleasuring you right now and I wouldn't have to touch an inch of your skin to do so."

I think I may be sick, seriously, do I have to put up with this? -send.

Reply - Yes, please just be patient, play along.

Lilliana sighed out loud. She couldn't help herself.

David took this as a sign to continue.

"I'd start with that gorgeous head of hair of yours. Imagine my fingers along your scalp and running through your hair. Drifting down your face, your neck, brushing lightly over your sweet, soft flesh. Mm, I can almost taste your skin."

Her eyes remained on his. She could not move an inch. She would not show him how sickened she was at the thought of his hands anywhere near her.

"Imagine my lips, sliding down your neck, to your breasts." He smiled a little.

"I'd have to bite you of course. I wouldn't be able to help myself. You'd be frightened, but I'd soothe you. I'd suck your nipples until you came, begging for more." He smiled slowly. "I could make you come, so easily."

Lilliana glanced across at the mirror. She saw how pale she'd gone and hoped Johnson gave a damn.

She glanced back at David and lowered her lashes. He was leaning closer, the chains around his ankles stretching taunt.

"Enough, it's my turn. Tell me the locations of your head organizations. I need names of those who have been linked to the illicit trafficking and money laundering. Those responsible for the kidnapping, raping and murdering of hundreds of men and women in..." Before she could continue, he interrupted.

"Only if you open your legs." He said quietly, sitting as close to her as the chains would allow.

"No." She shook her head. "Tell me now."

His handsome face tilted to one side. His silky blonde hair fell over one eye. Eyes that were so pale, alien, almost familiar. "Five one twenty, Holy Lane Texas." He whispered.

Lilliana stilled, not believing how easy that had been. She glanced across at the mirror and was sure Johnson was on the phone then and there to his contacts to raid that address.

"Now, if you want the other locations, or any intel, open your *fucking legs.*" He said it softly, politely even.

"Give them to me and I'll do it. Promise." Lilliana leaned forward, revealing her generous breasts for his full viewing.

She was going to kill Johnson for this assignment.

He quietly gave them to her, then lurched forward with his long arms and grabbed her knees with his long, strong fingers before she had a chance to blink, and he spread her legs wide open.

Her hand reached forward and slapped his face as hard as she could and jumped up as the door burst open. The guard stepped in with a prod stick and told David to remain still.

"Are you alright?" The guard addressed Lilliana.

She pushed her hair off her face and straightened her dress. "Fine, thank you."

She marched out of the room, Johnson stepping out of the room next door. "Lilliana, please step in here till he passes."

Lilliana walked into the small room and watched the guard through the one-way mirror; unlocking the chains around David's feet.

David had turned towards the mirror, giving it a wink.

Johnson had closed the door and walked up behind Lilliana. "Are you alright?"

She turned to face him. Tall and handsome, in a very rustic way was Johnson, at the age of forty-eight. Sandy brown hair, crinkly, smiley eyes, when he wasn't looking so serious anyway.

"Look, to be honest no, I'm not alright. I do not like being in that man's presence. I was sick reading his file. There is something about him that puts me right on edge." She ran her hands up her arms, shaking her head. "Please, please tell me I don't have to see him again?"

Johnson sighed, hating to make her unhappy. "It depends how these leads run, hopefully we can make some sort of headway."

Johnson reached for the phone as it rang, cutting off any further comment he had wanted to add. Lilliana listened to the changed enthusiasm in his tone. "That is fantastic news. Make a start on the other locations and get back to us ASAP. Cheers."

He clicked off the phone, smiling at Lilliana. "Bingo on location one. Here's hoping that you will not have to be in the same room with that man again."

Lilliana blew out a breath. "Thank the stars for small favours. Good luck Johnson."

He smiled and shook her hand. "I'll be in touch. Thank you for being so brave."

She waved her hand behind her as she left the room, relieved they had at least gotten one secure location. A bit of discomfort was definitely worth it. She headed for the exit. She could not wait to be out of this section.

Just as she reached the guard a voice called out behind her. Dr Clair.

"Lilliana, I've just had a call from Dr Richard. You are needed in Psych right now."

"Thank you Clair." Lilliana turned on her heel and left as the guard opened the door and gate for her to leave.

****

Twenty minutes later she walked down to Psych and saw Richard waiting a little way down the corridor.

Just what I need, she thought to herself.

"Lilliana." Richard said, peering over his horn-rimmed glasses. She nodded hello and followed him as he started to walk down the corridor and down a deeper section of the wards, where they branched off into larger rooms.

Rooms full of different sized bathtubs, chairs with leather straps, where hands and feet were held firmly in place to stop a patient from harming themselves, or an assistant when treatment was required.

"Felicia seems to be pregnant." Richard began, as they walked down another long corridor. "You can perform the abortion. Good training for you."

He hadn't realized that she was no longer walking beside him but had stopped ten steps behind.

"I will not." She said firmly.

He turned around and pushed his glasses up his long, narrow nose staring at her. "Why must you always argue with me?"

Lilliana placed her hands on her hips. "I don't mean to Richard. Really. But I don't agree with what you are saying. I will not abort her baby."

Richard sighed, shaking his head. "Come," he said, turning on his heel, "you may change your mind soon enough."

Lilliana dropped her hands and followed him a little way further before they came to a small room with a mirror like the one Johnson had watched her and David through.

Richard kept his eyes on Lilliana as she watched the woman in the room.

Felicia was dressed in white shorts and a white singlet top.

She was sitting in the middle of the room, trying to slice her wrist open with the longest fingernail she had.

As Richard had cut them beyond the quick the only blood on her arms was that of her own bleeding fingers.

Lilliana folded her arms and looked at Richard. "So what do you want to do? Take away the baby she has growing inside her, when she's already lost a baby?"

"Well, Miss Lilliana she can't keep it, can she? And I don't think the father wants it." He smirked at her.

Lilliana shook her head. "What are you doing to treat her, have you considered any of my suggestions?"

"She's a psychopath, she'll receive the treatment I deem imperative to her condition and then she will go to the Black Ops division." He looked back towards Felicia.

"But first an abortion is in order. Shall we?" He raised an eyebrow, then turned to open Felicia's door.

"Shall I get one of the nurses to prep the room?" Lilliana asked.

"It's already set up." Richard said over his shoulder as he walked into the room.

"Good afternoon dear," He smiled at Felicia. "how about a little stroll?" He bent down and grabbed her thin wrist, pulling her up towards him. As she rose, her other thin arm shot out, her fingers stretching to scratch Richard's face.

He simply moved his head back, and grabbing her behind the neck, forced her in front of him and out of the room.

Lilliana inwardly shook her head. She would never get used to the often-barbaric ways Richard dealt with those destined for Black Ops.

She followed them further along the corridor and into a room where Joe, the psych attendee, was setting up sterilized surgical equipment.

"Here we go." Richard said to Felicia. He nodded to Joe and together they grabbed a wrist and an ankle each, and deposited the screaming woman onto the upright seat, forced her hands and ankles through the leather straps, securing her tightly.

Lilliana uncomfortably folded her arms. "You don't need me Richard. I'm going." She turned to go, when Felicia screamed at her. "No, Dark Angel, stay! Please, don't leave me alone with them. Please!"

She begged, her voice sounding pitifully desperate.

Lilliana walked over to Felicia and placed a hand on the crying woman's head.

"It's going to be okay," She soothed in her gentlest voice, "it will all be over soon and then we'll get you settled."

Felicia looked panicked. "What will be over soon? What are you going to do to me?" Her pale eyes filled with tears and she started tugging as hard as she was able on her restraints.

Lilliana looked over at Richard. "Well, are you going to give her a sedative?"

He was pulling on rubber gloves, snapping them into place over his wrists as he stared at her.

Like he wasn't creepy enough, she thought.

"No." He said and turned to face Joe. Taking the offered scissors, he started cutting off Felicia's shorts.

Joe tightened the belt around her waist which was attached to the chair so she would stop bucking.

Lilliana felt sick for the poor woman.

"Richard, I insist you give this woman a sedative right now." Lilliana said firmly, holding onto one of Felicia's hands.

Richard removed Felicia's shorts, and pushed her knees into the stirrups where she could not move, her vagina wide open and exposed.

Lilliana was glaring at Richard. She released Felicia's hand, about to walk out when Felicia's fingers gripped around her wrist and tightened like a steel vice.

Richard slid the brace into Felicia's vagina, none too gently and then proceeded to insert the scraping tool.

Lilliana turned her head away and closed her eyes as Felicia's screams pierced her ears.

"Where's Will? Where's Will? Why hasn't he come for me? He'll kill you for this, all of you!" She threw her head from side to side, tears pouring down her face as she screamed. Then, shockingly, hysterical laughter burst from her.

Lilliana stared into the woman's pale blue eyes. Her laughter stopped as suddenly as it had begun. She went rigidly still as Richard removed the tools.

She stared into Lilliana's eyes before whispering, "You're all going to pay for this."

Lilliana could understand her grief, her humiliation.

She tried to pull her arm free, but Felicia was surprisingly strong. "Richard please, a little help here." She hated asking him for anything.

He reached over and using his gloved hand which had the woman's blood all over it, grabbed Lilliana's wrist and pried Felicia's fingers from around it, releasing her.

She rubbed her wrist, staring angrily at the man she close-to loathed.

"I'm leaving. See she gets the correct after care or I will put in a complaint. Is that clear?"

He raised an eyebrow at her and snapped off his bloody gloves, whispering, "Crystal."

She shook her head and left the room as quickly as she could.

She did not even stop to sign out and exited the hospital as fast as she could without running. She broke into a jog when she hit the staircase and bolted straight for the showers.

Everything she had on went down the chute. Even her shoes. Let those downstairs in the laundry department figure it out, she thought, stepping into a steaming shower.

She scrubbed her skin till it was red raw, especially where Richard had touched her.

After soaping and conditioning, she piled her hair on top of her head with hair clips, which were in a drawer and settled into the spa, putting the bubbles on full.

She must have sat there for almost an hour, staring at the green Jade tiles on the wall.

She was considering a change in career. Maybe laundry where she could simply wash clothes, make the beds, fix the clothes back into the wardrobes of all the Given. A simpler life.

She leaned her head back and squeezed her eyes shut as thoughts of what Damon might be up to, slammed into her mind. She jolted as a voice called out her name.

"Jessica." She reached over to hug her friend who had joined her in the warm water. Tears slipped out of her eyes.

"I'm so sorry I haven't been able to catch up with you Lilly." Jessica hugged her back, and then held her at arm's length.

"How are you?"

Lilliana shook her head, leaning back against the wall of the spa, looking up at the ceiling. "I'm tired, overwhelmed, pissed off and want to shoot a particular Doctor!"

Jessica thought that was a good start.

"Of course you're tired. You never stop. Who are you pissed off with?"

Lilliana shook her head.

"Okay, next, do you want to shoot a particular creepy Dr R?" Lilliana nodded.

"Well, these things I can understand." Jessica thought she might take Lilliana's mind off her situation for a few minutes and chat about what her group had been up to. "We have this new girl, Vanessa. We thought we had our hands full with Natalie. Let me tell you, Natalie is as sweet as apple pie compared to this girl. She cannot keep her hands off Orlando."

Lilliana smiled at her dear friend as she listened to her chat about her day and all the comings and goings of settling new Given into their home. Out of all the girls, Jessica and Lilliana had the least amount of free time together as their routines kept them apart.

Jessica had bloomed into a stunning woman. Her legs had gotten longer, browner. Her eyes such a bright blue, with her stunning long blonde hair, she was as pretty as a peach.

"You look so well, so happy." Lilliana said quietly.

"Oh, I am Lilly. I just love my role as Team Leader. Marcus told Orlando the other day that we are the best paired Team Leaders he has seen in the fourteen years he has been here. Cool huh?"

"Very cool." Lilliana smiled.

"Have you seen him yet?" Jessica asked. Not needing to mention who 'he' was, feeling a little hesitant to bring him up.

Lilliana shook her head. "I feel so frustrated with the fact he is here, under the very same roof after all this time, yet still has not come to talk to me!" She was surprised to find tears of frustration fall from her eyes, disappearing into the bubbling water.

She had been holding them in for days now whilst trying to function and get on with her work. "I mean, I am bursting at the seams to lay just one eye on him, for even half a second! It's been taking every ounce of my self-control not to hunt him down like an animal." She could feel herself working into a coiled spring with each word she spoke. Jessica could see clearly how tightly strung Lilliana's nerves seemed to be.

"Oh Lilly look, hardly anyone has seen him. Jose says he's in a pretty bad way. We can only imagine what he's been through. Please babe, don't take it personally okay?"

Lilliana took a deep breath and pulled herself together. Nodding, she slipped under the water to wash out her conditioner.

Popping back up, she looked at Jessica. "I need to go for a ride." Stepping out, she went under the drier and was dried in seconds. She remained under long enough for the warm, steamy air to dry her hair.

She grabbed a robe off the back of the door and turned to smile at her friend. "Thanks Jessica. I appreciate you seeking me out. I really needed to have a chat with you. Even if it was quick. If you need me to do anything for Vanessa, let me know. I'll see you soon."

"No worries Lilliana. Take care." Jessica smiled as she watched her friend leave.

***

The next morning, Lilliana awoke feeling relaxed and refreshed.

She'd ridden Beauty for hours and hadn't come in till late, had skipped dinner and gone straight to bed.

She stretched her muscles before getting out of bed and strolled over to her window.

The day was alive with sunshine, a gentle breeze and the scent of Jasmine in the air.

Lilliana considered what she had on this morning. No Johnson, Cam or Dr Richard was scheduled. A group with Allie, which she always looked forward to and then nothing in the afternoon.

Today was a good day.

She pulled out a soft lemon sundress and slipped on some high yellow pumps.

She brushed her hair till it shone and pulled it over one shoulder and did a braid.

She popped large silver hoops through her ears, added a collection of silver bracelets and a squirt of perfume.

She was starving and headed down to breakfast within ten minutes of jumping out of bed.

She walked to the buffet and poured an orange juice, drank it down, then grabbed a bowl of fruit and a cup of tea.

"Drank that fast didn't we?" Leon smiled at her, reaching for a mug of coffee.

Lilliana smiled. "How are you Leon?"

"Good. A busy day ahead, so I want to refuel the right way." He reached for a plate of toast, piled it high with a banana, a tub of yogurt and a slab of bacon.

Lilliana raised an eyebrow, popping a piece of mango into her mouth, she nodded. "Too true."

He winked at her before taking a seat with a group of colleagues.

She shook her head smiling, as she raised her cup of tea to her lips and glanced around the room, spotting Allie heading her way.

Allie smiled. "How are you darling?"

"Good, good." Lilliana nodded. "It's a new day."

"That it is my friend. I'll see you in group in a couple of hours." Allie left to find Christopher.

Popping the last piece of fruit in her mouth and swallowing her tea down, Lilliana headed out.

She said hello to Orlando as they crossed paths and walked out the front door.

It truly was a stunning day; the scent of blossoms filled the air. The freshly grown assorted bulbs that Rupert had been working on lined the paths with glorious colours. The gardens had increased in their beauty since Rupert, Josephine and their team worked together.

They created not only magical blooms for the establishment but colourful, glorious scented and edible varieties for the world outside their gates.

Lilliana planned on picking some for her office after her walk to see

Beauty. As she started down the steps, the direction of the stables in her mind, a voice called her name behind her.

"Lilliana."

She froze. It was the voice she longed to hear, for what felt like forever. The very voice she had dreamt about these past years.

She slowly turned, her eyes looking upwards towards the tall figure on the top of the entrance steps.

She found it difficult to breathe. How he had changed so little, yet so much?

His beautiful chiselled face looked guarded; his intense, blue eyes frowned slightly, as he watched her, watching him.

His body looked fit and muscular in his tight black jeans and dark steel blue shirt.

Five years, and she felt like she had the last time she'd looked at him. She watched his lips part, as he said her name again.

He frowned slightly, knowing she had heard him. She stood still, gazing up at him, her stunning green eyes wide and wistful. Her red lips parted, as if she was trying to catch her breath, unsure whether to walk towards him or run. He could see it in her expression.

He knew if she ran he would chase her. He prayed she would not.

He walked down the steps slowly towards her, stopping a step just above her.

"Hello Lilliana." He said quietly, staring at her with an unwavering intensity.

"Hi." she gazed up, breathless.

The look of him. It shattered her in so many ways. Being this close after so long apart. He looked more beautiful than he had five years ago, if that was at all possible, she thought.

The scent of her, this close, had him stepping back. "Would you mind coming into my office for a chat?" he offered her space to walk ahead of him.

She nodded and broke her gaze away from his, and walked up the steps, and towards his office. As she walked in, with him close behind, the door slid shut behind them.

She crossed over to the mantel and turned to watch him as he walked over to his desk.

He thought sitting behind it would better serve his male needs, which were taking over without his permission.

"Please Lilliana come, sit." He beckoned to the chair across the desk from his.

She walked over and gently sat down, crossing her legs, placing her hands nervously on her lap.

She could not take her eyes off his face. Nor he from hers.

He forced a smile. "You have been doing an excellent job in all your fields. I've read most of your cases and have been updated by some of the staff members, on all your achievements. I must to say, you are exactly where I thought you would be."

She raised an elegant eyebrow "Am I?" she asked quietly.

He twined his fingers together and held them to his lips, watching her intently.

Mm, it appeared she was a tad upset with him, he thought.

"I had Allie here last night, she was telling me about the room you designed. I'm hoping you'll take me along to see it."

Lilliana nodded. His hair, she noted, hung a little bit longer over his collar. Silky, black locks. His fingers, near his lips, looked long and strong.

She remembered how they felt around her throat, running down her sides, gripping her hips.

Oh brother, she thought. Calm down. His feelings have obviously changed; otherwise he would have sought you out as soon as he'd arrived.

She glanced away from him, resting her eyes on the edge of the desk.

"Will you not speak with me Lilliana?" He leaned back in his chair, folding his arms.

Her eyes flashed to his. "Yes Sir, of course." She stood.

"We have a couple of hours until our group today, would you be interested in coming along to see our room now?"

"Certainly." He stood and followed her as she walked towards the door.

So much to say. No way to say it all at this stage.

He wanted to reach out and grab her arm, spin her towards him and crush her lush mouth beneath his.

But he would not do that to her. Not after what he'd done already.

They walked out of the office, past the library, towards the back section where the stairs led down to the hospital.

They did not speak to each other but had plenty of people stopping them along the way for a quick chat, a question or a simple hello.

It took them half an hour to reach the door to Lilliana's office.

He noticed the two photographs of her on the outside wall.

One where she appeared to be asleep, covered in blood and he knew what else, the day she had arrived at this establishment after being abused for weeks on end.

The other, the stunning photograph of her in the prayer position with her Dark Angel outfit on, making her look like the real thing.

How very far she had come.

She was watching him as she had stepped into the office, waiting for him to follow. His gaze left her past and found her watching him, again.

He smiled and walked through her door.

"Wow." He was surprised and impressed. "This is stunning."

He walked into the middle of the room, appreciating the space. He absolutely loved the Buddha fountain, marvelling at the sheer size of it.

He walked over to the tank to have a closer look.

"Very impressive." He commented as he noted both the girls workspace, the library that offered a younger, fresh, yet professional feel about it. Offering all who came to speak with them, a very comfortable, relaxing place to sit and chat.

"What a brilliant effort Lilliana." He faced her after he'd had a thorough look around.

"Yes," She smiled her beautiful smile. "Allie and I absolutely love it down here, as do all of those who come here. We even have a few of our old friends' pop in to chat. Cam wants me to design his rooms for him."

"Well, who can blame him? It is sensational. Maybe I'll get you to do my office next door?" He hoped very much that they could come to some agreement.

She looked away from his eyes. Not trusting herself to say anything else.

She felt so confused. She wanted to rush into his arms, push her fingers through his hair. Feel that strong, male body close to hers.

But no, he was holding himself as a professional, aloof even. Surely she could do the same.

His eyes flickered up and down her body as her gaze was diverted.

Fresh, strong, clean, so purely Lilliana.

Her phone buzzed and she looked at him, excused herself and went to answer it.

"Lilliana. Hello Clair. No. Can't Richard deal with that?" Damon heard her sigh deeply, watching as she rubbed the back of her neck. He almost smiled. She still did that when nervous or uncomfortable, or so it seemed. "Can't you get Shelley or Jaycee to attend? Did he now? Fine. I'll be there in ten minutes. But I have group in an hours' time, and I am not missing that."

She ended the call, blushing a little with the intense way Damon was staring at her.

He'd left an intelligent, strong young girl and found a sensational woman. He too, knew that that would happen.

"I'm sorry but I have to go to Black Ops. We have a patient, Felicia who apparently has a thing for wanting me attend her." She shrugged a shoulder.

Damon tensed; his body stance became rigid. "Not at all. I understand. Thank you for the tour." He turned abruptly and left the room.

"You are welcome." She whispered to the empty room, puzzled at his quick change of manner but pushed it away as she headed up to Black Ops.

She arrived to find Johnson waiting for her. He seemed agitated.

"Hello Johnson." Lilliana smiled kindly, not liking to see this sweet, hard-working man conflicted. "What's wrong?"

"So very much," he said quietly, "come."

He led her to a cell where Felicia was sitting on the ground pulling out pieces of her thin, long blonde hair.

"Felicia, what are you doing? Is something the matter?" Concern filled her voice.

Felicia's eyes looked coldly at Lilliana. "Yes something is the matter you fucking *slut, you cut my baby out of me.*" She screamed, jumping up and rushing forward. She grabbed hold of the bars, pushing her face up hard against the cold metal.

Lilliana sighed. "Felicia, I'm sorry you feel that way. In time, you will come to terms with the decision made by Dr Richard. It was a decision made with the best intention for the foetus. Is there something else I can do for you?" Lilliana was trying to be positive and supportive but could also feel her best intentions draining away every minute she was here in Black Ops.

Felicia reached a thin, pale hand up to her head, grabbed a handful of hair and pulled it slowly out of her head. Not even screaming as a piece of scalp came away with it. Lilliana had seen a lot, even as a child before she came to the Given, but sometimes every now and then, someone did something that made her skin crawl. This was one of those moments.

Felicia threw the piece of scalp, with hair clinging to it, towards Lilliana, who luckily had seen it coming and dodged it in time. It landed outside the cell with a wet sounding splat. Lilliana looked away from the repulsive clump towards Johnson. "Why am I here?"

"Her maiden name was Reid."

"Oh." Lilliana said quietly, as it all clicked into place. "My god, but they are as sick as each other."

"Yes well, that's not all Lilliana." Johnson was trying to figure out how to tell her the rest.

"*STOP.*" Cam's voice called out.

Lilliana and Johnson turned to see Damon and Cam walking towards them with purposeful strides.

Felicia's head snapped up; eyes locked on Damon's handsome face.

"Will, *WILL, WILL.*" She screamed. "You've found me Will, I knew you'd find me, finally. Get me the fuck out of here, get this bitch away from me Will!"

Lilliana's face drained of blood. She looked at Felicia, then back towards Damon.

Will. Damon. Was Damon Will undercover? Oh, Lord. Her hearing started to fade. She looked back at Felicia. It made sense. The time Damon arrived was the same time Felicia arrived.

This woman had to be the 'blood-baby' wife. Oh, the baby! Was that Damon's baby she'd seen scraped out, the blood on her wrist when Richard had pulled her free from Felicia's grip?

She looked over at Damon, tears burned her eyes and confused emotions clogged her throat.

Damon was pained beyond belief to see Lilliana struggling with her emotions.

Felicia was in a total screaming frenzy by this stage, her thin pale arms reaching through the bars towards her Will, crying, begging him to get her out of there.

Damon did not even acknowledge her, his worried eyes remaining on Lilliana's face.

Her ears were ringing, she saw Damon's mouth move, but no sound registered. He went to lunge forward, wanting to stop what was about to happen, but was too many feet away.

With Lilliana's eyes on Damon, she completely forgot about the screaming Felicia, as Felicia's long arm reached out through the bars, grabbing a handful of Lilliana's hair, and with such force, jerked her backwards, slamming the back of her head hard against the metal cage.

Johnson sprang into action, buzzed the cage open and forcefully pulled Felicia's fingers from Lilliana's hair.

Lilliana closed her eyes, then opened them briefly, trying to clear the black and white spots which were dancing across her vision, as she saw Cam race towards her.

All in good time, although she tried to fight it, she unwillingly passed out in his arms.

"Bloody hell, what a fucking mess!" Cam yelled at his brother.

"Calm down Cameron, Johnson knew all about it."

Damon looked ill, as he glanced at Felicia, now restrained and locked up tight, then at the woman in his brother's arms. He ran his hands through his hair, desperate to take her off him.

"So, that psycho in there is your legal *wife*?" Cam practically shouted.

He knew he was out of line, and being irrational, but it was hard not to when faced with this entire situation.

"Cameron," Johnson said firmly. "Please calm down, you know it was undercover and we are doing everything we can to annul the marriage with the Officials legal team. Relax, let's just get Lilliana somewhere else before she comes to. Okay?"

Cam turned on his heel with Lilliana in his arms, fuming.

What a mess. Bloody Richard knew all about it, he was sure of it, and the bastard had involved Lilliana knowing that she'd find out about it all in the end.

He marched out of Black Ops and headed towards his rooms. It was closer than her office, or her room.

Damon was not far behind.

He paused briefly outside his door while the security scanner identified him, before opening the door for him to enter.

Josephine was lying on the ground designing a garden on numerous sheets of graphic paper. She looked up, ready to smile at her love, but the thought of a smile quickly vanished as soon as her gaze fell on the woman in his arms.

She jumped up, standing on her designs as she rushed forward.

"What's happened? Lilliana?" She placed her hand on her friend's forehead.

"Let me put her on the bed." Cam walked into the next room and placed her on their king-sized bed. "Jose my love, could you get me an ice pack?"

"Sure baby." She got to it, handing it to him within moments.

He placed it gently against the lump on the back of Lilliana's head, holding it place.

Damon stood in the doorway.

Cam looked over at him. "Look, I'm sorry brother, but I think she would be better off, by you not being here when she comes to."

Josephine looked between Damon and Cam. Seeing Lilliana was in very good hands, and seeing the expression on Damon's face, she walked over and linked her arm through his.

"I think we need a drink, in your rooms Damon. It has been too long since I've been in that part of the house."

"Okay." He said quietly, so unlike himself.

Josephine was worried, and Cam too, was anxious at his tone.

Josephine offered Cam a small smile, as she led Damon from their room, to his.

Josephine walked straight over to Damon's small bar and poured them both a rather large shot of honeyed whiskey; as Damon went and sat on one of the couches, head in hands.

Josephine slowly walked towards him and sat close beside him bumping her knee against his.

When he looked up she wanted to cry, the expression on his face was one which she had never seen, and it was full of despair.

"Hey." She whispered, pushing the whiskey into his hands, "It's going to be alright. Whatever it is, it's going to be alright."

Damon threw the shot down his throat as if it were water. If only it could get rid of the disgust he felt within himself when he'd looked at Felicia, followed by the pain that had flashed across Lilliana's face.

He dropped the glass onto the table as his head fell heavily back into his hands. Josephine put her full glass down in front of him, feeling he needed it more than she did. Rubbing his back, she leaned into him, offering any comfort she could. "I'm so worried about you right now. What can I do to help you Damon?"

He shook his head not daring to speak. He felt so devastated.

Devastated by what he had been through the past five years. The things he had done to prove himself trustworthy. The despicable woman he had had to marry to remain deep undercover. The woman who almost made him sick every time he had to touch her.

How he hated her guts! He wished her every hell possible.

And after two hours talking with Josephine it all came out.

From the first meeting with Johnson's contact, followed by vile, illegal activities to form solid relationships with the underworld scum, concreting his place in their society. Then, meeting Felicia, acting the part of a successful drug lord, and having her fall deeply in love with him, taking him to another world of crime and its many contacts.

The feeling of hatred when he had first injected a pregnant woman, creating a blood-drug baby, to partaking in using the blood, becoming a hateful parasite himself, and then sadly, ending the lives of many of the older blood-drug children as they reached the age of eighteen, when their blood became defective. It was almost too much to think about.

He kept the most horrific stories to himself, for Josephine's sake.

When he'd been debriefed by Johnson, Richard, Clair and Hillary he had held nothing back. That had been ten hours of another kind of hell.

Josephine was beyond devastated for this strong, conflicted brother of hers.

He had put himself through five years of hell and had destroyed the future growth of six of the biggest blood-drug divisions in two countries.

To say she was proud of him did not cut it.

She knew Lilliana would understand once all was explained.

"I think what you need," Josephine said pulling his head around so he could look her in the eyes, "is no thinking for an hour, but simple enjoyment of a ride, fresh air and peace with the knowledge that you are safely back home, after all your hard, selfless work, with a good life in front of you. Starting now, what do you say?"

He looked at her ever pretty, honest brown eyes, and smiled. "You may be onto something." He nodded, standing up, pulling her up with him and holding her close. "I'm blessed to have you Josephine."

She looked up at him. "And how blessed have I always been to have had you? We've always been lucky, you and me. Now tell me Damon, do you love her? Lilliana?"

Damon smiled down at her and whispered. "Always and forever."

"Brilliant. Let's give her some time to digest all this information, okay, she's been through a lot lately."

"Yes Ma'am." He kissed her nose.

"Good Sir, now off you go!" She smiled over her shoulder at him as she left through the doorway in search of Cam.

CHAPTER 7

Lilliana came back to the land of conscience, to find Cam leaning over her, a concerned look on his face.

"I think I'm going to be sick," she whispered, humiliated. He had a bucket ready and pulled her up, holding her hair while she vomited.

Once she was finished, he wiped her mouth, gave her a glass of water to rinse and spit and then went into his bathroom to wash and flush.

When he came back to her, she was sitting up, legs dangling over the side of the bed. Her fancy heels adding to the charm as she almost looked like that young girl who had first come to them years earlier. Lost. Unsure. Scared.

He knelt at her feet, looking up into her pale face.

"All will be well Lilliana. We've sent a file through to your office. I think it would be helpful for you to go over it today, after group."

"Sure." She said quietly. "I'd better go, I don't want to let Allie or my group down." She waited for him to stand, then slid off the bed, touching the small lump on the back of her head, wincing slightly.

She glanced up at Cam. "Thanks for catching me." Sounding a little embarrassed.

"Always my Angel, always." He kissed the top of her head.

"I'll make sure a meal gets delivered to you. The file is over ten hours long." He smiled.

She nodded, squeezing his hand as she left, having no words at this moment, and knew she had to put herself in a positive state to get through group, and give them all the attention they deserved.

***

Lilliana arrived just as their last patient entered.

She'd had enough time to change into a comfortable pair of blue jeans, heeled boots that came up to her knees and a white shirt. She'd brushed her teeth, and hair gently, trying not to hit the lump.

She had needed a bit of makeup to cover her paleness and add a sparkle to her eyes.

Allie smiled at her as she sat in her usual position, giving her a nod of approval. Josephine had contacted Allie an hour beforehand and filled her in on all the recent events.

She had been shocked and didn't expect to see Lilliana in group. Had almost called Hillary when Cam had rung through to let her know Lilliana would be attending group.

Luckily, group was smooth sailing this day.

There was one minor incident, but Allie sorted it out effortlessly.

Lilliana held herself together, answering any questions directed at her, or offering a gentle opinion, giving advice and simply being one-hundred percent present for all in the group.

When they smiled, and said goodbye to their last patient, the door sliding shut, Lilliana plonked down on a soft chair and stared sightlessly towards her fish.

Allie pushed a hot tea into her hands.

Lilliana smiled up at her, snapping out of her thoughts. "Thanks."

"Are you going to be alright?" Concern filled Allie's voice.

"Yes, eventually," Lilliana replied, sipping her tea.

"Do you want me to stay and review those files with you?" Allie gestured to Lilliana's desk.

"Oh, no Allie, no that's fine. I'll be fine." She forced a small smile. "I think that's something I have to do on my own."

Allie squeezed her shoulder. "You know where to find me if you need me. Lock the door, okay?"

"Yes, okay. Please don't worry Allie. Enjoy the rest of your day, It's the first mostly free day you've had in months."

"Yes, yours also and look what happened." Allie headed over to the door.

As she stepped out, before it slid shut, pointed firmly and said, "Lock it."

Lilliana smiled, getting up to lock the door and placed her empty teacup back on the tray.

Walking over to her desk, she grabbed the data system, no bigger than a tennis ball and placed it on to the surface of the rounded table, in the centre of the room. Pressing the centre of the disc-like-object, she projected a large screen which hung mid-air, so she could sit comfortably, or stand.

She set the atmosphere to make the task as peaceful as possible, lighting some scented candles.

Thinking it was going to be a long ten hours was an understatement.

The session seemed to start well. The screen ever watchful on Damon's face. His interrogators, Johnson and the three leading Doctors, were behind camera, not making an appearance once. Just their voices demanding answers to unnerving, uncomfortable and never-ending question after question.

It took her back to a time when she herself had been assaulted by unwanted questions.

Damon appeared in control, relaxed, leaning back in his seat, hands loosely clasped together.

He started off, by talking about why he had chosen to leave their facility and go undercover. After hearing about the parasites that impregnated women, to infect their babies blood with the drug that would ultimately deliver the babies into a life of slavery and an early death.

To first, contacting Johnson's men, who were a part of the Officials network, then forming the necessary relationships with the Underworlds unsavoury individuals.

It was a dark, dangerous world, full of despicable souls, like Felicia

Reid.

It made Lilliana sick to hear her name on his lips. She paced the room as she watched and listened.

Four hours in, she had to pause it. Hands on her hips, she could not stop shaking as she paced back and forth. Her head reeling at the things Damon had been informing his 'interrogators'.

The tests he had done to prove himself. He said he could never forgive himself for some of the tasks he had performed.

He had leaned forward at one stage, head in hands, his voice choked.

Johnson had assured him, if it weren't for his deep involvement undercover, they could not have shut down all the organisations that they had.

Her meal arrived. She could not touch it. It was enough of a chore just drinking tea.

She heard Dr Richard's voice asking about intercourse with the enemy. She froze.

Damon had shot him down with a look of disgust and told him that was irrelevant to the outcome of the case.

Dr Richard had then replied, obviously not, as he survived successfully and happily married undercover for those five years.

Damon had cursed and Johnson had calmed everyone down, with the help of Dr Clair.

It was gruelling, emotionally exhausting and due to pausing it often, took Lilliana twelve hours to complete the entire debrief.

She pressed pause on the last image. It was all Damon. His tired, ever-handsome face, glancing into the camera.

She sat and simply stared at his face, taking in all that she'd heard.

Common sense told her he had done everything in his power to make this world a better place. He always had.

Even here, he had constantly done everything he could, daily, to soothe anyone who was in pain, or try to find a solution to his people's problems. Always.

She couldn't hold on to the fact that if he hadn't left in the first place, he wouldn't be suffering now, and they may have had five years of blissful happiness.

No, she wouldn't hold onto that. Not in the end when he had succeeded at his mission. She shut the system down, glancing at the clock. Two a.m.

She walked around the room, blowing out candles, leaving the small light above the Buddha on.

Crossing to her desk she pulled open the bottom drawer, took out a soft mink blanket and a small pillow.

Pushing the draw closed with her foot, she made up a make-shift bed on the soft chairs, positioning her-self cosily where she could watch the fish drift lazily.

The trickling of the fountain and the emotional day had her asleep in no time.

***

In the morning Lilliana had a quick bite to eat, after a run with one of the early running groups. She had slept poorly, her dreams filled with the ache of Damon's voice and all he had endured. After a quick shower, she dressed and headed down, behind schedule for her first Group of the day. She only just made it in time.

Allie was talking to a young boy of seventeen who liked to wear a different mask each day as he said it was a part of him.

Today he had an eerie mask of a clown on.

Lilliana apologized quietly to everyone and sat down.

"And why have you chosen a clown face today Rick?" Allie asked the boy.

"Because I want to kill someone today. I can feel the urge. The shadows are coming."

Allie glanced across at Lilliana.

This was their second Group with this lot of Given, and Allie had assessed Rick herself and had deemed him low risk.

Today, with what had come out of his mouth so far, it didn't seem that way.

"Would you feel safer being somewhere else Rick?" Lilliana tried not to feel freaked out, as the expressionless clown face turned her way.

"I feel safe," he said slowly. "do you?"

"I'm sorry, but why do I have to be in a room full of nut bags?"

Sophia, a sassy blonde girl looked fed up.

"I mean, I get fucked up the ass by my brother my entire life, try to kill myself, that didn't work. Finally get a break, although now, that seems debatable, am sent here, and have to suffer and listen to this bullshit." She stood, putting her hands on her hips, and turned to Rick. "There are no shadows, you moron. And if you feel like killing anybody, do us all a favour and kill yourself!"

Rick stood slowly and took a step towards Sophia.

Lilliana quickly got to her feet and moved between them, holding a hand out to each of them.

"Rick, sit, calm down. Sophia, that kind of talk is not tolerated nor helpful, not only in this room, but in this entire establishment. Sit."

Sophia glared at Lilliana then at Rick. "Sorry Lilliana." She sat slowly.

Lilliana went over to her seat and sat, keeping a close eye on Rick for the remainder of the session.

It was a heartfelt hour, as they gave Ruth a chance to purge her story of watching her mother and sister being murdered in front of her. Then she herself was held prisoner for four years by the same man.

He never touched her or spoke to her. But she had been terrified of him always.

She still had gruesome nightmares and often blacked out to escape her world and thoughts.

It was a good session for Ruth, as she talked openly and with gentle persuasion.

"Well done Ruth," Allie applauded her. "Well done."

Lilliana stood as the session drew to a close. "Thank you everyone for a great session, make your next class on time and have a good day. Rick, stay behind please."

A few of the Given thanked them, others just nodded and left.

Rick slouched back in his chair, swinging his arm over the back of it.

As the door slid shut, Allie joined Rick. "What's this about killing urges Rick? Do we need to place you in a different division?"

Rick turned his gaze away from Lilliana and looked across at Allie.

"No, I was kidding." He muttered; his voice was as flat as his clown mask.

"I don't think you were," Lilliana said. "Allie, excuse me for a moment."

She walked over to her desk and hit the switch for her glass panel to slide across, offering her phone call the privacy that was needed.

Dr Hillary arrived with a security escort minutes later.

Rick was as sweet as pie, going with them calmly and readily, not causing a fuss what-so-ever.

Once the door shut behind them, Allie looked across at Lilliana. "Good call, we'll see what comes from it."

Lilliana nodded. "Hopefully all will be well. I've got Eric in five minutes."

There was a knock on the door.

"Or now," Lilliana smiled as the door slid open to reveal Eric.

Tall, and good looking, with a troubled darkness about him that had always been there.

"Hello Eric, come in." Lilliana watched as he walked past Allie.

Natalie turned up moments after him, to go into Allie's room.

They both had an hour session, but Eric's time ran over by an extra twenty minutes.

"Thanks Doc, I appreciate the extra time. Some days are hard. Harder than others you know." Eric looked down at her as they walked to the door.

"We deal with trauma the best way we can, and you've made great progress Eric. Your role as Watcher, really suits you." She stopped to face him as they stepped out into the corridor.

"You should be so proud of yourself." Lilliana rubbed his arm before crossing hers.

He nodded, his eyes frowning as he looked at someone behind her. Glancing over her shoulder, she saw what had caused Eric's frown.

Damon, walking briskly towards them, hands in his jeans pockets, black shoes tapping on the marbled floors.

She turned back to Eric and smiled. "Well, I'll see you around Eric."

He smiled at her and stepped close, leaning down, he whispered, "If you have any problems you know, you can talk to me."

He stepped back and walked past Lilliana, saying nothing to Damon as he left to retrieve his Given from solitude.

Lilliana took a deep breath as she heard Damon come up behind her. She turned to greet him and practically bumped into his chest.

She laughed quietly, taking a step back. "Sorry." God, he smelt good.

"Don't be. How are you this morning?" Her scent wrapped around him, as he glanced down at her body, noting how her blue dress clung to every curve, her black belt cinched at her waist. Black heels affording her extra height, making her eyes almost level to his.

Her long, silky waves were pulled back loosely with a clip, a few tendrils escaping here and there.

How he wanted to touch her. Desperately!

Him standing so close, inspecting her like a prized horse was not only making her nervous, but dizzy as well.

"Can I help you Sir?" Her voice, breaking the spell.

His eyes flicked back to hers, as he straightened, realizing he was slowly leaning down towards her.

"Yes." He glanced back at her lips. "You can help me." He cleared his throat, which was what she was looking at.

Allie left her office area and walked up to them both. "Morning Damon." She smiled.

"Allie, good morning." He returned her smile. "I am borrowing Lilliana for an hour or two, as I checked your schedules today. I have asked Hillary if she will help you with this afternoon's group."

Allie looked across at Lilliana. "No worries. It's a pretty casual group. I'll see you later then."

"Fantastic. Lilliana, if you will please come with me."

Lilliana said bye to Allie and went with Damon. They walked to the rear of the Hospital and stepped into a hidden doorway, leading to the secured passageway.

As they walked along Lilliana was very aware of the man beside her. She could hear his breathing. Feel the heat of his skin.

She was desperate to say something about his undercover work. Ask him how he was doing. Tell him how proud she was of him, but instead asked, "Where are we going?"

"Johnson wanted me to come get you; he needs your help with David Reid."

Lilliana stopped short.

He turned to face her when he realized she wasn't walking with him. "Is this a problem for you? If it is Lilliana, I can do something about it." He pushed his hands deeper into his pockets. If they came out, even a fraction, he would put them on her, and now was not that time.

Lilliana glanced back down the direction that they had come, before looking back at Damon. Thinking of Johnson, knowing he wouldn't ask her if he didn't need her help so desperately.

"No," she said softly. "It's no problem."

He nodded. "Come then." He continued down the length of the corridor, before heading up the steep stairs.

Lilliana watched his long, strong legs, saying nothing. Hoping whatever was to come next, would be over soon.

They walked on in silence for the next few minutes, going up to the higher levels, finally coming across the narrow bridge leading to Black Ops. Damon opened the gate for her, then the door and nodded at the guard as they passed.

"How are you Mr Night?"

"Good thanks Henry, yourself?" Damon smiled as Lilliana walked past.

"Good Sir, things have been busy."

"As always." Damon replied, as he continued along the way, and going up another flight of stairs, he took Lilliana into Johnson's office.

It was a large, spacious room with thick glass tables lining one wall, security monitors on the opposite one, showing around one hundred different areas of the Given rooms and grounds.

Lilliana was amazed at what one could see.

From Christopher in the kitchen, teaching a few young Givens a challenging technique working with pastry, to Thomas in the stables with a vet checking on the mares.

Jessica and Orlando were out in the meditation garden with a small group, working on mindfulness.

And was that Natalie in the laundry room, trying on one of Fox's outfits? And that was most definitely Rupert and Luke making out behind the pool house.

Dr Richard walking around his classroom, hands clasped behind his back, lecturing away.

"Interesting what you see people doing, isn't it?" Damon said behind her.

She was about to reply when Johnson stepped in.

"What you're seeing there is the latest high-grade CCTV by the military's Department of Homeland Security." He indicated to the opposite wall, which held just as many screens, all images of the outside world.

"Impressive."

"Thank you, Lilliana. I was hoping you'd come." He walked over to her and put his large hands on her shoulders.

"I need your help badly." He squeezed her shoulders gently before walking over to his desk.

"I know," she sighed, "you would not have asked me here if it's not important. But I need to remind you Johnson. I hate being up here."

"I hope this is the last time, in a long time, that I have to ask you here." He looked up from downloading files onto a tablet, looking her in the eyes. "But the fact is, you are my very powerful tool with this sick bastard."

Lilliana nodded as she watched Damon lean his hip against the desk, watching her, she quickly averted her eyes back to Johnson.

Why did his simple glance make her want to melt?

Make her want to walk over and throw herself in his arms?

Stop it. She internally scolded herself, be cool, calm and carry on.

Be professional.

Johnson, watching Lilliana and Damon, wanted to chuckle. It was so obvious they wanted each other. Stubborn people!

"Lilliana, you'll need to go over these files quickly, just to get updated. I'll go make you a tea. Damon?" He turned to the man he respected, feeling his pain. He had been through so much the past few years. Damon had confessed to both himself and Cam the other night, that he would not touch Lilliana, and taint her with his filthy hands. He and Cam had argued with him, reasoning that that was not the case, but, he was punishing himself for the wicked things he'd done, whilst undercover.

He was having nightmares and was needing to speak to Clair every spare hour she had, to deal with his guilt and to try to cleanse and heal his mind, so he could operate to his full potential for all his people.

For Damon, it was torture to be near Lilliana and not touch her. To see her, to hear her. It was his way of punishing himself.

"No, I'm good thanks." Damon leaned back and folded his arms.

"I'll wait here."

Johnson nodded passing the tablet to Lilliana as he left the room to go make her tea.

Lilliana sat in a chair close to where Damon stood.

She tried to ignore the fact that his legs were in reach if she stretched out her hand.

Ignore the fact that he was right there, looking down at her.

She focused on what needed to be read, for a few minutes, with difficulty, but could not handle the intensity of his proximity, for one second longer. She looked up, her green eyes connecting with his piercing blue ones.

"Can you please stop that? I can't concentrate!" She opened her hands above the files, as if to say, -trying to read and absorb.

"Sorry. I can't seem to help myself." He knew exactly what she was implying but did not look away.

Johnson broke the awkward, wanting tension as he walked back in, handing Lilliana her tea. She thanked him and continued reading for another twenty minutes.

She stood, setting her cup down on a side table, and placed the tablet on Johnson's desk.

"Is this true?" She looked Johnson in the eye. "Is David Reid's father the man who took Orlando's sister?"

"Yes. The very one. We've reviewed some of the footage we've had access to. You can actually see both David and Felicia in the background of an orgy at a particular event making out with each other." He glanced across at Damon.

Damon remained still; eyes ever watchful on Lilliana.

She had reached up to grab a long, silky lock and curled her finger around it as she paced.

"Can it get any more disturbing?" She whispered, and stopped pacing, turning to face Johnson. "What do you want me to do?"

"As you know, Mr Reid is an ex-Diplomat, and extremely powerful still. He has been linked to several mass terrorist and bio attacks in Australia, Ireland, and China and has recently targeted these countries, abducting the Presidents' youngest children." Johnson ran a finger around his collar, then popped the top button of his shirt.

Lilliana knew the gesture showed how much duress Johnson was under with this situation.

Damon's voice cut into her concern for Johnson.

"It is up to us to find out where this location is. The Presidents' have offered this facility one million if we get them back, in any condition. We'd do it for free of course, but they insist."

Lilliana looked at Damon. "Even if they are dead?" she shook her head.

"That's correct. Johnson believes you can get David to give us the location, or locations." Damon didn't doubt it.

Lilliana rubbed her arms and then folded them. "How am I supposed to get this information out of him? Last time was not my idea of a picnic." She looked across at Johnson. "What do you expect me to do?"

Johnson sighed, not liking what was to come. "As you know, David is a complete, although extremely talented, Psychopath. He has done horrific things, but his greatest weakness, the only one we have discovered, is his total inability to hurt anything that is beautiful, that turns him on. He has a weird sense where he just wants to please a beautiful woman." Johnson shrugged. "It takes all sorts."

"Going through his files last night," Damon addressed her, "we came across a case of a series of kidnappings, where several female victims stated, that although he held them against their will, he did not hurt them, but seemed to only want to please them. Dressing them in the highest fashion, having chefs cook for them, spa treatments. The only thing he demanded of them was that they use their manners and treat him with respect. He held them for three weeks each, before releasing them to the exact location he took them from." Damon did not think it necessary, to inform Lilliana what David Reid had done to the women that had not used their manners.

Lilliana rubbed her forehead. She didn't like what she was hearing. "Well, he didn't seem to want to please me the last time we had a discussion, and I really don't think me being in a room with him for any amount of time is going to make him give me the locations of his father's Crime Houses."

"The youngest child taken, is four-years-old Lilliana, we have to try." Damon had walked over to her and said this quietly near her bent head. She looked up at him, then across to Johnson.

"Let's get this over with then, I suppose you want to give me a script?"

"Script and costume," he forced a smile. "Sorry Lilliana, but trust me, the more to his taste I can present you, the less time you will be in the same room with him."

"Oh great." Lilliana placed her hands on her hips and shook her head. "This just gets better and better. I really should have taken those acting classes Richard suggested in my early days of group."

Damon hid a smile recalling those days and was about to comment when a voice called out.

"Are we ready?" Fox, with a large carry bag in hand, crossed over to Lilliana and put her arm around her shoulders, smiling down at her.

"How are you darling?"

"Just swell." Lilliana hugged Fox back. "If you want a drop-dead gorgeous woman, why not let Fox do this?"

"Because Lilliana you are trained for this and he has a thing, for you." Damon felt like a wolf leading a lamb to slaughter.

"And because," Fox said, "I would rip that bastard's jugular out in five seconds!" She smiled, stunningly, looking like a very sexy, sly Fox indeed.

"That wouldn't be such a bad thing." Lilliana muttered.

Damon wanted to laugh looking at her expression. It was the second time he'd seen her close to sulking.

"Right, Fox, ten minutes, let's get this done. We'll be up in section E, room five." Johnson turned and left the room.

Lilliana looked at Damon as Fox was taking a slip of a white dress out.

He smiled at her and turned away leaving Fox and Lilliana alone in the room, closing the door behind him.

"Right, we need you apparently to appear sexy, sweet and classy. Nothing out of the ordinary for you." Fox turned to Lilliana. "Come on sweet cakes, get undressed."

Lilliana kicked off her heels and slipped out of her dress.

"No, that underwear won't do." Fox said, tapping her lips.

"Well, I'm not planning on showing him my underwear Fox, so it shouldn't really matter." Lilliana folded her arms.

"Darling, when you play a role, everything matters." Fox clicked her fingers. "Now strip!"

Lilliana got naked, and Fox handed her a gorgeous matching strapless bra and G-string in pearl white.

Then Fox slipped the elegant and sexy short white, silk dress over Lilliana's head, and helped her step into high heels.

Lilliana looked down in dismay. "It's practically see through!" She glared at Fox.

"Hence the sexy underwear dear," Fox smiled. "Let's go."

They left the room, Lilliana not too happy. She kept her mind focused on the four-year old child who was in the hands of another type of lunatic.

They arrived at their destination within five minutes, after going up a flight of stairs and past cells where quite a few prisoners got a good eyeful of Lilliana.

When Damon spotted her walking towards him, his mouth went dry. She looked like a goddess.

He could just make out her underwear and was privately thanking Fox for her creative imagination.

"Let's hope he doesn't eat her alive," Johnson said quietly behind him.

"Not going to happen." Damon replied just as quietly, as the two ladies joined them.

"Hope that's what you wanted gentlemen."

"It's perfect Fox, thank you." Johnson smiled at her.

"You can go now." Damon did not take his eyes off Lilliana.

Fox saluted before winking at Lilliana. "Knock him dead tiger, and I mean that literally!"

Johnson was going through a list of things he expected Lilliana to ask, how to act, what to say. She was nodding trying to take it all in, but she was all too aware of herself being practically naked, with Damon one foot away, eyes pinned on her.

"Ready? Let's go." Johnson nodded towards the door. As Lilliana stepped forward, Damon grabbed her upper arm and pulled her back towards him.

She turned to face him and froze as his hands went up to cup her face, he gently stroked the side of her cheek, then slipped his fingers into her hair. She reminded herself to keep breathing, struggling not to put her hands on him. His scent overwhelmed her, standing so close, watching him swallow, as the tip of his tongue peeked out between his lips as he concentrated on his task. Her hands reached up to grab his wrists, but he stopped her further movement with a slight shake of his head. His fingers unclipped her hair, and putting the clip into his back pocket, ran his fingers over her scalp, releasing all her long, silky locks, allowing them to fall over her shoulders and down the length of her back.

Johnson cleared his throat, feeling like he was intruding on a moment.

"That's better," Damon said softly, stepping back, giving her a small smile.

She nodded to him, a little lost for words. Had loved his hands on her.

Those long strong fingers running along her scalp. She wanted them there again. And now, she was supposed to concentrate and seduce a psychopath to talk?

She took a deep, nervous breath.

"Think of it as modelling Lilliana, it's just another role," Damon suggested, wanting to soothe her somehow.

She nodded again and stepped through the door which Johnson had opened for her.

CHAPTER 8

Stepping into the room, Lilliana channelled the character she had to play, to get this individual to talk to her.

There was a long mirror on one wall where she knew Johnson and Damon would be watching and recording this session. Two chairs were placed in the room.

"Hello Doctor," the handsome, yet creepy man said. "You've come to pay me a visit I see. I've been asking for you. Good to see people around here listen."

David Reid sat, unchained, legs crossed, fingers linked behind his head, looking like he had just attended the theatre and had finished a good meal.

He was all in white. Straight-legged pants, a white tee shirt and running shoes.

They matched, she thought.

"Hello David." She forced the smile she needed to display and elegantly sat opposite him, crossing her legs, allowing the white slip to slide further up her leg to reveal a strong, tanned thigh. "How are you today?"

"Fine, now that you're here. How are you?"

"Good. Thank you." She tipped her head a little, letting her hair fall over her shoulder, past her breast, where she could see his eyes fixated. She took a long lock and twirled it around and around her finger.

"And what shall we do with ourselves today?" his eyes roaming up and down her legs.

"I was hoping you'd talk to me about your father?" She stopped twirling her hair and let her hand slowly slip down her front and rest on the top of her thigh, tapping a long, clear fingernail against the hem of her dress.

"Well, you know Dr Lilliana, you need to do something for me, if you want me to do something for you." He voice, chillingly quiet.

Lilliana shrugged, glancing away, looking down at the floor then, slowly up at him through her long, dark eyelashes.

"What do you want?"

"I want to massage your feet."

Lilliana remembered what Johnson had said. The slightest physical contact, and David would be sure to give them a truckload of vital information.

Damon could clearly see her shoulders stiffen. "I'm not sure she can do this."

"No," Johnson replied, "you're just not sure you can watch her do this."

"True." Damon folded his arms, legs spread, ready to run in there and put a stop to this precarious situation in a second.

"Relax. She's done this and more in the past five years and you weren't here to protect her." Johnson said, not unkindly.

"Thanks for the reminder," Damon snapped, keeping his eyes, like Johnson's, on the two people in the other room.

Lilliana raised her foot, stretching it out, looking so pretty in those beautiful heels Fox had put on her.

"Of course," she said holding it raised. "But first I want the name of one of your fathers' locations. I know he has several. I want them all."

David's eyes clouded over, so close to beautiful soft, smooth flesh. He wanted to touch her, badly. When else would he get this opportunity?

Once in The Givens Black Ops walls, forever he would remain. There was no getting out, not unless you considered death that unlucky ticket.

He leaned forward in his chair, reaching a hand to touch her shoe.

She pulled her leg back just out of his reach. "Uh-uh." She shook her head. "One location first." A delicate whisper.

He shot off a location in Cavan, Ireland, as fast as lightening.

This will be too easy, she thought to herself.

She slowly extended her leg, offering him her foot, mentally preparing herself for his touch.

He sighed as his hands claimed her foot, pulling himself and his chair closer, he placed her foot near his groin.

Lilliana froze, but quickly forced herself to relax. Her hands had gone to the sides of her chair ready to bolt but slowly, taking a deep breath, she placed them in her lap, trying to appear demure.

David had gone very quiet and was extremely focused on the pretty heeled shoe, on Lilliana's foot.

"Another location?" she asked, pushing her foot forward a little, feeling his swollen erection under the toe of her shoe.

She swallowed hard, as his creepy pale eyes looked directly into hers. "I want to fuck your foot," he said simply.

Lilliana shook her head. "Not an option."

He flicked off her shoe and his fingers pulled on her foot, pushing it hard against his groin and he yelled out two more locations.

He opened his legs wide and moved his swollen penis against the arch of her foot, as he continued to massage her.

"Stop!" she cried out.

"Open your legs," he commanded.

Lilliana glanced across at the mirror, wanting help, but knowing she had to get those locations.

She shook her head once at the mirror letting Johnson and Damon know she was alright, and didn't need them coming in.

She knew what she had to do. She'd been through worse and survived it.

Surely she could give this perverted prick what he wanted, to save a few innocents.

If Damon could do what he had done the past five years, to save so many, then so could she.

She looked at David. "How wide?"

His eyes nearly fell out of his head as he responded, "As wide as they'll go."

He released her foot, placing it gently on the ground.

She ran her hands down the length of her thighs, then up again. Holding onto the chair, Lilliana spread her legs open, so he could get a good look at Fox's sexy panties.

David moaned and rubbed his growing erection.

Lilliana swallowed the bile that was rising.

David called out three locations, including Australia and China, as he ejaculated in his pants.

Lilliana slammed her thighs together, scooped up the shoe, pushed her foot into it before crossing her legs.

"You know," he said quietly, "I've seen and done a lot in my young life." He leaned back in his chair, crossing his legs, either oblivious to, or not caring about the wet patch that was evident for all to see.

It was like they'd just finished a good game of tennis and were about to have cocktails by the pool.

"I have to say, I love kiddie flicks. The more fucked up the better. Probably because my Dad put me in them at a young age." He shrugged a shoulder. "Must be in your blood to really get it."

"I wouldn't know." Lilliana stood, she had to get away from him immediately, as her threshold for plain wrong had hit its limit. Walking towards the door, she asked over her shoulder, "Is that all the locations?"

He just smiled. "I'll finish this story, then I'll tell you one more." She swallowed her sigh and stood against the door, watching him.

"I have a particular memory of these two girls. Best video series I'd seen in ages." He placed his hands behind his head and shook it.

"Man, what these fellas made those two young things do to each other. It was like an ongoing series, my dad just had to purchase the next exciting episode. Cost him a small fortune, but it was so worth it. These girls were so beautiful, especially that dark one. She had real fire in her belly, fought like a hell cat, which of course, only got herself into more trouble. Brilliant for the viewers though." He chuckled. "Man, what they did to her, what they made her do, although, in the end I think she secretly liked it. I was desperate to watch her get it in the end, I would have liked that, I bet she would have too."

Lilliana had frozen like a deer in the headlights.

Of course, sick bastards like this would have enjoyed the suffering and pain inflicted on innocent girls like herself and Jessica. Not caring an ounce of the damage done, torture, endured. Internal and emotional wounds they would carry for the rest of their lives.

"The shame was, the night we were going to view the de-flowering of those two girls, we got nothing but a blood bath. Although, that was entertaining in itself." He smiled eerily.

Lilliana could not breathe, could not move. As David stood and slowly walked towards her, she continued to simply stare at him, feeling like that fifteen-year-old again.

He stepped close, putting his hands around her throat and whispered right against her ear, his breath hot. "I've never wanted to hurt anyone as beautiful as you. But you got away from them." He shook his head slowly. "You shouldn't have." His fingers tightened.

Lilliana snapped, she reached up to her ear and pulled out her earring, which was made up of solid, silver spikes, like spears of flowing ice crystals.

She grabbed hold of it, and as his fingers tightened around her throat she thrust upwards, a sharp spike striking into the side of David's neck.

He flew backwards, holding the wound where the blood started to flow, his eyes widened, almost with admiration, as Lilliana flew towards him, screaming all her rage as she punched him under the chin, making his head fly back.

As David fell over a chair, Lillian launched herself at him, determined to inflict bodily harm, but strong, firm arms reached around her waist, lifting her feet off the ground.

Her hands continued to reach outwards, as she screamed at David. Johnson entered with security, who shot David with a tranquilizer.

He went down quickly, saying softly to Lilliana, "We will end you."

She struggled to get free of those iron-like arms that gripped her waist.

"*Let Me Go!*" She screamed, her hands pulling at the arms around her. "*Let Me* go." The last word ending on a sob.

Damon kept his arms firmly around Lilliana, as she continued to struggle.

He carried her out of the room and walked further down the corridor, before placing her feet on the ground, but keeping his arms firmly around her, her back pressed against his chest. She would not be still.

His face pressed into her hair, his lips against her ear, "Lilliana, stop." He said soothingly, yet firmly. "Stop."

Her breathing was coming hard and fast, like so many unwanted images flooding her memory. She just had to get away, to be alone and shut herself down until she felt calm. She slipped off her heels and stopped fighting Damon.

She knew if she was still, he'd release her.

He did, against his better judgement, his arms slowly left her warm, rigid body.

She could feel his solid warmth behind her. She did not want to step away from him, but she had no choice. She waited five seconds, then sprinted off in the direction of the stairs, and flew down them. Her mind flashing back to that beautiful sunny day, before everything had turned black.

When Simon and Orlando Grey had cruelly taken her and her friend, drugged them and deposited them in a world of pain.

She sprinted to the main door, Henry opened it quickly, as he could see the tears streaming down her face. Eyebrows raised in concern but stepped out of her way as she bolted through, pushing the gate open and out, running across the bridge.

Which way? Left and straight, she ran, trying to block unwanted past turmoil. Remembering first waking to the sound of Jessica crying, the dripping faucet. Feeling so groggy, cold and terrified. From the first confronting abuse. Over, and over again.

She could hear footsteps catching up to her and bolted for the stairs that would lead down to the hospital. If she could just lock herself up in her office.

As she reached the top of the stairs, about to head down, large, strong hands gripped around her waist, lifting her off her feet once more.

She could smell Damon, wanted to turn to him, to allow his solid warmth to comfort her. But she didn't want him seeing her like this.

"No, please, just let me go!" She cried softly, but firmly, shaking her head.

"I don't think so Lilliana." His arms bound around her as he walked away from the stairs and moved back into the corridor. He placed her on the ground, one hand leaving her waist to run along her arm and stop at her wrist, his strong fingers gripping, like a handcuff. Then his other arm released her waist.

She slowly turned to face him, eyes meeting his.

His heart nearly broke seeing such emotional pain flash across her beautiful features.

"Lilliana." He whispered, feeling her devastation.

She dropped her head back, crying quietly, closing her eyes to block out his concerned, ever handsome face.

He swooped her up in a flash. Her head fell against his chest, keeping her eyes shut, her hands slid up his chest and went around his neck, pressing her tear stained face against his throat.

He walked quickly, knowing what he needed to do for her.

It took him minutes to walk to his rooms. Going in through the secured entrance, the panel sliding shut behind him.

He walked into the open lounge, and lay Lilliana on the soft couch, placing a small cushion under her head.

Her eyes remained closed, she placed her hands together and held them under her chin.

He gently swept her long, soft hair off her face and caught a tear on her cheek, wiping it away.

She heard his footsteps leave, only to return moments later. He ran a hand along her back, gently tugging her short dress down to cover her gorgeous bottom. He forced himself not to linger and placed a soft, mink blanket over her.

Walking to the fireplace, he hit a switch and flames burst through about the hearth, sending out heat and soothing light across the entire room. He stood watching her for a few moments, before quietly leaving the room to make a phone call.

Lilliana must have slept, for when her eyes opened again the room was darker, the window outside was showing late afternoon. The fire light gently flickering shadow-shapes around the room.

Sitting up, she looked around. No sign of Damon. Pushing the blanket off her, she saw a tray on the large coffee table with a note.

Lifting the lid, she saw a plate of sandwiches and a bowl of soup, still steaming.

The note read. - You are on lockdown. Do not leave this room. - Damon.

She wasn't sure how she felt about being told she was on lockdown, but if she was honest with herself, she did not want to leave. The room was cosy and warm, despite the fact she felt naked. She had a complete feeling of isolation, but not in an uncomfortable way. She crossed over to the mantel to see what photographs Damon had on display. There was one that made her smile. A very handsome man, clearly Damon's father, stood with his hands on his two little boys' shoulders, all happily smiling into the camera. The same man standing beside an attractive woman. Lilliana presumed it to be Damon's mother. There was one of Damon and Cam, both in archery gear, aiming their arrows towards the camera. Late teens, both very handsome. Of course, there was a photo of Damon on Beast.

And surprisingly, in a large silver frame, sat a photo of Lilliana in her Dark Angel outfit. It wasn't the sweet innocent shot that had been blown up and displayed near the Christmas tree, all those years ago. This was a close-up, where Lilliana's face dominated the shot, her eyes looking huge, green and bewitching. She looked coolly into the camera; a touch serious.

She even had to admit it was a sexy shot. And Damon had it on his mantel! She turned around, eyes surveying the rest of the room.

She could not believe she was standing in his private domain.

His scent was in the air, his presence, everywhere. It was a very masculine, sexy environment.

She looked over at his amazing bookshelves, filled with not only hundreds of old books, but bottles of wine, candles, awards and photographs.

She ran her hand along the back of one of the couches as she walked down to his desk at the end of the room.

It was a beautifully crafted old oak desk, and Lilliana thought of all the hours, upon hours Damon must have sat here, sorting out complications and dilemmas in which helped this establishment run so efficiently. She sat down in his leather chair and tucking her feet up under her, glanced at the items on his desk, before turning the chair around to the large cabinet that stood against the wall. She reached out her hand and gently swung one of the doors open.

Inside were thousands of small disks and tiny USB sticks.

Each had a title or name on them.

Of course, she saw her name, amongst others she knew.

She sighed and swung the door shut and swivelled the chair back to face the desk. Getting up, she walked over to the balcony and pushed the wide, clear glass doors open.

She stepped out into a stormy atmosphere, the wind, furious and ice cold.

She embraced it, placing her hands on the rails, as she looked down upon the stunning grounds of the Given, the wind forcing her hair to fly around her head and back like a black cape.

Almost a decade. She'd been here for what felt like forever, was grateful to be.

Her friends without whom, she felt she would have shrivelled and died. The consistency of their friendship, strength, love, and easy laughter over the years was invaluable to her. She knew she was extremely blessed to have them.

Her mind wandered to her mother. The pain was immediate. How she had missed her, beyond belief, whilst getting on with the life she was given. Her tears came in a hot flood. She was as immune to them as she was the heavy rain that began to pelt down on her already chilled skin.

She thought of how old her mother would be now, how she may have dealt with the loss of her daughter all those years ago. Hoped her dad had been kind to her.

She squeezed her eyes shut and let her sobs get carried away with the wind.

Her heart ached for her friends and all the pain they had endured before coming here, for herself, for Jessica, those two young girls who had been through so much devastating torment!

For all the children who suffered so cruelly in this forsaken world.

She cried for everything Damon had been through, how he had put himself in the pit of hell, to help those poor women and children.

Human beings, she thought, the deadliest creatures on this planet. Her eyes took in the darkening sky, the trees being thrust around by the howling winds.

She slipped down onto the balcony floor, hands clutching at the rails like prison bars, her eyes became unfocused on the surroundings in the distance as her mind plagued her with unwanted, horrid images of a cruel world that could not be cleansed.

***

Damon entered through his main door. The room was dark, apart from the blaze the firelight threw here and there. 'Lights on' He commanded sharply, the lights went on as he crossed over to the table and lifted the lid on the serving tray, noting she had not eaten a single bite.

Looking towards the open balcony doors, he quickly marched to the other end of the long room and stepped out into the torrential rain. He frowned when he saw Lilliana appearing asleep on the balcony floor, totally drenched and clearly shivering.

He cursed under his breath as he walked over to her and bending, scooped her up and took her back inside, shutting the doors behind him.

He glanced down at her face. He could see she'd been crying, but the rain tracks masked her tears.

He walked out of the main lounge and crossed towards his bedroom area.

"Damon," she whispered.

He wanted to freeze and just look at her. It was the first time he'd ever heard his name, on her lips.

Entering his large, immaculate bathroom, and keeping his arm around her, he settled her bottom on his raised knee, and got the shower running hot and pelting.

He stepped into the shower with her, fully clothed, cradling her in his arms.

The water sprayed from four separate jets in the walls and they were blanketed in warmth immediately.

Damon settled his chin on the top of her head, leaning back against the wall, he took a deep breath and let it out slowly.

He kept his eyes trained on the opposite wall, not wanting to glance down at her for a second. The slip of a dress was practically see-through when it was dry, but wet, you could see every inch of her delectable body perfectly.

And what had been left to the imagination, proved to be every bit as stunning as he'd imagined.

Her shivering slowing, she raised a hand and pushed her hair off her face. She felt his strong body stiffen at her movement.

Lifting her eyes, she could see his throat take a swallow. Her finger reached up and touched him there. Velvet soft, so smooth.

She pulled her head out of the hollow of his shoulder and looked up into his breath-taking face.

It was taking all his strength to remain still, his eyes boring down into hers.

She could feel his energy coiling, ready to release at any moment. She was both thrilled and terrified at the same time. She wriggled out of his arms.

His hands gently let her slide to her feet but remained holding her.

Her fingers gently stroked his wrists, before gliding up his arms, to rest on his firm biceps.

She looked up slowly, her eyes finally meeting his.

They remained still, the steam of the shower moving seductively around them. Being so close, touching, having their eyes fill of the other. It was enough. For now.

She stepped forward and slowly tiptoed up, placing her lips near his.

"Damon." It was a Siren's whisper She brushed her lips across his, and then went to step back down and away.

He moved fast, like a snake striking its prey, and jerked her back toward him, his mouth crashing down, collecting her lips in a deep, wet kiss, sucking, tongue stroking, sliding, seeking.

Her hands shot forward, and held his face, pulling him even closer.

Their lips devoured the others. His hands around her waist, slipped to her hips and pulled her against his groin.

She could feel his erection through her almost invisible dress.

Her fingers thread through his hair as she kissed him like there was no tomorrow.

He was blown away by the irresistibility of her.

His memories of the young lady he'd wanted badly was nothing compared to what Lilliana, the woman, was doing to him right now.

He was ready to take her right here, on the shower floor.

"Lilliana." He lifted his mouth from hers, staring into her clear, lustful green eyes.

Her mouth open, wet, and panting.

"No, not again. Do not stop." She grabbed him behind the neck and pulled him down towards her, her breasts pressed into his chest, she whispered, "I want you, now." Then claimed his mouth again with hers.

Her other hand ran down his wet shirt and her fingers slipped into the top of his jeans.

He moaned, not wanting her to stop, not ever.

But he would not take her here. Not like some randy, out of control teenager.

He reached back, still kissing her deeply, and flipped a switch.

The water stopped. Lilliana did not. Her fingers were working on undoing his top button, as she rubbed herself against him, like an eager cat wanting cream.

She almost cried when he gently, but firmly, held her away from him.

She closed her eyes, dropping her head forward. "You don't want me, do you?" She sounded devastated.

Damon chuckled, making her glare at him.

"My sweet Lilliana, did that kiss feel like I didn't want you? If I didn't want you, do you think I would have brought you up here, to my private rooms?" He gently took her by her wrist and pulled her out of the shower and over to the drier. They stood under it together, letting the delicious warm air dry them and their clothing in minutes. Damon ran his fingers through her hair combing her long, silky locks as the flowing, warm air dried it.

She sighed and leaned back against his chest, closing her eyes. Loving the feeling of being able to lean into him, the feeling of his hands on her.

She did not want to wake from this dream.

Once they were dried Damon put his arm around her shoulder and led her into his bedroom.

"Hop up onto the bed Lilliana." His voice husky, quiet as he walked over and pulled the thick, heavy blankets back.

She stood there, so beautiful, in that ridiculously sexy outfit.

Looking innocent, yet all too seductive.

"Are you coming in?" A sexy, dark eyebrow raised.

"Oh, I'll be coming in Miss Lilliana, but first, I'd like a change of clothes, and I want to get you into something else."

She walked over to his bed, deliberately brushing against him as she sat. She tucked her legs under her as he placed the blankets around her hips.

Tipping her chin up, he bent to kiss her open lips. He deepened the kiss within a moment, her hands reached up to hold his wrists, not letting him get away.

He moved his head back, staring into her eyes.

"You certainly have an appetite." He stroked his finger along her cheek.

"For you." She said simply, grabbing his wrist, she bought it to her lips, her eyes on his, she kissed his skin.

Damon sucked in his breath and gently pulled his wrist out of her grasp.

She wanted to pout, but instead, fell back against the pillows, pulling the blankets up to her chest.

He took a step back, not wanting to take his eyes off her, reached for his phone on the side table, and punched in a number.

Lilliana could not believe she had just had a fantasy full filled. To be kissed and held by this deliciously handsome man. In his shower, and now, she was laying in his bed, after all these years. She lifted the sheet up and buried her nose into it, closing her eyes, breathing his scent in.

She never wanted to take her eyes off him.

Never wanted to be separated from him. She opened her eyes to see him staring at her, a strange look on his face, as he spoke to Christopher, then Cam.

Hanging up, he slipped the phone into his back pocket.

He bent down, placing his hands either side of her body on the mattress.

"You and I are going to spend the next day here. You're not going anywhere."

He watched her eyes widen, her breath hitch.

"I am finally going to have you Lilliana, as I've always wanted to have you, to claim you."

It was the sexiest threat she'd ever heard in her life. "Promise?"

He chuckled, straightening. "Hell yes. But first, I have a bit of business to tidy up."

He walked into his walk-in robe and came out minutes later dressed in fresh blue jeans and a black t-shirt.

He dumped his other clothes down the chute.

"While I'm gone please undress, and everything you have on now, go place it in the dumpster chute near my kitchen. I have Josephine bringing something up for you to put on. Okay?"

"Yes Sir," she replied to his ordering tone.

He smiled. She returned it.

He walked backwards watching her, then as he reached the doorway, spun around and left the room. She waited a few seconds hearing the entrance door close.

She jumped up and tiptoed out of the room, a sense of surreal happiness took over her. Could this really be happening?"

She stripped off the beautiful garments that Fox had dressed her up in, and gratefully dumped them down the chute. Happy to never see them again.

Standing totally naked she ran into the lounge area and wrapped herself in the mink blanket.

Josephine entered five minutes later. She dumped the bag she'd been holding and walked straight over to where Lilliana was standing in front of the fire, reached out and grabbed her friend. She pulled her against her and held onto her tightly.

Lilliana's arms gratefully went around her friend. "Jose."

"How are you Lilly?" Josephine held her friend at arms-length, to get a good look at her.

"I hardly know." Lilliana shook her head. "The last eighty odd hours have been like a roller coaster. I feel like I have emotional whip lash. Jose, look where I am!" She finished off with a laugh.

Not quite hysterically. But close enough to make Josephine raise an eyebrow.

"Sit down."

Lilliana sat exactly where she was. On the rug near the fireplace.

Josephine walked over to the mini bar and shuffled through, pulling out an orange Baileys.

She poured them both half a glass, and walked over to Lilliana, before sitting down on the floor with her. She held the glass out to Lilliana, who happily took it.

"Cheers." She clinked her glass against Josephine's, before throwing the entire contents down her throat.

Josephine did the same thing. "Mm, that's yummy stuff on a stormy night, and by the looks of you, I think we'll have another."

By the third drink they'd both had enough.

"Are you going to be okay up here?"

"I believe so my dear friend, I've never felt safer." Lilliana stood and walked over to the bag that Josephine had packed some of her clothes in.

Pulling out her matching purple bra and panties, she dropped the blanket and stepped into them.

Then she slipped her knee length black soft dress over her head.

Loving how warm and safe it made her feel.

"Thanks Jose." She yawned.

"Right, you need to lie down and get some shut eye. Damon has errands to do before you both ditch your responsibilities." She winked at her friend.

"Nice one, bring that up." Lilliana rubbed the back of her neck, thinking of Matilda's one on one with her in the morning.

"Please. I'm kidding. If anyone deserves a break," She grabbed Lilliana's arm, and dragged her to the couch, pushing her down, she kissed her on top of the head, and squeezed her shoulder. "It's you my friend." Josephine waved as she walked to the door.

"See you later Josephine." Lilliana nestled back into the couch and stared into the fireplace. It wasn't long until the flames mesmerized her to sleep.

***

Damon had been gone two hours. He popped in to see Allie and organized Lilliana's appointments, and any shifts in the Psych ward, to be covered for the next two days.

He had a quick chat to Cam and a handful of Team Leaders about the next week's assignments and classes and a chat with several of the senior staff.

He felt everything was covered, before popping into the kitchen to double check things with Christopher and Cook before going up to see Johnson.

He wanted to make sure Lilliana hadn't put herself through hell for nothing.

They had found the Ex-Diplomats hidden locations, and all the children had been rescued. The four-year-old was the only one not abused. It was one small blessing.

Ex-Diplomat Reid was not amongst the locations, but they were not giving up hope.

After running down to check in with Rachael and Billy regarding several new Given who had just arrived, he felt he had covered all the important tasks before he selfishly stole himself away to spend uninterrupted time with the woman he desperately wanted. Needed.

Loved.

He ran up the stairs, and punching in the code to unlock his door, stepped into his rooms.

He walked past the couch and his heart melted at the sight before him.

Lilliana fast asleep, her hair flowing and spread out beneath her. Her cheeks had a rosy tinge, her long dark lashes brushing them.

One arm was thrown above her head, the other resting on her stomach.

One leg stretched out, the other lazily dangling off the couch, making her dress slip further up her thigh.

He didn't know how long he simply stood there, staring at her, watching her breathe. Sleeping deeply - in his rooms. It felt like he had wanted her up here with him, forever.

He sat on the side of the couch and placing his hands either side of her waist, leaned in close, and watched her.

He moved one hand up near her neck and slid his lips gently over hers.

The taste of her, soft, sweet. He enjoyed the moment of claiming her, feeling her slowly come awake beneath him.

She kept her eyes closed, enjoying the sleepy sensation of waking to those gorgeous lips on hers. She opened her mouth beneath his, letting him sink in as far as he would.

His tongue pushed into her mouth seeking hers.

She moaned as his hand slid up along her hip, to slip behind her back and hold her to him.

Her hands reached up to grasp around his strong back pulling herself up against him.

They kissed deep and long, sinking into each other.

When Damon drew back for air he shook his head, looking down at her.

She raised an eyebrow, smiling. "Something the matter?"

"Yes actually. I don't know how I'm ever going to keep my hands off you. I think I'm going to have to lock you up here forever."

"Do it then." She pushed herself up, leaning on her elbows, arching her neck; she pushed her lips closer to his.

He slowly kissed her, open mouthed and softly.

His hand around her back, slid up her front, and gently went around her throat. Holding her there, kissing her thoroughly.

She moved his hand, and spun her legs around him, sitting up, and pushing him back into the couch, she straddled him.

He smiled.

She wriggled as close as she could to him, feeling his erection push firmly against her. Her eyes on his, she watched his darken to a deep, intense blue.

Keeping her eyes on his, her hands stroked his neck, ran down his chest, then up again.

She leaned forward and licked her favourite spot near the base of his throat, before kissing it.

His hands clung to her hips, pushing her down harder against his large, swollen flesh through his jeans.

She wiggled against him, wanting to be closer.

She tugged his tee shirt above his head and flung it behind her.

Her eyes, like that of a hungry wolf, took him all in, from his firm solid chest, right down to his hard-abdominal muscles, running her small fingers all over him.

He wanted to throw her down, and drive himself hard into her, again and again. But he would not. He wanted her to have this experience at her own pace. Her own pleasure.

His head tipped back, leaning on the couch as his eyes watched hers widen, as she explored his body.

Her fingers reached to his jeans button and popped it open.

She pushed herself up and tugged his jeans lower over his hips. He tilted his hips and helped her get them down around his knees. He loved the feel of her hands wandering over his body.

His black briefs clung to his tight hips, firm buttocks, and swollen flesh.

Lilliana could hear herself breathing heavily and was hoping he could not hear her irregularity. She may have felt desperate to have him but didn't want to appear desperate.

Her eyes glanced up, and she smiled shyly.

He nearly came then and there. This beautiful, sweet woman!

He cupped the back of her neck, and pulled her hard up against his chest, his lips dipped into hers, his tongue showing her what he wanted to do to her.

She melted into his arms, pushing herself back on top of him, ever so close.

"Oh Lilliana, you are killing me." He moaned softly into her mouth.

His hands cupped her bottom, and as his fingers found the hem of her dress, he gently grabbed the edge, and pulled upwards and over her head, until she was sitting there almost as equally naked as him.

He tossed it close to where she tossed his tee shirt. Then, he had his eyes full.

The deep purple bra and knickers clung to a firm, curvy, strong body.

Her dark hair swirled around her like a silken cloud.

His hands sat on her thighs, either side of his legs. His fingers slowly stroking her soft flesh, backwards and forwards.

It was making her dizzy. Her head fell back, and she sighed deeply. He leaned forward, his lips slid along her neck, one arm behind her back, keeping her in place as he kissed her. His other hand came up slowly to cup a heavy, swollen breast.

He squeezed, ever so gently, his thumb stroking her already peeked nipple through the silky material.

Lilliana moaned loudly and pushed herself harder against him, wanting him inside her already.

She started rocking against him, feeling something stir deep within her belly.

He pulled her towards him, his mouth slipping over her nipple, and sucked her through the material.

Her hands flew to his head, holding him there whilst she whispered, rocking against him. "Now Damon, please."

He nearly chuckled. She was driving him crazy, pushing herself against him like she wanted to devour him.

He unclipped her bra, and setting her firm, high breasts free, was nearly his undoing.

"Oh my God Lilliana, you are beautiful." His hands reached up, stroking her neck, and he gently tipped her head, so he could stare into her eyes.

He pulled her down, and his lips slid over hers, kissing her softly.

She felt his other hand slide over her back, to her front, feather soft fingers played over her waist, and her heartbeat quickened with new excitement as his fingers dipped with purpose, into the front of her wet knickers, slick with her wanting juices.

She gasped as his fingers slid over her throbbing, swollen bud and she eagerly pushed herself harder against his pleasing, clever fingers, feeling something like a dizzy wave building deep within her.

Her mind was reeling with the fact she was in Damon's strong, toned arms, feeling his ever-sexy body warm against hers, and those hands assaulting her in the most pleasant, mind numbing way, his scent wrapping around her possessively.

Damon adored the soft, desperate moans slipping from Lilliana's lips, and swallowed them up as his mouth continued to assault hers, his tongue mimicking his fingers, sliding back and forth, taunting, teasing, pleasing.

Her nipples rubbed erotically against Damon's dark chest hair, as she rocked against him, arousing her soft flesh, sending a delicious pull deep within her belly.

He loved the feel of her soft weight, sensing she was close to peaking. His thumb rubbed her wet clit firmly, as his fingers slid back and forward along her swollen lips, hitting her bottom, sending fire inside her core.

She pushed herself harder against his fingers, her hands slid up his arms, his chest, to finally sink into his glorious hair, holding his head to deepen their kiss. Sucking his tongue, imagining his shaft deep inside her, had her crying out against his lips as her body began to tremble and seek that final release of an explosive, deep sated orgasm.

His finger gently massaged her, until she was spent.

He removed his hand, but continued gently kissing her mouth, as she panted softly, trying to catch her breath.

He reached a hand to stroke her smooth back, before claiming a handful of hair, tugging gently until her head fell back, and her swollen, wet, open lips fell away from his.

His eyes held her still as they bore into hers. She smiled slowly and her fingers touched his jaw, stroking lovingly.

"Lilliana." He gently took her hand, and kissed the soft skin inside her wrist, his eyes not leaving hers for a moment, ever watchful.

Lilliana shivered, watching him kiss her wrist with an open mouth. She could not categorize the many thoughts and feelings that were consuming her, as this very moment, as she sat upon this man's lap.

"Damon." She replied simply.

He sighed and kissed her throat, before pulling her gently against him.

She fell limply in his arms, her head falling onto his shoulder.

She closed her eyes, wanting to cry from sheer happiness.

She felt wet and throbbing below and wanted more. More Damon.

Her hand slid between them and sought his hard flesh. Moving back a little so she had room, her fingers found his swollen shaft, and her hand went around it, and the material of his briefs.

Damon pushed against her hand, gritting his teeth not to come all over her like a teenage boy with no control.

She moaned, and that was it, he leapt up taking her with him. Grabbing her wrist, he turned and walked the distance into his large bedroom. He threw the covers back and fell backwards pulling her with him.

She laughed as she landed on his stomach. "In a hurry, are we?"

"No," he shook his head. "I've only been waiting for you, forever." Her heart melted. He was so serious.

Her hand ran along his chest, down, down, but he grabbed her wrist, stopping her.

She looked up into his eyes. He shook his head, saying nothing. Her breath caught with the intensity of his gaze. Always!

He slowly, gently rolled them over, so she was on her back.

His hand ran up her side, starting from under her knee, brushing her bottom, hip, along the sensitive side of her belly, feather-light strokes to the side of her breast.

Her breathing hitched again. He chuckled.

She looked at him.

"I love it when you do that," he whispered. "When you used to do that, it did crazy things to me. It was always so hard being professional around you. Trying to do the right thing with you. Mm." He dipped his head to her breast. "But now it looks like I can do, pretty well as much to you, as I want to."

"Promise?" She whispered, as his tongue whipped out and circled her nipple, then he blew gently making it peak larger than life.

She wriggled beneath him, moaning. His lips sucked her nipple into his mouth, his other hand brushed over her stomach to slip into her panties, sliding them down her hips. Her hands left his back, to grab them, and lifting her hips, pushed them lower, kicking them off with her feet.

She could not believe how totally unembarrassed she was, being naked in Damon's arms.

She reached up to gently take his head and lift it off her breast.

He raised his dark eyes to hers. Then, he glanced down her body, looking at every inch he could feast on before his gaze returned to hers.

"This is so surreal." He shook his head. "And as beautiful as every fantasy I've ever had about you was, it is beyond nothing compared to having you right here, right now, at my fingertips."

She felt her insides turn to liquid, as his voice echoed her deepest thoughts.

"You may in fact, need to pinch me, extremely hard, just to confirm this is actually happening." He smiled down at her.

A throaty, rich laugh burst from her. "I've been saying that to myself the past few hours." Her hands stroked his hair. "To touch you freely." She relished his hands, stroking her, as she stroked him. Damon Night.

"I'll never forget the first time I saw you, you frightened me so much with your intensity, but in such a good way." She couldn't take her eyes off his. She shook her head. "I've loved you for what seems like forever Damon."

His eyes closed; his breath caught. His forehead gently found hers.

She tipped her head up, her lips slid along his.

As he kissed her, his hand slid down to tug off his briefs.

When his large, swollen flesh sprang free he almost chuckled at her gasp.

Her fingers reached towards him as he nuzzled her soft, smooth throat.

When her fingers wrapped around him, he moaned deep in his throat. "You'll have to stop that if you want me to last the distance Lilliana."

He gasped as her thumb brushed over the sensitive tip, releasing a clear pearl drop.

He reached down and grabbed her wrist, pinning it above her head.

He looked deep into her eyes as he slowly shook his head, and whispered, "No you don't."

She pouted and he burst out laughing.

"You are so hot when you pout." He shook his head again.

"I don't mean to pout." she whispered, wanting to say what she thought of those that did pout, but all thoughts of wanting him made it difficult to focus on an intelligent come back.

Her lips were waiting, as his mouth claimed hers in a greedy gulp. They kissed long and slow. Taking their time exploring the depth of their desire. Each gentle thrust of Damon's tongue, a nip of her bottom lip with his teeth, a suck on her tongue and the gentle glide of lips over lips had Lilliana reeling into a black hole, flicked with bright lights of never-ending pleasure, building tighter in her belly.

She wanted to get as close to him as she could, and wrapped a long smooth leg around his hip, pushing herself against him, loving the feel of his hard body. Her fingers gliding over hard flesh.

He continued kissing her as his hand slid down between them, pushing a finger between her legs, feeling how wet and ready she was.

His finger circled her throbbing bud again and again as his tongue invaded her mouth. She was panting and ready to explode, pushing herself hard against his hand.

He quickly withdrew, and she felt him guide his penis tip to her entrance.

She moaned, knowing very soon she would have him. All of him!

Her other leg joined her ankle, and gripped his hips hard, kissing him deeply.

"Now, please now." She whispered into his mouth as her hips rocked.

He stroked her nipple, kissed her deeply, and thrust up, filling her with his entirety.

She threw her head back and arched towards him.

Losing herself, she could feel her body rise, higher and higher. The fever tight in her belly, growing.

She thrust hard against him, again and again, rocking, her fingers sliding down his back, covered in a light sheen of sweat.

He kissed her throat while he kneaded her firm, full breast, flicking his finger over her nipple, pinching gently.

He pumped his hips slowly, savouring her tight, wet sweetness.

He never wanted this sensation to end.

He pulled his head back, to look at her as she moaned and writhed beneath him. His sexy little angel.

"Lilliana," He whispered, running a finger along her soft cheek bone. "Open your eyes. Look at me." He commanded as he stroked his engorged shaft in and out in a hypnotic rhythm.

She was lost in the new sensations her body was delivering her, she wasn't sure she could focus on what he asked.

She turned her head and opened her eyes.

Her large, green liquid pools swallowed him up.

Her hands made their way to the back of his neck, her fingers looping in his soft black hair.

"Kiss me," she whispered. "Damon."

He moaned, feeling her legs tighten around him, she was so close. Leaning down, his eyes ever on hers, his lips slid over hers, as his tongue thrust, and his rhythm increased.

Lilliana felt him pushing into her core, stroking every part of her in a delicious, slippery path to erotica. Her legs dropped off his hips as he pumped into her, opening her body for each delicious thrust and glide.

His tongue matching his rhythm below, had Lilliana crying out loud into his mouth as her orgasm exploded within her.

That's all Damon needed to hear, to finally allow himself that sweet release, and as her lips slid down his throat, he came hard and deeply inside her. He groaned, loving the sensation of being lost within her, feeling both bodies throbbing with release.

They lay in each other's arms, breathing heavily. She, stroking his hair. He, nuzzling her neck.

She sighed happily and stretched her sore, tired body along-side his. Like a sleek black panther, he thought. He ran his hand along her side, cupping her bottom, bringing her close to him again.

She smiled sleepily and raised her lips, seeking his, her eyes closed.

His hand cupped her chin, his lips slid over hers briefly before he stood and walked away from the bed.

Lilliana sat up leaning on her wrist; she pushed her heavy waterfall of hair off her shoulder.

"Where are you going my love?"

He stopped walking, and turned around, his face looked so pleased.

Looking at her, sitting so beautifully, proudly. She was not the slightest bit embarrassed sitting there like a queen on her throne.

As naked as he liked looking at her.

And she had softly, lovingly, called him her love.

She tipped her head to one side and raised an eyebrow, "Penny for your thoughts?"

He walked slowly back to the edge of the bed. She'd risen and shuffled over to him on her knees. They were inches apart, her proud, firm breasts jutting towards him, beckoning to him.

He reached out his hands, and circling her waist pulled her up towards him.

Her hands rested on his shoulders.

He bent his head and kissed her softly, slowly. He watched as her eyes fluttered shut.

She moaned and pressed herself against him, her arms circling his neck.

He chuckled and gently pushed her away from him. "You beautiful witch, stop or you'll be my undoing."

She sighed. "Okay."

He tipped up her chin. "Don't worry my darling. You are with me for the next forty-eight hours. We have plenty of time to pleasure each other. But you need food, and we need a shower. Okay?"

"Okay." She smiled, liking the idea of having him to herself for the next two days. Alone!

He took her into the shower and got the jets on hot and hard.

They lathered each other's hair and body. Lilliana loved running her fingers up and down Damon's hard, sculptured chest, over his firm, toned biceps, dropping kisses here and there. He watched her through half closed eyes as he leaned back against the warm shower tiles, allowing her time to explore him. His hands, itching to take hold of her, to bend her over and thrust into her time and time again. To hear her moan his name in pleasure. He was hard just thinking about it.

When Lilliana soaped her hands up and started stroking Damon's throbbing shaft, his eyes closed. He could feel himself close to coming and went to stop her.

"No," she said, shaking her head, holding a finger up against his lips, "I want to, let me. Please?"

He looked down into her eyes and could see how much she wanted this. She lowered to her knees; keeping her eyes on his as her hand started too firmly, yet slowly pull him.

"Ah!" He moaned his head dropped against the tiled wall, eyes closing. "Lilliana, what are you doing to me?" His eyes burst open seconds later as he felt her lips slide over his length. He couldn't stop himself if he tried and exploded in her sweet mouth within moments. He took a few deep breaths, feeling Lilliana's hand gently wash him.

He reached down, and taking her under the arms, helped her to her feet, and wiped the side of her mouth for her, then bent down to kiss her deeply.

She linked her arms around his neck, pushing herself against him. "Incredible," he whispered. "I want you again."

She could feel that he did and smiled up at him.

He shook his head, shutting off the water. "Food."

He placed them both into the drier booth, then pulled her out and into the lounge, and offered her a seat near the fire.

He left to go into the other room and returning with a pair of jeans on, and his black tee shirt for her. He slipped it over her head, his fingers brushing the sides of her breasts as he tugged it down.

She grabbed his hand as he was about to walk away and kissed his palm before releasing it, and sitting back into the chair, crossed her legs.

He smiled down at her as a knock sounded at the door, and went to open it, to find Christopher standing with a large tray in hands.

"Perfect timing, thank you Christopher. I'll take it from here."

"No worries Sir, hope it's all to your liking."

"It always is." Damon smiled.

"And may I say, thank you for this day off. I'm really grateful".

"Well, it is after all, five in the morning, I think you and Allie deserve a few quiet hours together. Enjoy." Damon smiled as he took the large tray off Christopher.

"You too Sir."

Damon shut the door and walked over to Lilliana. He placed the tray on the table and lifted the lid.

Lilliana didn't realize how very famished she was. She moved forward to the delicious aroma of roast pork sandwiches with gravy and apple sauce. Cucumber and cheese, chicken and cranberry jelly.

"Oh yummy." She selected a sandwich.

Damon chuckled, pouring her a tea. "Yummy, is it? I haven't heard a fully grown, yet delicious woman, say that word in many years." He handed her the tea.

Lilliana shrugged an elegant shoulder, clearly not worried. Eating two whole sandwiches and moving on to a pile of fresh cherries and chocolate dipping sauce.

Damon sat back in his chair opposite hers, eating his sandwiches, drinking his water, watching every bite she took.

"What would you like us to do together Lilliana in the time that we have?" He watched her over his glass of water.

"You mean, apart from the obvious?"

He smiled, placing his glass down. "Yes beautiful, apart from the obvious."

"Well, I'd like to go riding with you, and I'd like you to teach me how to shoot an arrow without killing anyone."

He linked his fingers in his lap, casually crossing his ankle over his knee.

He nodded. "I recall you doing archery with Natalie a very long time ago. You weren't very good at it." He smiled.

"That's because I had a crappy teacher." She sipped her tea. "No offense to Natalie."

"Oh no, of course not." He chuckled drily, knowing too well the difficult relationship she had with Natalie over the years.

"Well, she hasn't made my time pleasant here. I do try to be gentle with her." She smiled. "I have so many bad memories of her, things she has said and done, and even with all my training, my knowledge, sometimes I just can't get past the things she does and how it affects the people around her." She finished her tea.

"Another?" He offered.

"Yes please, I'm so thirsty." He took her cup, and bending down, claimed a kiss. She was only too happy to oblige.

"Mm," he said, straightening. His finger hooked her chin, marvelling at her beautiful face. "Delicious." He let go of her chin and turned to pour her tea.

She shivered. She had just made love to the man of her dreams, and here he was pouring her a cup of tea, and she simply wanted more of him.

She smiled up at him as he placed the cup in her hands, his fingers brushing hers, before he sat down, picking up an apple and crunching into it.

She watched the juice ran down his chin, wanting to lick it off.

He wiped it off with his fingers, watching her right back.

The butterflies started to flutter in her stomach, and she shook her head, gazing across to the flames in the fire.

"And what's that cheeky look all about, Miss Lilliana?"

She leaned her head back against the chair, her eyes roaming over his features.

"I keep thinking back to all those times you confused me, or more truthfully, when I confused myself, about you." She shrugged.

"Can you elaborate on those memories for me?" He took another bite of his apple.

She laughed. "It sounds like we're back in group."

He smiled. "Yes, you were never very good at sharing, in your early days were you darling? You gave Richard hell, apparently are still giving him hell." He looked almost proud.

Lilliana tucked her legs underneath her, getting comfortable.

"Let's not talk about Richard, if you don't mind, Sir." She smiled.

He nodded, flicking his apple core across the room, it went straight down the rubbish chute.

Lilliana raised an eyebrow. "Impressive."

"Thanks, now, a memory please."

Lilliana nodded and smiled. "My first one, where I was really impacted by your presence, was when you made me eat those favourite sandwiches in my first evaluation. You were so kind, yet commanding, gentle and firm. There was something about you that jolted me, every time I was near you." She smiled across at him, into his beautiful eyes.

She shrugged, taking a deep breath. "You turned me on from day one, but I was so lost, confused. I thought my thoughts about you were evil. That I was impure because of what I'd been through. Plus, I was so young, I didn't truly understand what was going on between us. You just confused me all the time."

He nodded, letting her know he got it.

"You were always there when I needed you." She continued. "I felt you. It was like this charge went off whenever I saw you, thought about you. And that second photo shoot I did, with you and Beast," she shrugged again, "it just about blew me away. Having your hands on me, where I secretly wanted them. Having you so close." She finished on a whisper.

He silently watched her, his heart so full.

"Everything you are telling me I can relate to. Come." He stood and held out his hand.

She rose, taking his hand as he led her to the couch. Sitting down, he tugged her gently and she lay down, placing her head in his lap looking up at him, as he stroked her hair.

"It seems like a lifetime ago, doesn't it? You were such a beautiful girl that pulled at my very core. Every time you were in trouble, or in need. I just wanted to protect you. But more selfishly, when you were in trouble, it gave me secret pleasure to be able to spend that extra five minutes in your company. Even if it was only to lecture you!"

He ran his hand along her cheek, watching her eyes drift shut. It was, after all getting close to seven in the morning. It had been an emotional roller coaster for her the past 18 hours, and more.

"Let's go to bed sweetheart." He said quietly.

When her eyes shot open, looking hopeful, he laughed, and kissed her nose. "To sleep beautiful, we have all day."

He helped her to her feet, and placing his arm around her shoulders, hers about his waist, they walked into the bedroom.

He walked over and pulled the covers back for her. She smiled and slipped beneath them as he slid in beside her, pulling her towards him. Her head cushioned on his chest.

"Lights off." He quietly commanded, and the room fell into a peaceful darkness.

She closed her eyes, breathing him in, and whispered. "Good night, Damon."

His lips gently swept over hers. "Goodnight Angel." She was asleep as soon as the words left his lips.

CHAPTER 9

Lilliana woke and stretched her hand out to feel that firm, delicious body, only to find an empty space beside her. She sat up, glancing around the large bed and saw a yellow rose sitting on Damon's pillow, with a small note, which read.

-You are still on lockdown Miss L. Be back soon. Yours only, Damon. X-

She smiled and held the rose to her nose, breathing in its sweet aroma.

She slipped off the bed, grateful for some moments of privacy and went to the toilet, then into the bathroom to find a new purple toothbrush sitting on the vanity, which she used after washing her hands with the sweet-scented soap.

Looking in the mirror she couldn't believe how fresh she looked, grateful not to be looking tired. She brushed, spat and rinsed, then decided to find something else to put on.

She wandered back into the bedroom and stepped into Damon's walk-in robe and could not believe what she was seeing. Half the robe was full of women's clothing in her size.

Her hands riffled through, wondering when Damon had done this.

She felt a warm flush.

Reaching for a yellow sundress, she slipped it over her head, bra and knicker free.

She slipped her feet into low, yellow heels and found a brush to pull through her hair.

She walked out of the room and down the corridor to see if she could find Damon, and entering his small kitchenette, put the hot water on.

Opening the fridge, she pulled out the juice, and went in search for a glass.

As she reached up into the cupboard, strong hands slipped around her waist. Damon. His face pushed into her thick hair at the back of her neck, as he breathed her in, his hands running up her waist to cup her breasts.

She smiled, leaning back into him. "Good morning.

"Good afternoon," he moved her hair aside to kiss her neck. "It's half three." He turned her around, reaching for her hand to place the juice down on the countertop.

She smiled, her hands running up his chest, as his ran down her back, cupping her bottom, pulling her slowly against him. She tipped her head back as his mouth come down to slowly devour hers.

She moaned, stretching up on her toes to get closer to him, wanting him right here.

His hands moved under her dress, pulling back as he realized she was not wearing any underwear.

He raised an eyebrow as his fingers swept over her soft flesh.

Then his fingers swept down, between her buttocks, to stroke her backside, sending shivers down her spine.

She returned his deep kisses, as his fingers reached between her legs, massaging her wetness.

He whispered against her mouth, "So ready." He slipped two fingers ever so slowly, gently inside.

She rocked against his hand, desperate for the dizzy fog to claim her, but wanting it to claim him also.

She quickly pulled away from his hand, it took a lot for her to do so, as she had been so close to that magical abyss.

"I want you with me."

He yanked his tee shirt over his head, as she walked backwards, towards the bedroom. He slowly unzipped his jeans, his eyes on hers, following her. Her knees hit the bed, and she went down.

He yanked off his jeans and briefs, kicking them free with his feet.

Leaning over her he helped her pull her dress over her head.

He ran his hand down her body, slowly starting from her neck, leaning forward where his hand had been, his lips kissed her, her breasts. He fondled her till she withered beneath him.

She stroked his back, but he shook his head.

"Let me touch you, my sweet."

She nodded, letting her hands fall to her sides.

His head bent to suckle a nipple, as his hand stroked the flesh of her stomach, feather light and seductive. Her back arched, her fingers gripping the sheets.

Her breathing hitched, she felt so greedy, wanting more.

His hand cupped her sex, and she moved against it.

Then she felt his hands move her legs gently apart, and cupping her bottom, lifted her up a fraction. She felt his breath against her wet, hot sex, and her belly tightened in anticipation.

He kissed her thigh, up and down, his tongue flicking out to leave a warm, damp trail, heading towards her centre, which was throbbing with need.

His lips sought her bud, as his finger pushed up inside her wet core, another finger stroking her backside. She nearly screamed as his constant, thorough, continual lapping and stroking, had her coming hard and fast, in a silky spiral of throbbing, luscious heat.

He pulled himself up the length of her body, and as he shared with her the taste of herself, he pushed his throbbing shaft into her quickly, increasing her orgasm as he thrust repeatedly, smoothly, deeply, coming with her.

He gathered her in his arms and rolled her over, so she was on top of his chest, her hair falling over them like a sheet of silk.

Silence surrounded them, as they were both in a blissful moment of contentment, heart rates slowing, breathes flowing, bodies relaxed as lush throbbing eased.

Lilliana felt a rush of emotions and tried to compartmentalise them and was slightly shocked to find herself in tears.

He felt her tears before he heard them, alarmed he sat up, bringing her with him.

"Lilliana! What's wrong?" His handsome face looked panicked. He stroked her hair away from her face. "Did I hurt you?"

She shook her head, trying to stop the tears, but they just kept flowing.

She pushed herself up on her knees, and tightly wrapped her arms around his neck, pushing her face into his throat, shaking her head, trying to reassure him. "No, never Damon, you could never hurt me. I'm crying because I love you so much. Because that was so beautiful, and I cannot believe I am here with you."

He wanted to laugh, so grateful at her reaction. But held her gently, feeling his love for her bloom even deeper. "My beautiful, sweet angel. I love you. I will try forever, never to hurt you. I'd rather die." She looked up into his eyes, feeling such a deep contentment. Cupping his face, she lovingly stroked his jaw before kissing him. "Hungry?" he asked.

"Not anymore," she smiled.

He shook his head. "Cheeky girl, I mean food."

"Yes, I am." She snuggled her face into his chest.

"Excellent, food, then how about that horse ride?" He pulled her up, kissing her forehead, before stepping back.

"Is that where you were, organizing Thomas?" she bent down to scoop up his jeans before passing them to him.

He took them, shaking them out before pulling them up his long legs. "Yes, I thought I'd grant you that wish first."

"Just looking at you, being able to touch you whenever I want is a wish come true for me." She smiled.

He ran a hand over her hair. "For me too love." He said quietly. He walked away and into the robe, coming out with her Jodhpurs and a riding jacket with a white singlet top.

"When did you organize this wardrobe Damon?" She pulled the

riding pants up.

"It was a fantasy of mine, to have your size clothes here." He shrugged. "Creepy?" He looked a little unsure whether she would think him strange.

She shook her head, slipping the singlet top on and popping her arms in her riding jacket.

She walked over to him, and wrapped her arms around his waist, landing a kiss in the middle of his chest. "Possibly, to some. Not to me. But I would be happier if we could pass them onto some of our other Given, it's greedy having more than one wardrobe." She dropped another kiss onto his chest before looking up into his eyes.

He smiled down at her. "Stop looking at me like that, or we will never leave this room." His arms slid around her, and he bent down for a deep, slow kiss. Sighing, he drew back. "Time to eat, slip on your boots."

She did, and quickly pulling her hair over one shoulder began a long braid as she followed him out into the kitchen for a quick breakfast of juice, a bowl of fresh fruit and yoghurt, with stolen kisses in between.

When they finished, he offered her his hand.

Smiling she took it as he led her out of his front door, and down the winding stairs.

She could not believe this. His large, strong fingers gripped hers as they went down two flights. He stopped and turned to face her before they hit the next landing where many of the staff rooms were.

"I'm debating what to do about us in public Lilliana?" He stroked the inside of her wrist, so smooth.

She tilted her head, looking up at him, her wide, green eyes taking in his handsome frown "As in, you are worried what some people will think, or how they'll react?"

He smiled down at her. "Yes, exactly to both. It's just so soon after my return, I wouldn't want damaging tongues to wag."

She ran a hand up his chest, sliding it around his throat, her thumb stroking his soft spot. "If we need to act like colleagues, and nothing more for the sake of sparing us possible criticism and you worry, I can do that Damon, if, at the end of the day, we can be together."

His grabbed her wrist, her stroking his neck drove him crazy, and made him want to drag her back upstairs.

He quickly, softly, kissed her lips before straightening. "Yes, I knew you'd get it. We'll give ourselves a trial, shall we? If we can keep our hands off each other in public, we will remain professional. If not. Well?" He sighed shaking his head, running his hand along her face. "We can only try."

"Right, Sir," she smiled, "let's go, shall we?" She turned on her heel, and quickly went down the several flights of stairs.

He watched her perfect, generous bottom move in her tight jodhpurs as he followed behind her at a distance.

Many staff and Given who were out and about, heading towards their four o'clock classes or shifts, greeted both Lilliana and Damon.

They returned smiles and hello's, occasionally stopping for a quick chat.

She continued down the stairs as Fox stopped Damon to introduce him to a new member of the household who was also keen on horses and photography.

Lilliana reached the bottom of the stairs and ran into Cam.

"Hello Darling." He smiled and bent to kiss her cheek. "And how are you on this fine afternoon. Mm, but you are looking mighty pretty. Shall I ask what you are up to, and where is my brother?"

Lilliana glanced behind her, still not seeing Damon. She stepped closer to Cam and whispered. "We are not together, in public, for the sake of anyone thinking it unsuitable so soon after Damon's return." She played with the end of her braid, which brushed her waist.

"Right." Cam nodded. "Well, good luck with that one." He tapped her nose and smiled. "If he hurts you, I'll kill him." He said softly.

Lilliana shook her head. "He is not capable of hurting me Cameron."

"I hope not. Now, off you go and enjoy your ride."

"What are you up to?" she walked backwards, towards the entrance doors.

"To find Josephine and Rupert, we have a delivery to prepare for this week." Cam went to walk off.

"Give her my love," Lilliana called over her shoulder as she turned, walking past the library.

She waved to Jessica, who was sitting with a group of fifteen young Given.

Jessica flashed a smile, so relieved to see Lilliana looking refreshed and happy.

Lilliana headed out the front door and down the steps, wondering how far behind Damon was.

She arrived at the stables, twenty minutes after leaving Damon.

"Hi Thomas."

"Hi." Thomas shouted to be heard from eighty stalls down.

Lilliana smiled as she jogged down to watch Thomas gear up Beast for their ride.

"How've you been?" She rubbed Beast's nose.

"Pretty good thanks Miss Lilliana, been flat out this week. We're flying out twenty horses tomorrow. I have to tell Mr. Night that the cargo plane will be here at Two pm sharp."

"Yes, he'll want to be here for that." Lilliana agreed.

"Be here for what?" Damon stepped into the stall.

Lilliana's gut clenched looking at him. She felt dizzy remembering all that he'd done to her. All she wanted to do to him.

She was not a blushing schoolgirl, but her cheeks heated of their own accord, with the thoughts of his hands on her.

Damon's eyebrow rose at her flaming cheeks. What was she up to in that mind of hers? He wondered, as he tried to focus on Thomas's detailed list, regarding the horses' departure the following day.

"Excellent, sounds as if you have it all in order as usual. A gift of your choosing will arrive as soon as you can email me the details and I'll run it through with the Board."

"Oh no Sir, it's enough just loving what I do." Thomas started to say, but Damon clapped his hand on Thomas's shoulder, stopping any further protest.

"Thomas, there is no one I trust more with these animals. They are more than just horses to both you and I, so please, there must be something you have been needing. It is yours and not another word."

Thomas smiled. "Sir, thank you so much, I have busting to deck out my room upstairs and the entire stables with the latest surround sound."

"Good man, easily done." Damon turned to see Lilliana smiling that beautiful smile of hers, staring at him.

"As you can see," he said, watching Lilliana, "Miss Lilliana and I are going for a ride together on Beast. We are going out the back way to hopefully avoid prying eyes."

"No worries Sir, all is quiet, only two horses have been taken out this afternoon, and they are due back in fifteen."

Thomas passed the reins to Damon, who thanked him, and held out his hand to Lilliana. She placed her hand in his, and said bye to Thomas, as Damon led her and Beast toward the rear door. Once they were out of the stables he released her hand and sprang up on Beast. Thomas had placed a thick saddle blanket on Beast's back. Damon had ridden bare-back many times and with the thick blanket the ride was very comfortable. It had a strap under Beast's belly so it would not slip around. He gathered the reins in one hand and held the other out to Lilliana.

Reaching up, her eyes watching his, feeling so excited to finally go for a ride with this man. He pulled her up and sat her in front of him. Her back pressed against his chest as he placed his arms around her and gently nudged Beast into a walk.

Lilliana took a deep breath, feeling the magnificent horse under her pick-up pace as they trotted away from the stables in minutes.

After five minutes silence, Damon kicked Beast into a canter. Lilliana had her fingers wrapped gently in Beast's mane, Damon's thighs pressing against her bottom keeping her in place, his chest pressing into her back as the pace quickened.

It was a muggy afternoon; the air held the moisture from last night's storm.

The ground beneath them was muddy in places, but Beast kept his footing, not slipping once as they took off into a gallop when they hit the open fields. Both had their minds full of the time they had spent together so far, excited for what lay ahead, and enjoyed the relaxed atmosphere, riding in the fresh air together.

After some time, Damon slowed Beast down as they headed towards the dense forest.

He placed the reins in one hand, the other sliding tightly around Lilliana's waist, pulling her closer against him, pushing his face into her smooth, warm neck and kissed her behind her ear.

Her hands wrapped about his arm, holding it to her tightly, leaning her head back against his shoulder she sighed deeply, so content.

His lips sucked in her bottom earlobe, making her laugh. She couldn't help but pull away.

"Hey, come back here." He tugged her back against him, kissing her noisily on the cheek whilst she laughed.

"Not fair when I can't reach you."

He dropped the reins over his foot, and grabbing her by the waist, lifted her and turned her around, hooking her feet around his hips and behind him.

"Mm, I remember this feeling, having a gorgeous young thing this close to me, a few years ago. Feels even better now," he murmured, as his head dipped towards hers.

She slipped her arms around him, as Beast set a lazy pace, occasionally stopping to graze.

Her fingers stroked his back through his soft shirt. She looked up at him and lost her breath as his lips captured hers for another hungry, deep kiss.

She dug her fingers into his hair, holding him in position to ravish his mouth. The movement of the walking horse set an erotic rocking motion beneath them.

Damon slipped his hands up the back of her riding jacket, past her singlet, to scrape over her soft skin, pressing her as close as he could, kissing her thoroughly.

She pulled back, breathless, staring into his hungry eyes. She stroked his face lovingly. "What is it about you? I'm constantly overwhelmed with any look you cast in my direction."

He rubbed her back, up and down, and gave her a lazy smile. "Really? Well, that's good to hear, now you know how I have felt being around you pretty much the entire time we have known each other."

She moved forward to receive another warm kiss, and slipped her tongue into his mouth, finding his and gently sucked.

Damon sucked in his breath as she sucked cleverly on his tongue, then nibbled at his lips, pushing herself against him, he felt himself grow hard, and kicked the reins up into his hands as he pulled away from her.

"Time to get you back to where I can have you." Grabbing her, he turned her around, clamped his arm around her waist, and gently kicked Beast into action towards the stables.

Lilliana could feel his muscles through her thin riding jacket, loved hearing him breathe in her ear as they raced back, her belly full of knowing butterflies.

As they reached the front entrance of the stables he quickly kissed her neck, after glancing around for any eyewitnesses, and then helped her down.

"The code for our room is 5192723. I'll be there shortly." He glanced at her for a few more seconds, before taking Beast into the stables.

Our room, Lilliana thought, he called it our room. She set off at a jog, looking forward to a hot shower and some food. And then, hopefully, nothing but Damon.

She ran up the front steps, a little breathless and then slowed to a walk with a bit of decorum.

As she headed to the main staircase, a ruckus caught her attention, coming from one of the common rooms.

Knowing a staff member or a Watcher was probably around to deal with the situation, Lilliana almost veered up the stairs, but her instinct to care and protect kicked in.

Surely Damon would understand, as he'd do the same thing.

Stepping into the room, she saw the Watcher was Eric, and he was on the ground, blood seeping from his shoulder and his Given, Sam, was in a bloody scrap on the floor with Rick.

Lilliana rushed over to Eric and dropping to her knees, pushed aside his ripped shirt so she could get a clear look at his wound. It was deep enough for her to be worried; he was losing a lot of blood.

She pulled off her jacket and pushed it hard against the bloody gash. She glanced around looking for a familiar face she could use, to send for Billy or Rachael.

A young girl started screaming as Rick stood up, holding Sam's eyeball in his hand; Sam's screams matching the hysterical girls.

Lilliana glanced back at Eric. "Will you be okay for a second Eric? I have to try to stop him."

Eric, pale, but focused, nodded. "Be careful," he whispered, holding her jacket against his shoulder.

Lilliana stood slowly, trying to figure out the best way to get a hold of this situation and stepped away, circling to the back of the group. There were a lot of young girls in this room. It must have been their break time as staff were nowhere to be seen, and as Eric was the only Watcher on, it was obviously a quiet group.

Rick must have come in here for god only knew what reason. Well, that reason was now, pretty obvious.

Today he wore a gruesome mask, of a butchered cows face. Blood was dripping down his neck, and it was tied and held around his head with a piece of wire. The smell was overwhelming, in the worst way possible.

Lilliana wondered what had happened to the rest of the poor cow.

As Rick appeared to be focused on the bleeding boy on the ground, and the hysterical girls, Lilliana crept up behind him.

Eerily enough, just as she was about to grab one of his arms and pull it up behind his back, he surprised her with his speed and strength, as he spun around and grabbed her arm, jerking her up against him hard, bringing the gory blade up to her throat, the eyeball with it.

"Keep back!" He screamed, as Dr Richard stepped into the room. He had been in the library and decided it time, to come and see what all the fuss was about.

Richard glanced down at Eric, pulled a phone out of his pocket and quickly ordered Billy up here, along with added security.

He looked across at Lilliana and suppressed the smirk he felt growing. Right or wrong, he enjoyed seeing her in sticky situations.

"Everybody here needs to understand, that I am in control *OF EVERY SITUATION!*" Rick screamed; his words muffled by the mask.

Lilliana looked at Richard as he stepped forward.

Rick pushed the knife harder against Lilliana's throat, a line of blood appeared.

"Richard?" Lilliana snapped out. Was he trying to get her killed? Seriously!

He stopped and folded his arms, always looking arrogant, no matter what situation they seemed to be in.

"Everybody get out or I will *SLICE HER THE FUCK UP!*" Rick screamed, stepping towards a young girl, flicking the blood of Sam's eyeball onto her. The young girl pitched forward and vomited. Her friend grabbed her by the arm and dragged her out.

Billy stepped into the room taking note of the situation. "Lilliana," he called softly in despair. How did she get herself into these situations?

"I'm okay Billy, really! I can handle this, just help Eric." She sounded surprisingly calm, even to her own ears, happy to see two security guards arrive with Billy.

Richard had ushered all the young girls out of the room, and as Billy got Eric up and out, a security guard scooped up a limp, pale Sam. It just left Richard, a guard, Rick and Lilliana in a twisted face off.

Damon entered the foyer and was greeted by the young girls, sobbing hysterically. He spied Billy taking Eric towards the hospital stairs, and rushed over, hoping Lilliana was upstairs having a nice shower, whilst he quickly dealt with whatever situation, that had arisen.

"Billy, what's happened?" He placed his hand on his friend's shoulder, glancing at Eric.

"Stabbing incident. Another kid lost his eye, and now Rick has a knife to Lilliana's throat in common room three. Sorry Sir, I have to go."

Damon had already turned, and cursing under his breath, took off at a run to the room.

He pushed past Richard and the guard before stopping dead in his tracks. He could feel the blood drain from his face.

A very tall, strong looking, cowman, had a sharp, filthy knife pressed to his beautiful woman's neck. Blood already seeping slowly from a cut.

"Stop or I'll ram her through." Rick's voice was oddly
chilling.

"He means it." Richard said drily.

"Fabulous." Damon breathed out an angry breath. He placed his hands on his hips to stop them from shaking. His eyes glued to Lilliana's.

"*I SAID. I. WANT. EVERYONE. OUT!*" Rick grabbed Lillian's arm, and jerked the knife along her wrist, opening it up deeply.

She cried out before she could stop herself, as blood flowed quickly.

He then jerked the knife upwards and Damon froze as it looked like he was about to slam it into Lilliana's chest.

"*STOP!*" Damon screamed out. "What the *hell* do you want Rick? Whatever it is, it's yours. Just let her go." He felt desperate as he pleaded, hoping for a calm confidence he did not feel.

Lilliana was feeling dizzy. She tried to stay upright but could feel herself sag against Rick. Her arm was on fire.

"Stay up Doc," he said against her ear, "or I'll cut you through."

Lilliana blinked hard, trying to focus on Damon. There was no way she was going down. Not now. This was not the end.

"Rick," she forced herself in group mode, "you know you need to talk about your feelings. Your wants. You know Rick, doing this will only make you angry, disappointed in yourself. I can help you. We just need to sit down and talk. I know you don't want to hurt me. You know that too, don't you Rick?" She hoped whatever Allie had been doing with him during his one-on-one, was working, regarding his guilt trips, after he had hurt something or someone.

Rick paused, looking down at the top of Lilliana's head.

Lilliana eyed Damon hard and then looked down at the ground. He nodded.

As Rick was preoccupied in his deep thoughts, two things happened simultaneously. Lilliana dropped to the ground as fast as she could, the knife slicing shallowly along her collar bone, as Damon flew in the air, landing a solid kick to the middle of Rick's chest. Rick flew back, hitting against a couch hard, then the guard was on top of him, zapping him with a prod bar.

"Perfect for a cow." Richard muttered under his breath.

Damon scooped Lilliana up in his arms, cursing as he walked past Richard, and off to the hospital.

"Richard," he barked out. "Walk with me now!"

Lilliana was trying to grip her wrist to stop extra blood loss, but it was pointless. Her wrist was so slippery, and she couldn't concentrate. "I can walk, put me down. I'm okay."

Damon glanced down briefly, noting Lilliana had no colour in her face whatsoever, and gently squeezed her as his pace quickened.

Richard kept pace with Damon as they headed toward, and then down, the hospital stairs.

"Who was responsible for his evaluation? He is bloody high risk for Christ's sake. What the hell was he doing in main house? I will have whoever is responsible hauled over the coals for this!" He stormed down the corridor and headed for the nurses station.

He felt it the moment Lilliana lost consciousness. She flopped limply in his arms.

He shouted to Rachael as they neared the nurses station.

"This way." She led him quickly to a room.

He laid Lilliana on the bed, pushing her hair off her shoulders. Nurse Rachael got started on the pain medication and then started cleaning the deep cut on her wrist.

"Bloody hell." Damon muttered. He ran his hands though his hair.

He turned to Richard, when he thought he heard the man snicker.

"Do you have a problem Richard?" His voice, dangerously quiet.

Richard held up his hands. "No, not at all. But it was her, and her little friend, who sent him out there."

Rachael looked at Richard. She'd heard Rick went off the deep end, when Billy brought Eric and poor Sam down.

"Rick was not Lilliana's patient, Richard. He was Allie's. He had only attended Lilliana's group twice." She looked quickly at Damon, before concentrating on applying sterile suture gel, which brought the two sides of the gaping wound on Lilliana's wrist back together.

She smeared a small amount over the sliced collar bone after cleaning the area.

Stepping back, she sighed and turning to Damon said, "She needs plenty of rest."

"Anything else, apart from the pain meds?" Damon asked.

"No." Rachael went to move past Richard. He disturbed her almost as much as he did Lilliana. She had talked to Johnson about her feelings for this man.

But he was very efficient in his role, and he never put a foot out of line whilst working. Although that could have been debated, depending on whom one spoke to.

"Richard, leave please, I'd like to speak to Rachael alone. I'll see you around five." Damon folded his arms.

Richard nodded, and left the room.

Rachael turned to Damon. "What can I do for you Sir?"

"I want to care for Lilliana in my rooms. Would that be a problem?" He waited.

She held in her smile. "Not for you. I'll send Leon up with any medication, according to Billy, it was a filthy knife," she shook her head. "I'm hoping infection doesn't set in. We'll keep our eye on her and she should be fine. Rest is the key." She raised an eyebrow.

He felt he was being told well and truly, to keep his hands-off Lilliana. Anyone else, he would have said something, but his respect for Rachael was abundant.

"Yes Ma'am." He wanted to salute but smiled instead. "Can I take her now?"

"Yes, that's fine." Rachael smiled and left the room.

Damon turned to Lilliana. Out like a light he thought. He walked over and bending, pushed his hands under her warm, soft body and scooped her up, cradling her against his chest. He left the room and headed to the back entrance of the secluded passageway, up to his rooms.

Once in, he adjusted the heat system to leave the room comfortable and flipped the auto flames on in the bedroom fireplace to add ambience.

He undressed Lilliana, bathed her gently, washed her face, and slipped a long black night gown on her. He laid her in the bed, tucking the blankets around her chest. He went to have a quick shower himself, poured a coffee, ordered some food and then settled in a chair near the fire.

He reached for a book on a low shelf, sipping his coffee he read, listening to her soft breathing from the bed.

It wasn't long before a knock sounded at his door. Putting his book down, he answered it, to find Leon standing there, equipped with the required medicines for Lilliana.

"Please come on in." Damon stepped aside for Leon to enter.

"How is she?" Concern lined his voice, and a tinge of something else Damon suspected.

"Sleeping." he replied shortly, leading the way for Leon to follow.

As they walked, Leon took in Damon's surrounding rooms. Very nice, he thought. As they should be, the guy hardly slept, and worked like a machine to keep this place running.

He followed Damon into a large, warm bedroom. Firelight flickered across splendid dark furnishings, and a relaxing contemporary painting was on the wall above where an angel slept.

Leon stared at Lilliana and quickly crossed over to her. Damon stood near the fire, arms folded, watching Leon closely.

Leon placed his case on the side of the bed, and leaning down, gently picked up Lilliana's wrist, inspecting the red, angry line. He shook his head and muttered something.

"What's that Leon?" Damon asked.

Leon looked across at Damon. "Nothing Sir." He looked away from Damon as he placed Lilliana's arm back down.

Lilliana groaned in pain, opening her eyes. "Leon, that really hurts." Her eyes glanced around the room, to find what she first had wanted to see when she opened her eyes.

And there he was, looking dark and dangerous, a frown on his face.

Lilliana held up her good hand, reaching for him.

He crossed to the bed in an instant, and sat near her, taking her hand in his.

"How are you sweet girl?"

"I'm fine. How is Sam?" Damon looked across at Leon.

Lilliana pulled her gaze away from her loves face, to look at another man she thought highly of.

"He's still in surgery with Dr Ryan." Leon saw the concern in Lilliana's eyes.

"I hope he'll be alright."

"He'll be fine," Leon soothed, "how are you feeling?"

"I'll be fine too," she said quietly. Not wanting to let Damon know how much pain she was in. Her wrist throbbed as if the knife itself was still lodged there.

"Well, sleeping is the best thing for you right now Lilliana. I am going to increase your pain medication, which should knock you out for half a day." Leon smiled down at her.

"Okay then." Lilliana smiled across at Damon. "Maybe we can get my archery lesson in after all that."

Damon squeezed her hand, not answering. The thought of her in danger, or trouble of any kind pained him. He was seriously considering keeping her locked up here forever.

"Lilliana," Leon poked around in his case, bringing out a large needle, "this should knock you out for about twelve hours. Have you eaten recently?" He looked down at her.

Lilliana forced her eyes away from Damon's face. "All my hours have been jumbled up lately. I'm not really hungry, just thirsty."

Damon squeezed her hand and left the room, returning with a large, cold orange juice.

"Drink this sweetheart," he said softly, placing it in her hands. "Leon, I can give her that, and anything else you need me to. I'd like to speak to Lilliana privately before we place her in a sedation trance."

Leon placed the needle down on a small tray on the bedside table. He added to that, four small, silver tablets. "These will help increase the healing process." He pointed to the needle. "The trance will last twelve hours or so Lilliana, but it has added antibiotics to fight any infection which may spread. That knife was beyond filthy."

"Thank you Leon. Where did he find that poor cows face?"

"A cow passed away after it delivered its calf. Rick cut its face off after it died."

"That's something to be thankful for I guess." She sighed.

Damon's phone rang as Leon clipped his bag shut. As Damon left the room to speak privately to Hillary about Rick's situation, Leon bent down to Lilliana.

"Are you alright?" His hand reached out to brush hers.

She smiled up at him. "All is well Leon, please don't worry about me, I'm totally fine." She squeezed his hand.

Leon leaned down as if to kiss Lilliana's forehead when Damon cleared his throat behind them, making Leon jerk upright.

"Right, well. If you need me, please just send for me." Leon nodded to Damon as he briskly walked past.

Lilliana raised an eyebrow to Damon and called out thank you to Leon. Damon left to follow the other man out.

Lilliana placed her good wrist across her forehead and closed her eyes. Not quite the night she'd planned. She let out a deep sigh. She did not want to spend her last uninterrupted day with Damon, asleep.

Maybe if she could just get up, act normal, show no pain.

She pushed herself up and noted the gorgeous black nightgown. She threw the covers back and slid her feet onto the cool floorboards.

A little wave of dizziness came over her. She took a deep breath and pushed herself up and walked across to the bathroom.

Closing the door behind her she relieved herself, washed her hands and splashed cold water onto her face.

She glanced in the mirror, shocked at how pale she actually was. Her black hair against her skin, making it seem more so. Her green eyes were frowning in pain. Taking a deep breath, she soothed her features to look calm and relaxed.

She nodded, feeling in control as she slid the door open, and walked out through the bedroom, down the corridor and into the main living area.

Damon had his back to her as she entered. He was on the phone, talking quietly, yet sharply. A dangerous combination to anyone's ears with a clue.

"I'm not quite sure what to do about this situation Allie? Someone with your qualifications should have been aware that he was high risk, I feel that a demotion of some sort is certainly in order here." He had one hand placed on his hip, his back ramrod straight, listening to Allie. "It could have gone a whole other way today; you are aware of that aren't you?"

He looks so tall, Lilliana thought to herself. Taller than usual, especially when he had his serious voice on. Serious mood. Poor Allie. Damon was quiet for a minute, as Allie must have been justifying her case.

"I'll take that into consideration Allie, but this isn't over. I'll talk to you in the morning. My office, eight sharp!" He clicked the phone down hard. He placed his other hand on his hip and dropped his head back, with a loud sigh.

"Damon." Lilliana said quietly behind him.

He turned to face her, noting how pale she looked.

"What do you think you're doing? I need you to stay in bed." He crossed over to her, and cupped her chin, pulling her face gently upwards.

He bent down and kissed her gently. Lips closed.

Her hands by her sides, slipped up his shirt, running her fingers along his abs; she tiptoed closer and opened her lips, wanting him to do the same.

He wanted to do the same, and more, but forced himself to gently take hold of her upper arms and push her away.

"No," she took a step forward. "I want you. I do not want to waste one second of our time together sleeping. Damon, please?"

He stepped back as she took another step forward. "Lilliana, baby, you need to sleep. I promise I will stay with you, I have work to do anyway." He gently ran his hand over her hair, and quickly turning, he walked to his desk, grabbing his tablet.

He faced her, opening his arm for her to slip under his shoulder, he smiled down at her. She looped her arm around his waist.

As they walked towards the bedroom, a knock sounded at the door.

Damon looked down at her. "You pop yourself into bed. That will be our food."

"Okay," she nodded, walking towards the bedroom. Food was good. The slower she ate, the longer she could be with him. Awake.

She went and settled herself amongst the pillows, sitting on top of the covers. Maybe if she made herself look presentable he would be unable to resist her.

He returned in minutes, glancing at her as he walked in. A small smile on his lips, he placed a large tray on the end of the bed, then walking over to the chair and small table near the fire, placed his Tablet down.

He kicked off his shoes and threw his socks down the chute. He sat opposite her on the end of the bed, in jeans and tee shirt, looking very delicious in Lilliana's eyes.

"You let me know the minute you're not feeling well, okay?"

Like an hour ago, she thought to herself, but smiled and said instead, "I'm fine."

He passed her a freshly made shrimp salad, with a bowl of mango sorbet.

Pouring a glass of water, he leaned over and placed it on the bedside table, near the needle and medication.

He brushed her cheek with his lips as he sat back down, grabbed a fork and passed it to her, then he lay on his side, along the end of the bed, and forked up a large mouthful of salad, chewing slowly, he watched her.

It blew her mind, that him just staring at her like that, made her totally melt.

His eyes did not blink. Just stayed focused on her face, her body, as he chewed.

She glanced down and stabbed a cherry tomato, wondering if she could keep it down. She flicked it off and reached for her mango sorbet.

"You know, I have to say something in regard to Allie." She glanced up. This was new territory for her, addressing him professionally, about a work colleague.

"Oh." he slowly took a mouthful of water. Watching. Waiting.

"Yes." Lilliana placed her spoon back down in her untouched bowl. "Allie processed Rick for three months in Psych, along with Dr Hillary. He was deemed low risk, and he was quite alright in our first group, only showing mild irritation in second group, which was when I called in for a second opinion. After Dr Hillary and security took Rick from our rooms, the decision for Rick's placement was out of Allie's hands. I am certain, that she had no idea he had been processed for main house.

So, I think you'll need to look for someone else to blame." She reached for her glass of water and took a nervous swallow.

He had not moved an inch. Just stared at her, unblinking.

He lowered his eyes finally and took another jab at his salad, before placing his fork in his mouth, and as he chewed, collected his plate, and her untouched food and put them on the tray, then stepping off the bed, walked out of the room and put them in the kitchen chute.

Lilliana drained her glass and nervously placed it back on the table.

She stared into the fireplace, wondering if, in future she was going to discuss business with him, she'd schedule a meeting. This was all new territory for them both.

He returned shortly and walked up to her and sat on the side of the bed.

He was so close. She could see the deep flecks of grey and blue in his deep blue eyes.

He smelled divine. She reached up her fingers and stroked a lock at the back of his neck.

He bent towards her lips, red and partly open. He could hear her breathing. She was nervous, he could tell.

He smiled as he gently took her fingers that had played with his hair, and turned her hand over, kissing her wrist, he pulled her closer and kissed her lips, sweetly softly.

He pulled back as she went to deepen the kiss. It pained him to do so. He wanted her, badly. The light sheen of sweat indicated the pain she was feeling but trying to hide.

She pouted. He smiled and pulling her into his arms, chuckled quietly, his hands running down her back, and up again. Sighing, he took a deep breath of her hair, kissing her neck through the silken mass.

Her arms went around his waist. "You're not angry with me, are you?"

"I don't think I could ever be angry with you." He leant her back in his arm, as his other hand was busy doing something near the table, and kissed her, this time sinking into her, letting the kiss go as deep as they both wanted it to.

He kissed her for a few minutes, letting them both enjoy the feelings of deep desire.

Lilliana moaned, her fingers pulling his head as close as she could, as she melted back into the pillows, pushing her body against his.

He could so easily lose himself in her right now but forced himself to pull back. Both breathing heavily. He shook his head.

"Can't seem to stop myself," he whispered.

He sat up straight and pulled a hand through his hair. Grabbing the pills up, he popped them near Lilliana's lips. She looked down at them, then across at the needle.

"I don't want to." She folded her arms.

"Mm, I was thinking Doctors of any kind never make the best patients." He moved towards her lips and brushed his across hers gently. "For me," he whispered leaning back, his intense eyes staring directly into hers, giving her no-where else to go.

She couldn't breathe, simply nodded.

He smiled and popped the four silver pills between her lips, then held the glass of water up against them for her to drink.

She did, her eyes never leaving his.

When she swallowed them all, he kissed her nose, then placing the glass of water down, picked up the needle.

She held up her hand to stop him. "When I wake up, and we get back to our schedules, are we sticking to the plan of remaining work colleagues in public?"

"For a little while baby, until we get back into full routine. I haven't been back long, and I need to feel how the land is laying with some people. But I promise we will have time together soon." He stroked her cheek. "We will always be together."

She was filled with relief. "That's all I need to hear."

He bent down, and placing his mouth over hers, poured his love into her.

She sighed, then gasped against his lips, as the sharp prick of the needle went into her arm. She was out in a second.

He placed her gently back on to the pillows and tucked her in making sure to be gentle near her collar bone and wrist.

He sat there for a while stroking her soft long hair.

He couldn't take his eyes from her, feeling so blessed that here she was, finally, safely, in his bed.

"Hello." A voice called from the hallway. Cam.

"In here." Damon called softly.

Cam walked in to see his brother, like a guardian angel, sitting over an angel of another sort.

He leant against the doorway and folded his arms. Watching.

"Can I help you Cam?" Damon asked keeping his eyes on Lilliana as his hand swept along her hair.

"Yes, you can actually. I want to marry Josephine next week and thought that would give Fox and the girls enough time to organize something just right for my honey."

Damon turned to face his brother, a smile on his lips. "And what would you like me to do Cameron; it seems that you can organize all this without me. The man who organizes million-dollar photo shoots and horticultural projects worldwide doesn't need of my help." He left the bed and walked over to pour himself a coffee. "Want one?"

Cam shook his head, "Nah, I've got to get back to Josephine. Promised her I'd give her a report on how Lilliana is doing." He made his way over to inspect her healing wounds. "How is she?"

"She's one tough little thing, but, I always knew that. She'll be fine, she just needs to sleep." He took a mouthful of coffee, watching Lilliana over the top.

Cam smiled. "You've got it bad hey, but then, you always did."

"True." Damon said simply.

"So, what is it that I can do for you Cameron?" Damon set his cup down, and folded his arms, waiting.

"I was wondering if you'd not only give Josephine away to me, but be my best man at our wedding?" Cam asked.

Damon smiled and crossed over to his brother, pulling him into a brotherly hug. "It would be my absolute pleasure. I'm so happy for the both of you."

He held him at arms' length and looked him in the eye. "You know, the past nine years, you've come along way. There was a time I could have killed you on a weekly basis."

Cam chuckled. "Well, I have to admit, I wouldn't have blamed you. I was a hard case."

Damon clapped him on the shoulder before turning to walk over to Lilliana. He sat on the side of the bed, looking down at her.

"Maybe a double wedding?"

Damon chuckled. "Don't tempt me. No, Lilliana and I are just getting started on our phase two."

"Okay," Cam asked. "What was phase one."

"Where I could look, but not morally touch. But we are on even ground now. I just hope that ground stays flat for a while and we can stay on our feet."

He stroked Lilliana's cheek, then rose and walked over to his chair. Sitting he picked up his Tablet and clicked on several files.

"Well, I think that's where you are missing the point," Cam smiled. "In the early days, you shouldn't be on your feet, but flat on your back. I can give you some pointers."

"Goodbye, Cameron." Damon said, with a smile in his voice.

Cam saluted as he left the room.

Damon got straight into viewing a pile of reports, scheduling conference calls for tomorrow when Lilliana would still be sleeping, re-scheduled Richard till after he spoke with Allie in the morning and checked out the budget for the next six months.

He was seriously considering building another main house further out in the property. Somewhere else to put senior staff and working couples.

Open another level in the main house for new Given.

He was also considering getting rid of the Black Ops unit. But in agreement with the government's Officials, they got paid the big bucks to keep the bastards of society, using them to acquire information, to shut down bigger underground activity.

He worked for six hours straight, going into his office area to take a phone call from the Chinese ambassador.

Leon came up around three am to check on Lilliana. After he left, Damon had a hot shower and finally, slipped into bed with her.

She was in such a deep sleep. He took pleasure in burying his face gently into her neck placing his arm around her, and then fell asleep breathing her in for the next five hours.

***

Damon was up at six, went for a run, then showered, had his meeting with Allie at eight, and then called for an assembly for ten.

After a week of being back, Damon thought it time he showed his face to all the Given again.

Cam introduced the newer Given to his brother, who had already read most of their files, and reviewed any of their footage that was available.

He was happy to greet older faces and catch up on their general progress.

So many scarred children formed into happy young adults.

He was quite impressed with Eric, despite the young man barely saying a civil word to him.

He went down to the H D to check in with Josephine and Rupert and was impressed with how very far their profits had skyrocketed in the past five years.

It was so rewarding to see the crops and advanced methods, Rupert and the scientists had put together, in developing such healthy, wonderful eats and flowers.

The fields in which they grew the horse feed, and feed for all the other livestock thrived all year round.

He made his two pm sale with Thomas at the stables; it took fifteen men, plus Thomas and Damon, to lead the horses into the field where the cargo plane came to fly the animals out.

Watching the plane leave, Damon felt a satisfaction he had not felt in years.

Damn it was good to be home, getting business flowing again and looking after his people.

Speaking of this, he thought it was time to get back to Lilliana, but first, a quick meeting with Richard.

Damon arrived at his office to freshen up. He washed his face and hands, then ran his fingers through his hair. Drained a cup of water, before pouring himself a strong, black coffee, then sat in his office chair, and waited.

Three minutes later a knock sounded.

"Enter." Damon called out, leaning back in his chair.

Richard walked in looking as arrogant as always.

"Hello Damon."

"Richard, please, sit." Damon indicated the chair opposite his.

Richard crossed over and sat.

"Coffee?" Damon asked.

"Yes, thank you." Richard smiled a frosty little smile.

Damon placed his cup on his desk and walked over to the side table, pouring Richard a coffee. Handing it to him, he stood, looking down at the man for a moment, before walking back behind his desk, sat and picked up his own mug, taking a mouthful. Watching Richard all the while.

"It seems we have a little problem that needs to be sorted out immediately."

"Oh?" Richard took a sip from his steaming mug, glancing at Damon. "And what would that problem be?"

"Your attitude regarding Lilliana," Damon set his cup down, leaning his arms on the desk. "I want to know why you treat her with such contempt."

"Why, I don't know what you're talking about, I give her as much respect as I do any other when we're working together."

"Like making her help abort that child, that I helped create with that monster. Almost spelling it out to her! Letting that filthy woman suffer, and putting Lilliana through that torment, to assist you?" Damon's voice had dropped below zero, his voice as cold as ice.

"What game are you playing at Richard? I may not physically have been here the past five years, but I have eyes and ears everywhere, and they are loyal and thorough in their reports to me." He leaned back in his chair, crossing his ankle over his knee, and folded his arms.

Richard looked at the handsome, younger man.

So similar to his father.

Yet he knew things about his father, which he imagined Damon had no idea about, what-so-ever, that would kill him, and this facilities reputation if it ever got out. But he had always been loyal, despite what others thought of him.

"Look, I have nothing to say. The fact is, I do my job here Damon. And I do it well, as I have for many years. I worked loyally for your father for years, enjoyed working for him. I also, enjoy working under yourself and Cameron.

I may not always do things the way you like me to, but I get them done. No one suffers. Not really." He shrugged.

"Would you like to work in Russia, China?" Damon asked.

Richard froze. "No. I would not. And, unless you want things to get ugly, do not threaten me, with placing me elsewhere."

Richard stood, placing his mug down on the desk. "Now, Sir, is that all? I have three evaluations that have just arrived early this morning. Cameron is waiting for me."

Damon stood. "What do you mean, unless I want things to get ugly? Elaborate." He placed his hands-on hips.

"Damon, if my role here is secure and you leave me, as you have done, to just get on with my job, I will not have to pollute that deep mind of yours, with murk from the past. Let it go. It is irrelevant. Now, unless you want your brother to be at me for tardiness, I must go."

Damon nodded, remaining silent, and sat down in his chair, as Richard left the room, wondering what the hell he was talking about? Taking a deep breath, he buzzed Leon, to see if he had finished with Lilliana.

CHAPTER 10

It was three days before Josephine's wedding. Lilliana's injury's had healed, the cut's invisible thanks to this generation's miracle healing vitamins, medicines and creams.

Jessica, Lilliana, Allie and Josephine were up in Cam's rooms, with dresses, seating cards, and other wedding paraphernalia spread all around them.

Four bottles of sparkling wine had already been consumed and a platter of savouries had been devoured. The feeling in the room was relaxed and festive.

It was four in the afternoon; they had all finished with their tasks for the day and were enjoying some down time.

Josephine was sprawled out on her back, her head across Lilliana's lap, holding her flute glass carefully.

Jessica was seated at the desk, giving up on organizing the seating arrangements, as there were over one thousand guests and no one else in the room seemed to be as worried about it as she was.

Allie, onto her second bottle, was spinning around and around the silver pole in the middle of the room, trying to master a flip spin.

"I mean, you have definitely chosen the right kinda guy to marry

Jose, it's just not normal these days to hook up with a guy, who doesn't have a pole in his rooms. You know? That's why I've held off with Christopher, he needs to understand that all it takes, is a giant thick pole."

Jessica burst out laughing, as Allie slid down the pole, the remainder of her champagne taking a slippery journey of its own all over Allie's chest.

"Oh Allie," Josephine sighed, "I thought Christopher's pole was all you needed."

Both Lilliana and Josephine had a laughing fit, knowing that the wine was putting them in a very relaxed, carefree mood. And why the hell not? They deserved to totally let go and enjoy this moment of having the entire afternoon off with their friends, and fingers crossed not one interruption.

At least that's what Damon and Cam promised them.

Damon. Lilliana felt those butterflies stir up again just thinking about him. She promised herself, for the next twelve hours she would totally concentrate on her friends, and her friends alone, but she couldn't wipe the smile off her face. She shook her head and looked down at Josephine who was staring up at her, smiling.

"Share Lilliana, it's only fair." Josephine pointed a finger under Lilliana's nose, it almost missed and poked her eye, but Lilliana moved her head and saved her eyeball.

"Yes, ditto to what Jose just said." Allie plonked down in the middle of the rug, with a fresh bottle of wine. She had done away with the glass and drank straight from the bottle.

Jessica grabbed her own glass and sat next to Allie on the floor, passing her friend her empty glass for her to top up.

"Yes, this is like a deeply entertaining novel, where the next chapter just must be read," Jessica nodded, taking a mouthful of the cool wine. "I mean, this has been coming for years, we really need details." She leaned her shoulder against Allie's.

Lilliana smiled down at Josephine and shrugged, taking a mouthful from her own glass. She looked out the window, a secretive smile on her face.

"It's like the cat that got the cream!" Josephine chuckled, pushing herself up.

Lilliana sighed happily, glancing at each of her friends warm, loving faces. "I don't know if I will ever be able to put into words, just how happy I am. It's like a dream I don't want to wake from. It's possibly the happiest I've ever been."

She took a cool, long swallow of her drink before continuing. "We are all so blessed. You are not only my dearest friends, but my sisters." She held her glass up to them all. "And not everyone in this life is so blessed."

Allie and Jessica jumped up to sit on the extra-large king-sized bed with Lilliana and Josephine, and the four clicked their glasses, and one bottle together, cheering.

"As a bonus," Lilliana said, "I think it's fair to say, we have fallen in love with very special men."

"Absolutely," Allie nodded, "our best friends to be sure."

"Come on Lilly, spill the beans. We've been sharing with you for years. I want juicy Goss!" Josephine nudged her.

Lilliana smiled and started by telling them about the first time he touched her, when she was asleep on the couch, to how her heart just about stopped when he claimed her for the first time. To their horse ride.

"Everything about him just about makes my heart have palpitations. The slightest touch, I feel like I'm going to pass out. The sound of his voice. A smile, even a frown. I just want more. Just the way he looks at me. Even if we are in a room full of people, and he's not looking at me. I can feel him, it's like my soul is so connected to him. We just feel each other?" Lilliana shrugged, "I think I'll totally die if he ever leaves me. I feel like I've felt this way forever about him."

She drained her glass and poured another. "Even being here, with three of the most important people in my life, having a ball, I simply cannot wait for the next second to lay my eyes on him."

"Oh yeah, you have it bad sister," Allie grinned at her. "And it's about time too."

"How is the, no touching, in public working for you?" Jessica popped a giant strawberry into her mouth.

Lilliana reached for a strawberry and dipped it into the melted chocolate.

She contemplated before answering. "It's fine. I think it's for the best. I haven't been with him since the afternoon Rick attacked me. He has been very careful about trying not to hurt me and making sure I get plenty of rest. Then he had an emergency and has been flat out the past three days."

"So basically," Allie walked over to the pole, and placing her leg around it, slid slowly down, then up, "You are ready to *EXPLODE.*" she screamed out, faking an orgasm, sliding back down the pole.

Josephine and Jessica burst out laughing, Lilliana shook her head smiling, and reaching for a strawberry, tossed it at Allie, who caught it neatly and popped it into her mouth.

"I've missed this," Lilliana said.

"Me too," Jessica smiled at her.

"Yes," Josephine agreed. "All busy and professional like now, aren't we? But I insist we do this, at least once a month. Agreed?"

They all agreed, and totally booked out Lilliana's and Allie's rooms in their office for the next meet. This excited Jessica as she hardly ever went downstairs.

Another hour passed and then there was a knock at the door.

Josephine looked pained.

Lilliana had organized Fox to come in and help order the perfect dresses.

Natalie was assisting.

"Just be nice," Lilliana kissed her friend's hair, as she walked backwards to the door, whispering, conspirator like, "she will do the best job out of everybody here, to make you look perfect."

Josephine saluted, and pretended to zip up her mouth.

Lilliana spun to open the door, smiling at Fox. "Hello, so good of you to come, please." She stepped back so the sexy red head could walk past. She kissed Lilliana's cheek as she did so.

Lilliana forced herself to smile at Natalie, as the girl walked in with the sample materials for the dresses.

"Hi Natalie," Lilliana said as Natalie strode into the room, "how've you been?"

"Like you care." Natalie spat out, as nasty as ever.

"Play nice Natalie." Fox snapped out. "Special occasion here."

Lilliana walked over, drained her glass and filled it up, smiling at Josephine as if to say, See, two can play this game.

Josephine leant close to Lilliana's ear and whispered, "Dutch courage putting up with this shit." She also drained her glass, then pushing back her brown curls, turned and smiled at Fox.

"So good of you to come help me Foxy-Loxy!"

Lilliana put her arm around her friend's shoulder. "Just excuse us Fox, we've all had a bit to drink. Would you like a glass?"

"Yes, thank you." She smiled a radiant smile at her younger friend, always appreciating her elegance. "Can we get one for Natalie please?"

"Absolutely." Jessica got two more glasses, and filling them, passed them over to their guests.

Fox simply drained the glass and held it out again to be refilled.

Natalie did the same after watching how fashionably Fox did everything.

"Right." Fox smiled, enjoying the effect the bubbly drink had on her. None of them drank, apart from special occasions. Like Christmas, maybe a birthday. But a wedding? She would certainly enjoy hanging out with these girls for another hour or two.

"Here, we have any colour you can see yourself wearing, any fabric you want to feel caress your skin on the day." Fox was so in her fashion mood.

Explaining how each material would best fit on Josephine's frame, what colour would suit her to look like the perfect bride. She was being very kind to Josephine.

And Josephine was being such a good girl also. No smart comments were being passed back and forth, like their usual tennis match.

Lilliana walked across to Cam's balcony and stepped out into the fresh, afternoon air, leaving Allie and Fox to have a happy argument on what each thought best for the bridesmaids' outfits.

Jessica joined her, bringing a bottle, topped up their glasses, and the two friends gazed across the beautiful grounds.

"You haven't said much about Orlando, Jessica. Is everything alright love?" Lilliana turned and gazed at her friend.

Jessica turned to face Lilliana. "Things are great." She shrugged. "We had a break for a while, we were just so exhausted with our roles. But now we make our time together count. Sometimes it feels as if I've known him forever, other times like I'm just getting to know him."

Lilliana bumped her shoulder into her friend's. "Eight and a half years is a long time and you've both been through a lot before, and during, that time. And in here, it's not like you have days or weeks to just be alone with that one person to communicate all your thoughts and feelings."

"Yeah, that is it exactly. Quality time is so important." Jessica nodded, and drained her glass. "I think I'm going to have a headache in the morning."

"Come on," Lilliana nodded inside "let's drink a bucket of water and then hit the good stuff. Allie is making cocktails after."

"Oh god no, excellent." Jessica chuckled. "I just hope Vanessa behaves tomorrow, or I may just end her," she joked, referring to a new, young Given, who had a constant, angry attitude towards all.

The two went inside, where Fox was standing, back ramrod straight, and having a stare-down with Allie.

The two girls were nose to chest as Allie being such a little thing, had to have her head thrown back to look up into Fox's eyes.

"What's going on?" Lilliana poured herself and Jessica a water.

"I think the girls are about to have a moment," Natalie said, almost dreamily.

"Really?" Lilliana poured her water down her throat, had another. "Can we do cocktails first, so I can enjoy and evaluate the show before it gets really steamy!" Josephine wondered.

Fox backed away from Allie. "How 'bout that cocktail, sugar." She turned and sat on the end of the bed where Josephine was lying up-side down, watching all.

An hour later there was no other sound in the room apart from five women, in hysterical fits of laughter, as Fox was telling stories about her fat Santa shoot one year, amongst other modelling stories.

Natalie looked happily tipsy but didn't add much in the way of conversation.

Lilliana felt, once again for her, and was glad she was part of tonight's celebrations. If she would only be like this more of the time, keep her mouth shut and her hands to herself.

At twenty-four, she had become an attractive girl. Curves and roundness in that sexy womanly way, her brown hair hung to her shoulders, her once mean eyes, always surrounded in frown lines, had rounded out to a prettier shape. When she smiled, she was actually very pleasant to look at.

She looked across and caught Lilliana staring.

"Problem, princess Lilly?"

It was always her mouth and attitude that stung. "Not really." Lilliana shrugged, and finished the rest of her drink.

"That was delicious. How about another one?"

The room was totally spinning, and everything was hilarious to them all.

Fox made sure they all had water in between drinks.

After another hour passed, they had a gallon of water and another cocktail.

"Alright, we have your colour and style all sorted, but what about your bridesmaids?" Fox wanted to know.

"Well, if I'm antique white, maybe the girls should be in a soft green, or something that looks like a light leaf?" Clearly Josephine had no idea but loved the thought of bringing her beloved nature into the day.

"How about purple with polka dots" Allie jokingly suggested.

"Oh, really? Nice, I don't think so, no more alcohol for you." Lilliana tossed a pillow at Allie, knocking her backwards.

Allie came up laughing. "Who the hell cares what colour we are in Fox, it's Josephine's day. She is the only one who needs to stand out."

"Right," Fox nodded, "how about Jade Green then?"

"Easy. Done." Josephine agreed. "But I want the girls' dress's to be off the shoulder, and knee length. Elegant. No flounces or fluff."

"Agreed," as Fox stood. "Thank you ladies for having us." She wavered a little.

"I don't suppose anyone feels like skinny dipping?"

"Hell yes, I am in." Allie stood.

"Shallow end only." Jessica said, trying to sound all, Team Leader-like and responsible.

Lilliana looked across at Josephine, and they both cracked up.

Lilliana shook her head. "Let's just stick to the spa. We won't have any drowned bodies three days before the big event that way."

"Hang on, foods about to arrive," Allie said, and sure enough, a knock at the door, revealed Christopher and a trolley, brimming with sandwiches, anti-pastas and salads.

Allie pounced on Christopher, wrapping her legs around his waist. He laughed before kissing her thoroughly.

After another hour, the six of them ate themselves a little sober, and then, greedily had another cocktail.

They each got into their bikinis, Natalie chose a one piece, and grabbing their drinks, quietly made their way downstairs.

They could hear a late, night detention going on in the library and they froze.

Lilliana scoffed, "Please, if we want to sneak out for a night swim, what are they going to do, put us over their knee?"

They all laughed quietly.

"It wouldn't be such a bad idea for some of you." A calm voice said from behind them.

Their laughter stopped and they slowly turned to face the man who melted Lilliana's insides, simply with the sound of his voice.

Damon stood, hands in his pockets, shirt half unbuttoned down his chest. It was after all, nearly midnight.

He could see the sparkle in their eyes, their ice cubes jingling quietly in their glasses.

Lilliana stepped forward through the girls, passing Josephine her glass.

His eyes roamed her splendid curves, her breasts almost falling out of her skimpy bikini, but in such an attractive way, it made him grow hard instantly.

"Hello Sir," she whispered, "If you are handing out punishment, I'll be the first in line." She wanted to smile, but the serious look on his face stopped her, making her the teeniest bit nervous. Once again, new territory.

"Ladies," he said quietly, "Lilliana will join you shortly. Off you go, quietly and carefully please. We still have other Given to consider."

They all bid 'Mr Night' farewell, and quickly left the hallway and down the front steps. Their laughter could be heard from where Lilliana and Damon stood, eating each other with their eyes.

He held out his hand for her to take. She stepped forward, placing her hand in his.

As soon as their skin made contact, he spun her around, almost like a dance move, as she followed him into his office across the hallway.

As the door slid shut behind them, he flicked a switch, locking it.

She turned around to face him. He ran a hand down her long hair that gently brushed her back.

She heard him sigh. Butterflies started to attack her stomach.

She reached up behind her back and pulled her bikini strap undone, letting it fall to her feet.

He took a step back. She took a step forward. He pulled his shirt over his head, and kicked off his shoes, taking another step back.

She dropped her bikini bottom. He dropped his jeans and briefs. Reaching out, he grabbed her around her waist, and jerked her hard up against his chest.

She smiled as his head lowered, her fingers sliding into his thick, soft hair.

"This is all I've been wanting," she sighed, as his lips slid gently over hers.

She stood on her tiptoes, pressing herself closer. He grabbed her around her hips and raised her up. She wrapped her legs around him, her mouth devouring his before trailing along his jaw, his neck.

He sighed, kneading her bottom, as she nuzzled him.

He tugged her hair making her head fall back so he could look into her eyes.

"Lilliana, I've missed you." He brushed her lips with his again.

"And I you, love," she whispered right back.

He walked backwards with her, until his knees hit the couch, and he sat with her, placing her close.

They kissed forever, taking their time, enjoying the fever that built up within each of them.

He placed his hand just under her neck pushing her slowly backwards, supporting her with his arm behind her. He kissed along her neck and downwards towards her breasts. He flicked a nipple with his thumb, whilst his tongue lazily swirled the other one, around and around.

Lilliana moaned. She was experiencing the same sensation between her legs.

He could feel her wetness against his swollen flesh.

She reached down to stroke him, bursting to ride him.

He felt her small hand grab hold of him, and nearly came then.

He pulled his head up to stare into her eyes. He ran his hands slowly down her front and back, massaging her skin. Then, he grabbed her hips, and raising her up, gently placed her on his hard, throbbing shaft.

Lilliana moaned, and started to rock against him. He too pushed up into her soft wetness, loving the feel of her ride him, her frenzy burning deep.

He massaged her breasts, then cupping her face, pulled her down to kiss her long and deep and she rubbed herself against him, driving him harder and deeper within herself.

His tongue thrust deeply in her mouth sending her over the edge.

They clung to each other as their orgasm surged, sweeping them in a delicious spiral of glory.

When she stopped moving, he wound his arms tightly around her, both breathing heavily, she wrapped her arms around his neck, pushing her face so close to him. Breathing him in.

They sat like that for many minutes. Not speaking, just holding each other.

He gently pulled her back, and kissed her deeply, she could feel her butterflies swirling gently. "Again," she whispered.

He chuckled and stood, carrying her up with him before placing her back on her feet.

"Soon enough my angel. Josephine will kill me if I interrupt anymore of your girl time."

Lilliana nodded. "Yes, dear Jose deserves this time." She kissed his cheek, before bending for her bikini top, then her bottom. She heard Damon suck in his breath, and turning, saw him pull his jeans on, with his eyes closed.

She put her top on, then her bottoms, feeling a sense of happiness.

He may not have her again right this moment. But the fact was, he wanted her, as she wanted him. She turned to face him.

He stood, jeans on, hands on hips, watching her. He shook his head slowly.

"What?"

"Do you need to ask?" he smiled, then, lifting a finger, pulled it towards him.

She walked over, and standing on tiptoe, reached up to place her arms around his neck.

His strong arms went around her, holding her closely, gently. He kissed the top of her hair. She sighed and kissed his neck.

He stroked her soft skin. "How has your day been baby?"

She leaned back in his arms, to smile up at him. "Awesome. Brilliant. Better now."

He kissed her first on one cheek, then, slowly the other. She'd stopped breathing, in anticipation.

His lips found hers and kissed her like she knew only he could.

"Off you go Lilliana, before I take you again." Gently holding her away from him.

She smiled, walking backwards. "I'll see you soon?" She only hoped.

He flipped a switch to open the door, and as she stepped through it. "I'm certainly counting on it."

"Bye Damon." She blew him a kiss.

He smiled as he watched her walk out, and down the front steps, towards her friends.

***

The night before the wedding Josephine wanted to bunk down in Lilliana's room, and had asked Damon if she and her bridal party could get ready in his rooms the following day. He graciously said, of course.

Lilliana and Josephine were tucked into bed, quietly talking about life. Men. Dreams. Life outside.

A knock on the door sounded, followed by Cams voice. "Are there a couple of angels in here that need a good night kiss?"

Lilliana looked at Josephine. "You want me to step out, give you two five minutes?"

"Only to talk, Lilly, make sure you tell Mr. Tentacle-hands out there. No touching."

Lilliana smiled, thinking, whatever. Knowing that if Cam sat down to talk, Josephine would be all over him. She checked the time. Two am.

"I'll duck down to the kitchen, heat us up some milk."

Lilliana opened the door to Cam. He looked her up and down, taking in her short, pink nightie. "Nice. I wish pyjama parties looked like this when I was a kid." He bent to kiss her cheek.

"You've got until I come back with hot milk. Talking only." she smiled at Cam. She could see his eyes widen hungrily, as he looked at Josephine sitting on Lilliana's bed, in a black teddy.

"What do you girls get up to together, looking all ravishing?"

Lilliana heard a pillow hit the door behind her as it closed. Shaking her head and smiling, she slowly set off down the stairs, making sure she gave them extra time if they needed it.

She remembered a night, similar to this one, where she'd walked down the stairs. The house entirely quiet, feeling like home.

Hitting the bottom step, she strolled past the library and over to the front entrance. The door was locked this night, and all forbidden to leave main house till sunrise, as outside, Damon had flown in an all-night crew to set up for tomorrow's celebrations. Out in the field opposite the stables, crews were setting up marquees with a kitchen area, dining tables, dance floors and any other wedding paraphernalia that the day would need, for a celebration to cater for around three thousand people, in a style that was befitting Cam's station at the Given.

The huge spot lights no doubt would see a few unsettled horses this night. Lilliana glanced over her shoulder, worried about Beauty, Beast and the other horses. Of course, they would be in good hands with Thomas nearby, but she was wanting to see for herself that all was well. Her hand reached for the door slightly hesitant, thinking of all the obvious reasons why she should not break Damon's rule. Then, thought of the fresh air, people out there being too busy to look for trouble, and her desire to make sure the horses were in fact, okay. What harm could there be in going out? She'd simply dash down, check on the horses, then dash back, get the milk and would have given Josephine and Cam their much-needed time together.

Taking a quiet breath, she undid the lock and slipped out into the night, and lightly jogged down the blue stone path following the direction to the stables. Behind her it was pitch-black. She was grateful that if someone looked towards the house she would not be seen.

But from the house, penetrating eyes, could see a figure in pink running towards the stables, a frown of disbelief marred his features; that of all the people to break rule this night, it was her.

The noise outside was rowdy. Stagehands laughing and telling jokes. Strong coffee was in the air, keeping cold bodies warm and sleepy minds active.

Although, most of the workers brought in knew they were working an all-night shift and had made up their sleep before getting on the plane.

Lilliana slowed to a walk as she reached the dark entrance of the stable. She knew this place like the back of her hand and walked confidently along, shushing some of the restless mares, stopping to stroke their noses, or whisper calmness gently to them.

As she walked past Thomas's upstairs quarters, she noticed his lights were off. Hopefully he was getting some sleep.

She finally reached Beauty's stall and put her arms around her beautiful horse's neck, kissing and stroking her, whispering gentle words. Spending many minutes enjoying her company.

"How are you Bella, are those silly men being noisy out there? It's alright; it's only for one night." Beauty pushed her nose into Lilliana's chest, snorting gently. Lilliana ran her hand along her neck, patting her, before moving onto Beast. She heard a shuffling behind her and froze. She held her breath, turning to face whoever was there. She could not see a thing.

She took a quiet step back, and Beast snorted behind her. She did not jump, so used to him and all the horses' behaviour in general. She waited, then heard a sniffing, wriggly body near her legs.

She laughed softly, "Is that you Rusty?" she said, bending down to give him a pat. "How are you boy?" She scrubbed her hand up his soft old chest, he snuffled against her hands, full of doggy appreciation.

"Off you go, back to bed." She ordered, after one more pat.

She sighed as she turned to face Beast and screamed as her body came up hard against another. Firm, tall, strong.

Steele like fingers, gripped her upper arms, and shook her gently.

"What am I going to do with you Lilliana?" Damon, his voice pained and frustrated.

She sighed, and gave a soft, nervous laugh. "Oh Damon," she leaned forward, dropping her forehead onto his chest. "You scared me half to death."

He remained rigid. She stepped back as far as she could as he still held her firmly.

"You're cross with me?" She asked quietly, feeling his vibe.

"You think? What do you think may have happened, if it wasn't me you just innocently bumped into, in the middle of the night, whilst you are practically naked." His last few words were clipped. Harsh.

"Damon, I was worried about the horses. That's all. I just wanted to quickly check on them, make sure they were alright." She wasn't sure if she should be nervous or mad.

She swallowed, feeling more than a little nervous. She tried to move back, pulling her arms, but his fingers were like a steel vice.

She could hear his breathing, irregular. Angry. "Let me go." She whispered, not wanting to frighten the horses by saying it loudly.

"Damon." She could hear the unsureness in her voice He had never hurt her before. She knew him to be incapable of it. Yet, just now, she sensed he wanted to teach her a lesson.

They stood, quietly, their breathing the only thing that could be heard amongst the horses' general noises.

She could feel tears well up in her throat. She could let them spill over, after all it was basically pitch black in here and, her insecurities at this late hour, and his uncharacteristic behaviour towards her, was setting her on edge.

The lights flickered on, setting the horses on edge also, their soft whinnying breaking the silence.

"Is that you Mr Night?" Thomas called from the front of the stable door.

Damon spotted the tears on Lilliana's cheeks. Hating himself instantly.

He released her arms and then quickly reached up to wipe a tear away.

Keeping his eyes on her, he called to Thomas. "Yes Thomas, sorry go back to bed, I was just leaving."

"Yes Sir." Thomas went back into his quarters, flicking off the light as he left.

As soon as it was black, Lilliana spun on her heel, and marched out of the stables.

Damon reached for her arm, running his hand down the length of it, before his fingers twined with hers. Holding her hand, he slowed her down, and they walked together towards the house.

"Darling, I'm sorry I'm cross with you. I can't help it. The thought of you placing yourself in unnecessary danger, frustrates me to no end. Can you understand where I'm coming from?" His voice was gentler.

She remained silent as they walked up the steps to the house.

Lilliana stopped a few steps above him, the lights behind them were reflecting her beautiful face, her tears dry, but still there.

He placed his hands on her waist, dropping his head onto her chest.

"Baby." He whispered, his strong fingers tightening.

She sighed, and ran her fingers gently through his hair, kissing it.

"No, I'm sorry. I don't mean to cause you worry Damon. Truly."

He leaned back, looking up at her. He stood up two more steps till their mouths were level. "Can I kiss you?"

"Like you ever need to ask that question." She leaned into him.

It was a soft kiss, a sorry for upsetting you, kind of kiss, that developed into an, oh my god I want you right here, right now, kind of kiss.

She stepped back, smiling. "I have a milk delivery, and a sister to save from sin."

"Oh, that sounds like fun. Can I help, before I tuck you into bed?" He took her fingers in his again, walking her into the house, locking the door soundly behind them.

"Of course, it's always more fun having someone along for a midnight adventure. I'll have to remember that in future. I might save myself from getting into trouble."

"Mm," he said doubtfully. "I think if there's trouble to be found, you'll find it no matter what."

She scoffed quietly, as he led her towards the kitchen, calling 'lights on', as they entered.

"So, that's what you think of me is it? A troublemaker," she, walked to the fridge to get out the milk jug.

He leaned against the bench, watching her. Arms folded, enjoying her walk around his kitchen, getting out mugs.

"Yes, amongst quite a few other things, which we will not go into tonight, or my sister will kill me, from keeping you up all night."

She poured the milk, went over to the froth machine, and heated up the two mugs, making frothy milk.

Damon walked over and picked up the milk jug before putting it back into the fridge.

Walking over to her he took the mugs out of her hands and placing them on the bench, turned and cupping her face in his hands, kissed her deeply, open mouthed and hungrily. She sighed contently, returning the kiss.

Pulling back, he looked her in the eyes and said quietly. "I'm sorry if I hurt you Baby girl, but please, in future," he closed his eyes briefly, as if in prayer, hoping she would hear him, "please follow my house rules. They are there to protect you. Okay?"

"Yes Sir." She pushed her lips up against his again.

He smiled against her lips and muttered, "Someone, give me

strength."

She laughed quietly.

"Righto, let's go deliver milk to the bride to be." He released her and stepped back, picking up the mugs.

They arrived as Cam was heading out the door.

"Well good evening, night owls." He smiled slyly.

"Keep it clean brother, just helping Lilliana deliver milk to my sister, if that's alright?" Damon stepped into the room, smiling at a very pleased looking Josephine. She smiled at Damon and blew Cam a kiss as she took her mug off Damon.

Sitting on the bed, she sipped it watching Lilliana take her mug off Damon. He bent down and brushed his lips across her forehead. "See you tomorrow ladies." He winked at Josephine, then, looking at Lilliana once more, left the room.

As the door slid shut, Lilliana sank gratefully onto her bed and taking a mouthful of milk, turned to tell Josephine about her two am adventure.

Josephine shook her head at the end of the story. "Poor Damon, you will be the death of that man. But in a totally good way, if there is such a thing?" she chuckled.

Lilliana drained her milk and snuggled down into the covers. "Thank the stars it's an afternoon wedding."

"Amen to that sister, goodnight my darling Lilly."

"Goodnight Jose. Dream well." Lilliana was asleep in moments, her dreams of a dark, tall man, standing in the distance, always just out of her reach whenever she got close to touching him.

CHAPTER 11

The day was beyond perfect for Josephine and Cam's union. By the time afternoon rolled around the sky was a deep blue, with sun rays seeping through the fluffy storm clouds.

Josephine had spent the morning with her friends, getting pampered by the H.B.R therapists, with strict orders from Fox to use all energy boosting lotions.

After being waxed, scrubbed and soaked in superb fruit body masks, they were buffed and polished, before slipping into their gorgeous dresses.

Looking out Damon's window Lilliana could see a mass crowd.

All Given and staff were in the groups down below, with champagne or lemonade in hand. Cam had also invited friends and from outside these walls, bringing their guest list to just under three thousand

Tim and Pier were amongst some of his guests and had another set of photographers flown in to take the shots of this magnificent wedding, along with a news crew that had been invited.

For the outside world, this was equivalent to the royal weddings of days past.

There was a knock at the door, as Fox was fixing a simple, stunning antique white veil into Josephine's hair. "Come in if you're not Cameron." She called out.

Lilliana stepped back into the room, as Damon entered through his front door.

He walked in, shutting the door behind him. "Don't fret gorgeous," he smiled at Josephine, "he is safely where he should be, waiting for the woman of his dreams to go commit herself to him. Forever."

He walked to stand in front of her. "You look stunning sweetheart." He gently took her hands and bent down to kiss both her cheeks.

She smiled up at him. "Thank you Damon," she sighed, "a big day for you, giving me away and being the best man."

He shook his head, smiling into her eyes. "That's the easy part love. The hard part," he said, looking over at Lilliana, "is keeping away from you today."

He squeezed Josephine's hands before letting them go, to walk over to Lilliana, looking stylishly elegant. Heels in antique white, which matched a belt sitting neatly around a gorgeously styled soft leaf-green dress that showcased her body beautifully. She wore her butterfly diamond earrings which Fox had given her, for her first Christmas.

Her hair was swept up, with long black curls slipping here and there. Make up fresh and light, she looked breathtaking.

"I think we'll wait outside girls," Allie said. "Two minutes Sir," she called, as she stepped out to Christopher's waiting elbow. Orlando was waiting for Jessica. Josephine and Fox stepped out, the door shutting behind them, leaving Lilliana and Damon alone.

Lilliana smiled up at Damon as he stepped close cupping her chin. "You, Miss, look ravishing." His other hand slid around her back, pulling her close.

She bent her head back to gaze into his eyes. "So do you."

He had on a steel grey suit pants and jacket, with a white shirt and grey tie.

He looked relaxed and formal at the same time.

She took a deep breath, his after shave making her want to bury her face into his neck. She would not smudge Fox's make up.

They stared into each other's eyes, as he said quietly, "As hard as it will be to stay away from you today, I feel it's for the best. The media will be on alert for anything of interest and not what they are actually here for. It's best if our being together isn't broadcast just yet to any of the Heads of the other establishments."

She ran a long, French tipped nail along his jaw and said, "I understand."

"Just for now, and as some of them will be here today, I want us to be careful." He was distastefully thinking of one person in particular.

A knock sounded on the door. Fox called out. "Time's up, Sir."

He smiled down at Lilliana before he bought his lips down to brush hers, back and forth.

Her tongue gently flicked his lips wanting to eat him up.

He moaned as he opened his mouth and deepened the kiss to a level they both wanted.

Her other arm reached up and around his neck pressing herself close to him.

He chuckled against her lips. "I know Baby, I want you too." He heard her sigh as he stepped away, and taking her hand led her to the door. He looked down at her as it slid open wondering how the hell he got to be so lucky to have her.

Her green eyes penetrated his. He quickly dipped down once more and kissed her lips before straightening, and walking over to Josephine, offered her his arm.

"Right Lilly," Fox said, "Off you go."

Lilliana took a deep breath and walked to the front of their line and started down the stairs. It took them ten minutes to get down to the front steps, and another ten minute to walk across the grounds, towards the elaborate marquee where the guests, now standing, were eagerly watching the wedding party come towards them.

There was the most amazing piece of music flowing from the band. Flutes and violins sang together in such a beautiful melody. Even the birds seemed to be joining in.

The paths were lined with cheerful flowers, leading Josephine to her love.

Cameras started to flash as they got closer to the path that led to a very dashing man down the front, waiting happily.

Lilliana walked proudly in front, smiling happily as heads turned her way.

This was such a special day for her friends.

Followed closely behind were Allie and Christopher. Then Orlando and Jessica, then finally the woman they'd all been waiting for. The one that Cam Night had chosen for his bride, on his handsome brother's arm.

Once she reached her destination Lilliana sat on a bench seat beside her friends and their men.

Damon passed the woman he considered his sister, to his brother, and after kissing her on the cheek, stood beside Cam.

The number of cameras clicking amazed a lot of people. The wedding had only just started, and they must have taken hundreds of shots already.

The ceremony was simple, perfect, and so like Cam and Josephine.

They vowed to each other in front of witnesses, and the Officials Marriage Celebrant, to love, cherish, respect and serve each other till their dying day.

After they kissed, a kiss that was long and passionate, they turned to the crowd's applause, and got ready for many hours of celebrating in style.

Josephine and Lilliana hugged as Damon congratulated Cam.

Lilliana had tears of joy flowing down her cheeks. As Josephine was embraced by their friends, Cam stepped forward and pulled Lilliana into his arms, dropping his chin on her head.

"Hey beautiful, thanks for always being a solid rock to Josephine. She loves you so much, and I'm sure you already know what I think about you."

Damon watched as Cam tilted Lilliana back, and kissed her full on the mouth.

Lilliana laughed and was happy when Josephine joined in for a group hug.

She turned and watched them both walk into the crowds of people wishing them well. Her heart swelled with happiness as she watched

Allie hug her sister's, Emile and Katy, and brother, Adam, who each had a Watcher standing close by.

Her eyes met Damon's, and she smiled before quickly turning her eyes away, and went in search for some cool punch before she was required to join in the wedding photos.

She found Leon by the punch bowl, a waiter filling his cup, spotted Lilliana, and filled another for her.

"They look so happy," Leon nodded over to Josephine and Cam.

"Yes." Lilliana drained her glass and handed it over for another refill. "Thanks. Yes they do. They are. How's the hospital going?" she smiled at him.

"Busy as usual. I had an interview the other day from New York's largest hospital magazine. I'm hoping my Mum gets to see it." He took a slow swallow of punch.

"You should be so proud of yourself Leon. And I know your Mum will be if she sees it." Lilliana rubbed his arm.

"Lilliana," Tim's photographer friend, Luke, called out, "Photo time."

Leon laughed at Lilliana's sigh. "Come on, you are perfect in front of the camera, what's that sigh for?"

She placed her glass on the table. "Nothing. Just wish I could skip this part."

Leon nudged her with his elbow, and whispered conspiratorially near her ear, "It's an old tradition, the maid of honour appearing in at least one photograph with the bridal party. Off you go. I'll save a dance for you."

"I will look forward to that." She smiled before she dashed off.

Damon had watched her chatting with Leon. He had to admit, they looked good together. Although Lilliana would make anyone look good.

Once she reached the group where all the girls stood, she joined in for some fun, happy snaps. Then some serious ones, then Cam joined in surrounded by all the beautiful girls, then Damon, and eventually, the entire bridal party with Christopher and Orlando.

Luke had all the men standing behind the women, their arms about their lady's waists. Damon slid his arms around Lilliana, slowly, trying to make it look just as the photographer was asking of him, as he knew that the world's media was watching.

Lilliana placed her hand on top of Damon's, her finger stroking his hand once.

His breath close to her ear, warm and familiar.

"I want you so badly right now," he whispered so quietly, smiling into the camera.

"Mm, I know," she whispered back.

Once the shot was done everybody kept their arms around each other, laughing or kissing.

Damon stepped back from Lilliana, placed his hands in his pockets, and turned to speak to a man who approached the group.

"Okay, we are done here for the moment. Cam and Josephine, I'll do ten minutes alone with you two then you can go enjoy your own party." Luke smiled his thanks to the rest of them.

Lilliana walked slowly back to the party by herself.

The others were hurrying to hit the drinks table.

She found Luke and Rupert and was happy to see them openly holding hands, very relaxed. Rupert hugged her as she drew near. "How's it going Doc?" he asked fondly.

"It's going well," she smiled, nodding. "It's a beautiful day," she squeezed Luke's hand.

"That it is. How stunning does Josephine look? She deserves every happiness." Rupert nodded.

Lilliana smiled proudly. "Oh yes, absolutely. Have fun, I'll see you around, save a dance for me later you two."

"Bye sweety." Rupert called as she walked into the crowd of people.

The atmosphere was both vibrant and relaxing. Laughter flowed, people talking non-stop. Lilliana was content drifting from one group to the next, enjoying all the relaxed, happy conversations.

She had a lovely chat with Johnson and Rachael, it was the first time in ages that she'd seen them together with their arms around each other laughing. Such hard workers, so dedicated to this facility.

She ended up at the bar, and Fox joined her, along with Tim and

Pier, and she placed a glass in Lilliana's hand, winking. "It's a good drop that one."

Lilliana burst out laughing as Pier demonstrated his latest martial art move he'd been learning and kicked a tray of food out of one of the servers' hands.

Luckily no one was harmed and the server, used to this kind of behaviour, at weddings such as this one, handled the situation beautifully.

Lilliana drained her glass and moved on, after kissing Tim. She saw Natalie, Naomi, Vanessa and another Given she hadn't yet met, all huddled in a group, talking about who they had on their hit list.

Lilliana planned on just walking past, when Natalie called her over. This will be good, she thought to herself, forcing a bright smile. "Hello there, are you all enjoying yourselves?"

She wished she had another drink, glancing around the crowd, she was wondering where Damon was, as she could hear a groovy beat start up and the dance floor was beginning to fill.

"Are you ladies going to dance?" she aimed at neutral ground.

"We were wondering Lilliana, how many people you have slept with here, or do you just enjoy giving them all hard-ons?" Natalie raised an eyebrow.

Ok, so that wasn't going to work, not surprisingly, with Natalie.

"Well, let's see Natalie. Less than those you've felt up after all these years. And as far as giving anyone a hard-on, well, that's completely out of my control. Now, did you ladies have an intelligent question, or can I get on with enjoying my sister's wedding?" She raised an eyebrow, and without waiting, walked off on the four of them.

A tray with drinks came past. She grabbed one and walked over to Shelly and Jaycee. "How are you going Lilliana?" Shelly asked.

"Fine now that I'm away from the brat gang over there," Lilliana shrugged to the girls behind her.

"Some people never even try to better themselves," Jaycee shook her head.

"This music is beyond brilliant," Lilliana tapped her foot to the beat.

"Care to dance Doc?" A voice said behind her.

She turned and smiled at Eric. "Why, I would love to, thank you. Bye girls." She smiled at them as she was dashed off and onto the dance floor.

Eric was a brilliant dancer, as was Lilliana, and they made a spectacular sight, twirling and flowing around the dance floor, amongst many abled bodies.

"You are a good dancer Eric" she said, as they slowed to a more sedate beat.

He slipped his arms around her waist.

"Yeah well, I have many hidden talents," he smiled down at her.

"It was hard on you, coming here." Lilliana looked around them. "So many kids have suffered so terribly but look how far we've come." She smiled up at him. "We are the lucky ones."

"Yes. Aren't we though," he agreed, softly.

She heard him sigh looking over her head as the song finished, another tap on her shoulder.

Eric smiled at Leon. "Your turn, but I think a drink is in order first."

"Thanks Eric. Good call." Leon offered Lilliana his arm. She leant up, and kissed Eric's cheek. It was something she had never done before, but this was certainly an appropriate occasion.

Leon escorted her to the bar.

Damon watched from afar, watching Eric, watch Lilliana walk off, whilst trying to keep track of the conversation with a diplomat from Italy, and a relative of Johnsons, arguing about the correction facility's protocol.

"Hey, this is a wedding fella's." Johnson arrived, saving Damon from this conflicting conversation when he should be having fun at his brother's wedding.

God, he just wanted to dance with Lilliana.

He winked at Johnson before, he slipped away and spying Fox, offered her a dance.

Once Lilliana and Leon had another drink, they too joined the dance floor.

Strung from above and around were thousands of the prettiest white, silver, and gold fairy lights, making it look like shiny stars filling up the night sky.

Leon spun Lilliana around, laughing when he accidentally stepped on another dancer's toes.

"At least they weren't mine," Lilliana laughed when he apologized.

They danced two songs together, ending on a high, he bowed, kissed her hand and left. She smiled, looking up at the pretty lights as she swayed to the music. Who said you can't dance on your own?

Fox joined her, followed by Allie, Rachael, Jessica, Shelly, Jaycee and Josephine.

The beat got fast, as did the girls steps, laughing and expertly twirling to a very funky beat.

In no time, there was a huge circle of women, getting as many of the other women to join in their laughter and catchy steps.

They danced another forty minutes, applauding the band loudly when they finished that section of songs.

Cam came over to claim Josephine, as did the other girls' dates.

Fox linked her arm through Lilliana's, and they headed out to the drinks tables, soon joined by Tim and Pier.

The night moved on and conversations flowed from Environmental to Education, Political to Economy and Arts, to finally the latest fashion, which was what Fox had been waiting for, leading with her opinions and asking many intricate questions to those that held the answers, giving Lilliana the opportunity to politely step back from the conversation, and have a good look through the crowd.

Lifting her glass to her lips she spotted Damon talking to a drop dead, gorgeous blonde woman. She looked much older than Damon, but that did nothing to take anything away from how extremely sexy this woman was.

Damon's eyes flickered straight across to Lilliana's, like he knew she'd been standing there, watching him.

As the blonde woman turned to follow Damon's gaze, she stared at Lilliana, a frown marring her beautiful features.

Lilliana sipped from her glass and stared right on back. She felt an arm go around her shoulder and gently turn her away.

"There's a good girl, we don't want you turning into stone after staring at dear cousin 'Medusa' for too long." Cam kept his arm around

Lilliana, whilst Josephine handed him a cocktail.

"Cousin?"

"Yes, twice removed. She's had a thing for Damon for years, constantly trying to get in his pants. Almost had him once! Ugh," he groaned, as Josephine elbowed him in the ribs.

"There's a dear, shut up now," she smiled sweetly at him.

He flung his arm around her shoulder, pulling her close for a deep kiss. "Yes, thank you dear soul mate."

"When are you two going to get a room?" Fox joined in the conversation, handing Lilliana a pretty pink cocktail.

"Soon, Foxy." Josephine came up for air. "But first the speeches!"

"Oh, really?" Fox raised an eyebrow.

"Yes, a quick one from Damon. That's it." Cam smiled down at his beautiful bride.

"Excellent." Fox finished her drink.

Josephine kissed Lilliana's cheek as Cam started to pull her in Damon's direction. Lilliana sipped the tasty pink liquid as she watched Damon introduce Josephine to his cousin.

"Sneaky looking bitch if you ask me." Fox confided.

"Mm." Was all Lilliana felt she could politely say.

Damon turned and walked to the band on the stage. A microphone was handed to him. The music stopped.

"Thank you everyone for helping mark this sensational day, where my baby brother has finally become a man and married one of the most beautiful girls on this planet.

To Josephine and Cameron, may this day, and every day forward bring you both the happiness you deserve. Please, raise your glass in wishing the happy couple all the very best, and for all those that can handle it, please, continue dancing and celebrating.

For everyone else, good night, and joy be with you all."

Damon raised his glass, as did everybody in an enormously loud, "CONGRATULATIONS." Accompanied by a thunderous round of applause.

Lilliana clapped happily as she watched Josephine and Cam wave as they walked off to go to their apartment.

Damon had offered them the cottage in the woods, but Josephine wanted to stay in their rooms, which she loved so much.

"So," a cool voice addressed Lilliana, "you're Miss Lilliana, are you?"

Lilliana turned to the striking cousin, who was more beautiful up close.

"Correct. I'm afraid I'm at a disadvantage and don't know who you are?" Lilliana lied, taking a sip of her drink, wishing just this once, that she was taller.

"I am Sapphire." She placed a hand on her hip, fingers adorned with diamonds, sparkling as she tapped her fingers. "I am a doctor of Psychiatry, amongst other talents. I have been helping run the Given facility in Russia."

"How interesting." Lilliana tried to sound convincing, not wanting to be rude to Damon and Cam's cousin.

"Yes, it certainly has been. Are you interested in travelling to other facilities, to help them run efficiently?"

"I feel that any establishment should run efficiently if it has the right driver in the seat for head position, and I'm quite happy with fulfilling my role here, helping this place run smoothly. This is my home now and I certainly don't plan on going elsewhere." Lilliana was waiting for someone to rescue her. Where was Fox?

"Mm, well we shall see." And with that, Sapphire, or Sap, as Lilliana now thought of her, flicked her long blonde hair and sauntered off.

"What was that all about?" Allie came up to Lilliana.

"I think I was getting a talking down to, by Damon's cousin."

The music had started up again and Allie and Lilliana watched as the beautiful woman walked over to drape herself around Damon as they danced to a slow beat.

Lilliana had been oblivious to the cameras, still snapping away after the photo shoot, but could see them flashing away, as the head of this establishment, and the co-ordinator of another, danced closely.

Lilliana placed her empty glass down and smiled at Allie. "I am totally exhausted. Kiss Jessica and say good night for me will you Allie cat?"

They kissed, as Allie said, "No problem babes. Sleep well."

Lilliana waved behind her as she slipped off into the crowds, heading past the stables. She pulled off her heels and pulled the pins from her hair, her curls floated down her back.

She shook her head and laughed softly. Evil bitch all right, she thought of Sap. Good riddance to her in the morning.

She went upstairs and into her rooms, too exhausted for a shower.

She stripped the beautiful dress off and pulled on her singlet and shorts.

Sitting at her window seat she pulled a blanket across her lap and watched the figures in the distance party on. She sighed, so happy that this day went so well for Josephine and Cam.

She wondered how long Damon would stay out. Probably right until the last guest was still standing. He was the perfect host and provider.

How handsome he had looked, dancing with Fox and any other partner he'd had that night. Her heart, just a little sad that she hadn't gotten that chance to dance with him at such a special event.

She took the blanket with her and slipped into bed, falling asleep to the music and laughter in the distance.

***

The following morning, after a fabulous hot shower, Lilliana joined Jessica and Allie for breakfast. They chatted about their favourite parts of Josephine's wedding, between slurping tea and orange juice, with mouthfuls of eggs and focaccias with delicious toppings, hoping she was enjoying her time-out, alone with Cam.

They said hello to Leon and Rachael and had a quick laugh with Fox, who was being a drama queen with her hangover, complaining about a demanding photo shoot she had to do with Tim and Pier before they flew out.

Damon walked into the room, and his breath caught in his throat looking at Lilliana, her head thrown back, beautiful neck exposed, with a dazzling smile as she laughed with her friends.

He poured a coffee and grabbed a piece of toast off the side table, nodding and responding to a staff member who had just asked him a question.

He glanced back at Lilliana, who in turn was watching him, sipping her tea.

He looked at her for another moment, before turning and leaving the room, coffee cup in hand.

Lilliana checked the time, she had twenty minutes before her and Allie's first group.

She murmured a quick goodbye to her friends and getting up, popped her teacup on the tray and followed Damon, hoping he'd gone to his office.

Knocking on his door, it slid open and she breezed in.

"Please, come in Lilliana," Damon said, in a very professional manner. He glanced back down at a file on his desk as he stood above it, before sitting down.

Lilliana was about to ask Damon if everything was alright when a figure turned from the bookcase. Sapphire.

"Well, good morning." Sapphire smiled, folding her arms across her perfect breasts. "It is nice seeing the staff pop in so early, isn't it Damon dear."

Lilliana looked at the woman, almost instantly disliking her as much as she disliked Richard.

"Yes Sapphire," Damon replied looking up, "our staff here are our family and always welcome to pop in if they have any problems, or simply need to talk." He smiled over at Lilliana, as he would have smiled at Rachael or Johnson.

"Can I help you with something this morning Lilliana?" He was so good at this 'no showing emotion in public' thing. God, he looked even more irresistible when she couldn't put her hands on him.

"Yes Sir." She could be just as aloof in front of the blonde one. "Allie was wondering if you could pop down later this morning and check over a file with her."

"Absolutely, I'll be there after her first group. Anything else?"

"No Sir. Thank you." She turned and left the room, getting out of there as fast as she could.

Taking a deep, steady breath, she went down to the hospital and into her and Allie's paradise, for a two-hour group, which, thankfully went without too many dramas.

A fifteen-year-old girl decided it would be alright to pee where she was sitting, not an ounce of embarrassment. Declaring that she thought she was in the loo anyhow, with the amount of shit talk that was going on around her.

Lilliana buzzed Billy to come take her out and please inform Shelly that the girl may need an extra evaluation. She was not ready for main house just yet.

Once that session was over, a cleaner removed the chair, cleaned the rug, sprayed and brought in a new chair from storage.

"Always a pleasure," Allie said, pouring a tea.

A knock sounded. Allie pressed the switch and the door slid open, to reveal, not only Damon, but also his charming cousin.

Lilliana suppressed a groan and walked into her office, pushing the button, which had her glass panels sliding shut, and cutting her off from the conversation which would take place with Allie. She wanted nothing further to do with Damon's, 'Sap'.

She kept her head down, and her fingers flying over her reports and updates on her Givens' progress.

She felt eyes boring into her but did not look up once to see the dirty look that was cast in her direction.

Damon had a quick chat to Allie, who luckily did have something to discuss with him, so Lilliana's cover story for entering Damon's office earlier was not blown. There was a tap on her window and she slowly looked up, or otherwise pretend she was deaf. Damon.

She held in her smile, as Sap was behind him, watching closely.

She pressed the button, allowing her panels to slide open. "Yes Sir, can I help you?" She rested her hands over her desks glass keyboard.

"Yes, we are having a staff meeting this afternoon. I require all heads there" Damon said, not a flicker of warmth entering into his voice.

She glanced down, and continued typing, answering similarly. "Not a problem Sir. I'll be there."

"Excellent. Don't be late."

She did not glance up again until Damon and Sap had left.

"What the hell?" Allie sat opposite Lilliana.

Lilliana sighed and leaned back in her chair. She'd have to go back and delete the last several lines she wrote, knowing it was a jumble of nothing. She shook her head. "I know, right. The whole 'cousin' thing is bizarre. Damon hasn't had a chance to clear anything up and I have no idea why she's following him around like a puppy dog, or even why she's still here?" She shrugged.

Allie folded her arms. "I don't like her shitty attitude. What does she want asking me questions like I'm in Grade Three? I'm a bloody excellent qualified Psychologist, amongst other things! I can't wait till she hightails it and fucks off back to where she came from."

Lilliana laughed at her friend. It felt good to do so, as there was an uneasy pit of tension growing in her belly. It was not a good feeling.

Her phone beeped.

"Dr Lilliana," she answered brightly. She rubbed her neck instantly, looking across at Allie as she rolled her eyes.

"Yes Richard. No, I have a Given coming in twenty. No I don't think that's the kind of thing that can be rushed." She paused whilst he rambled on. "Shall I send you Allie, Sir?"

Allie was shaking her head no. Lilliana closed her eyes, wishing she'd gotten to bed just that little bit earlier last night.

"Yes Sir, I'll be there immediately."

She stood as she dropped the phone down. Sighing, she forced a smile at Allie.

"If Penny comes before I'm through, please give her a tea, and pop some music on for her."

"Of course, what did Dick want?" Allie walked Lilliana to the door.

Lilliana shook her head. "No time, we'll chat soon." She left and headed down to the Psych ward. She stepped in front of the eye scanner, and then entered through the large metal doors to the desk and signed in, smiling at Brad who was at the desk today.

"Hey Lilly, how are you?"

"I'll be just fine when I get back out of here Brad." She smiled over her shoulder as she hurried off to find Richard.

Brad knew she couldn't stand working with Richard and he sympathized. He couldn't stand the unfeeling bastard either.

Lilliana walked down the corridor, till she came to the room Richard had instructed her to. She tapped on the door once before pushing it open and walked in.

There on the bed was a fifteen-year old boy, staring at the ceiling, an angry, defiant look on his face. His wrists and ankles were strapped down.

He had long white pants on and a white singlet top.

Basically, the uniform for any patient first brought down to the Psych ward.

Richard was standing at the side of the boy's bed. He pushed his glasses up, looking at Lilliana.

"Richard."

He simply nodded.

"What is it you'd like me to do?" She walked over to the boy and leaned over so she could see into his eyes.

"I need you to get him to communicate. He is not acknowledging me at all," he replied coolly.

Lilliana focused on the boy. She could see no evidence that the boy was physically injured, but she knew there was so much more than physical abuse to make a person snap.

"Hello there, my name is Lilliana," she spoke in her most calming voice. "I am here to help you, in any way that I can. Is there something I can get for you?"

The boy did not even blink but continued staring at the ceiling.

She leaned over further so there was nothing else for him to see, but her.

The boy's eyes flickered into hers, and after a few seconds of an unblinking stare, his eyes filled with tears, and slowly seeped down his face.

"Hey, it's going to be alright," she soothed, cupping his face.

She looked across at Richard. "Are you going to tell me anything about this boy?"

"His name is Scott; he entered our facility a week ago. Hasn't spoken a word. Was the only survivor amongst a pile of bodies the Officials found at his parents Casino."

Lilliana looked down at the boy. "Scott, whatever you have been through please know that I am going to do everything in my power to help you to deal with your new situation. Alright?"

She smiled softly, not wanting to overwhelm him anymore.

His hand started shaking, his eyes pleading for her to take hold.

She did so, slipping her fingers into his and squeezed gently.

"Richard, I insist that Scott be put in a different ward." She flipped the restraint holding one wrist, releasing his fingers as she reached across him to release the other. "He does not need to be restrained in his new room." Lilliana unclipped the boy's ankles.

Scott sat up slowly, his thick, dark blonde hair fell into his handsome, sweet, sad eyes.

He rubbed his ankles, not taking his eyes off Lilliana.

"How about a shower Scott and something to eat?" she smiled, holding out her hand.

Richard watched, but said nothing.

Scott nodded, slowly slipping off the bed, he folded his arms, but stood close to Lilliana, not looking once at Richard.

"Let's go." She invited, leading the way. She opened the door with Scott beside her and left the ward, and down into another less confined, locked-down section.

"Jaycee," Lilliana called, spying her colleague up ahead.

"Hi Lilly, what's up?" Jaycee smiled at Scott, placing a hand on her hip, waiting to see what she could do for Lilliana.

"Is there any available hand to see Scott gets a shower and a room? No restraints? I'd do it myself, but I have a one on one, in, well, now actually."

Jaycee nodded. "Sure thing. Scott, I'm Jaycee, and I'll introduce you to Joe in a minute. Is that okay?"

He nodded slowly but watched Lilliana.

She reached over slowly and rubbed his shoulder. "I will come back down this afternoon, okay?"

He blinked and allowed Jaycee to lead him off, with Lilliana looking on.

Poor, sad boy she thought, heading off to sign out with Brad and hopefully get to Penny on time.

As she headed back to her office, she got the creepy feeling that Richard had somehow just evaluated her. She shrugged it off, putting on her peaceful face as she entered her office.

Penny had only just walked in ahead of her, as Allie was pouring her a tea and spotting Lilliana, poured a second cup, placing it on Lilliana's side of the desk.

Lilliana squeezed Allie's arm gratefully as she said hello to Penny and shut them both away in her relaxing space so Penny could vent out her frustrations and pent up feelings. It took a good forty minutes along with another round of tea, but Penny left in a better headspace.

Lilliana filled in a report, responded to several emails, and opened an email Richard had forwarded to her, from Johnson. Some background information they had on Scott. It took her an hour to read through that.

She got up and strolled over to Allie's desk, tapping her glass panel.

Allie pressed a button and the panels slid open.

"We've missed lunch again," she smiled at Lilliana, "shall we get Christopher to bring something down?"

"Only for you, I'm okay for now."

"What time is this 'important' meeting this afternoon." Allie air quoted, important, with her fingers.

"Three pm, plenty of time for a horse ride and a quick bite to eat, then I want to take some magazines down to this sweet boy, Scott, he seems beyond sad."

Allie shook her head. "Aren't they all? Bloody assholes out there."

"Mm. Agreed. Well, enjoy Christopher." Lilliana winked as she headed out. "See you at the meeting."

Allie waved as she picked up the phone and dialled Christopher in the kitchen, hoping for more than just a chicken sandwich.

***

Lilliana got into her room and changed as fast as she could.

All black jodhpurs, boots and a snug fitting tee shirt.

She raced down the stairs, saying hello to friendly faces, she pulled her long hair back into a silken rope to hang down her back.

As she walked past the library she could see Damon, Sapphire and a group of staff in deep conversation. Sapphire had a Tablet and seemed to be tapping furiously away at it, a scowl on her face.

Damon's eyes met Lilliana's and he swallowed.

How he was missing her. Deeply. They had had such little time together and now, his bloody cousin, who was the co-ordinator for three Given facilities, thought it was time to come on over here, and stick her nose in where it wasn't wanted, more to the point where it wasn't needed.

She was definitely trying to win brownie points for someone, Damon just wasn't sure who that someone was.

And of all the times he needed Cam, to help him out with keeping Sapphire busy, he was off on his honeymoon.

His mouth went dry as Lilliana glanced away, pretending disinterest as Sapphire looked up, as she flung her ponytail over her shoulder and jogged out of sight.

How he longed to run after her. Sweep her up in his arms and crush her sweet mouth beneath his.

He nodded to Tina, ignoring the stare his cousin was giving him and concentrated on the here and now. Just.

Lilliana had a satisfactory two-hour ride, that was everything and more that her body and mind needed. Both she and Beauty were sweating up a storm by the time they got back to the stables. She spent a good half an hour cooling Beauty off, brushing her and letting her graze out in the pasture beside Beast. They pranced up and down together, the fence coming between them.

Lilliana knew how they felt.

She wanted to stay there, at the fence, the cool breeze caressing her face, but she had things to get on with.

Thomas came up behind her. "Hi Miss Lilliana."

She smiled, turning to face him. "How are you Thomas?" She always felt relaxed in Thomas's company. He was such a kind, dedicated man.

"Good, busy, beautiful weather. Mating season starts soon, Mr Night told me he wants to arrange for him to watch Beast and Beauty be put out together."

"Really?" Lilliana was wondering if he was going to let her know about that.

"They will certainly produce a beautiful foal, that's for sure."

"Yes Ma'am, an elite stock they will certainly breed."

"Well, have a good afternoon, I'd better head back."

"You too Miss Lilliana."

Walking into the house, Lilliana ducked into the Library. She could hear a class going on in the loft overhead, and quickly headed over to the magazines that held the latest Given activities, Horse magazines, Archery, and the latest technology that was going on in the H.D department, plus all the benefits their facility offered the outside world.

She bolted up to her room, dropped the magazines onto her bed and quickly took off to the showers. She was certain she had plenty of time before this meeting was starting.

The hot water and herbal lotions relaxed her tired muscles. Nothing that a good, large pair of hands couldn't fix, she thought to herself. But, beggars can't be choosers.

She leaned back against the shower wall, letting the warm water caress her body and rinse her clean of bubbles.

Lilliana heard her name being called. Fox. "I'm in here."

Shutting off the water, she walked over and stepped under the body drier, running her fingers through her hair.

"You have a meeting that is about to start, Allie sent me looking for you. Don't be late Lilliana, I do not like the look of that blonde bitch."

"Well, I can't go down naked, can I?" Lilliana slipped a robe on, heading out the door towards her bedroom.

As Fox strolled off, Lilliana heard her sarcastic comment, "I know at least two people who wouldn't be disappointed if you did."

Lilliana didn't waste a second once she was in her room, she quickly ran the brush through her hair, as she grabbed a simple white sundress out of the closet. Throwing it over her head, she pushed her feet into white, low heels, added a spritz of perfume, a dash of mascara and a dot of lipstick. Grabbing the magazines off the bed, she dashed out of the room, and raced down to deliver them to Scott.

Surely his needs were equally as important as a staff meeting?

She made it down to him in fifteen, and although his eyes remained sad, his small smile at seeing her, and the magazines in her arms, cemented the fact that any reprimand at being late for this meeting, was worth it. She squeezed his hand before she left, promising she would come back to see him before bedtime.

Racing into her office, trying to forget about Scott's solemn gaze, as he'd watched her leave, she grabbed her Tablet and once again raced upstairs towards this irregular meeting.

The meeting was held in the library, to accommodate the extra staff called in for this meeting.

The door was shut, which seemed odd to Lilliana. The large wooden double doors had never been closed in the nine years she'd been here, even on detention nights.

Taking a deep breath, she pushed open one heavy door and walked in, surprised at how many people turned around to look at her, the room falling silent.

Closing the door behind her she turned to apologize for being a tad late, but the look on Damon's face stopped her in her tracks.

He stood near the large fireplace. Seated in the chairs beside him, Sapphire, Johnson, Dr Ryan and Richard. The library chairs and settees had been turned to face the front row.

Damon slowly sat; ankle across his knee, Tablet resting on his calf, arms folded.

"Well, it is so good of you to finally join us Lilliana. If you would take a seat," he pointed to an empty one opposite him, beside Allie and Leon.

She felt herself blush, and quickly walked past the eighty or so staff, and took her seat, not daring to look at Damon.

Allie was busting to lean over and whisper something, but knew she'd be overheard, sitting so close to Damon, so instead, quickly typed a massage. - What, are we back in group and you're like, fifteen all over again?

Lilliana read it, and replied - What have I missed so far?

-Not much, heads are just giving their reports to Blondie.

Lilliana crossed her legs and risked a glance at Damon.

He was staring straight back at her. His eyes looking dark, dangerous, like he was ready to explode.

She too, knew how he felt. She looked across at Rachael, who was explaining in depth, to Sapphire, how she ran the hospital, answering any questions fired her way. Rachael's interrogation lasted fifteen minutes, and Lilliana could see the nurse getting more frustrated by the minute.

Sapphire turned to Hillary next, and began questioning her about the Psych wards.

Lilliana tuned out, as it went on and on.

When it was Leon's turn, along with Dr Ryan, she listened with interest on what he had to say. She loved the sound of his calm, smooth voice. His feathers did not get ruffled by this woman whatsoever. Lilliana was glad that one person seemed immune to her invasive nastiness.

"Now, Miss Allie. I believe, professionally, that your hair colour should not be blue. Don't you think it makes the wrong impression?" Sapphire looked at Allie as if she were beneath her.

Allie looked thoughtful and calm as she answered, but Lilliana, who knew her well, could sense her friend was about to attack. "I think what makes the wrong impression in my profession, is the wrong attitude. I, however, have an enormous amount of respect and well wishes for every one of my patients and my performance, which surely, if you are as thorough as you are making out here today, would know, my hair colour has nothing to do with the treatment they are receiving. If there is something important you'd like to bring up, please, feel free to do so, otherwise you are simply wasting all of our time here today." Allie sat glaring, as equally disgusted, back at Sapphire.

Lilliana was watching Damon, watch Allie, a look of pride on his face.

His eyes met Lilliana's, then quickly away.

Sapphire was typing, looking furious.

The room was quiet, all wondering what the hell was this woman about?

Sapphire got back on track and started talking to some of the heads in H.D which included Rupert. She was extremely impressed with his grafted plants. He had designed and grown many varieties of fruit trees, which grew up to seven different fruits per plant and had recently had similar success with a new vegetable tree. She had some high praise, asking him if he was interested in relocating to Australia, Africa, or China.

He replied no, absolutely not.

She tapped away again, then listened to the remaining reports on the developments that had occurred in the past five years, and how expanding graft and drought speciality species, would assist in the growth of this facility and benefit those beyond their walls.

After another hour, Damon called for a ten-minute break.

Leon smiled down at Lilliana as he helped her to her feet.

"Thanks Leon." She gently pulled her hand free, and left her Tablet on her seat, heading across to where one of four tea trolleys had been wheeled to.

She poured a chai tea, one of Rupert's blends, before heading up the steps to the loft above, wanting to get away from the noise below.

She sighed. It felt good to do so. What was going on here? When could things just get back to normal, without some Blonde Nazi stressing them all out?

Sipping her tea, she strolled to a window, trying to relax with the calming view of the gardens.

"Lilliana."

She turned to see Damon walking with purpose towards her.

Her eyes widened as he reached for her teacup, taking it out of her hands, he placed it on the windowsill, grabbed her wrist, quickly turned, and pulled her after him.

He led her behind a row of tall, carved bookshelves, and reaching for a knot in the wood, pushed it in. The entire case moved silently, to reveal a passageway.

He stepped in, pulling her with him. It closed behind them quickly.

She didn't have a chance to ask him a single question about what the hell his cousin was up to, or why he was going along with her.

She was pushed roughly against the wall, his body pressing hard against hers, his mouth devouring hers thoroughly. She clung to him, kissing him back as deep and as hard as she could, trying to take the taste of him in.

His hands, running up her back, then down again, gripping her hips, he pulled her against his groin.

"I want you, now," he whispered fiercely against her mouth. "It's been killing me not being able to touch you, talk to you the way I want to." His lips sank deeply into hers, his tongue thrusting, meeting hers with equal pleasure.

She moaned as his fingers swept up to gently massage her breast.

"Damon." She pleaded, wanting him to take her right here, right now. "I miss you, so much." She kissed him over and over, pressing herself up as hard as she could against him.

"I know baby, I want to, but we need to be careful, even this could put you at risk, and I don't want that."

She pulled back, staring into his eyes, as she reached up to hold his face. "What do you mean, put me at risk?" She stroked the side of his face, loving the feel of his skin against her hand. She tiptoed up to kiss him again. She did not want to miss the chance to breathe him in, taste him. Her fingers swept into his hair.

He kissed her lovingly, his hands stroked her and held her close before he eased back.

"I don't have much time to explain, I have to get back before she assumes where I am, and who I'm with. Sapphire is here, as part of the recruitment program. It's been going on for generations, where a selected family of co-coordinators travel the globe, visiting all the Given establishments, making selections of staff to rotate, and make permanent placements. The world has been talking about you for years, and the co-ordinators have viewed your files, and how your role here with us, has benefited our establishment greatly. They are questioning what you could do for them."

"What? No, they can't force me to leave, can they Damon?"

The pleading in her voice broke his heart.

He pulled her up against his chest, his hand bunching into her soft locks. "I am going to do everything in my power to change their minds. The last time something like this happened was four years before you came. These rounds between the co-ordinators and the Given diplomats usually occur every fifteen years. Sapphire is two years early; I don't know why." He stroked her back, as she stiffened in his arms.

She'd pushed her face hard into his chest, her head reeling. There was no way on earth she was leaving her home, Damon, her friends and those she cared for.

"We have to get back. Lilliana, please keep a low profile, and Baby, don't take anything I say to you in public, to heart. Okay?" He kissed her forehead, sensing her shock.

When he stepped away, she wrapped her arms around herself.

"You go down, I'll have to go out another way to avoid suspicion." Damon pressed a switch, and as the bookcase clicked open, he pushed it open, and checking no one was around, nodded for Lilliana to pass through. She turned to look at him as he closed the secret door slowly. Her beautiful green eyes, watching his, until the door of books closed in her face.

She quickly walked over, picked up her teacup, and headed down the stairs, just as Sapphire was calling the room back into order.

Lilliana took her seat, a minute later, the library door opened, and Sapphire watched as Damon walk in.

He walked with such a calm authority, which only added to his allure.

Lilliana sat quietly, head down, she couldn't wait for this blasted meeting to come to an end. Glancing at Damon, as he sat, she felt like crying. There was no way she could survive this world without him. She'd done it before, but not now. Now that she had had him, been with him, felt his heart race against hers. No. She couldn't be parted from him and survive. She closed her eyes in a silent prayer.

"Keeping you awake are we, Miss Lilliana?" Sapphire's sharp tone snapped Lilliana's eyes open.

"No Ma'am," she said quietly, trying to sound respectful. It was like she had swallowed hot rocks.

"Right." Sapphire stood; hands clasped in front of her. "To clarify all my questions, that I'm sure have felt more like an interrogation. My family works directly for the Diplomats of the Given's worldwide organization. It has been my position to travel every ten years or so, and make sure all the Given establishments are kept running profitably, ethically, and to the best of their abilities in all areas. Firstly, the Louisiana's Given, creates at least six million every year, above any other facility. We need to share that profitable growth. The Officials, and Diplomats believe, that in rotating staff, we can equally benefit all establishments."

There was a murmur around the room. Lilliana moved uncomfortably in her seat, wanting to simply run away.

"Can you actually force someone to go if they insist on staying where they are?" Rachael sounded as frustrated as Lilliana had ever heard her. "I have been in this facility since I was three. It is not only the place I have grown up in, my home, but I consider the hospital mine. I don't just love working there, I put my soul, my blood, sweat and tears into all I do, every single day. I refuse to leave. There is nothing you can do or say, to make me leave."

"Well, that's the beauty of drugs Nurse. If we select you, and you refuse, we inject you. We move you. And you wake up in a different location. You will have missed the chance to say goodbye to anyone you care for, anyone you love. It really is so simple."

Rachael stood up, clearly shaking, looking at Johnson.

Johnson sat rigidly still, arms folded, his eyes remained unblinking on Rachael's face, wanting to go and hold her, but forced himself remain watchful. Things were about to get ugly.

"Well, trust me Ms Sapphire, I have the most elite drugs that will allow me to remain awake for many days, and still allow me to function. You and your thugs will not get anywhere near me, and if you were smart, you wouldn't even try."

"Is that a threat?" Sapphire stood.

"Take it as you will!" Rachael uncharacteristically spat.

The tension in the room was so thick, you'd need an axe to get through it.

Allie looked at Damon, Leon and Lilliana exchanged a glance.

There were murmurs to begin with, but heated voices began to rise.

Damon stood up. "Alright everyone, calm down." He waited till the room fell silent. "Any person who does not want to leave our home, be assured, I will do everything in my power to prevent that from happening. For those who want to experience a change of scenery, you will have my full support." His eyes landed on Lilliana, before glancing around the room, trying to reassure his people. Unhappy faces looked back at him, and he felt the responsibility of their future, weigh heavily upon his shoulders. "This meeting is over." He folded his arms, looking as unhappy as his people.

"I'm not finished." Sapphire turned her gaze to Damon.

"For the moment, yes, you are." Damon kept his eyes on Lilliana whilst he addressed Sapphire. He felt as drained as he had, when he'd first arrived back within his homes walls. This meeting had gone hours longer than was intended.

Lilliana rose, standing in front of Damon. They stood, like magnets, feeling the others pain. Lilliana was the first to look away, turn and leave the room.

She didn't want to interrupt Josephine or Cam, but she had to share this burden with her friends, get their feedback.

She walked past the dining room, where many Given were going about their normal routine. Most diners had finished eating and were just chatting, relaxing before any night classes, work, or bed.

Oblivious to the blonde enemy in the library.

Lilliana jogged up the stairs, lucky she didn't break her neck in her heels, and after finally reaching the floor below Damon's, knocked hurriedly on Cam's door.

It opened after a handful of seconds, revealing Cam in nothing but unbuttoned jeans.

He looked down at Lilliana and saw by her face, that all was not well. He pulled her into the room, and into his arms. "What's my brother done sweetheart? I'll kill him if he has upset you."

Lilliana rested her head against his warm chest, feeling comfortable for the first time in hours.

"No," she said, her voice tinged with pain, "It's not Damon, Cameron. It's your evil cousin."

"What's happened?" Josephine walked over, pulling Lilliana out of Cams arms, and walked her over to the couch, sitting beside her.

"I don't know where to start." Lilliana pushed a hand through her hair.

Cam poured them all a wine, then, perched on the arm of a chair, waiting for Lilliana to collect herself.

She took a big swallow of wine before placing it on the coffee table. She took comfort in the room, with its light wooden furnishings, and Josephine's green and white touches here and there, along with splashes of colour from throw rugs and pillows, to scented potted plants.

She met Josephine's worried eyes. "Sapphire is here to select staff that benefit this establishment, and place them in other Given facilities, in order to help them gain financial growth, along with shared experience. I am on her list, to go to Russia for Modelling, and work in the Psych wards. I mean, this is a total nightmare for anyone who doesn't want to be moved. Rachael is as furious as I've ever seen her, other staff members are panicking, and I am *seriously freaking* out right now." She ended on a high pitch. Standing, she started to nervously pace the room.

"What is Damon doing about this?" Josephine asked, shocked at this news. "I mean, how much power does Sapphire actually have? He will stop her won't he Cam?"

Cam downed his wine, and walked over to his phone, punching in a number.

Two sets of eyes remained on him. He certainly didn't look like his casual, happy-go-lucky self, who took everything in his easy stride. He looked pent up and furious.

"Damon. It's me. What the *fucking hell* is going on with Sapphire? I have Lilliana here, and I can tell you now, that bitch is not taking Lilly anywhere. Get your ass up here now!" He slammed the phone down and stalked into the opposite room.

Josephine looked at Lilliana, raising an eyebrow and whispered,

"I've never heard him talk to Damon like that in my entire life!"

Lilliana had her arms wrapped around herself. She couldn't stop the shivers that involuntary consumed her.

"I couldn't handle it Jose, if I'm sent away from you all. This is my home, my work, my passion, my life." She shook her head as fat tears of fright fell from her eyes. "It's the fear of not being in control, of having my voice, my wants, be totally irrelevant to people like Sapphire, and whoever else is in charge, of this situation."

"I completely understand. I'd be freaking out right now if someone came up to me and said, time to go. I'd be super pissed off as well." Josephine patted the seat beside her. "Come on, sit, we are not letting you go anywhere. There has to be something we can do."

She put her arm around Lilliana's shoulder and passed her the wine. "Drink, it will warm you up."

They had a calming mouthful of wine, settling into their individual thoughts quietly for a few moments, before the door slammed open making them practically jump out of their skins. Damon strode into the room, the door slamming shut behind him.

"Cameron!" He shouted, glancing over at Lilliana, he shook his head, seeing her tears. His hands were in fists.

"Hey, Damon," Josephine stepped over to him. "Please, calm down, don't be mad at Cam, please."

"Cameron is not the one I'm angry with." He looked at the doorway as Cam walked into the room.

"What the hell Damon?" Cam threw his hands in the air. He'd put on a tee shirt and shoes. "I mean can this bitch seriously do this?"

He placed his hands on his hips, looking furiously at his brother.

Damon ran his hands through his hair, then he too placed his hands on his hips. They were in a standoff, but not with each other. They were both as furious as all hell with Sapphire, and the Officials who gave her the power to make life changing decisions for others.

"You know she can. She claims that Lilliana is so gifted in her field that she can take her place in Russia, and she can step into Lilliana's role here. Plus, they'll make Lilliana do modelling shoots in between, to pull in the big money. They will work her like an animal Cam, to make as much as they can, as quickly as they can."

"I can scar my face," Lilliana said quietly. "They won't want me if I don't have my face." She looked up at Damon.

He walked to her, standing tall as he looked down at her. He cupped her face and stroked her cheeks. "You will do no such thing. Besides, they have the medicines to heal any wound you may inflict upon your face." He reached down and pulled her up against him, cradling her softly against his body.

She pushed her face into his chest, closing her eyes. Her fists clenched into his shirt front.

Cam walked over and sat near Josephine, pulling her onto his lap.

"What a mess," Josephine said quietly, "what are you going to do Damon? You simply cannot let this happen. End of story."

Damon forced a smile over Lilliana's head for Josephine. "Over my dead body they will take her, or anyone who doesn't want to leave."

"Well, what do we do Damon? I can't see Sapphire stopping. She will do everything in her power to better the other facilities, I mean, that's part of her job." Cam rubbed Josephine's back.

Lilliana pushed away from Damon, and walked to the window, an idea forming, but no, it was dark and ugly. And not what she was about.

"I have to go. I promised a new patient I'd be down before he went to sleep."

She turned to face them all. She looked so sweet in her pretty white dress. Sexy in her heels, eyes surrounded by sadness. "I can't leave here. I won't. But I don't want to cause you any trouble Damon." Her eyes flickered across to Josephine and Cam, before looking back at Damon.

She headed out the room, wanting a quick get-away so she could collect herself before she saw Scott.

She headed towards the back stairs to the hospital.

Damon caught up with her, making sure no one was around, linked his fingers through hers. They started walking down slowly.

"No more talk of you causing trouble Lilliana. None." He said firmly.

She stopped walking and turned to face him. "I feel like a prostitute, going to the highest bidder. I thought when I came here, after what I'd endured, that this is where I'd be forever. I am not a prize-winning mare. I am very good at what I do, yes I understand about benefitting the other facilities, but Damon, surely there is something I can do to persuade her she doesn't want me. Need me."

He sighed, pinching the bridge of his nose. Closing his eyes for just a moment. "Trust me. I won't stop thinking about a solution."

Leaning down, he kissed her softly. "Come on sweet girl let me meet your new patient."

They let go of each other's hands as they hit the hospital ward, then walking onwards, Damon approached the eye scanner to allow them access to the Psych ward.

He had a quick chat to Reline, who was filling out a form, as Lilliana signed in.

She asked what room Scott had been placed in, then thanked Reline, as she walked off to find the boy who somehow, pulled at her heart strings in a strangely familiar way.

She smiled at Damon before pushing open the door and stepped into the room. Scott was sitting up in bed with the magazines all around him. When he saw Lilliana, he reached out a hand to her.

She quickly walked over and taking his hand, turned her head smiling.

"Scott, this is Mr Night, who is the head of this facility, and will also help you with anything you need, to help assist your healing."

He nodded his head to Damon, who smiled and said Hello. Damon noted how strangely familiar the boy's eyes were.

Scott turned his gaze back to Lilliana.

"Did you have a nice meal?"

He nodded.

"Would you like to talk to me about anything at all? I can ask Mr Night to wait outside if you like?" She smiled reassuringly.

He looked down at her hands, slowly shaking his head.

A knock on the door sounded, before it opened, Scott's fingers released hers, and bunched nervously in his lap.

Jaycee put her head around the corner. "Time for lights out."

"Thanks Jaycee," Lilliana reached down and started gathering up the magazines and placed them down on the small table near the bed where a plastic cup and water jug stood.

"Alright Scott, I will come and see you tomorrow, maybe you'll feel like talking to me then? Have a good sleep, snuggle down, the lights will go off once we leave. Good night." She smiled down at him, before glancing at Damon, who said good night to the boy, and they left the room.

Once the door shut behind them, Damon stood, staring at Lilliana.

"What?" she turned to walk down the corridor.

He shook his head, running his hand through his hair. "You. Just you." He followed her as she signed out, and together they headed towards the main stairs.

Lilliana stopped and turned to Damon. "Can I come up to yours?" she whispered, looking at his chest, not able to meet his eyes if he rejected her.

He glanced about, and seeing no one, tipped his finger under his chin.

"Yes," he whispered back. Grabbing her hand, they quickly turned and headed towards the secured passageway. Once in, they hurried to Damon's rooms.

Stepping inside Damon's sanctuary Lilliana felt herself start to relax for the first time in hours and then realized she had only had tea to drink all day.

"I'm starving," she admitted.

He rubbed his hands up and down her arms, nodding. "I'll get Christopher onto it, how about a bath while we are wait?"

She smiled "Sounds perfect, I need one to wash away the drama of today."

He took her hand, kissing her fingers as he led her into the bathroom.

She looked at the deep, sunken pool-like bath. Damon set the water temperature perfectly warm and soothing, flicked a switch and it started to quickly fill.

He walked around the room, lighting many scented candles, then once the water stopped he undressed Lilliana, and offering her his hand, helped her into the tub. The water rose to her belly before she sat lower, then the water swirled gently around her neck.

She sighed, leaning her head against a soft pad, closing her eyes. "Thank you, I really needed this."

He bent and ran a hand along her jaw. "You're welcome Baby. Relax. I'll order food and will join you shortly. I just have a quick call to make first."

"Okay." She watched him walk out of the room, then closed her eyes as he vanished from her view, forcing herself to stop thinking about being sent away to Russia.

These were the stories she'd never heard about. The exchange of staff. The Diplomatic Heads. co-ordinators. Whatever they chose to call themselves. Lilliana had a few choice words for them all.

Damon stepping back into the room, took all her negative thoughts away, as her hungry eyes took him in.

He strolled around towards the steps, tall, dark, naked.

From his broad shoulders, to his firm pecks and abs, down to his narrow strong hips. His buttocks so firm, his thighs, as the water brushed over them, shaped, defined. His maleness standing proud and ready. He sat opposite her; his eyes just as hungry as hers.

He sat back, leaning his head into the padded cushion, lazily watching her. "How are you feeling Lilliana?"

She shook her head. "Content now." She felt his feet, find her ankles, and placed them either side of her.

His feet gently rubbing her ankles. His eyes unblinking, taking her in. "Come here."

She was more than happy to comply. She gently pushed away from the wall and glided towards him, and as she neared him he gently took her under the arms and pulled her towards him, his mouth waiting.

She nearly cried at the intensity of the kiss. Holding so much promise, that he would not lose her.

His lips firm, yet soft. She couldn't get enough, kissing him, her tongue meeting his in a mating ritual of their own.

His hands roamed down her back, placing his strong fingers around her waist, pulling her closer. Her arms circled around his neck, pushing her breasts against his chest, loving the feel of him being wet. She did not want to wait one more second and was grateful when he lifted her hips and slid her down onto his throbbing, waiting shaft. She was beyond ready for him and rode him fast and furious.

Their union was anything but slow and sweet, but pulsated with a deep frenzy of lust, need, and a desire to comfort the other.

Afterwards, she clung to his shoulders, kissing him deeply, tears falling down her face. Partly tears of joy, being with him once more, partly terrified of being torn away from him.

He wrapped his arms around her, trying to give her as much comfort and reassurance as he could in that moment.

She was beyond devastated, thinking about not being able to have him again. Leaving him. He was her world. Her safety net. Her reason for being who she was.

"Talk to me." Damon felt his gut tighten that his beautiful, sweet lady was feeling so much despair. "What can I do Baby?"

She leaned back to look at him, beautiful green eyes filled with tears. "Lock me away somewhere so she'll never find me."

"Sweet girl." He whispered against her lips, before kissing her. That thought was very appealing.

He pulled back, lifted her up and stepping out of the spa, he reached down and pulled her out with him.

They stepped under the drier, and the warm air flowed around them. "Don't think I haven't thought about that," he said, his fingers gliding through her hair to dry it, and comb out any knots.

"Cam is working on a loophole contract with Johnson, seeing if any monies you earn for this establishment, in the next five years, can be forwarded to Russia. That way, we may be able to keep you here."

Once they were dried he led her into the bedroom and together they got dressed before heading out to the main lounge.

Lilliana crossed to the fire enjoying the warmth, as her eyes wandered over Damon's photographs.

Damon walked to the door, opening it to reveal Christopher and the food trolley.

Christopher dropped his hand as he was about to knock on the door. Shaking his head, smiling. "How are you Sir?"

"Good thank you, how are you?" Damon pulled the trolley into the room, waiting for Christopher.

He looked a little unsettled, not his usual, confident self.

He pushed his black hair out of his eyes. "Well, Sir I'm pretty upset actually, and was wondering if I could talk to you for a minute." He looked past Damon, to Lilliana.

Lilliana smiled at Christopher, letting him know it was fine.

"Of course, come in."

"Thanks Sir, sorry Lilly, if I'm interrupting," he stepped into the room, the door sliding shut behind him.

"Please, do not apologize, you are family. If you have a problem, we all have a problem." She sat down, waiting.

"Thanks Lilly." Christopher took a deep breath and walked over to one of the couches and sat.

"I had a visit earlier, from Ms Sapphire, offering me a deal. As you know, before I came here, I helped run a soup kitchen with my cult family. We were known as the GK's, Goth Kitchen Heads. Anyway, my parents set up soup kitchens, to feed those in need, three meals a day." He nodded his thanks, as Damon passed him a cup of coffee. "We had a few friends of ours who would supply as fresh as vegetables as they could find, flour for baking breads, and occasionally my father and I would go out of town, to steal a sheep, or cattle, from the larger properties that had ways of surviving the drought. It was down to the stage where most families could only purchase one ration of meat per week and what with the restrictions getting the way they were, and prices going up, most people could barely pay for fresh meat once a month. We did what we could, to help the less fortunate, get by." He took a grateful mouthful, of the thick black liquid. "When the Officials busted us, my dad took two of them down while they were trying to arrest him and me for cattle theft. My Mum stabbed an Official, got herself shot in the process. I don't know what happened to our group after I got sent here, but I know they wouldn't give up. Ms Sapphire has informed me, that if I go to Russia, and cook in their kitchens, she will donate a million dollars to the GK's." He rubbed a hand over his tired looking face. "One million dollars will save so many people, and keep their families fed for years."

Damon, leaning against his desk, arms folded, silently formed a plan as he listened to everything Christopher was saying.

"I can't leave Allie, Sir, so I asked Ms Sapphire if I could bring her with me. She flat out refused. I won't leave without her, but I need to leave to help out my people."

Damon glanced across at Lilliana, who looked as grieved as Christopher, with this current predicament.

He stood and crossed to her, standing behind her chair, he placed his large hands on her creamy shoulders and squeezed gently, massaging her.

"How can one woman promise so much Damon?" she asked over her shoulder.

"I'm not sure, but I know for a fact that the GK's still operate and would benefit from her offer. Johnson has many contacts of good faith on the outside. How about we give them two million, and then we can tell Sapphire to forget her deal in the first place."

Christopher stood; his expression bewildered. "Would you do that Sir? I don't know how I could ever thank you, seriously, thank you!"

Damon squeezed Lilliana's shoulders, before walking around, and brushing her arm as he did, stepped over to Christopher and reached to shake the younger man's hand.

"I think you do enough Christopher, preparing wonderful meals for your family here. You are an amazing, gifted teacher, who has taught so many Given how to cook a decent, healthy meal. You have given Cook the break he needs. And you have made one very special lady, who has had a terrible start in life, smile constantly. I will deal with Sapphire, and Johnson and I will get onto sorting out funds for your old organization."

Christopher was beaming. "Yes Sir. Thank you so much. Bye Lilly."

"Kiss Allie for me."

"No problem there." He called over his shoulder as he briskly walked out the door.

Damon walked over to his desk and picked up the phone. Speaking quietly to Johnson for a few minutes while Lilliana dug into a plateful of sandwiches and hot finger food. She was so hungry, the food so delicious and fresh, she felt guilty eating so much, after the story Christopher had just told her about people out there not getting enough to eat.

And that was almost nine years ago. The thought of how much worse this situation could be out there, was overwhelming. Surely the Givens wonderful supply of fresh fruits and vegetables, that went out to the markets, were well priced for everyone to receive?

Maybe Damon needed to do something about that and donate to a sound cause, that would benefit the right groups, not the money hungry organizations.

She poured a tea as Damon was talking to Cam about a catch up in an hour.

She glanced over at Damon as she'd finished eating. He was leaning against the desk, watching her.

He looked frustrated, dark, dangerous in a sexy way.

"What is it?"

"I want you to stay here for a few hours. Just get some sleep, no wandering around. Can you do that for me Lilliana?" He had folded his arms across his chest, staring down at her as she walked across to him, stopping just before she reached his feet.

"Of course I can, why?" She placed her hands around his biceps, stepping closer.

She heard him take a deep breath, and unfolding his arms, wrapped them around her body, gently stroking her back, his chin resting on top of her head.

"Don't you worry yourself about it love, I just need to find a solution for all our problems, but you being here, will be one thing less for me to worry about." He raised his head to look into her eyes.

She brushed her lips across his. He deepened the kiss instantly, crushing her mouth beneath his.

Her arms wrapped around his neck, holding him closer.

His mouth left her lips, to brush her cheek, her neck, his fingers plunging into her long, thick waves. He broke the kiss. "I love you. I am going to do everything in my power to keep you, my darling girl. All I need you to do is stay here, don't let anybody in. Just go to bed, and I will see you in the morning."

Lilliana nodded her head, her fingers leaving his neck, to trial down his arms, to find his fingers. "I have a group with Allie first thing in the morning and then I want to see Scott. That's fine, isn't it?" She was hoping he would not stop her from doing her work.

"Of course." He kissed her nose and then walked around her, heading out the door.

"Damon."

He turned around to face her, as the door slid open.

"I love you."

He smiled, stepping backwards, as the door slid shut between them.

Lilliana walked around his room, running her fingertips over this piece of furniture, or that photo frame. She loved being here, surrounded by everything that was Damon.

She walked over and sat at his desk contemplating her options.

Surely if she had a meeting with Sapphire, maybe she could persuade her to see the benefits of keeping her here? Could she make a deal with her, offering her some of the income from her modelling shoots? Yes, a lot went straight into the establishment, but a small, worthy portion was put aside for her own personal use. She'd have to speak to Fox and Cam, to see what contracts were coming up, also how much she could offer her. She picked up the phone and pressed in three digits. Waiting a few minutes till the other end finally picked up.

"This had better be good as you're interrupting my personnel work-out" Fox said, a little breathlessly

"Fox, it's Lilliana, sorry, I know it's getting late." Lilliana wondered if she should just leave it till tomorrow but knew she wouldn't get any sleep if she didn't start working on an escape plan now.

"Foxy-girl, tell who ever that is to go away." A sexy drawl could be heard in the background.

"Shut up Zack," Fox snapped out, as only she could, and still expect the man to stay in her bed. "What's up Lilly?"

"I was just wondering if you and Cam are aware of any more contracts coming up. I need to get a bit of a stash together, and hopefully pay Sapphire and the Russian facility off, so I can stay here. She's told me she wants me gone. I'm thinking if I offer her enough she'll leave me alone." Lilliana ran a hand through her hair, waiting.

"I'll come to you in the morning. Do you have a group at nine?"

"Yes."

"Well, get some sleep honey, and I'll see you eight sharp in your office." Fox ended the call.

Lilliana rested the phone back down and went into Damon's little kitchen to heat up some hot milk. Hoping that that would knock her out, and she could escape from all her thoughts.

Once she drank it down, she walked into the bedroom and undressed. Calling lights off, she snuggled deep down under the blankets, wrapping her arms around Damon's pillow, breathing the scent of him in.

Remembering when times had been simple, and thoughts and worries were basically on how to benefit her patients.

She squeezed her eyes shut praying that tomorrow, with the help of Fox and Cam, she could come up with a plan to stop the evil blonde witch take her away forever.

CHAPTER 12

Damon, Cam and Johnson, with three of Johnson's best men, sat around Damon's down-stairs office the entire night, going over proposals, budgets, and basic brainstorming on what to do about Sapphire.

Damon had made contact, via one of Johnson's outside men, to locate and serve Christopher's old GK's, and offer them their generous donation.

Damon had emailed Sapphire and told her, professionally of course, to keep her sticky fingers off his people.

And then sent her the numbers he was willing to pay her, and her facilities, to send her back there, along with any willing Given.

It was after eight in the morning when the men decided to get on with their roles in this game of getting rid of Sapphire.

By the time Damon walked upstairs to his rooms, hoping to find Lilliana still in bed, he was disappointed to find her gone.

He showered briefly, made a strong coffee and then went in search for his woman.

***

Fox arrived promptly at eight. Lilliana had been waiting for her, with fruit smoothies and some freshly made muffins, from Allie via Christopher.

The two had been talking for about forty minutes, throwing around different ideas.

"Damon should just marry you and be done with it." Fox shrugged.

"Yes well, technically he is still legally married to Felicia Reid. I don't know how long until the Officials sort all those details out and finalise the whole ordeal."

"I think what we need to know first, is if this bitch will go for any sum we might be lucky enough to come up with, or if she just wants you gone to get her claws into Damon." Fox wiped a crumb of white chocolate and raspberry muffin from the corner of her mouth, and elegantly sucked on her finger.

Lilliana sat back in her chair, slowly nodding. "Yes, you're right of course. But if we can come up with some sort of impressive figure, she won't be able to refuse, surely?"

"Unless it's not really the money she's after?" Fox stood. "Don't worry, that feral whore is not going to take anyone away from here who doesn't want to go."

"Charming." A cool voice chided from behind them. Lilliana had not heard the outer office door open.

Damon.

"Oh Damon dear, the truth can be bitter." Fox smiled, flipping her hair over her shoulder. She raised one eyebrow and placed her hands on her hips as she stood. "What the hell are you doing about this meddling bitch? Surely you have some greater power here. You are almost bloody royalty yourself?"

Damon too, had placed his hands on his hips, glaring down at Fox with her attitude. He took a step closer to her and gently pointed a finger under her nose. "Don't need this shit from you right now Fox. Go. I need to talk to Lilliana."

Fox held up her hands. "Gone. Talk soon Lilly, we'll see what we can do."

"Thank you Fox." Lilliana was grateful for Fox's forwardness. She remained seated, legs crossed, fingers tapping on her desk.

Once the door closed, Damon strode around the other side of her desk, and reaching down, pulled Lilliana up against him, crushing his mouth hungrily to hers.

Her fingers gripped the front of his shirt, taking him all in, wanting more.

"It was strange being in your bed without you."

His cupped her face, holding her away a little so his eyes could take in her appearance.

He shook his head slowly. "I will never get enough of you. Ever."

"Hey you two." Allie called from behind them. "What am I missing?"

Damon stroked Lilliana's cheek before dropping his hand, and walked away, smiling at Allie as he passed. "Not much Allie. Enjoy group." He smiled at Lilliana over his shoulder, and quickly strode from the room.

Lilliana had no time to explain the situation to Allie, as their first patient entered the room, then several more.

It was a productive session, where one young girl who had done hard core drugs and stolen money from her family to support her habit, confessed that due to her parents' lack of communication, she felt unworthy, and had turned to drugs to make life seem more fulfilling.

Which was an age-old story, but for Lexi, the first time in months she felt she could talk about herself, so it was a very good step in the right direction.

Once group ended the two friends sat for another forty minutes, while Lilliana filled Allie in on all the happenings with Sapphire and Russia.

They both sat in silence, staring at the peaceful fish.

"It's total bullshit." Allie said quietly. "I mean, Damon is the head of this facility, it has been his family's business for generations. Surely she has no power here?"

"I guess it's complicated. Political if you like. I don't understand a lot of it." Lilliana shrugged. "Fox and I are working on a plan to pay Sapphire out, so she'll leave me alone. But then again, Fox doesn't think it has everything to do with money."

"Yeah well, it doesn't make sense Lilly. From what Christopher was telling me, about the deal she tried to make with him, she has plenty of money. Something is not adding up." Allie checked the time. "Marcus wants me to help out with taking Sap on a promotional tour, along with Natalie."

Lilliana stood, smiling, "Won't that be fun?"

"Oh yeah. A real hoot! Will you be okay?"

"Yes, I'll be fine. I may get a ride in before lunch, but first I want to pop down and see Scott."

"Alright, well, later Lilly." Allie gave her a quick squeeze, before she headed out.

Lilliana left, and headed down to the Psych ward.

After the eye scan she walked in and ran smack into Dr Richard. She could hear his strange intake of breath as he stared down at her over his horn-rimmed spectacles.

"Sorry." She apologized, and left that, as her greeting as she quickly walked around him and over to the desk to sign in.

"Hi Brad, how's it going today?" She asked as he handed her the sign in Tablet, to press her thumb against.

"Good thanks Lilliana, it was another busy night, I'm about to head off, catch up on some sleep." He did in fact look exhausted.

"How are you handling the rotation shift?"

Brad shrugged, "I think I'll be putting in for full time night shift, this two-week merry go-round isn't really working for me. The Awake Serum doesn't have a good effect on me, so that doesn't help anyone here much."

"That's the thing Brad, in your position it's not only important you look after you, but you need to be in the right headspace to look after everyone in here."

He nodded in agreement as she said goodbye.

"Bye Lilliana," he called after her as she headed down to Scott's room.

Screaming could be heard from a few rooms, crying from another. As Lilliana walked on she could hear a firm voice instructing someone that if they didn't settle down and stop biting, they would be shocked for a week.

Ouch! Harsh, Lilliana thought.

Lilliana knocked before walking into Scott's room.

The tall handsome boy was sitting on the end of his bed, drawing. As he wasn't allowed anything that could be made into a weapon, he'd been given black paper and white chalk.

He looked up and smiled as Lilliana walked in.

"Hello Scott. How are you this morning? Did you have a good night?"

He nodded twice, patting the bed beside him, wanting to show her his drawings.

She sat beside him, crossing her legs, leaning back on her hand to see.

His drawings were amazing. There was one of a horse galloping. He'd captured the movement beautifully, of stretching muscles, flowing mane in the wind. A full moon on the horizon.

Another, a spider. A very creepy, sinister drawing of the spider's fangs flecked with poison and a symbol, dripping in venom. Lilliana could not quite make it out.

Another, more horrific, a room full of bodies, their faces twisted in pain, all naked like they were in an orgy. One of the faces looked vaguely familiar.

The last drawing stopped her still.

It was a picture of her, from years ago, from one of the photo shoots she'd done, as the winter vixen, for a perfume commercial.

She looked dark, sexy and mischievous.

She looked at Scott, who was looking hard at her.

"You are very talented. Did you study?"

Scott stared at her, unblinking, and nodded slowly.

"I was told that you were tutored from the age of four, till you came here, is that correct?" He nodded.

"What do these drawings mean to you? Does it make you feel better expressing your fears, your desires, or happiness through your art?"

He nodded again.

She gently placed the picture of her down on top of the others. "You know you can talk to me? Don't be afraid. As soon as we talk we can decide where it is best for you to go Scott. You will absolutely love Main house. There is so much for you to do and learn with all the programs available, plus all the recreational activities. Horse riding, tennis, archery, which is something I am not very good at." She slipped off the bed and stood. "I'll be back this afternoon. Maybe you'd like to talk to me then? Enjoy your day. See you soon."

She turned to leave when a quiet voice reached her, calling softly. "Lilliana."

She forced herself not to freeze and put a relaxed smile on her face as she turned around. Scott was a foot behind her. His eyes, so green, deep, familiar, stared down into hers.

He reached out his hand, in it, the picture he'd drawn of her.

She reached out slowly and accepted the gift. "Thank you," she said softly, and stepping back, smiled as she turned and left the room.

As the door closed behind her she glanced down at the drawing.

How very talented he was.

Hopefully this afternoon he would speak to her.

Wanting to check out his background story a little more, she headed out of Psych and up to Black Ops to find Johnson.

After ten minutes, she walked through the iron gateway, and through the doorway, where the security guard smiled at her, and said hello.

Lilliana smiled back and walked towards Johnson's office.

Knocking on the door, it opened to reveal a room full of men. Damon standing in the middle, arms folded, with a very serious look on his face.

Her stomach clenched at the appreciative sight of him. "Oh, I'm sorry, I should have called." Lilliana went to take a step back, when Damon held up his hand, and opening his palm, extended his fingers towards himself, as if to say, come.

Lilliana stepped inside the office, and walked to Damon, he bent down so her lips could speak quietly in his ear.

"I just came to ask Johnson for some background info on Scott." Being this close to his tall, strong body, without touching him, with people looking on, did things to her.

The smell of him, his sharp, blue eyes taking her in. His lips, oh how she wanted to lay one on him right now. He was gazing at her, seeming aloof and professional. But she could see the hunger in his eyes.

She averted her eyes, not wanting to give herself away with flushed cheeks as Damon nodded over to where Johnson was sitting.

Lilliana quickly walked past the many men, apologizing as she reached Johnson.

"Johnson, forgive my intrusion, I should have called. I wanted your complete background report on Scott if that's okay?"

"Of course Lilliana." Johnson tapping at the glass keyboard on his desk, pulled up a file, and quickly sent the information to Lilliana's email.

"Done." He nodded.

"Thank you." She smiled and turned to leave the room.

Damon watched her, as did most the men in the room, with respectful, yet hungry eyes.

Her white skirt flowing around her ankles, clinched at her curvy waist with a green belt. A snug fitting white blouse and her long, black hair braided over one shoulder, tall green heels. She looked very tasty to any male still breathing.

Her eyes flicked briefly to Damon's as she turned to shut the door.

Smiling to herself, she quickly left Black Ops, and made it to her room, to get changed into her riding gear. A visit with Beauty was sure to get her mind clear with fresh, positive ideas regarding Scott opening up, and expressing himself to her.

She ran into Jessica on the way out and was so happy to see her friend. She was with a few Given.

"Jessica, how are you?" Lilliana hugged her, smiling hello to a few of the younger girls. Two of them in her, and Allie's, group.

"Good Lilly. Allie and Josephine filled me in about Sapphire wanting you for Russia. It can't happen, there's no way." Jessica frowned.

"I certainly hope there is no way," Lilliana agreed. "How's Orlando?"

Jessica smiled. "He is fantastic. He's just taken a group down to the tennis courts, where we are meeting him there in twenty. Do you want to come?" she asked, eagerly.

"I'd love to, but I owe myself a ride, before I have to get back to some work I have to get through. We must catch up soon. Okay?"

Jessica agreed and the two hugged before going off in their separate directions.

Once Lilliana saddled Beauty, she mounted and took off on the usual path for horse riding, slowly at first, then she let Beauty have her head.

For an hour, they rode hard, arriving to a part of the property that had long rope swings attached to some of the larger trees, set up as part of their therapeutic, relaxation and sensory integration programmes. Lilliana knotted the reins, allowing Beauty to graze, and chose a swing, where she could overlook the lake in the distance, allowing her mind to wander as she gently pumped her legs, leaning backwards and forwards, reaching great heights, before relaxing into the swing and allowing it to slow at its own speed.

So much to consider. Damon. She still couldn't breathe around him. Had so many unanswered questions about him. She didn't know how to ask him how he was feeling about his aborted baby, about Felicia. Let alone how he was internally coping with his thoughts regarding his time in the outside world. She didn't want to pry or upset him in any way. Was still slightly shy and a little intimidated by him at times. The fact that she'd slept with the man more than four times amazed her.

She shook her head, slipping off the swing, taking the reins as she stroked Beauty's neck, and began to walk with her. What would she seriously do if she had to leave here?

She pushed away the dark thoughts that had now crept twice into her mind. There must be other options. Surely there had to be.

The sun was warm, a slight breeze rustled the long grass.

Lilliana plonked down amongst the cat tails and wild daises. There was not a single soul in sight. She couldn't see anything but trees and grassed fields for miles around.

She lay back in the grass and closed her eyes, taking the deepest breath in and exhaling, soaking up the sun's rays, feeling it gently pull her into a lazy, heavy sleep.

She awoke to fat rains drops splashing down on her face, the sky had darkened dramatically.

She sat up and jumped to her feet. How long has she been asleep?

She did a 360 of the area. Beauty was nowhere in sight.

Oh, great! Fabulous! She thought. Hoping that her horse had the good sense to get herself back to the stables. Pushing wet escaped tendrils of hair off her face, she started for the path home, and put herself in a positive mood. This was an adventure, on a beautiful afternoon, where she didn't have any appointments, or meetings. Just a nice walk in the rain. She could hear an eerie, slightly familiar sound in the distance.

She continued walking for several minutes, arms wrapped around herself as the chill of the rain seeped through every inch of her clothing, erasing that spirited feeling of adventure. She was pondering what time it was, and how long-ago Beauty had headed on home when her breath caught in her throat.

There, looming ahead of her and drawing rapidly closer, was an enormous black figure, cloaked by the pelting rain. She froze trying not to panic and knowing she could see it, wondered if it could see her, after all there was nowhere to run, nowhere to hide. Finally, it was upon her, through the pouring rain, her eyes made out Damon on Beast.

She felt relieved but did not relax; his body language wouldn't allow it.

His eyes had a seriousness about them she had not seen for many a year, his lips held rigid. He didn't say a word, just reached down a large hand toward her.

As she reached up for him, he grabbed her wrist and pulled her up effortlessly behind him, then making sure her arms were tightly about his waist, kicked Beast into a gallop, returning them to the stables in twenty-five minutes.

Damon was breathing heavily when they arrived, and jumping down reached up for her, his long fingers digging into her hips as he pulled her off his horse. Her body bumping into his, sliding down against him, until her feet hit the ground.

She didn't know if he was angry, or worried and wasn't comfortable meeting his eyes.

As Thomas led Beast off, Damon placed a finger under her chin and pushed her face up so her eyes could be thoroughly sought by his.

He bent quickly and kissed her briefly, forcing himself not to deepen the kiss. He took her hand and led her towards the house.

Lilliana realized what the eerie sound had been. A sound she had not heard for many years. It was the siren that alerted all, that an emergency was upon them, and the entire facility would be put in lockdown mode.

"Damon, what has happened?" He was walking quickly up the steps inside.

He glanced down at her and gave his head a quick shake, just as a worried voice was calling out for his attention. Closing the door behind them, he let go of her hand and indicated she go into the large assembly room.

He took a small towel from Johnson who had been waiting, and quickly pulled it through his hair, rubbing it dry enough that, water was running down his neck. He had a quick chat to the staff member who had called out to him, before following Lilliana into the waiting assembly.

Finally, the eerie siren ceased.

Lilliana scanned the hall for a friend. She spotted Leon and headed over. "What's going on?" She started shivering, her bones chilled. Leon wrapped his arm around her and rubbed his hands up and down her arms trying to get some warmth into her.

"I guess this explains where you have been the past two hours Lilly," he shook his head, "thank God you're alright. I thought Damon was going to murder someone when he couldn't find you when the siren sounded."

"This can't be good Leon do you know what's happened?" Her teeth started chattering. She was desperate for a hot shower.

Leon shook his head, his eyes drawn to the stage where Cam and Damon, along with Johnson and Sapphire were now standing.

Sapphire looked furious. Her hair wet and clinched back as tightly as her pinched facial features. Her eyes scanning the room with an evil glare.

"Given, we are gathered at this assembly this afternoon, as an attack has been made on Ms Sapphire. We believe we have the culprit in custody. Ms Sapphire wanted this assembly to deliver a warning to you all." Damon spoke slowly, calmly, he too looked furious, but Lilliana wasn't sure if he was furious at Sapphire, or the situation.

He stepped back and held his hand out for his cousin to address the crowd.

Standing beside his brother, he folded his arms and looked out at his people, wondering what more he could do to protect them.

Sapphire's shrill tone cut through his thoughts and he turned his attention back to his cousin.

"Let me just say, some of you here have truly appreciated the marvellous offer I have made you, in regard to a new future. I have talked with close to two hundred of you who are interested in either going undercover, or stepping into roles at the other Given establishments, plus two new establishment's that are being built in both Glenormiston South, Australia, and in Enniskillen, Ireland.

These opportunities are for the very gifted and talented Given, who want to do more than just help themselves. I have also come across many of you who stubbornly, ungratefully even, refuse my assistance in helping along your careers."

Her cold eyes glanced here and there, resting on Lilliana and Leon before glaring out at others.

"That's right, it's called freedom of choice you bitch!" A voice screamed out in the crowd, setting off others. Obviously Sapphire could not know who that person was. But Lilliana did, and hoped Eric would just keep cool and quiet now he had had his say.

"Typical of scum that have been given too much freedom and squandered this fabulous opportunity." Sapphire spat out above the resentful voices. "Obviously things here are run a lot differently than they are at other establishments. That has to change!"

"Enough!" Damon stepped forward, cutting Sapphire off.

He turned his attention to his people, whose worried voices filtered around the assembly.

"Please, everyone, I need you all to keep calm. Mr Night and I will be here to answer any questions you may have, in regard to new placements. We will be available around the clock for the next twenty-four hours. Ms Sapphire will be leaving then, with those of you who have chosen placements elsewhere. For now, class, work, or appointments carry on as usual."

He glanced into the crowd, listening to something Cam was saying. He looked at his brother and nodded as they both hurried off the stage and out a side door, no doubt getting to the office to get ready for a barrage of people.

Lilliana let out a deep breath, shaking her head. "What else can possibly happen today?" She stood, turning to Leon, about to ask him what he had on next, but the unusual way he was looking at her, stopped her in her tracks. "What is it Leon?" she shivered, her wet clothes becoming more uncomfortable as the seconds ticked by.

He had a strange glint in his eye. He stood slowly and uncharacteristically, grabbed her by the shoulders and pulled her against him, kissing her full on the lips. He deepened the kiss, before the shock wore off.

Lilliana pushed against his chest, holding her hand to her mouth. "Leon!" she gasped. Trying not to think of the hundreds of people they were surrounded by. She waited for some kind of explanation, when he quickly turned on his heel and strode from the room.

Alright then? She thought as she glanced around, seeing many curious eyes watching. Dr Richard simply raised an eyebrow. Great! She flushed red, and walked briskly from the room, wondering where her girls were, and thought after a quick shower she would go and find them. Defrosting ten minutes later under the hot jets, she shook her head, mentally high fiving the person who had upset Sapphire, way to go! And then Leon. She guessed he had feelings for her, as she did for him in many ways. He was drop dead gorgeous, intelligent, funny, a hardworking dedicated man. But, at the end of the day he was simply Leon, her friend.

She was just hoping he wasn't beating himself up too badly about the kiss. She could move on past the embarrassing moment and hoped he could do the same.

She stepped out, dried and slipping on a robe, dashed to her room, to pull on a long sleeved, short, dark green dress, with leggings and black boots.

She added a black belt, brushed her hair out and gave herself a quick squirt of perfume.

She headed up to Cam's quarters, hoping Josephine would be there. No one answered. She dashed downstairs, then through the hospital entrance and down the steep hospital stairs, and along the corridors toward her and Allie's office, hoping to find Allie.

Walking into emptiness she placed her hands on her hips and jumped a mile when a large hand landed on her shoulder. Spinning around, she grabbed her chest laughing when she saw Christopher. "Oh brother, you gave me a fright! You'd think in my role I'd be used to people sneaking up on me."

She stopped talking as she noticed Christopher's face, his streaky mascara and eye liner indicated he'd been crying. Paler than usual, his shoulders were sagging.

Warning bells were going off in her head. "Christopher, what is it?" She stepped forward, taking his large, cold hands in hers.

"You may want to sit Lilliana."

"No, I don't need to sit, just tell me." Her voice, firm.

"Allie went out with Natalie and Marcus, to take Sapphire on the grounds tour, which included the archery section." He let out a shaky breath. "Natalie, Sapphire and Allie were having a bit of a competition." He swallowed, as if it were too much for him to talk.

Lilliana squeezed his hands gently.

"They were near the dense part of the forest, where boar roam and Allie claims one was heading straight towards Sapphire. She aimed for it, only Sapphire claims Allie was aiming for her, and took no chances, shot her."

Lilliana gasped and stepped away from Christopher, covering her mouth, waiting.

"It's okay Lilly." He stepped forward and grabbed her shoulders. "She's okay, but the arrow did go through her side. She's still in surgery with Dr Ryan."

"Did Marcus see the boar? Natalie?" she asked.

"Natalie says there was no boar and Marcus was five minutes in the other direction. Cam and Damon don't believe Allie was being malicious, but they only have her word against Sapphire's, and had to put the statement out that they had the culprit in custody, or Sapphire was going to insist on calling Allie out, as her right as a superior."

"What does that even mean, calling Allie out? Honestly, since that woman has come here she has caused nothing but disturbance." Placing her hands on her hips, she paced.

"What that means, is that she could take Allie out. End her. Kill her." Christopher almost chocked on the last word.

She stopped pacing and stared at him. "Oh Christopher, thank god she didn't. I'd kill Sapphire myself!" Lilliana rubbed his arm as she walked past him and out the door. She could hear him following her as she went to search for Rachael, or someone who could tell her about Allies' injuries.

Reaching the nurses' station, she smiled at Billy. "How are you Billy?"

"Good Darling." He forced a smile.

Lilliana reached across and grabbed Billy's wrist. His grey eyes glanced up and stared into her deep green ones.

"What is it? Are you alright?"

"I've been offered a position in Enniskillen, Ireland. Leon's been propositioned with Glenormiston South, Australia. I think he's considering it; it sounds like a phenomenal location." He pulled his wrist gently away, and grabbed a Tablet, clicking on a few files, he passed it to a waiting nurse, quietly giving her instructions before she left.

Lilliana watched him and guessed that may have been the reason why Leon had impulsively kissed her. He might be leaving here for good.

Billy turned back to Lilliana, Christopher standing in the background.

"Are you leaving us then Billy?" She waited, hoping that if that was the decision he made; she could be happy for him.

"I'm not sure yet." He smiled, this time more easily. "I've got time to decide, unlike some of the others here. The Ireland facility is still being built."

Lilliana nodded, as Christopher stepped forward. "Billy, any news about Allie?"

"I promise, as soon as I hear, I'll contact you both, but for now, I have rounds." He clapped Christopher on the shoulder as he walked off.

Lilliana looked at Christopher, who looked deflated.

He walked over to a seat and sat heavily. "I'm staying, I promise I will find you as soon as I hear anything."

Lilliana nodded, and bending to kiss his cheek spun on her heel and took off at a quick pace.

She knew what she had to do, before any judgement could be made against Allie. Knew only clear evidence would stop whatever wrong decision was about to be made. Even if Sapphire did not deal with Allie in the way she wanted, Cam and Damon would still have to pass a penalty of some sort. They would have no choice as; at this stage it was a co-ordinators word against the word of a worker.

Racing up the stairs, her mind reeling with the entire situation, and everything else that had been going on in the past twenty-four hours.

She tried to clear her thoughts and focused on finding Natalie.

If there was one person, who was full of bullshit and lies, it was her.

She walked towards the library, hearing angry, raised voices from Damon's office, and worried how he was handling everything, hoping he was okay.

Damon's door flew open and he stepped out, looking furious. His eyes met Lilliana's. She froze, wanting to comfort him somehow and went to take a step towards him, he held out a hand, indicating she stop.

She did immediately, as a shrill voice screamed out behind him. "If you take one more step you will find out *exactly* what I am capable of."

Lilliana could see about ten people in the room behind Damon, watching, waiting. Sapphire stood in the centre, looking like an arrogant, demonic being.

Damon took a deep breath, letting his eyes roam over Lilliana, as if to give him strength, he then straightened his shoulders and turning, stepped back into the room, the door closing behind him.

Lilliana pushed her hands through her hair wondering what the hell was going on in there.

She had to find Natalie. Now! She walked into the library and had a quick look inside. She saw Jessica with her group but did not want to interrupt her.

As soon as Jessica spotted Lilliana she quickly excused herself and walked towards her friend, a pinched, worried look on her pretty face.

"Have you heard, about Allie? Marcus told me before assembly. There is no way she would have taken that shot Lilly." Jessica shook her head, her soft blonde, silky hair shifting around her shoulders. "This cannot be happening!" Her voice broke, and she took a deep breath trying to calm herself.

Lilliana reached out and squeezed Jessica's hand. "It's okay darling. I am going to sort this out. If anyone is bullshitting, about this situation, it's Natalie. I need to find her. Have you seen her?"

"She is probably down in laundry." Jessica wrapped her arms around herself. "What's going to happen to Allie if she's found guilty?"

Lilliana's sweet, gentle friend, sounded as worried as Lilliana felt.

"Don't think about that, that's not going to happen Jess. I've got this." She hugged her friend briefly, before she spun out of the room and took off towards the back of the house, where the stairs to the laundry led. It was positioned behind the kitchen area, leading under the labyrinth of secluded passageways.

Lilliana walked down the thick, concrete steps. It was a strange feeling walking down here, a place she had not entered in nine years.

Reaching the last step, she viewed a huge room which had at least ninety industrial washing machines all rattling around.

It was quite noisy, with people in white tops and pants bustling around. There was music playing, and one man, Mick, was singing at the top of his lungs as he was taking sheets out of one machine and dumping them into a trolley placed on a track that was centred in the middle of the room. Flicking a switch, the trolley took off on its wheels, heading towards a door at the back of the room.

Above, attached to the ceilings were large rails, and hanging on those were many varieties of hangers and baskets.

Along the opposite wall of the machines it looked like an old post box of days gone by. Hundreds of chutes, some occasionally popping open to drop clothes into the clothes bags attached to them.

So, this is where my clothes come, Lilliana thought to herself, appreciating the busy people that worked laundry. Ten long tables held piles of clothes that were being folded, hung, and sorted into piles.

Lilliana walked over toward Mick. He seemed like a happy guy.

Surely he would tell her where Natalie was?

A few heads turned, watching her walk towards him.

"Excuse me." She waited for him to turn towards her. He sang a few more beats about, 'wanting to get down and dirty with you', before he flashed her a big toothy grin.

"Now what can I do for you little darling?" he asked in a friendly manner. He reached for another basket and dumped it into his machine.

"I was wondering if Natalie was around?" she smiled, hoping she looked like a friendly friend, not someone on a mission to rip someone's throat out.

"Yeah, she sure is. Down in the ironing rooms. Straight through that door, down past the dryers, all the way down till you reach a big door on the left, follow that through and you'll find the ironing room. Don't get lost down there." He winked at her, before turning his attention back to his job, whistling merrily.

"Thank you," Lilliana called, heading past many bodies to get to the door at the end of the very long room.

Lilliana walked through the doorway and was hit by hot air, where the biggest driers she'd ever seen, were silently spinning clothing around.

She smiled at a few faces who gave her a curious glance as to why she was down here.

Lilliana followed Mick's directions and finally came to the ironing room.

She took a deep breath before stepping through the doorway.

It was another enormous room, where large ironing boards were attached to walls, with giant presses that let out continuous puffs of steam as they pressed clothes, or sheets, tablecloths, towels, aprons, doona-covers, hospital staff uniforms and any other linen.

Lilliana scanned the room, looking for Natalie, walking further down until she finally spotted her.

Her long brown hair was piled up on top of her head, frizzing in the steam and the dampness of the room.

Right here we go, she thought to herself as she walked right up to Natalie's station.

"Oh goody, a visit from you." Natalie drawled, as she slammed the hot press down, steaming a set of towels. "And to what do I owe this unexpected treat?"

Lilliana knew attitude would flow in abundance with this conversation and was ready for it. Folding her arms, she prayed Natalie would be honest.

"I want to know what happened earlier today when you, Marcus and Allie, took Sapphire out."

"Nothing to tell, that hasn't already been told to the right people." Natalie shrugged carelessly.

Lilliana shook her head. "Look here Natalie, for once in your life, do the right thing. Tell the truth. Allie has been a friend to you. She's your goddamn therapist for Christ sake! What, you want to see her hurt, see her locked up? I know she would not have shot at Sapphire! What are you not telling them?"

Lilliana had taken a step closer, frowning furiously at the girl whom she had struggled to form any kind of relationship with for almost a decade.

Natalie took the towels and placed them on a large table behind her, where another lady took them, placing them in a large basket on wheels.

"Seriously, Allie won't get punished. None of your brat pack gets what they deserve. I think it's about time one of you do."

"This isn't a game Natalie! Stop being such a bitch, stop making bullshit assumptions, and tell me what happened!" Lilliana had taken another step forward, the two were nearly nose to nose. Natalie, being a head taller, so Lilliana had to tilt her head back to stare angrily into her eyes.

"What, a little thing like you, is going to what, make me? Please, get over yourself you little slut. You think I don't know you are sucking Damon's dick? Letting him fuck you up the ass? Why do you think that Sapphire wants you out of the picture? She wants Damon all to herself!" Natalie smirked down at Lilliana, enjoying the startled look on her face.

"Yeah, people talk to me, it's amazing what information one can gather when you seem irrelevant. And it is amazing what you can tell people, when they make you relevant."

Lilliana pulled her hand back and slapped Natalie hard across the face. The crack, shockingly loud.

Natalie slowly nodded and did not raise her hand to touch the hot, red mark.

"Truth hurts, doesn't it?"

"Not like this is going to." Lilliana slapped Natalie again, as hard as she could where the first slap landed. It felt so good, wrong, but good.

Natalie's eyes narrowed and as quick as lightening, snapped out her hand and grabbed Lilliana's wrist, jerking her hand towards the hot press.

Lilliana's back was up against the hard board, Natalie slammed against her, pinning her in place, her stomach hard up against Lilliana's, her strong arms wrapping about her.

"Bloody get off me Natalie!" Lilliana snarled at the heavier girl.

"Not yet princess Lilly." Natalie had twisted Lilliana's arm behind her back and was holding it down on the press board, pushing all her weight down into her.

She grabbed the top of the press and started to slowly bring it down towards Lilliana's hand.

"Natalie do not do this. You will be punished; you know you will!" Lilliana tried to sound calm but was slightly terrified of the pain a burn like this would inflict.

"I've always wanted something from you, and you will either give it to me, or I will burn your hand into a crispy crème, and your friend will be in lock-up forever, or dead." Natalie had an evil glint in her eye.

"What the hell Natalie!" Lilliana shook her head.

"Yeah, that's right, I'm YOUR bitch now, and I want those fucking lips of yours on mine." Natalie smirked, enjoying the thrill of seeing Lilliana panic, the shocked look on her face. She almost laughed.

"Fuck off Fran; this is not your problem." Natalie snapped out at a younger girl, had walked over. She did not take her eyes off Lilliana's face.

"Not going to happen Natalie."

"Really? Too bad then." Natalie quickly slammed the press down, sending hot flames of intense pain through Lilliana's hand before releasing the top upright.

Lilliana screamed, feeling like she had just fallen into a raging pit of fire.

"Just one little kiss Lilliana." Natalie leaned down a fraction. "What's it going to hurt, when it could do so much good?"

A quick flash shot through Lilliana's mind. If Natalie wasn't so ugly on the inside, she would be quite a pretty girl.

As Natalie's lips were about to claim Lilliana's, Lilliana turned her face away and Natalie's warm, wet lips collided with her cheek.

"Again then." Natalie reached back for the press lid; her body squashing Lilliana's hard.

"No! Wait!" Lilliana cried, trying to talk around the intense pain.

"Oh, what for?" Natalie tilted her head to one side.

"You tell me about Allie, you tell me the truth, and I'll do it." Lilliana's hand was throbbing. Her arm was hurting, being held at such an awkward angle. She could feel Natalie's belly pressed up hard against hers. Soft and warm.

"You kiss me like a wet dream, and I'll tell you anything you want to hear." Natalie said, her breath uneven at the thought.

"Just the truth Natalie. That's all I want. None of your bullshit. Let me go first."

Natalie slowly shook her head. "Not a fucking chance sweetheart." She bent her head down and her lips touched Lilliana's.

Lilliana waited; Natalie's lips were very soft.

"You need to kiss me, Princess." Natalie whispered against her lips.

Lilliana closed her eyes and kissed Natalie quickly, then leaning back so their lips broke contact.

"Am I about to have an orgasm? Kiss me till I am wet, or you get nothing."

Natalie brought her hand up to Lilliana's throat and stroked her neck, her other hand holding Lilliana's arm behind her back pressed down on the board.

Lilliana released a furious breath and nodded. She didn't know how much time she had and wanted this over quick.

She pushed her lips up against Natalie's. Her lips parted a fraction and she quickly licked Natalie's top lip, and then kissed her again.

Natalie moaned, her hand slipped down Lilliana's throat to gently cup her breast, opening her lips she deepened the kiss pushing her tongue deep into Lilliana's mouth.

Lilliana fought to pull back and jerked her head away. Natalie was breathing heavily, looking down into Lilliana's eyes.

She let Lilliana go abruptly and reached behind her for her next item to press.

Lilliana stepped away quickly grabbing her sore, burnt hand, and looked at it. Angry red welts appearing.

She glanced at Natalie, a frown upon her face. "Well?"

Natalie pressed the next item, and then looked at Lilliana. Her eyes roaming down her body, at her groin area. "I bet you taste just as sweet all over. Mm." She licked her lips, then grinned at Lilliana.

"God help me Natalie, if you do not tell me about Allie right this second I will knock you out!"

"All right keep your pants on. Then again…" Natalie stopped, as Lilliana had taken a step forward, a look of murder in her eyes.

"Alright, alright. Look, we'd been out for an hour and Marcus was filling Sapphire in about all our activities, programs, blah blah blah. She grilled Allie on questions about Christopher while we were having a bit of an archery comp. Then Marcus said he'd thought he'd seen a boar in the distance and took off to circle it, just in case it came our way. Sapphire had told Allie she wanted Christopher and would take him against his will anyhow, and how this facility was too well stocked where others were lacking. She apparently didn't care what Damon paid out to Christopher's charity. She basically said she'd have who she wanted, and in her position, no one would stop her. That she was arranging for the plane to arrive tomorrow with her people to get everything into place" Natalie shrugged.

"And she said this in your hearing, to Allie?" Lilliana asked, her hand burning.

"Yeah well, I was looking busy elsewhere like I couldn't hear. And then afterwards she made me swear to go along with her version, or she'd send me off to the worst location she could think of."

"And?" Lilliana waited for the punch line.

"And, there was a boar, mind you, it wasn't anywhere near Sapphire, and Allie took the shot. Missed Sapphire, then Sapphire did not miss Allie. End of saga."

"Why didn't you just tell the truth Natalie? Honestly, what the hell is wrong with you? We, all of us, could have been a good friend to you. Why?" Lilliana shook her head.

"Coz it's more fun this way princess. Now fuck off, or I'll make you lick me out."

Lilliana slowly shook her head at Natalie. "I've said it once, and I'll say it again, you are a complete bitch Natalie." Lilliana hurried out of the room.

"Tell me something I don't know!" Natalie called out, unfazed.

Lilliana cradled her hand to her chest. First she had to get something to stop this insane pain, then she would find Marcus.

She headed toward the hospital.

CHAPTER 13

Christopher stood when he saw Lilliana walk in, holding her hand protectively to her chest.

"What happened, are you hurt?"

"I'll be fine Christopher I just need some cream. We can relax. There was a boar, Natalie confessed." Lilliana pressed the buzzer on the unattended Nurses' station.

"What, did you break your hand smashing her face to get a confession?" He grinned, feeling lighter now that they had a confession to back Allie's story up.

Lilliana ducked her head and shook it.

Leon walked around the corner and noticed Lilliana holding her hand. He crossed over to her, noting the absence of staff.

He reached across and held out his hand for hers.

She looked up at him as she held her hand out. He gently took it in his and turned her hand over so he could look at her palm.

He smiled down at her. "Ouch. Come with me."

He turned around and walked down the corridor coming to a side room where there was a stretcher bed to sit on with steps to get up, and many shelves holding all sorts of creams and bandages.

"Please, sit." He pointed to the bed.

She perched up whilst he rummaged through and collected the required medicines.

"What happened?" He gently wiped her hand with a damp sterilizer pad.

She looked at him. Handsome Leon. He had always been such a strong, good friend.

"Oh, I fell on an ironing press." She smiled as his eyes met hers. "Long story."

He looked at her for a few more seconds, then pulled the lid off one of the tubes of cream and started to apply it.

"Lilliana, about that kiss." He started quietly.

"Please, do not apologize. I'm sorry if I ever led you on to believe, that I had deeper feelings for you, other than friendship." Lilliana reached out her good hand and touched his arm. "You have always been so good to me Leon." She finished quietly.

He stilled and looked down at her. "I had hoped at one stage we would have been more than just friends Lilly. But I see now it was my mistake. Not yours." He smiled. "Still friends?"

"As if you need to ask me that." She shook her head smiling. "Always, I will always be your friend. Even if you go to Australia."

He finished the second cream application before spraying a healing mist.

"Well, that's at least six months away Lilly. If I go." He popped the items back in the tray and turned to Lilliana, holding out his hand to help her down.

As they walked out of the room she asked. "How is Allie doing?"

"Dr Ryan is still working on her, but he has a good team. The next twenty-four hours are crucial. Did you know she will be sent to

Black Ops after surgery?"

"What? Oh that is beyond ridiculous, I have proof that she was not intending to hurt Sapphire." Lilliana felt pinpricks of panic and outrage. Black Ops, Allie! Seriously?

"Yes, well they have had a team of Johnson's men, Marcus, and Sapphire, in Damon's office the past two hours sorting it all out. Rachael is as mad as hell. Said she would have taken the shot and not missed if only she knew how." Leon shrugged. "Sapphire is definitely not a popular person right now."

"Not surprisingly." Lilliana headed off, calling over her shoulder.

"Thank you Leon, the pain is almost gone."

"You are welcome." He watched as she walked off, and then turned on his heel to go see how Allie was doing.

***

Josephine spotted Lilliana storming towards Damon's office. Noting her eyes full of purpose. She quickly raced towards her and grabbed her arm.

"Oh, Jose." Lilliana pulled her friend in for a quick hug, not oblivious to the rage that marred her usually happy features. "What's happening now?"

"You wouldn't believe it, Sapphire's calling for the death penalty. She's put the call out to her people, they should be here this afternoon. If that bitch kills Allie, I promise you, she will not be leaving here with her life!" Josephine was as furious as Lilliana had ever seen her.

She rubbed her friends arm. "Look, I need to go in there, I know she's lying. There was a boar, I have Natalie's word that Allie wasn't trying to kill Sapphire."

Another raised voice could be heard from the room. It almost sounded like thunder. Damon. And he was beyond furious.

The door opened and five of Johnson's men stormed out, Johnson in the rear.

Lilliana moved her head so she could see into the room. Cam and Damon were standing in the middle of the room. Arms folded. Scowls on their faces.

Sapphire calmly seated, looking like a lady of leisure, apart from her foot tapping impatiently on the wooden floor.

Lilliana and Johnson exchanged a nod as he walked past her.

She walked into Damon's office, Josephine on her heels. The door slid shut behind them.

She looked down at Sapphire as she walked past her and right up to Damon. She did not touch him, as much as she wanted to, but stood close and looked him in his beautiful, deep blue eyes. He too looked down at her with a hidden wanting.

"What's up Lilliana?" Cam asked, watching Josephine standing hesitantly near the door.

"I have new information to prove that, that woman," she turned and stared at Sapphire, "lied about Allie."

Sapphire stood, scoffing. "Oh, and like that is going to help. I think my word will be above any little rejects of the world. Wouldn't you agree Damon?"

Damon's eyes flicked from Lilliana's beautiful face to his cousin's, then back again.

"Are you actually serious?" Lilliana was furious with this woman's care factor. Did she seriously believe she could lie about this situation, and think that was the end of it? Not on her watch.

"Are you going to deny that the boar was there? That Allie was in fact, shooting at the boar and her intentions were to save your life?" Lilliana took another step towards Sapphire. Her rage increasing.

To imagine Allie being put down like a poor stray, wild animal, or having to spend time, if not life, in the Black Ops with those despicable people of society! Well she was not going to let that happen!

"Oh please, no one saw a boar. That little rag was trying to kill me so I wouldn't take her boyfriend away. Simple." Sapphire raised a sexy blonde eyebrow, and folded her slim arms, staring at Lilliana.

"The fact is, my dear Lilliana, my people are coming in an hour's time. I will take from this establishment, whoever I want. You have an hour to go pack your bags and say your farewells. Understood?"

Lilliana's vision clouded with fury, but she knew what would clear that vision. Stepping forward she closed the distance and slapped Sapphire as hard as she could across her perfect, cold face.

Josephine's intake of breath warned Cam that she was on her way to defend Lilliana, and he grabbed her arm as she briskly marched forward, tucking her securely under his shoulder. He knew Damon and Lilliana could handle themselves.

Sapphire raised a hand to her face. She looked at Damon and shook her head.

"I think we'll need to train her all over again when she comes to Russia, but we have certain methods that only need to be used once, and she will never step out of line again."

Lilliana went to leap at Sapphire, planning on strangling her, but Damon wrapped his strong arms around her waist, holding her close, giving her no room to move.

Her hands went to his wrists, trying to loosen them. "Please Damon, just let me end her!" She was so furious. Never in her life had she been as physically violent as she had this day.

"Cam get her out of here please," Damon nodded towards Sapphire.

Cam squeezed Josephine gently before releasing her and grabbed Sapphire by the arm and jerked her out of the room.

She looked her shoulder and yelled in glee, "I'll see you on the plane Miss Lilliana!"

Josephine threw a worried look at Damon and Lilliana as she quickly followed her husband out of the room.

Once the door closed, Damon buried his face into the back of Lilliana's neck, breathing her in through her silky hair. His arms loosened, giving her room to relax.

"Calm down baby, you're not going anywhere. We have her." He brushed her hair away, so he could run his lips along her neck.

She turned in his arms, shaking her head. "Poor Allie. If she doesn't make it…" She could not finish that sentence. She slid her hands up his chest, tipping her head back so she could look him in the eyes. She reached up, as he leaned down, and their lips met in a warm, soft glide, sending sensations deep down into the pit of her stomach.

She pressed herself closer, her fingers twisting into his hair near his collar, pulling him deeper against her mouth.

His tongue swept into her mouth, as he deepened the kiss, before he pulled away.

He ran a hand along her jaw, then down her throat, stroking her soft skin, his other hand stroking her back, eyes boring into hers.

She reached up to stroke his face.

"My beautiful girl, how I love you." He murmured quietly, noticing her red palm. "What happened?" His voice held such concern.

Lilliana shook her head, indicating it was nothing. "Why does she think she's taking me Damon, if you are clearly saying she is not? And what do you mean, you have her?" Lilliana asked.

His face darkened. He shook his head. He bent, kissed her quickly, then stepped back and walked over to his desk. He sat and reached for his phone.

"Damon, what aren't you telling me?" Lilliana was worried about his expression.

He picked up his phone and looked up at her. "It is better for you, and I, that you don't know. Now please Lilliana, I need to make some calls. Go check on Allie."

She looked down at him. Even with a concerned, angry expression, he remained handsome, in such a dark, appealing way.

She couldn't imagine what he had to deal with this day. But she knew he always had a full plate and did not want to add to it. She smiled a little, nodding, and walked out, heading towards the hospital.

***

Cam walked back into Damon's office fifty minutes later.

Richard stood up from the chair opposite Damon, nodded to Cam and left.

"What decisions have you come to?" he watched Richard leave the room, before turning his attention back to his brother.

Damon leaned back in his chair, placing his hands behind his neck.

"We can't let her get away with taking people who don't want to go. Our people who want a change, sure, no problem. They are happy to go in the next two, to six months, once placements are organized. Sapphire's people will be here soon, but we'll deal with them. Shouldn't be too hard, they won't be highly positioned, probably low-level." He rubbed a hand over his face.

"I have an hour to do what I have to do Cam. After the information given to me by Richard, that woman has no right to have the position she has. It disgusts me that she still has so much power after all she has done."

Cam frowned. "So, Richard does have his good qualities after all. Details?"

"I think it best if you don't know." Damon looked a little pale. He stood and poured a glass of water. He drained it, placed the glass back down on the tray, and ran a hand through his hair.

"Damon, come on! We are supposed to be in this together. Whatever it is, I promise you, I can handle it." Cam waited to see if Damon would spill the beans, hoping he would share the burden.

Damon leaned his hands against the desk, dropping his head, shaking it, before looking up at his brother, who looked more like their father than he did.

"It's not good news Cam. Not at all." He straightened and folded his arms.

"Richard has informed me that in the past, our father, amongst other family members, including Sapphire, were involved in several illegal operations that made money for all the establishments. Apparently, he paid Richard to drug Mother, for years, so he could continue to have affairs and perform these illegal acts. In the end, she suffered a heart attack which killed her. He shrugged. "It goes deeper Cam, but I don't have time to go into it all. Basically since I have taken, cleanly, over here, some of the other establishments have suffered money loss."

"Bloody Richard! How the hell did he get away with this?" Cam was furious. "And our Father, Damon?" He was grieved by the information.

"Our Father threatened to send him to another establishment if he didn't obey our fathers demand. Apparently, Richard was in love with another doctor here at the time and did not want to leave her. So, he drugged Mother. He has always regretted it. He didn't have to share this with me Cam. But he has given me information I can legally use in my position, as Head Heir to this establishment, against Sapphire and I intend to use it to its full potential."

Cam's mouth dropped open. "You mean…" He couldn't say it. Not yet.

"Yeah, that's what I mean." Damon picked up his phone.

"Thomas, clear everyone out of the stables, please make sure Zero is in his stall. Be careful with him, then clear out too, for an hour. Yes. Thank you, Thomas." Damon dropped the phone back down.

Damon looked across at Cam. "This is between us Cameron, no one can ever know. Deal?"

Cam nodded. "No one will ever know the truth from me Damon."

"Right, tell Sapphire I'm down at the stables. I want her there in five." He strode out the door, as Cam took off in the opposite direction.

***

Lilliana stayed with Christopher when they wheeled Allie out of the hospital ward and up towards the Black Ops unit.

She looked tiny and frail; her soft, blue hair lay in long layers around her head on the white pillow, she had the look of paleness one does when under heavy sedation.

Christopher clung to Lilliana's hand, swallowing hard.

"It's all right Christopher, I will go up with her, make sure she is settled in. Okay?"

"Yeah, thanks Lilliana. It sucks not having that clearance. I'll see you after dinner, you can let me know how she's doing." He squeezed her hand before releasing it, then took off upstairs to get on with his job.

Lilliana followed the team upstairs, and after twenty minutes had Allie settled in a room, which wasn't at all unlike a hospital room. The fact that it had padded walls and Lilliana knowing it was a cell, didn't make her happy for her friend.

She felt a large hand on her shoulder and looked around to see Johnson, who had arrived with Dr Clair.

"How are you going?" he asked quietly.

"Better than poor Allie here." She turned her attention to Dr Clair. "Just so you know, she is innocent and should not be treated like a criminal in any way."

"Yes well, we treat all equally here, until Damon decides her final punishment, she will be kept in this room."

"Did the arrow miss her spine?" Lilliana prayed her friend would recover in every possible way.

"The doctor will be up in an hour to give me all the details, he needed a short break after so many hours in surgery." Clair said.

"Of course. Well, I'm going out for a bit, but please, Johnson if you can, find me if you have any news." She smiled at the man she thought so highly of.

"Of course Lilliana."

Needing some fresh air, she took a deep breath and decided to head over to the stables, knowing the magic of her horse's company would help her relax.

***

Damon stood alone in the stables, dressed completely in black; boots, jeans, a tight tee shirt and leather gloves.

His hands behind his back, staring down the length of the stables.

His mind was reeling with some of the overwhelming information Richard had shared with him. His mind, black with ugly thoughts flowing through it. He was furious on the inside, appearing calm on the outside.

He looked devilishly sexy, dark, and dangerous. That was the first thought that ran through Sapphire's mind as she stepped into the stables and headed down towards him.

"Well, all alone and lots of hay to tumble around in. I might let you keep your Lilliana Damon, if I get to have you too." She purred, walking on.

Lilliana froze outside of Beast's stall, hearing Sapphire, but not wanting to be seen. She crept around the corner and sat on a hay bale, keeping out of view, but wanting to hear what Damon would say.

"Well, we can't always get what we want, can we Sapphire?" His voice was chilled. Colder than Lilliana had ever heard it.

Sapphire stood a few feet from him. "Pretend you are your horse Damon and fuck me like it's mating season. It's simple. You know I've always wanted you." She took a step forward.

Lilliana peeked around the corner, feeling like a naughty girl, spying on her parents fighting.

Sapphire ran her hand up Damon's chest. His gloved hand snapped out, like a striking snake, and grabbed her wrist in a tight, painful hold.

Sapphire sucked in her breath. "Oh yeah baby, you know I love it rough." She let out a throaty laugh, as her other hand ran down and cupped his balls through his jeans.

Lilliana was furious but stayed where she was. What was Damon's play here?

Damon grabbed her intruding hand and jerked it away from him.

She pouted, not attractively. "Come on baby, don't play hard to get."

"I know about you, you hypercritical bitch! I know everything you've done. You're a rapist! A murderer! A pimp!" His voice got colder with each accusation.

Sapphire gave a nervous laugh. "I can tell you now honey, there's no way you'd know everything." She raised an eyebrow.

"Do you really think you are going to get away with your crimes? I can make it so public you will be shamed forever and be locked up with the worst of them." Damon's words were clipped.

Sapphire had the sense to look uncomfortable.

"You wouldn't, I'd spill the beans about your Daddy so fast you would be out of here in a flash." She almost looked smug. "Oh, didn't know about darling Daddy killing Mummy, now, did we?"

"Yes, I've recently been told about my disgusting Father. But that has nothing to do with me. We are discussing you, and what I'm going to do about you."

He slowly pulled out a pocketknife from his back pocket and flicked it open. He watched as Sapphire's eyes widened in shock and held her wrist more firmly as she tried to pull away from him. He jerked her closer and with a swift slicing action ran the blade along her shoulder to chest.

The wound was not inflicted to kill, but to fill the air, with the scent of blood.

She cried out in pain as blood seeped from the wound, struggling to get away from him.

He held her wrist and tugged her after him, towards a stall.

Opening the door, he went to fling her in.

"No, Damon, please, what are you going to do?" She sounded a little panicked.

Lilliana's breath was shallow, listening to the impending demise of Sapphire.

She heard Damon's response. "Meet Zero. He absolutely loathes new people, especially women. I'd usually say that's unfortunate, but today..."

"Well," Sapphire interrupted, "maybe he'll meet your precious Lilliana, and trample that beautiful face of hers, off her head"

Lilliana heard a loud slap, followed by Sapphire's moan.

"Did I forget to mention it is mating season. Your blood is going to send him into a frenzy. I will have no regrets killing you." she heard Damon say.

Lilliana froze. Could she allow Damon to do this? Murder? He had been through so much already these past few years.

"Damon," she called out, stepping from around the corner. She walked slowly towards him, uncertain, stopping a few feet away. "Lilliana, what are you doing here? I need you to leave. *Now!*" Damon looked worried and frustrated at the same time.

Lilliana couldn't take her eyes off his face. "What you are about to do Damon, can you live with this?" She spoke softly.

"I'm living with worse, trust me on that." He said quietly, with a hint of disgust in his voice, his eyes penetrating hers.

Sapphire struggled to get her hand free. She went to kick Damon hard in the balls, but he blocked it without looking.

"Can you live with being an accomplice to murder you little piece of work?" Sapphire snarled.

Lilliana pulled her gaze away from Damon to look at the beautiful blonde woman.

If she had done the things Damon accused her of, then she deserved to die. So many others must have suffered under her hands.

If Damon could live with what he was about to do, then she would support his decision.

"I can live with anything Damon decides." She glanced back at Damon.

He nodded. "Go, I need you to leave. You cannot witness this."

She stood, not wanting him to suffer this alone.

"Now Lilliana. Please!" he snapped, needing her to go. A plane could be heard in the distance.

She stared into his eyes before turning and walking away.

As she headed down along the stables she heard Sapphire's screams after Damon had pushed her into the stall with the unpredictable stallion, who immediately went into a stampeding frenzy, kicking and trampling the woman, till the screaming stopped and the thick smell of blood filled the air.

Lilliana ran the rest of the way out of the stables and along the pathway. The plane circled overhead before returning toward the runway.

She didn't realize she was being watched as she headed inside, going straight to her office to wait for news on Allie, or for Damon to find her.

***

Damon made it back to his rooms in time to shower and call Cam, before the siren sounded.

As Cam walked into Damon's room he pointed up to the sound system. "Looks like Thomas has found the unfortunate accident."

Damon ran his fingers through his damp hair. "Best get downstairs, I'm sure Johnson has greeted our guests by now. We should be there."

"Right, let's go," Cam said heading out the door, Damon on his heels.

Reaching the bottom levels after ten minutes, battling the wave of Given on the stairs, exiting different rooms to make it to the assembly hall, Damon and Cam strode into Damon's office.

They both froze in their tracks, as Johnson was talking to a man they had not seen in many years, and certainly not low level.

Tall like their father, ten years his junior. Dark and handsome. Their Uncle Seth. He turned his attention away from Johnson to turn and look at his nephews for the first time since they were young boys.

"Damon, Cameron. How are you both?"

Damon was the first to walk over and shake his uncle's hand. "Uncle Seth, it's good to see you again." He lied. "How are you?"

"Please Damon, if I recall correctly, you will be thirty in a fortnight. You may officially call me Seth." He firmly shook his hand, looking over his shoulder at Cameron.

Damon stepped back, to let Cam shake their Uncle's hand. "Cameron, I hear you went and got married. Sorry I couldn't make it. Business and all. Hope you understand?" He forced a smile, shaking Cams hand.

Cam forced a smile also, not mentioning that no invitation had been issued to his Uncle whatsoever.

"I see I have arrived to a shocking incident in your stables, regarding Sapphire. I'm told it was an accident." He walked over to the fireplace to glance over the objects decorating the mantel.

"After all the resistance Sapphire has faced during her stay at this facility." He turned to face them. "I'll be the judge of that."

"Resistance? Hardly Uncle." Damon said, not using the man's name. "We have many here who are very happy to go to other establishments. It is my duty to protect those that do not want to leave. And murder? No, I don't think so."

Seth watched Damon. All the reports seemed to be true.

He was very protective of his Given, fiercely loyal in his role.

His father had trained him well. He wondered if he delved into the evils his father had. Time would tell.

"In regard to Sapphire, I have been informed that she was shot at, and now, she is dead. I would say that's a clear indication that there are people here, who are not happy with all the good she was trying to achieve. I will find the person responsible for her death and they will be punished." He folded his arms, waiting for their reactions.

Cam shrugged. "I guess we could question the horse, but at this stage I don't understand neighing or horse snort." He held his hand up to Damon. "But you're the expert on horses' brother, maybe you could help Johnson question him?"

"Still the comedian of the family I see Cameron. Do you think the death of your cousin funny?" Seth asked in a voice filled with anger.

"Nope." Cam looked him square in the eye.

Johnson cleared his throat. "Sir," he addressed Damon, "I think we'd best get to assembly.

"Right." Damon agreed. "How do you want to do this?" He looked at his Uncle.

"Oh, let me worry about that. Shall we?" He walked out the door, leaving Cam and Damon to exchange a worried look.

***

Lilliana was sitting next to Jessica and Josephine up the front of the assembly hall, when the four men entered the room, going up on stage.

Lilliana's eyes widened as she noticed the strong family resemblance.

Josephine moved closer, whispering, "That's Cam and Damon's Uncle."

Lilliana watched Damon closely, wondering how he was feeling right now after the Sapphire incident.

His eyes met hers briefly before glancing out around the room, as the loud marching of boots in unison thumped against the hard-wooden floor, as a group of fifty or so armed-soldiers in black, filled the hall.

Jessica nervously folded her arms.

Seth stepped forward, holding up a hand, indicating that the soldiers halt. They did so, placing themselves evenly around the hall.

"My Name is Seth Night. My brother ran this establishment till his dying day, as my nephews do now." He indicated to Damon and Cam. "I came here today, to assist Ms Sapphire in relocating some of you. Unfortunately, there has been a ghastly incident in the stables and Ms Sapphire was killed. Whether this was an accident or murder, I will be here with my team to find out what has occurred. The murderer will not get away with killing an Official co-ordinator of the Givens establishments." His eyes roamed around the room.

Lilliana slipped lower in her chair, not liking the way he looked at any of them.

When his eyes dropped down to hers, she froze. It was like when Damon sometimes looked at her. Like he could see into her soul.

"I will begin interviewing people immediately, starting with you." He pointed right down at Lilliana.

She swallowed, not glancing at Damon. Not breathing. She felt Josephine take one hand, Jessica the other.

Muffled whispers floated around the room. Lilliana felt the need to calm some of the younger Given down, hoping they would be okay until the assembly ended.

"To help you all understand the horror of Sapphire's end, here is a picture of her to take with you. If someone has information about what they think may shed light on this case, please feel free to come share your thoughts with me."

He nodded to Johnson who flicked a remote switch in his hand and a hologram of Sapphire, appeared larger than life above the four men standing on the stage.

It was horrific. Her face trampled, half ripped off, showing a bloody skull, eye hanging out of its socket, her mouth appearing to be screaming. Her body bloodied and smashed.

Lilliana hoped she had died quickly. Whether she deserved the punishment Damon had inflicted, or not, it looked beyond brutal. She heard cries of anguish, along with people gasping in horror, and some of the more sensitive souls throwing up. She glanced behind her and noticed Penny, and a few of her friends, looking extremely distraught, along with some of the boys in their group.

She whispered to Jessica. "This is not good, there's a few that will need extra TLC from all of us this afternoon."

Jessica glanced around the room, nodding, "May as well get started."

Amongst the crowd, Ruth had thrown herself on the floor, screaming for the image to be taken down.

Lilliana quickly stood and went to walk over to Ruth.

She only got to the end of her row when the snapping of Seth's fingers had two soldiers in black, walking towards her. She quickly took two steps back, when they lurched forward and roughly grabbed her by her arms.

Jessica rushed forward, only to be stopped by more impending soldiers.

"Hey, back off!" Eric had stood and was hurriedly walking towards Lilliana.

She quickly shook her head as one of the other soldiers stepped forward and zapped Eric in the back with a Taser rod.

"No." Lilliana cried as Eric went down hard, smashing his face on the floor as he fell.

She glanced over at the stage and watched as Damon jumped down and headed straight towards her.

Leon was making sure Eric was alright, angry voices filled the hall.

Cam's eyes met Josephine's. He could see how furious she was.

Damon reached Lilliana and said to the men holding her. "Take it easy with her. She just wants to make sure that the young girls are alright.

There are a lot of fragile Given here." He glanced down at Lilliana. Her beautiful green eyes looked worried. He wanted to reach out and stroke her face.

He looked across at the stage and saw his Uncle watching them closely.

"Alright everyone," Cam called out, "back to class or work. If you need to be interviewed, Mr Night will get one of his staff to collect you. Do not be frightened or worried, we want everyone here to be reassured that we do not think Ms Sapphire was murdered, it is simply routine. Thank you for your time." He indicated that they could leave.

The room became bustling with people getting up to leave, looking distressed and uncomfortable as they navigated their way around the soldiers. Rachael was waiting for Johnson to approach her. He reached her side and gently took her arm, leading her to a corner of the room.

"Should I know something?" She looked worried.

He quickly stroked her cheek before turning his face away, looking at Seth on the stage. "No Rachael," he said softly, "all will be well. You just go back to the hospital and charm that prick if he comes your way." He smiled at her, as her fingers squeezed his.

"I have to get back to this mess." He looked around at the distressed faces.

Rachael nodded and quickly kissed his cheek before taking off in the direction of the hospital.

Seth approached Damon. "It looks like your office will do for questioning to start with. Shall we?" He smiled and strolled past the men holding Lilliana. Cam and Johnson in tow.

***

Josephine grabbed Cam's arm as they walked past the library.

He stopped, looking down into her warm, concerned brown eyes.

"Hey Baby," he said softly.

"What the hell do they want with Lilly?" she hissed.

He pulled her towards him, holding her close and kissed the top of her soft, brown curls.

"Don't fret sweetheart, they've got nothing on her."

He kissed her softly, glad it wasn't her in the line of fire with his

Uncle. She kissed him back, squeezing his arm. "Look after her." She ordered before they came apart, and he left to head into Damon's office.

***

As Cam entered he saw three things clearly, simultaneously.

Damon, looking beyond pissed off.

Lilliana, looking more scared than he'd ever seen her, and Seth pacing, looking like the cat that'd got to lick the last bit of cream out of the bowl.

"This is cosy." Cam strolled in, the door closing behind him. He thought he would go with the cool, laid back approach, hoping to knock Seth off his arrogant perch a tad.

Lilliana was seated in between the two black-clad guards. She was sitting forward, knees together, hands clasped around them.

"Seriously Uncle, you don't need the armed guard with Lilliana. She is one of our finest role models and I'm sure would be more than willing to assist you on this investigation." Cam walked over to the fruit bowl sitting on Damon's bookcase, and grabbing an apple munched loudly as he sat on the arm of a chair, he winked at Lilliana.

"Thank you Cameron. I can assure you, I know enough about Miss Lilliana here, as it was under my instruction that Sapphire bring her to our Russian facility." Seth turned his gaze towards the beautiful young woman.

He could truly see what all the fuss was about. He strolled over and sat directly opposite her.

Her smell was pure heaven. He wondered what she'd taste like.

He'd been married to his wife for thirty-five years, and often had affairs with younger women. Younger men too if the truth be told.

He could sense Damon, standing in the corner ready to lunge forward to protect her if anyone so much as breathed on her.

He could understand his nephew's obsession.

He sat back in his chair, waiting for Lilliana to look at him. She didn't, so he started with, "So, shall I address you as Miss Lilliana, your Given name, Dark Angel, your modelling name, or Doctor?"

He clasped his fingers in his lap, as her eyes lifted to his.

"Lilliana is fine." She said quietly, hoping not to draw too much attention.

"Let me tell you what I know, Lilliana. You were an extremely gifted student, arriving here after a horrific tale of abuse and suffering. You worked hard and dedicated a lot of your free time volunteering before you became the qualified Therapist, etcetera that you are today. Plus, a beautiful young model when the desire takes hold. How am I doing so far?" He smiled.

Lilliana glanced at Damon. It was so hard seeing the older, handsome man, smile a similar smile to the one she saw on her loves face.

The whole thing disturbed her.

Damon stood behind his Uncle; arms folded across his chest. He nodded at her, letting her know anything she said would be okay.

"You're doing fine, only I don't model when I desire, I model when I'm asked." She noted Johnson looking uncomfortable with her answer. Or perhaps it was just the entire situation?

She returned her gaze back at Seth.

"Oh, I see. So, you go above and beyond for the greater good of your community?"

Lilliana shrugged. "Everything we do at this establishment is for the greater good. All of us spend our time helping others, a lot of us give our free time to continue helping other sections of our community if need be." She knew she was waffling but couldn't help herself due to her nerves.

Seth nodded. "So if you were asked to fit in more modelling around your patients, you would?" He waited.

Her eyes went to Damon, who nodded quickly.

"Yes."

"Well, let's hope you get that chance to do more for your community, and don't end up in the Black Ops division with your friend." He smiled, liking the way her beautiful skin paled.

"Can we just cut to the chase Uncle?" Damon snapped out. "Lilliana has many people to see to this afternoon." He defended.

Seth turned around slowly to look at his handsome nephew.

No wonder Sapphire had wanted him so badly. If he wasn't his nephew, he'd almost feel the same way.

He turned back to face Lilliana. "Do you often go to the stables in the middle of the day?"

"If I'm lucky enough to get a break during the day, I find it relaxes me and enables me to be more present for all those that need me."

"And do you often run away from them?" He waited.

"Yes, if I lose track of time and I'm in a hurry." She said quickly, forcing herself to sit still and not rub her neck, or fold her arms.

"Really, and what was I seeing you, run from, or to, this day as my plane flew over, Mm?" He leaned forward, watching her closely.

Lilliana did not miss a beat. She reached forward, taking the glass of water Johnson had filled for her when they first entered. She took a mouthful, watching Seth over the top of the glass and draining it, set it back down.

"I was visiting my horse, as I'd had some upsetting news, and the reason I was running, is because I was hurrying back to the hospital to see how my friend was doing." She answered smoothly, not at all uncomfortable with the lie. She would lie till the cows came home to protect Damon.

Seth nodded. "Alright then. Did you see Sapphire enter, talk to her?" Lilliana shook her head, wondering whether Damon or Johnson had taken care of the CCTV that ran throughout the stables. She was certain they would have.

"Lilliana," he said her name, liking the way it rolled smoothly off his tongue. "Did you see her?"

"No." she answered, shaking her head once more. Her dark green eyes met his blue ones steadily, hoping this would be over soon.

"Right. Well, off you go, back to work. Just be ready to be available at any time if I need to speak with you again." He enjoyed her view from the front but watching her walk off was just as enjoyable.

He noted Cam scowling at him and chuckled.

Damon headed out the door behind Lilliana. "Oh Damon." Seth called out.

Damon turned to face him, "Yes Uncle?"

"Don't be too long, we have forty interviews to get through. Thomas, your head stable vet guy, will be joining us in a few moments."

Damon nodded and quickly turned following Lilliana out of the room and down the corridor.

Once they were out of sight from all, he watched her sag against the wall. Her head fell back against it, eyes closed. She let out a long sigh.

Her eyes opened as his hands went around her face.

"Lilliana." His lips brushed her forehead.

Her arms went around his waist; she breathed him in, fingers stroking his back.

"Are you alright love?" he placed a finger under her chin, tilting her face up, so her eyes could meet his.

"Yes." She felt centred as she gazed into his eyes, like they grounded her. "Are you?"

He pulled her into his arms, running his large, strong hands along her back. He kissed her hair. "If you are alright, I'm alright love." He pulled her back and bent so his lips could find her raised, willing ones.

They kissed quickly, deeply, before he pulled away. His hands framed her face, taking her in.

She nodded, letting him know all would be well.

He dropped his hands and quickly walked off, back to the interviewing.

He arrived just as Thomas did.

"Hi Sir." Thomas nodded.

"Hello Thomas, please come in." Damon indicated for Thomas to go in ahead of him.

"Ah, Thomas. Please sit." Seth stood near the fireplace. Hands placed behind his back.

Thomas sat, not looking uncomfortable whatsoever. Which seemed to be the other man's intention. He sat crossing an ankle over his knee, like he'd seen Damon do many times. A relaxed, confident pose he liked to think.

"What can I do to help you Mr Night?" He asked in a very friendly manner.

Seth wanted to chuckle. A very loyal man here to be sure.

"Just wondering where you were this day when a murder occurred in your stables?" Seth asked.

"Ah, yes. I was down in the back pasture doing stock take with a few of my hands. It's this time of year we often go through our feeds, grains and such. It is a real shame I wasn't in the stables at the time Ms Sapphire came for a visit, I could have warned her about Zero. A real shame." Thomas nodded his head, looking perfectly sorry.

"And have you any idea how the video feed got cut off?" Seth tapped his fingers on the mantel.

"Yes Sir, we have a family of Vermillion Flycatchers that took nest near the main power cord. It appears rats got up there to get the young ones and chewed right through the cords. Not too cheap to fix, but, I should have it all sorted by the end of the day." Thomas nodded, looking very helpful.

"Right then. That shall be all for now Thomas." Seth sighed. This was getting him nowhere.

Thomas got up and smiling at Cam and Damon, left the room.

And that was how the next few hours went for Seth. Very unhelpful, happy, loyal people.

He wasn't getting the answers he desired.

CHAPTER 14

Lilliana had two scheduled groups. Dr Hillary sat in for one and unfortunately, Dr Richard sat in for the other. She truly missed Allie's presence for that session.

It was getting late when she had finally gotten around to finishing reviewing all the files on Scott, that Johnson had emailed her.

Hours of reading documented activity and looking through photographs had her head spinning with the many Casino events. Amongst some of the photographs, were pictures of her father, her mother and herself. She certainly had vague memories of the casino, and the longer she looked at the pictures, memories flooded back to her.

There was one photograph capturing a big event. She knew it was her Mother in the photograph holding a little dark-haired girls hand. She knew it was her. There was a small boy next to her, looking up at her.

Was it Scott? It looked so like him.

She had been through all the files and could not believe the bold, cold facts and evidence indicated that her father had many illegal affair, that looked to include the casino owner's wife? Was Scott her brother? Her father's son?

She leapt up from her desk and headed out towards the Psych ward. After the eye scan, she walked in quickly, murmuring a hello to the person behind the desk as she signed in.

She took a deep breath before knocking and walked into Scott's room. She stood waiting for him to acknowledge her.

He glanced up from his book and smiled.

She smiled back. "Hello Scott. How are you today?" she asked, genuinely wanting to know. Amongst a thousand other things.

He nodded his head, whispering. "Good."

She walked over and sat in a cosy chair opposite his bed, where he was perched. He placed the book down so he could focus on her.

"I think we need to have a talk." She smiled. "Where, hopefully you actually talk to me."

Her smile was beautiful, just like how she looked in the photographs. His breath quickened.

She held out a hand, mistaking his excitement for nervousness.

"It's alright Scott. Please, relax. It's just you and me here. No one else." She nodded, trying to assure him.

"I am relaxed." He said quietly.

"Good. I was wondering if you still have those drawings, the ones you showed me last time?" She was hopeful.

He nodded and got up, walking over to a drawer and opening it, he pulled a stack of papers out.

There were so many. He walked back and handed them to her. She took them, smiling thank you, as he turned and sat back down on the bed.

She flicked through them, searching for one in particular, enjoying the others for what they were.

A picture of four steer's feet got her attention. It was quite unusually beautiful. Different. There were others, of animals, faces, grotesque drawings of twisted bodies in sexual positions, spiders with human eyes. Many of Lilliana. And then, the one she'd been looking for.

The pile of human bodies. Naked. Their faces twisted in pain, screaming, clawing to escape their impending death, and then finally, the familiar face. Her father's.

She held the picture around and tapped his face, looking at Scott.

"Do you know this man?" Her green eyes met his.

He nodded. "Yes, he is our Father." He said simply.

Lilliana nodded and swallowed. "Was he here this night, or did you draw him from memory?"

"Yes, he was there that night. Now he is dead." Scott didn't blink.

Lilliana dropped the picture on top of the others, the air rushing out of her lungs in surprise at his candidness. She placed them on the table beside her.

Right, she told herself, be calm. You are not the patient here, he is.

She smiled at him, hoping it didn't look like a crazy person's smile who was about to lose it.

"So, my brother." She nodded. "Is that fact, or fiction?"

"Oh, it's fact alright. In time, my mother let me know that the bastard who repeatedly raped her and beat, her wasn't my real father. That my real father had connections and was powerful. That I had a sister who was one of the world's most favourite models. I remembered you, from when I was little. You came for special events, when your father had a political thing on. Your mother was always busy with the ladies. She was a good person your mother. Always had time to give me a cuddle. But your father. He was a sick demented fuck bag."

Lilliana was shocked. Not so much with what was coming out of Scott's mouth, but the fact that he'd said so much in such a short space of time. It certainly had to be a good thing, progress for sure.

She nodded, letting him know it was alright to continue.

He leaned back on the bed, appearing comfortable. "Apparently, I was conceived when you were six. My parents hosted orgies funded by our father. People paid the big dollars for sex, drugs, and any sexy little young male or female." He leaned forward, a look of disgust on his face. "He was no better than the filth that took you. When your disappearance hit the news Lilliana, then three months later your placement with the Given, my mother couldn't stop laughing. Said it was ridiculously ironic that the daughter from one of the biggest drug and orgy organisers was taken herself." Scott watched, as Lilliana went very pale.

She stood and paced the room, pushing her hand through her hair.

"Does it never end?" She whispered. "The deceit, the lies, the filth?" She turned to face Scott. "How did they all die?"

"I heard one of the coroner guys say something about poison." Scott lied as easily as she had earlier to Seth.

Lilliana nodded. "I am sorry Scott; I have to go." She walked over and squeezed his hand.

He stood suddenly, frightening her with his speed. She stepped back, not sure of his next move.

His eyes looked sad as he shook his head. "Don't ever be afraid of me, for I will never hurt you my sister." He reached out a hand, taking her small one in his larger one.

"Sorry," she smiled. "I am a little jumpy today. At least I know why your eyes are so familiar." She squeezed his hand back.

"Yes," he said quietly, "just like yours."

He let go of her hand and walked backwards, sitting on the bed.

"I will see you later. Maybe after a few more sessions we can talk about you going to main house?"

He nodded. "That would be good. Thank you."

She smiled as she exited the room, leaning against the door as it closed beside her, her smile faded.

***

Lilliana was relieved to close herself in her office for five minutes of peace.

She poured a cold water and downed it fast, then poured another before walking over to her Buddha and sat down to gaze up at him.

Scott. Her brother.

Her father. Dead.

Her mother? How was her mother handling all this? Obviously, it had been months that her mother had had to deal with heartache.

Maybe years if she'd known about the affair.

What a mess.

Now that she knew about Scott, she would do everything in her power to help him, but then she was going to do that anyway.

She sighed, finished her water and walking over to her desk, picked up her phone and dialled three numbers.

After a few rings the phone picked up.

"Damon Night." His voice snapped crisply over the phone.

"Damon, it's Lilliana." she said quietly, hoping he was alright.

"How are you sweetheart?" He was obviously alone.

"I have just found out that Scott is my brother. Apparently my father had an affair with Scott's mother when I was little." She let out a deep breath.

"Where are you? I have ten minutes if you need to talk." He sounded worried.

"I'm okay. Have you finished with your Uncle?" She hoped he had.

"No. He just stepped out for a minute to talk to his associates. I need to know if you're alright. How have you taken this news?" Damon held his breath, waiting, ready to drop the phone and go to her side.

"I'm alright. I'm more worried about you." She would have given anything to just be with him. Alone. For a week.

"All will be well Lilliana. Have you been to see Allie?"

"I'm going up to see her now."

"Hopefully I will see you later, take care baby." He finished quietly.

"You too my love." She clicked off the phone.

Taking a deep breath, she ran her hands through her hair, and left to visit Allie.

***

With the long, busy, drama filled day, Lilliana had missed all meals and was starving. She knew Christopher would probably be finishing up in the kitchen. It was after nine pm.

She found him, running through the menus for the next day and placing a vegetable order for H D.

She stood in the doorway, watching him. Tall, well built. A serious expression on his face.

She thought of her love for Damon and felt for this man.

Christopher was not permitted in the Black Ops division. He must be going through another kind of hell, not being able to see Allie.

He was seated at the enormous marble bench top, pieces of paper spread out neatly, as he was writing this, scratching out that.

He had menus for the hospital canteen, Main house, Psych ward,

Black Ops and any other outside orders that worked different shifts throughout the establishment. He had helped Cook build a brilliant team to back them in the kitchen.

She remembered back to first seeing Christopher in their compulsory group therapy. He had seemed serious, dark. Wore blacker eye liner than any female she had met, and still did. Black nail polish. He was one of the sweetest men she'd ever met.

She hadn't noticed Cook enter through the other door and clearing his throat he addressed Lilliana.

"Can we help you?"

Christopher looked over at Cook, then to where he was looking.

Lilliana stood in the doorway, arms folded, leaning against the door frame.

He smiled at her. "Come on in Lilliana. Skipping meals again?"

"Not on purpose." As she walked over to Christopher, she smiled at Cook. "I'm fine, thank you Cook."

She sat on the offered seat Christopher pulled out.

"I've got everything sorted for tomorrow's meals Cook, why don't you call it a night?" Christopher took a sip of his black coffee.

"Yes, well, Mr Night needs a delivery of these items before eleven if you can handle that." Cook dropped a small piece of paper on the bench top in front of Christopher.

Christopher picked it up, nodding. "Will do, goodnight Cook."

"Night," Cook said to them, as he left through the same door he came in.

Once he left, Christopher dropped the note, and headed across to the fridge.

He started pulling out fresh salads and salmon to make Lilliana a sandwich.

Lilliana picked up Damon's order and went through it.

"I'm going up to see Allie shortly. When I come back down, can I help you make these, and deliver them?" She enjoyed watching him butter bread, and expertly slice the salmon, popping dill and capers along with the salad into the sandwich.

He slid the plate along the bench till it came to a stop in front of her.

She smiled. "Nicely done.

He shrugged, "It's all in the wrist."

She moaned in appreciation at the first mouthful, watching him put everything back in the fridge. He dropped the knives and breadboard into the sink, and walked over to Lilliana, picking up Damon's list.

Lilliana swallowed and asked, "How are you doing?" before taking another mouthful.

He forced a smile. "Pretty crappy if the truth be told. What can I do? I need to keep going here. Just have to hope for the best, that my baby comes through this okay. If she doesn't Lilly, I don't think I'll be able to stand staying on here." He reached for his coffee and drank deeply, turning his gaze on her, happy to see her eating her sandwich.

"How was your interrogation? I mean, what bullshit, to interview you in regard to Sapphire's accident. Bloody idiot." He shook his head, noting she had gone a little pale.

"What is it? Do you know something?" He reached across, grabbing her wrist.

Lilliana's eyes met his, unblinkingly. "No, of course not." She shook her head, slipping off the tall seat; she walked over and took a glass out of the sink. Rinsing it she filled it with cold water, her back to him, she drank till it emptied.

She turned to face him and smiled. "I'm going to pop up and see Allie, and talk to Johnson, see what we can do to get you a bit of clearance for a visit. Okay?"

He nodded slowly, wondering what it was she did not want to tell him. Lilliana was one of the smartest people he knew. If she was keeping something from him, it was probably for a good reason. "No worries Lilly. See you soon."

Lilliana walked past him, rubbed his back and left to visit her friend.

✱✱✱

She arrived up in Black Ops twenty minutes later, to find Josephine sitting by Allie's side, reading to her.

It brought a tear to Lilliana's eyes. She leaned against the door frame watching her two friends, wishing Jessica was here also.

Allie was still heavily sedated and looked peaceful, yet pale, in her drug induced sleep.

Josephine was curled up in the chair, reading out all the latest crops she, Rupert and their team had harvested, plus what she had just planted in her garden, which was a new plot she could see from her and Cam's window.

She glanced over at Lilliana and smiled.

"Hey, my friend. Long day huh?" She stood and walked over to her, pulling her into a hug.

Lilliana wrapped her arms around Josephine, and breathed her sweet friend in. Grateful that she got clearance to sit up here with Allie. "It has been the longest day ever." Lilliana replied, squeezing Josephine before releasing her and walked over to peer down at Allie.

She smoothed her soft blue hair off her forehead, listening to her breathing, quiet and slow.

Lilliana stroked her cheek and said to Josephine. "Has the Doctor said anything about her condition?"

"Only that she should be fine and will probably come to in the next day or so. Her spine wasn't damaged." Josephine went back and sat down.

"I'm going to speak to Johnson. See if we can't get Christopher some clearance. Are you staying long?" Lilliana asked her.

"Well, I've been here a couple of hours. Leon popped in. It looks like Cam is going to be in a meeting till two am, so, I am going to sit and read till he comes and collects me." She smiled at Lilliana.

Lilliana shook her head, smiling at Josephine. "You are the most beautiful friend anyone could ask for. You know that, don't you?"

"Thank you sweetie. And right back at you. Are you feeling okay? Cam told me about your to-do with Uncle Weirdo."

"Yes, I'm fine. I just want things to be normal around here again. Well, as normal as anything gets around here." She headed towards the door.

"Yes, as soon as things are normal, we must get together, and celebrate boring. I could do with a bit of boring." Josephine nodded.

Lilliana laughed quietly. "I definitely agree with you on that one. Speak soon." She waved as she disappeared, in search of Johnson.

She found him in his office having a chat with five of his men.

Lilliana knocked on the door then entered as he waved her in.

She smiled hello to the men and waited by the door until he finished talking to them.

She watched Johnson tell his men about seeing to the departure of Seth's men the following day.

Lilliana felt a great deal of relief knowing that they would all be leaving tomorrow. She couldn't imagine what Damon was feeling.

As Johnson's men streamed out, bidding her goodnight, Lilliana smiled at Johnson. As the door shut behind the men, leaving them alone, Johnson let out a sigh and went behind his desk and sat.

"So, they are all leaving tomorrow? That is brilliant." She walked over and sat opposite him.

He gazed steadily at her face. Her green eyes looked huge. She was pale this night, her dark, glossy hair framing her face prettily.

Damon had told him quickly what he had done to Sapphire, and after a deep conversation regarding rights, Official Law, and the crimes which Sapphire was connected to, Johnson finally convinced Damon to come clean to his Uncle.

"Yes, they are departing first light. Damon will be in a meeting with Seth, and they will be holding a conference call for a few hours with the other establishments in regard to finances, Sapphire's reports and other issues. And of course, deciding on what to do with Allie. I'll be joining them shortly." He was watching her closely to gage her reaction.

Lilliana stood. "I think the only decision to make regarding Allie, is to let her heal and place her back where she belongs. Seriously, can the whole situation get any more ridiculous?" Lilliana placed her hands on her hips.

Johnson sat back in his chair, crossing his arms. "I know, but one step at a time. Let's just deal with the next few hours until Seth and his crew leave. Okay?"

She nodded, taking another deep breath. "Listen, I wanted to see if I could get Christopher a pass to see Allie? Even for just five minutes. The poor guy is suffering, and Josephine was up here, so…" She trailed off, hoping Johnson could see where she was coming from.

"I can't do that just yet, sorry. Josephine has authorization, as she is married to Cam and one day she may be running this establishment, or one like it and will need to be familiar with all sections." Johnson looked her in the eye, hoping she would understand.

Lilliana nodded. "Okay. Just wanted to check. Thanks anyway." She glanced at the time on the wall. Ten fifteen pm.

Enough time to shower, change, and go back down to the kitchen.

"I'll get going. Have a good remainder of the night Johnson," she smiled as she walked over to the door.

"You too Lilliana. Good night." Johnson watched her go, before finishing off filing his reports and heading off to find Rachael.

***

Lilliana was exhausted after her shower, and looking at her bed, would have loved to just sink into it and sleep for days.

Her mind flickered to Damon and she quickly walked over to her robe and reaching in pulled out a soft, knee length, long sleeved dark green dress.

If she couldn't put on her pjs, this was the next best thing. She slipped on flat black ballet slippers, brushed her hair, and left the room heading downstairs.

She arrived in the kitchen to find Christopher preparing a trolley with freshly baked biscuits, and on the bench, were an assortment of sandwich fillers.

"Ready?" Christopher asked spotting her.

"Absolutely." She walked over, pulling up her sleeves.

"We'll make some salmon, turkey, and roast beef fillers, with a batch of salad on the side. I've made biscuits and I had a slice prepared earlier, so I'll just slice a few pieces off that, and get the coffee hot while you're doing the sandwiches. How does that sound?" He smiled down at her. She looked up at him. "It sounds fab. You are amazing Christopher."

"Well, it's not rocket science," he said, shrugging.

"Don't knock what you do. You feed hundreds of people every day. And work around the clock." Lilliana nodded. "You are amazing. I'm qualified to say so."

He laughed, shaking his head. "Well, thank you Lilly. I'll own that, now let's get started so we can feed this mob on time. I don't think Damon's eaten today either."

It took Lilliana a good half hour to make up all the different sandwiches. She was wondering just how many people would be in this meeting.

As she placed her two trays on the trolley, Christopher had finished the slice, coffee, and sorted out a few other eats.

"Do you feel like wheeling this in?" He asked her.

"Absolutely. Look, I want you to know I talked to Johnson about getting you in to see Allie. He says not just yet, but I'll talk to Damon about it." She watched disappointment flicker across his face.

She reached out her hand and rubbed his arm. "Sorry." she said quietly.

"Don't be. It will all be okay in the end. It will have to be." He forced a smile. "Off you go."

"Yes Sir." She smiled cheekily as she pushed the trolley out of the kitchen, and down the long hallway past common rooms, stairways, and the Library, towards Damon's office.

***

Damon was listening to the head of the Australian Given establishment, talk about taking justice into their own hands, regarding other Head Directors.

His name was Russell Meek. Aged thirty-four, he ran his establishment with a firm, fair hand, for the past ten years after his father had been murdered by an unstable Given. He would also be in charge, of setting up the new Australian Given establishment, in Victoria's Glenormiston South.

He was a well-adjusted man. Loved what he did and had always had a good rapport with Damon and Cam. It was he who had recommended Dr Clair to them.

He was completely on Damon's side in this, the situation regarding Sapphire, and the way Damon had dealt with her. He was letting Seth know in no uncertain circumstances, would the Australian Given be prosecuting Damon in any way, and he would have their complete support.

He also called Seth out on how he could have had no idea regarding Sapphire's illegal activities, when they worked so very closely together.

Damon watched Seth's face closely and had an idea that his heart was as black as his father, and his cousins had been.

It did him a little good knowing Sapphire got what she deserved, although, he would have liked her to have suffered more than she had.

He didn't know what that said about him. He didn't care much right at this moment.

"Damon, if there is anything I can do for you in regard to any of these matters addressed tonight, please, let me know." Russell said after finishing his conversation to Seth.

"Thanks so much Russell. As always, it's a pleasure talking to you. Until next time." Damon ended the call, as a knock sounded at the door.

"Come in." He called, leaning back in his chair and placing his hands behind his neck, stretching. He glanced across at Cam, who had Josephine sitting close at his side.

Cam had gone up to Allie's room to collect her for part of this meeting. As she was his wife he thought she might like to start some training in listening to phone calls, and other business matters. Plus, he just wanted her by his side if he had to be here this hour of the night.

There were five other men from Seth's group sitting not far from Seth around the coffee table.

Dr Richard was there also as he had evidence to help Damon's case.

And Dr Clair, she had worked in other establishments and had a connections with two of the Directors, including Russell.

Johnson and Rachael had been called in for the last twenty minutes.

As the door slid open Lilliana wheeled the trolley in. She glanced up as all eyes were on her. She smiled at Josephine, and glanced across at Damon, ignoring Seth.

"Supper is served Sir." She addressed Damon.

Damon felt his stomach tighten just looking at her. Even this late at night she looked as fresh and delicious as always.

He wanted a taste of her lips, not a goddamn sandwich.

But, he stood and smiling walked across to her as he said to the room. "Let's break for ten minutes. We have a long night ahead of us, so refreshments will do us all some good."

Josephine and Cam came over and Lilliana started pouring tea and coffee.

She handed Josephine a cup as Rachael walked over.

"Hi Lilliana, how are you doing?" She took a sandwich and a piece of slice, popping them onto a small plate.

"Good Rachael." She leaned closer to Rachael and said quietly, "I'll be better when all this is over with." Rachael nodded and smiled. "Agreed." She took the cup Lilliana offered her and went to sit back down, handing Johnson the sandwich.

Richard approached Lilliana and helped himself to a plate of food. She said nothing to him but handed him a sweet tea she knew he liked.

He took it from her and nodded his thanks before sitting back down.

"So, you serve tea also. Talented." Seth said as he strolled up to her.

"Hardly." Lilliana replied drily, passing Cam a plate of sandwiches.

"Helpful though." Cam winked and went to sit back down with Josephine.

She could feel Damon standing behind her. She turned around to smile at him, not realising he was standing so close.

Her breath caught in her throat. She wanted to wrap her arms around him and just lay her head against his chest. To feel his warm skin. Smell him. Hear his heartbeat.

He watched her, watch him. He knew what she was feeling. He was feeling the same way.

"Excuse us for a moment." He said to the room, before walking out the door.

Lilliana followed him, knowing he wanted her too.

As the door slid shut behind them blocking them from the room's eyes, he turned around and pulled her up against him. His hands ran along her back, running through her hair. His eyes looked deeply into hers, just looking.

She stood on tiptoes, her lips parting as they got closer to his.

He took his time leaning down, breathing her in, watching her eyes go dark.

His lips claimed hers in a soft brush, backward and forward.

His hands, sliding down to cup her gorgeous bottom, bringing her hard against him.

Lilliana could feel him through her dress and moaned softly. He deepened the kiss instantly, and they were both so desperate to simply be alone.

He pulled back, his hands framing her beautiful face. "Don't go back to your room. Go straight to mine. You remember the code?"

She nodded. He stroked a hand along her cheek. "I don't know what time I'll be up baby. But do not leave until you see me. Okay?"

She kissed him again, placing her hand behind his neck to hold him to her.

The kiss was sweet, tender and quickly became hot and heavy.

They parted. Lilliana breathing heavily, Damon shook his head. He stepped back running his hand through his hair. "What am I going to do with you?"

She smiled. "Oh, I could think of a few things."

He raised an eyebrow, loving her playfulness. "Really?"

"You better go, eat something. I helped Christopher make those, so, enjoy."

"Oh I will. You go get some sleep." He pointed a finger at her as the door opened behind him.

She nodded and turning headed for the stairs.

He went back into the room, piled a plate high, poured a steaming coffee then went to his desk for many hours of debating.

CHAPTER 15

Lilliana was so happy to be back in Damon's rooms. She walked to the small kitchen and poured a cold water before heading to the bedroom.

Sipping the cool liquid, she stepped into Damon's dressing room and could smell him immediately.

She reached for one of her nightgowns in the drawer, but she stopped, turning to Damon's side.

Running her fingers along his shirts, her fingertips brushed over his steel blue shirt.

She loved this shirt on him, it made him look so devilishly handsome.

She tugged it off the hanger, and walking over to the bed, she placed her glass on the bedside table, pulled her dress over her head and folding it, placed it on the chair near the end of the bed and pulled Damon's shirt on.

She wrapped her arms around herself and walked back out into the living room.

She decided a glass of wine would do well with helping her relax,

And went to Damon's bar and found a bottle of Penfolds Grange

2000.

Taking a delicious mouthful, she appreciated the aromatic spices with fig and plum flavours.

She walked over to the music pod and put on a haunting piece where Monks sang in such glorious, sweet harmony, it almost brought tears to her eyes.

She pressed it on repeat and wandered out onto the balcony.

The rain had stopped, and a muggy warmth had settled into the sweetly perfumed air.

Lilliana leaned against the balcony rail and happily looked across at the stables where the lights, dimly lit, made the entire area look hauntingly romantic.

She finished her wine and going back inside poured another before heading over to Damon's bookcase.

Her fingertips ran along the spines of books and photo albums. She loved being amongst Damon's things. She walked over to the couch and sat down, tucking her feet up under her.

Snuggling back against the soft leather her eyes trailed over his photographs on the mantle-piece. Her eyes landing on the photo of him on Beast's glistening black back. She finished her wine and jumped up and placed her glass on the coffee table, then snatched up the photograph and went into the bedroom.

Dropping the picture on the bed, she continued walking into the bathroom, happy to see her toothbrush was still in the drawer near Damon's.

After brushing her teeth and going to the toilet she washed her hands and face and went back into the bedroom and slid under the warm covers.

Grabbing the photograph, she looked at Damon then tucked it on her chest and called the lights off.

Listening to the glorious sounds of the Monks, she was asleep within minutes.

And that's how Damon found her at seven the following morning.

His shirt wrapped around her, the top buttons undone, revealing creamy soft, smooth skin, and ample breast to tempt a saint.

Her long silky black hair was spilling over his pillow and sheets.

One arm thrown above her head, the other near her stomach, loosely hanging over a framed picture.

He smiled to himself, so enjoying seeing her here in his bed.

It was exactly where she belonged.

Her quiet breathing, and being in such a relaxed and unaware state, stole his heart.

This woman, the young girl she had once been, was practically his.

Gently picking up her wrist so he could remove the frame, he glanced at it noting it was himself and Beast, and smiling again, placed it on the bedside table.

He sat down beside her and ran his hand down her face and along her throat, his fingers gently stroking.

Her hand slowly went up and her fingers wrapped around his wrist.

Her lips smiled and her eyes slowly opened.

Deep sleepy green eyes stared into his dark blue, unblinking ones.

Her fingers stroked his wrist, her other hand reached up to slip around his neck, and gently bring him towards her.

He came toward her, his lips slowly slid along hers.

She sighed as she felt the weight of him on her, his breath over her mouth, everything she'd been waiting for. His scent, everything she needed to get though the day.

Her lips smiled against his, her fingers stroking his black locks along his neck.

He deepened the kiss and stretched out on top of her, the covers between them.

He bunched his hand in her hair, loving the feel of the weight of it, the silkiness.

He lifted his mouth from hers, leaning back a little so he could just look at her.

"Good morning." He murmured, liking the way her lips looked after he'd kissed them thoroughly.

"It is now." She smiled up at him. "It would be even better if you were in here with me." She invited.

He licked his lips, tasting her, and then leaned down again to kiss her open mouth.

Both her arms wrapped around him, stroking his back, feeling his strong, firm body through his shirt.

She moaned into his mouth as his tongue tortured her.

He chuckled, leaning back once more. "There is nothing I would rather do, then get into bed with you right now Baby, but I have five minutes to get back downstairs and put my Uncle and his puppets on a plane." He stroked her face before getting off the bed and walked into his dressing room.

Lilliana jumped up after him and stood behind him, watching him strip off his shirt and pull on a fresh one.

She took the one he removed and walked over to the chute and dropped it down.

She turned around to find him watching her as he was doing up his buttons.

She shook her head, disbelieving that she was actually watching this gorgeous man get dressed.

"Penny?" He asked.

"Oh we don't have time." She slowly started to undo the buttons on his shirt which she wore, placing her hands on her hips, making the shirt reveal her perky, full breasts, and a very sexy black G-string with her firm, athletic legs looking like they were going all the way to heaven.

She almost burst out laughing just watching his reaction.

His hands had stilled as he was doing up the button on his cuffs. His eyes darkened and he practically stopped breathing.

His eyes met hers and before she knew it, he pounced on her.

She gasped as his hands lifted her and carried her backwards towards the bed, with no effort he dropped her down and spread his body on top of hers.

His kisses before had been deep and loving. Appreciative.

Now they were hungry and plunging, like he wanted to eat her up entirely.

He tugged his shirt off her and moved back so her fingers could undo the front of his. He grabbed her G-string and effortlessly ripped the fine material in two, appreciating her whoosh of breath leaving her body in excitement.

Whilst they continued ravishing each other's mouths he rolled over onto his back, taking her with him, her fingers working on his jeans. She tugged them down with his briefs.

Once they were removed he rolled her back over and ran a hand down along her soft stomach.

She nearly cried out at the thought of him touching her down there, it had been too long, and she was desperate to have him.

His fingers sought her wet warmth and he moaned, kissing her deeply.

Her fingers were stroking him, loving the feel off his large erection, hot in her hand.

His fingers slid inside her and she cried out softly. "Now," she whispered, "please Damon."

He was happy to give her exactly what she wanted and pushed himself deep inside her.

He pumped slowly at first, kissing her throat, her ear, then her mouth over and over.

Her fingers running through his hair, she moved rhythmically with him.

They fit together so beautifully.

He ran his hand down the length of her body, then up again to cup her breast, his finger gently squeezed her nipple.

Her legs wrapped tightly around him as she felt she was close to fever pitch, running her hands along his back, then grasping his firm buttocks tightly, pushing him closer towards her core.

He thrust faster, deeper, then slipped a hand between them to rub her sweet, wet bud. She felt dizzy, like she was floating as his body and hands worked their magic, taking her somewhere else where only he could take her.

She felt so slippery down there, his fingers stroking over and over as he pumped faster, harder, deeper as he kissed her, his tongue matching their rhythm.

She came as he pumped into her, crying out his name.

He thrust deeply and came with her, breathing heavily, he dropped his head on her chest, kissing her in between her breasts, close to her heart.

They lay there for a few minutes catching their breath, enjoying holding each other.

She sighed and ran her fingers through his hair.

He raised his head to stare into her eyes.

"You are the most beautiful woman I have ever met."

She smiled up at him.

He kissed her before getting off the bed, pulling her up with him.

"Time to get back to my duties, although, this was one interruption I'm not sorry about."

"I should think not." She slapped his bare backside playfully, as he bent to pick up his pants.

He turned to look at her as he tugged them up his legs, his shirt hanging down his back; he pulled it up and started to button it back together.

He shook his head. "Please go cover your gorgeous self before I take you again and they send a search party up here for me."

"I'd love a hot shower first, if that's all right?"

"Of course sweet girl, enjoy. Can you make it quick though? My Uncle has requested you be there for his departure." Damon slid his feet into his shoes.

"Lovely." Lilliana groaned as she walked into the bathroom, running a perfect shower, loving the way her body felt after it had been ravished by that delicious man in the other room.

Once she finished and stepped out of the body drier she rubbed a lotion all over her body and face, brushed her hair, and pulled on blue jeans, a white shirt and pushed her feet in brown boots.

After a quick squirt of Damon's after shave, she found her silver bangles and earrings and walked out into the kitchen.

Damon turned to face her while drinking freshly squeezed orange juice.

His eyes took her all in and he murmured his appreciation.

"What?" Lilliana asked, taking the glass of juice he offered her.

He shook his head. "You Lilliana. Just you."

She drank her juice down, watching him right back. Placing her empty glass on the sink behind him she slipped her arms around his waist and laid her cheek against his warm, strong chest. "I know," she said quietly, "I feel the same way."

He kissed her hair, and she moved her head to look up at him.

"I love you so much Damon." She stroked her fingers along his back.

He dropped a sweet kiss on her lips, before saying "I love you Lilliana."

He ran his hands along her hair. "Now, we have to go. Ready?"

"If it's to say good riddance to that Uncle of yours, yes absolutely." She stepped back, allowing him room to walk around her and go over to his desk to collect his phone.

Slipping it into his back pocket, Lilliana watched his sure, confident moves, constantly surprising herself with how greedy her eyes were when he was around.

It was his turn to catch her staring. "I know that look well," he smiled, crossing over to her, he took her hand and lead her to the doorway. "Time to go."

She smiled to herself as they headed out the door and down the stairs. She liked the fact that he was as desperate to have her as she was to have him.

As they walked further down the stairs she glanced up at him. His dark features gave him that glint of danger when he looked serious.

She could imagine he could not wait to get rid of his Uncle.

His eyes flickered down at her, and his lips turned up into a slow smile.

"Problem?" He stroked his thumb along her fingers.

"Only that we never seem to have enough time alone."

He smiled. "Agreed."

Reaching the bottom of the stairs, Lilliana was curious that Damon had not released her hand, and went to pull it from his, but he tightened his fingers around hers, keeping her close to him.

Damon led her over to his office and as the door opened it revealed Cam and Josephine already waiting with Seth.

"Good Morning," Cam called out happily. A smiley Josephine tucked under his arm.

"It will be soon," Lilliana murmured quietly so only Damon could hear.

He smiled down at her, before answering Cam. "Morning."

He glanced at his Uncle. "Ready?"

Seth smiled ever so coolly. "Oh I must say I am." He rose from the chair he was sitting in and smiled at Lilliana. "It has been such a pleasure meeting you in the flesh Lilliana. You are even more beautiful in person than your photographs portray you to be. Don't get too comfortable here. I may be coming to collect you soon." Lilliana's fingers tightened around Damon's.

Damon looked at his Uncle with distaste. "I think after last night's and this morning's meetings you would have finally realized you have no more bargaining chips left. Lilliana will never be yours to use. Nor anyone else in my establishment, unless they wish. Now, I suggest you get on your plane, and hopefully never return in my life span." He pulled Lilliana in front of him, placing his large hands on her shoulders. She felt a rush of protective love for him.

Cam nodded his head in approval. "Well said brother. Let me escort our charming Uncle, shall I?"

"Thank you Cameron. Now Josephine, would you like to come with Lilliana and I after breakfast to visit Allie?" Damon asked.

She smiled at him. "Thank you, I will." Josephine kissed Cam before he turned to walk out with Seth.

Damon kissed the top of Lilliana's head. "I'll meet you up there after breakfast; I just have to make a call or two." He gazed into Lilliana's eyes.

She looked back up into his beautiful deep blue ones.

He smiled, stroking her cheek, loving the softness of it. He slowly leaned down as her hand reached for his neck, their lips happily meeting halfway. The kiss was soft, smooth, sweet

"Hm, maybe you two could get a room," Josephine joked, laughter in her voice.

Damon deepened the kiss, his hand on the back of Lilliana's neck before he drew away and eyes on Lilliana, said to Josephine, "Don't tempt me. Now, off you both go. I'll see you soon." He turned around and walked across to his desk to sit down whilst flicking on the phone screen for a conference call.

Lilliana was smiling at him, watching his every move.

Josephine reached for her arm and grabbing her by the wrist, pulled her backwards out the door.

"I actually need to eat with my mouth, not my eyes, so please come on, I am starving, and tired. You know, being the wife of one of these establishments is exhausting, all night meetings, dramas, accusations, blah blah blah."

Lilliana smiled at Josephine's ramblings as they headed into the breakfast room.

It had been way too long since she had a relaxed moment with a friend, where she could let down her guard.

"God it's good just to hear you talk," Lilliana said, piling up a plate.

She realized she was starving as soon as they entered the room, and the aromas of pancakes, muffins, toast and coffee hit her.

Josephine smiled. "And it feels good to talk to you. God, I have missed you all."

Lilliana nodded, pouring a tea. "I know."

"Morning," Leon said behind her.

She turned around, smiling at him. "Morning Leon. How's your day looking?"

"Busy." He took a mouthful of coffee. "Have to do some teaching today, but I find that enjoyable when the students are willing to listen. Doctor Ryan will be with me as back up." He noticed how fresh and relaxed Lilliana looked. He hadn't seen her like this for a while.

"You look good," he said quietly.

She was halfway putting a strawberry in her mouth as she looked up at him.

She smiled and shoved it in, nodding her thanks as Josephine grabbed her arm and tugged her towards the tables.

Lilliana waved goodbye to Leon and sat down with her plate.

Josephine plonked down beside her and chatted to Samantha on her other side.

The sounds of chatter filled the room. Lilliana looked around for Eric but realized he may be breakfasting in the other dining area. She hadn't had a one-on-one with him for a couple of weeks now and was wondering how he was doing.

Samantha finished her breakfast and saying goodbye to Josephine headed out for her morning run.

Josephine turned her attention to Lilliana.

"How's Christopher holding up?"

Lilliana shrugged one shoulder. "Remarkably well considering. He wants to see Allie but understands the protocol. It still sucks though." Lilliana reached for the lemon and sugar and topped her pancakes off the way she liked them, jabbing a forkful and placing the fluffy cakes into her mouth, almost moaning at the deliciousness of it all.

"It so totally sucks. Cam and I almost had our first fight over it." Josephine had a definite twinkle in her eye.

"What is that look?" Lilliana noted the amused expression on Josephine's face.

"Well, it's just that Cam is so damn hot when he is mad, I couldn't argue with him for more than a minute before I dragged him into the library toilets and had my way with him." Josephine snickered. "I felt a bit like Natalie, remember in detention years ago," she laughed, "but it was four in the morning, not a soul around."

Lilliana smiled at Josephine, shaking her head. "Well, as long as it ended on a positive note." She finished up her pancakes and downed her tea.

"Hopefully Allie will get better fast, and Damon and Cam can sort out this situation, and put Allie back where she belongs. I don't think I can handle any more groups with Richard."

"God, no!" Josephine agreed, standing. "Ready?"

"Absolutely." Lilliana stood and together they made their way out of the room and headed up to Black Ops where they would meet Damon.

As they came to the entrance of the stairway a voice called out to Lilliana.

Turning around she saw Fox walking quickly towards them.

The three smiled at each other.

"Lilliana, you've been assigned a lingerie photo shoot for this Christmas." She flicked her long red hair over one shoulder, a tablet clutched to her chest.

She wore a tight, white dress, fitting snugly to her knees, and long sleeves adorning her long, slim arms. A deep plunging V-neck, which had all the males who joined her for breakfast, basically in a daze.

"Not if it involves a fat Santa," Lilliana said. Referring to the Christmas where Fox had had a photo shoot and had to drape herself practically naked over a very grotesque Santa Claus.

Not a merry Christmas.

Fox turned the tablet around, her fingers flicked across the screen. She held the screen up for Lilliana to see.

"Oh, gorgeous, I think Cam would like to see me in that." Josephine commented on one of the beautiful outfits Fox was showing them.

Fox watched Lilliana, hoping she would appreciate this assignment.

"The shoot is to show how all sizes can look amazing in these outfits. Athletic, slim and a little larger than average. So, it's Natalie, you and I."

"Oh, no thanks, you can forget it." Lilliana shook her head. The last thing she needed was to be anywhere near Natalie.

"Oh please Lilliana, it's not like you can actually say no." She tilted her head. "We'll make it fun. Cam's going to do the music, make it funky, sexy."

Lilliana looked at Fox. "Who is doing the shoot?"

"Tim. And there will be some of the models you've already worked with. We can even arrange to do a portrait for you to give Damon for his Birthday."

How had she never known Damon's birthday date?

"Wouldn't he just love one of you all spread out and gorgeous?" Fox said, hoping that would cheer Lilliana up from the prospect of working alongside Natalie.

It did. Lilliana nodded slowly. "Yeah, okay. Can you promise that I won't kill Natalie?"

"Well darling, that is completely up to you." Fox smiled, happy she had Lilliana on board. Due to an anonymous source outside these walls, Fox would get five thousand, just for that one accomplishment. Her money was going to a very good cause.

Her brother.

"Right, this sounds like too much fun, is it an open set for anyone to come and watch?" Josephine asked.

Fox raised an eyebrow at her. "I'll talk to your husband, but as you are his wife, you can pretty much go where you want."

"Cool." Josephine said.

"We have to go, was there anything else?" Lilliana asked.

Fox shook her head. "I'll get the details to you later. Looking forward to it. See you." Fox turned and walked off, calling out to someone she spotted near the library.

Josephine sighed. "How does she pull it off, always so cool and in control. She is one sexy woman."

"Yes, she is. Let's go."

As they headed up the stairs and into Black Ops, Josephine filled Lilliana in on the sordid details about Seth and some of the family members.

She left out the sad, gruesome tales about Damon and Cams father. She believed that was something Damon needed to share with Lilliana himself.

Lilliana shook her head as she pushed the gate open, reaching for the door that the security guard would be behind.

"How can those that hold such positions of importance, abuse their roles, use their power, to do so much evil?"

"Yeah well, people huh?" Josephine smiled at the guard. "Hi Henry."

Henry smiled. "Morning Ladies."

Lilliana smiled as her stomach tightened. It always did when she came up here.

They headed to the left corridor, and up three small flights of stairs towards the section where they kept unstable patients.

As they rounded the corner, Lilliana spotted Damon up ahead. He had his back to them, hands in his pockets, leaning against the doorway listening to Dr Clair.

One absolutely, gorgeous male, Lilliana thought to herself. She didn't think she would ever get over what a complete spunk he was.

Tall dark and handsome just didn't cut it.

"Get a grip girl." Josephine chuckled beside her, noting the way her friend's cheeks flushed as they drew nearer to Damon.

"You're one to talk." Lilliana said softly as they approached Damon and Clair.

"True." Josephine smiled.

"Hello Lilliana, Mrs Night." Clair addressed them over Damon's shoulder.

"Hello." they chorused as Damon turned to face them. Checking his watch, he glanced back at them. "Long breakfast, was it?" He looked slightly annoyed.

"Oh, sorry, we got held up briefly with Fox." Lilliana said, hoping he wasn't too upset.

"Mm, well we have to make this quick. Shall we?" He pointed to the door for the ladies to go ahead of him.

Clair and Josephine walked into the room.

As Lilliana went to follow, Damon stepped in front of her blocking her way.

She looked up at him, her breath caught in her throat. His handsome face, so serious, so intense!

His eyes so dark, as he slowly bent his head down towards her, his lips brushing her ear as he whispered quietly to her, "I had Richard pop in to see me quickly this morning. Scott is being very difficult."

He couldn't help himself, or their location. Her smell, being this close to her, his lips kissed her ear, her cheek, before pulling up.

He glanced down to see her beautiful, worried expression.

"Why didn't Richard tell me himself?" Lilliana shook her head. "Never mind, I have a group and a one-on-one in two hours' time, I'll pop in and see him after here."

Damon nodded and together they walked in to join the others.

"Look who's awake," Josephine was beaming.

"Oh Allie," Lilliana cried happily and quickly walked over to her friend who was sitting up in bed, a small smile on her face.

Lilliana leaned down and put her arms gently around her, a tear of happiness slipped from her eye.

"Hey Lilly," Allie hugged her friend.

Lilliana smiled down at her, stroking a hand over her soft blue hair.

"It's so good to see you." She smiled at Damon and Josephine.

Damon stood at the end of the bed; arms folded loosely. "How are you feeling?"

Allie nodded, looking Damon in the eye. "I'm feeling good. I have been told I am in the Black Ops unit. Why? And why hasn't Christopher been allowed to visit me? I asked Johnson these questions at four this morning when I woke. He won't tell me anything!" Allie didn't bother to hide her frustration.

Lilliana took hold of her hand, as Josephine went to the other side of the bed and took her other hand.

"Don't stress Allie," Josephine said. "We will tell you everything. Won't we Damon?" Josephine raised a cool eyebrow in her brother's direction.

"Of course. Now that you are awake Allie, we will try to make clear what is happening. Cam should be here any moment." Damon checked his watch again as Cam strolled into the room, right on queue.

"Morning all," Cam said cheerily as he walked over to Josephine, kissing her on the cheek. He smiled down at Allie. "How was dream world?"

"Dandy thanks." Allie said looking back over at Damon.

"Clair, you can go, page Johnson for me, will you?" Damon said.

"Of course." Clair nodded and left the room. The door slid shut behind her.

Lilliana noted that Damon appeared concerned. What decision was he making here? What needed to be made clear?

She squeezed Allie's hand before letting go and walked towards Damon.

Cam was talking to Allie quietly, whilst Josephine had grabbed some lotion and sat on the side of the bed to give Allie a hand massage.

"What is it Damon?" Lilliana asked.

His eyes dropped to her face. He wasn't looking forward to what the next twenty minutes would bring.

Lilliana wanted to reach out and stroke his arm, but she could see he had put up his professional wall. She began to get a bad feeling.

She stepped away from him and turned back to Allie, not wanting to see that cool look in his eyes.

The door slid open and Johnson strode in. "Morning." he said briskly to all, nodding to Damon.

Everybody greeted Johnson as he walked over and stood near Damon. Almost like he was there for back up.

"Allie," Johnson began, "I need you to be honest and tell me everything about your outing with Sapphire, Marcus and Natalie."

Allie reached out for Lilliana's hand. She took it and squeezed it reassuringly.

"We went out to show Sapphire some of our therapy and relaxation activities. She spoke mostly to Marcus. Sleazy bitch! Sorry!" She held up a hand.

Lilliana almost smiled with relief to hear her friend sound like her gutsy self.

"Anyway, we'd been at it for almost two hours when I'd had enough of her making her innuendos about taking the best from here, spreading the labour to other Given establishments. And she just wouldn't stop going on about Christopher. The size of his hands, watching him knead bread. She was basically telling me it wouldn't take her long to have him kneading her. We were having a bit of a competition in Archery, as Natalie wanted to show off her skills. Marcus had thought he'd seen a boar and wanted to circle around our area, make sure it was safe. When he left, Natalie wandered around our perimeter to keep Sapphire safe as she is as good as shot as Marcus. So, it was just Sapphire and I for a little while." Allie swallowed and Lilliana, seeing she was nervous, went to the small side table to pour her a water.

Handing it to her friend, she squeezed her shoulder. "It's alright Allie," she said softly, "take your time."

Allie looked up at Lilliana and nodded, taking a few mouthfuls of water before passing the cup back.

Damon watched them, rubbing a hand over his mouth, his eyes flicking to Cam, who, meeting Damon's eyes, walked to the end of the bed and stood on the other side of Johnson.

Three opposite three. A fair fight, Cam thought.

"Go on Allie." Damon said.

Allie nodded. "Well, I did see a boar and it was big. I aimed for it and apparently, my aim headed for Sapphire."

Johnson was watching her eye movement. Body language. He knew she was lying. He looked at Damon before saying to Allie. "Be honest Allie. I don't want to give you the truth serum. It can be painful."

"What!" Lilliana snapped out, giving Johnson a look. "That's hardly called for."

Damon kept his eye on Lilliana; she was beautiful when she was angry. He felt a stirring of concern in his belly, along with a hint of lust.

"Lilly, relax," Cam said, hoping to diffuse the situation.

Lilliana looked across at Josephine, who said, "Let's hope we can all relax, get this over with. What is going on?" She turned her brown eyes towards her husband, not liking the way he looked uncomfortable.

If he knew something, he should have shared it with her; she was his wife after all.

Johnson held up a hand. "Please, we all need to stay calm, give your answer please Allie. Was it your intention, when aiming your arrow at Sapphire, to kill her?"

There was a silent pause in the room. Allie swallowed nervously again.

All eyes were on her.

"It was. Yes." She confessed quickly, eyes on Damon.

He closed his eyes briefly, worried about Christopher. Opening them to study Allie, who looked small and pale. He feared for her. Glancing at Lilliana, her face looked pained for her friend.

"Well, what's all this going to mean? Where do we go from here?" Josephine asked, folding her arms.

Johnson looked at Damon, as did Cam.

"What that means, is that Allie will be appointed a cell here in Black Ops and become a permanent resident." Damon said smoothly, calmly. Flatly.

The room went into an uproar, from Josephine throwing her hands on her hips, shouting, "That is total Bullshit!"

To Allie shaking her head, hands running through her hair. Tears pouring down her face, crying out, "*No, that cannot happen to me, please Damon, no.*"

Lilliana too shook her head, placing an arm around Allie's shoulder, trying to offer some comfort.

The look she was giving Damon was one of utter disbelief. "That is the absolute *wrong* decision. This *cannot* be happening. Seriously."

"Seriously is an *understatement*." Josephine burst out.

"This is ridiculous Damon, surely you realize that this is not the right decision? Lilliana stared at him.

He stared right back, about to have his say, when Josephine continued. "Absolutely no way is that going to happen. No way in hell Has the world gone totally fucking insane?'

Johnson held up his hands, "Please, everyone. This was the only decision we could make, there was an eyewitness and now Allie has confessed. We need to treat all equal as an example. You know that Lilliana." He looked at her, trying to implore her to see reason.

Lilliana shook her head again, trying to keep her emotions in check whilst she comforted Allie. She whispered to her friend, "It's going to be alright, there must be something we can do. Don't worry." She kissed her hair.

Allie looked up at Lilliana. "I can't be locked up again Lilly. I can't, not after everything I've been through." Allie looked beyond panicked, sick and afraid.

"It's alright, I promise you, it's going to be alright." Lilliana felt it was all she could say to her friend at that moment. Her mind was a whirlwind of how she could possibly help her get out of this situation.

Her eyes glanced down at the end of the bed, Damon had his head bent, agreeing to something Johnson was saying.

He didn't look happy, and how could he after making a statement like that?

Josephine was as mad as a cut snake; she kissed Allie, and then stormed down towards Cam. "Did you know about this? Don't answer that now." she snapped out, holding up her hand. "We need to talk. Immediately." She turned and marched out of the room, heading off to their shared quarters. What she was about to say to her man, needed to be said in private.

Cam nodded to Damon, as he walked quickly out of the room to follow Josephine, knowing he had one hell of a battle before him.

Lilliana bent down and quietly said to Allie, "I will be back later this afternoon to come see you. I know it's hard, but try not to worry, I think I have a plan, okay?" She forced a smile for her friend.

"Thanks Lilliana. I can always count on you." Allie squeezed her hand before releasing it.

Lilliana turned to walk out of the room quickly, hoping to make it out before Johnson and Damon finished their talk.

She walked down the stairs and out through the gateway, wanting to visit Scott before her sessions started.

"Lilliana." Damon called out.

She could hear his footsteps approaching. Damn it! She was too angry to talk to him right now. She continued, as if she hadn't heard him.

"Lilliana!" His voice clipped.

She stopped and turned around, folding her arms to stop them from shaking.

She didn't know she was frowning and had an angry look on her face.

He slowed as he drew near her.

Her body language said it all. She was furious. He'd never seen her so angry in all the years he'd known her. He wanted to reach out, and smooth her features, calm her down and kiss her happy.

But this was a completely different situation they found themselves in.

And kissing was not the answer.

Two mature adults. One being the head of this establishment.

The other, a Given and now a valued worker of this establishment, required to follow the orders of her Director.

She watched him stop before her, placing his hands in his pockets, his dark features frowning slightly.

This beautiful, caring man who helped so many.

How the hell had he come to the wrong decision?

They were certainly in a standoff right now, neither saying a word, just staring.

"Go ahead," he said quietly, "get it off your chest."

"How could you?" Lilliana burst out. "You know where Allie has come from. And you just want to lock her up, like that is the answer here?" Lilliana pushed her heavy hair off her face, placing her hands on her hips, shaking her head, lost for words. Wondering what angle, he would take in this conversation.

"I mean, the fact is, Allie did not even *hurt* Sapphire. She simply took a shot at her and missed for Christ sakes. There has been no injury caused here by Allie. No murder, and I am not going to let this go. Allie does not deserve to be punished like this. Sapphire is dead and you and I both know who ended her!" Lilliana jabbed a finger towards Damon's chest.

He flung his head up, like a stallion that had been startled, placing his hands on his hips, glaring down at her.

Her beautiful features paled as she looked up at him, realizing she may have gone too far.

Was this the man who had worshiped her body less than two hours ago?

She dropped her hand and stepped away from him.

Damon nodded, and said dangerously quiet. "Tell me what you really think Lilliana?" His tone had a hint of zero in it. Frosty and cool.

Lilliana shook her head, taking another step back and turned around walking away from him.

"Oh no you don't!" he snapped out and reached down to grab her wrist, pulling her to a stop and back towards him.

She turned around to face him again, her eyes meeting his, breathing heavily after her outburst and contained tears of anger.

They both stood, angry for their own reasons.

Footsteps approached and a figure came around the corner. Richard.

"Ah, Damon, I was running a bit late for the staff meeting, but I can see I'm not alone." As always he had an arrogant look on his face as he glanced at Lilliana coolly before looking back at Damon.

Damon did not take his eyes off Lilliana's face. "I'll be there in five Richard. Just tell everyone to help themselves to tea, would you?"

"Well, I have a busy morning myself Sir, so if you are going to be too much longer I suggest..."

"NOW RICHARD." Damon raised his voice, running out of patience.

"Right Sir." Richard walked past them and towards the hospital stairs, to the small staff meeting that was going to be held in the canteen, on how to better some of their services in the hospital and psych wards.

Damon pinched the bridge of his nose, closing his eyes briefly.

It softened Lilliana's anger immediately.

He opened his eyes to her fingers lightly touching his arm.

He could smell her, the sweet scent of her as she stepped closer. See her worried eyes coloured with marvellous light green flecks throughout the deepest of greens.

"I'm sorry Damon. I know Sapphire got what she deserved. No one should be allowed to get away with what she did, the way she abused her position.

But surely you can see how wrong it is to punish Allie this way?" Lilliana dropped her hand, stepping back again.

He ran a hand through his hair, gazing down at her.

"What do you want me to do Lilliana? We have a witness who has spread the story of Allie's attempt to harm Sapphire. No, she did not hurt Sapphire, but the fact is we need to let everybody know that any deliberate harm towards a head of any establishment, will not go unpunished." He hoped she would understand what he was trying to do here. "What if her aim had been better? What if she had killed Sapphire?"

Lilliana shook her head, "But she didn't. I don't believe you are the type of person who would let such a good person, a brilliant therapist, my friend, sit in a cell for a non-existing crime."

Her face, so trusting of him. Of the man he was. He could see love in her eyes, hoping he wouldn't let her down.

He didn't want to let her down. Never wanted to see disappointment, or pain, flicker across her beautiful features.

But that wasn't reality, and he was in a position where he had to set an example.

He wanted to reach out to her, pull her against him.

But instead said quietly, "I don't have time to discuss this in full right this minute, we both have a lot on this morning. I'm sorry Lilliana." he quickly checked his watch again.

Lilliana nodded, knowing she had to get a move on also. "Alright then. Just know I'm not letting this go until Allie is where she should be." she felt a little nervous challenging him.

He sighed, looking down at her, his strong, stubborn, intelligent woman.

"Fine. Do what you need to. Shall we?" he indicated to the stairs leading down to the hospital section as they both had to go in that direction.

They walked down silently, both deep in their own thoughts.

As they arrived downstairs and into the hospital Damon went to walk towards the canteen, Lilliana towards the psych section.

"I'll find you later." Damon called after her.

"I'm sure you will Sir." she called over her shoulder as she continued along the corridor.

So, he thought to himself. Sir, is it? Interesting. He shook his head to clear it and continued along toward his second meeting of the day.

CHAPTER 16

Lilliana's day flew by in a whirlwind. She had forty minutes of trying to get Scott to talk to her about why he refused to cooperate with the staff, and why he insisted on being rude to Dr Richard. Not that she could blame him.

He simply asked her if she'd ever been in a room with the man longer than ten minutes.

She could easily see how this young man would get annoyed quickly with a man like Richard.

She assured him the sooner he calmed down and complied with the rules, the sooner they could put a tick in all the right boxes, and he could join main house.

He had nodded and apologized, saying he was just uncomfortable with the arrogant bastard, then apologised once more with the look on Lilliana's face.

She wanted to tell him she agreed with him, but that wouldn't have been professional.

Lilliana promised him that she would ask Cam to organize some activities in the fresh air soon.

Her group without Allie was a difficult session, as quite a few of their people were unhappy that Allie was not with them, again.

A newer Given, thirteen-year old Bliss, cried and said she had heard rumours that Allie was going to be executed in public.

Lilliana assured them all that nothing like that was going to happen and hoped that Allie would be with them all again soon.

It was a long session and not as productive for some of them, as Lilliana would have hoped for.

She had enough time to quickly write an email and send it to all the appropriate people before her one on one arrived. She felt nervous hitting the send button, wondering what it would mean for her and Damon.

Pushing her nerves aside, she greeted Rose for her session, and her nerves soon developed into a splitting headache as Rose divulged more details of the nightmare she had lived before coming to them here.

Although the session ended with Rose feeling better, it left Lilliana exhausted. Most days she could take a deep breath and shake it off. Today was not one of those days.

As she walked Rose to the door Natalie barged in.

Lilliana inwardly cringed, forced a smile and said. "Goodbye Rose, I'll see you next week."

"Goodbye Lilliana, thank you." Rose smiled before walking off.

Lilliana turned to Natalie, folding her arms. "Can I help you?" she asked her.

"Probably not." Natalie snapped out.

Lilliana shook her head and walked over towards her desk.

Sitting down she flicked on her screen to see if she had received any replies to her earlier email.

Natalie strolled around the room and stood near the Buddha. She had her long, curly brown hair out today, and a lot of green eye makeup on to match her green one-piece jumpsuit. On her feet were white wedges to match the thick white belt around her waist.

Lilliana glanced at her, sighing quietly. She presumed Natalie was here as she was missing out on her sessions with Allie.

"Can I help you or not Natalie? I'm certainly happy to listen to you if you need someone to talk to." Lilliana waited.

Natalie turned around, staring at Lilliana. "I keep having the same nightmare over, and over again."

"Would you like to sit and have a cup of tea?" Lilliana offered kindly.

"No," Natalie replied shortly.

Lilliana waited, not wanting to press Natalie for information. If she wanted to talk, she would.

Lilliana's eyes flicked over the screen and saw that she had at least seventy emails concerning her mission in regard to Allie.

She smiled inwardly. Surely Damon would have to do something about this situation now.

"Have you ever been strangled before?" Natalie asked.

"Yes." she replied.

"My stepbrother used to strangle me in my sleep. I'd wake, to my step-sister, sitting on top of me, licking me out." Natalie talked as easily as if she were discussing the lunch menu. Walking around, looking at this picture, or picking up that object.

Lilliana sat still, not wanting to move in case she put an end to Natalie's story. It was obvious she needed to get this off her chest.

Lilliana wasn't sure she wanted to hear this from Natalie, but as her friend wasn't here, she would help Allie out this way.

"I wouldn't be able to help myself at times, I couldn't stop the orgasms. It's like my body betrayed me. Some nights I would wake to a knife at my throat, my stepsister holding it whilst my stepbrother had his balls in my face. I was forced to suck his dick and hairy balls, even if I choked on them, whilst he was licking me out. Truth be told, I looked forward to waking up with her licking me out, more than him. I orgasmed really hard with her." Natalie shrugged.

Lilliana inwardly groaned. "Would you like to take some hypnotherapy sessions, to try to stop the dreams?"

Natalie shrugged. "Dunno."

"Well if the dreams or nightmares, are upsetting you, we can try to do something about them. Help is here Natalie."

"The thing is, yeah, they are more like a dream than a nightmare, kind of a wet dream if you know what I mean." Natalie smirked.

Lilliana was getting a bad feeling. "No, I don't know what you mean." she wondered where this was going, and unkindly, how long it would take.

"My step-sister in the dream, after she makes me orgasm really hard, her naked vagina sitting on my stomach, smearing her wet juices all over me, looks at me over her shoulder, smiling. Well, it's not her face I see, it's yours. And I can't help myself, I am so fucking turned on, I wake up and masturbate. I orgasm real explosive like, imagining your lips, your face, going me hard! It is fucking sensational!" Natalie smirked at her again.

Lilliana sat very still in her chair, not wanting to show Natalie exactly how pissed off she was. She was in her office. She would remain professional.

"Alright Natalie. Sharing time is over. Thanks for popping in. I think in future if you need to talk whilst Allie is away, go see Dr Hillary."

"What 'ev's."

"Also, when you see Fox, tell her I won't be doing the lingerie shoot."

Natalie strolled over to the door waving her middle finger in the air as she left.

Once the door slid shut behind her Lilliana leaned back in her chair and ran a hand over her face, shaking her head.

Bloody Natalie! Seriously some days she was surprised she hadn't knocked her right out.

She took a deep breath and got back to her emails, reports, and a few evaluations that she had to send to Damon, regarding some new Givens.

She had a lunch tray sent in and enjoyed a quick, refreshing meal, followed by a trip to the psych ward, and after another hour or so of reports, she was thinking about a swim or a horse ride before dinner, maybe catch up with Jessica. Her phone rang, breaking her thoughts of action.

"Lilliana here." she answered.

"Lilliana, it's Damon. My office. Now." he said quietly, coolly, before hanging up in her ear.

Lilliana sat, staring at the phone. Okay then. Lots of polite people to deal with this day.

She reached into her bottom draw and pulled out her deodorant, perfume and brush, quickly freshening herself up.

It took her another twenty minutes before reaching Damon's office.

As she drew near, she saw a crowd of people exit the office. People she'd emailed today about her quest to release Allie from her situation in Black Ops.

That sure was fast, she thought to herself, a feeling of nervousness coming over her.

She was in unfamiliar waters here.

Fox approached her. "Well, I hope you know what you've gotten yourself into." She smiled at Lilliana and rubbed her arm.

Josephine and Jessica came up behind Fox.

"By the way, don't think you are getting out of that photo shoot."

"Oh no Fox, please. If you only knew about my visit with Natalie today. I cannot handle her." Lilliana pleaded.

"Don't fret love, I'll be there to look after you." Fox winked and sauntered off.

Josephine watched Lilliana closely. "Are you alright?"

Lilliana met her friend's eyes. "Theoretically, yes."

"That email was brill. Gutsy. You really told him hey." Josephine had a twinkle in her eye.

Lilliana shrugged. "I just had to do something for Allie. It was the only thing I could think of."

Josephine nodded. "I hope he doesn't eat you alive. I've actually never seen him so, emotionless."

"It was a bit frightful confessing to him what I really thought." Jessica agreed, squeezing Lilliana's arm.

Lilliana's stomach dropped. Oh no.

Billy walked out of the room, along with Nurse Rachael, Rupert, Luke, Reline, Jaycee, Leon, Eric and so many other familiar faces.

She peered into the room and saw Damon standing in the middle of it. Arms folded; a dark look across his features.

Lilliana forced herself to swallow.

Cam walked out and took Josephine's arm. "We'll see you later love," he said quietly to Lilliana.

"Find me when it's over." Jessica murmured before heading towards the library

She nodded, and as the crowd dispersed, walked slowly into the office, the door sliding shut behind her.

Lilliana could feel herself start to shake. She clasped her hands in front of her to stop the physical evidence of nerves and slowly took a very deep breath, her eyes finally meeting his across the room.

Damon stood like a statue. Staring calmly at her. He raised his hand and ran his fingers along his lips. Tapping them twice before turning around and walking over to his desk.

He sat and tapped, bringing up the emails on the projection screen for them both to see.

He looked across at Lilliana. He could see how nervous she was.

Trembling even. Good, he thought.

He pointed to the chair opposite him and said quietly. "Sit."

Lilliana held up her head and walked over and sat opposite him. Crossing her legs and placing her hands in her lap, hoping she looked calm and in control.

She almost did.

He glanced at the list of emails sent to him. An impressive list to say the least.

He sat back in his chair and crossed his ankle over his knee, his fingers slowly tapping against his thigh.

Lilliana's eyes were drawn to those fingers.

"So," he said, drawing her eyes back up to his, "I can see you've been busy since our chat this morning."

"I did say I was not going to let this go." she said quietly.

"Yes. You did. I must say Lilliana, you have surprised me with the direction in which you have gone to get my attention on how very serious you were." His eyes, unblinking, intense.

Lilliana got the feeling he wanted to wrap his fingers around her neck, and slowly squeeze.

"I have over eighty, well educated, Given that help run this establishment to perfection, who signed your petition to release Allie immediately. If I do not release Allie, you will all go on strike until she is released."

He raised an eyebrow. "Very clever," he said softly, "to even have my own brother sign it, most heads in all major fields."

Lilliana folded her arms, ready for her defence.

"Can you imagine what that would do to this establishment?" His voice was steely.

"Yes," she replied with more confidence than she felt. "I can."

Damon dropped his foot on the floor and leant his elbows on his desk, placing his fingers against his lips, removing them to say. "I don't know why I am so surprised at the lengths you would go to, to protect and help a friend. You've done it before."

Lilliana straightened in her chair. "Do not bring that up." She felt sick that he would. That he would even think to mention her childhood and the abuse she suffered to protect Jessica.

He shook his head. "I did not bring it up to hurt you, only to point out how very loyal you are."

Lilliana stood up quickly and walked over to the fireplace. Her back to him, she viewed his statue of Beast on the mantel, remembering the time she had given it to him.

How very deeply she had felt for him as her protector. Her leader. Teacher.

She turned around to face him, folding her arms.

"I was surprised though that you felt you had to mention to so many the fact that it was I who ended Sapphire. What did you think to gain by that?"

Lilliana felt a little flustered. Like she was a small girl again, who had been caught with her hand in the candy jar.

She hoped he would understand, she had never meant to betray him. "I knew you were within your rights to punish her, end her for the crimes she had committed. I know that all those I sent the letter to would understand that also. I just wanted to show you how ridiculous it was to keep Allie locked up for possibly causing harm." She shrugged one elegant shoulder.

Her eyes met his, unsure of where they would go from here.

He stood from his chair and walked to the front of his desk, leaning his hip against it, he too folded his arms across his chest.

They found themselves once again in a silent standoff.

"Good Lilliana," he said after a few silent moments, "you have your formal request answered. Allie will be released tonight, after a briefing with Johnson and Clair, along with Richard and myself. No doubt she will be back in your office by tomorrow morning."

Lilliana felt so happy inside. She wanted to go over and kiss Damon thank you but was unsure how he would react.

He stood unmoving, and she was startled to find herself unusually intimidated.

"Thank you Sir," she said quietly, "our rooms are all the better with her in them. She has many Given that are comfortable talking only to her, and as we both have different tactics to get our patients to express themselves, we will certainly function more positively with her back." she finished.

Silence again.

Very professional, he thought. He could see how unsure she was of the situation they found themselves in.

Thinking of the way she was beneath him, only this morning, naked, trusting and open.

And now here she stood. Professional. Quiet. Her deep green eyes filled with uncertainty.

His phone rang. He sighed as he turned to answer it. There was a tap at the door at the same time. "Damon," he said into the phone, to turn and watch as Lilliana quickly stepped out of the room, as Marcus and four new Team Leaders walked in.

Marcus and Lilliana smiled their hellos, and Damon watched her disappear as the door slid shut blocking her from his view.

He would deal with her and their new feelings soon enough.

He turned his attention to six new problems, and continued with his afternoon, trying to push the hurt expression on her beautiful face, out of his mind.

***

Lilliana went in search of Jessica. She found her above-stairs in the library with a small group of Given. They all had specific acid scarring over their faces.

Lilliana wondered who was counselling them as she had not seen these youngsters before.

Jessica excused herself politely and quickly walked towards Lilliana. By the smile on her face Jessica guessed that things had gone well.

They clasped hands. "It's done." Lilliana's voice was filled with relief.

"Thank you so much for participating Jessica. I saw what you wrote in your email. That wouldn't have been easy for you."

"And it wouldn't have been easy for you to read it Lilly. We do what we need to do, to help a friend. I'm only sorry if it made you uncomfortable in front of Damon." Jessica looked apologetic.

Lilliana shook her head. "Don't worry. Sorry for the interruption. I just had to let you know." She nodded to the group behind Jessica. "Are they going into the new scar removal program?"

"Most of them want to. A couple of the older boys have refused, saying their scars are what defines them. We're all different."

"That we are." She kissed Jessica's cheek before leaving.

She checked the time and decided, she felt the need to go for a ride, and raced upstairs. Reaching her room in record time, she threw on her riding gear and pushed her feet into her riding boots.

She left her hair out long and wavy down her back and ran back downstairs.

"Lilliana," Cam called out, stopping her near the entrance.

She turned to face him as she pulled on her fingerless riding gloves. She smiled. "You've heard?"

"Oh yeah, big time baby, way to go Tiger Lilly, you certainly put brother dearest into a very fine mood," he smiled cheekily down at her.

Lilliana shook her head. "That was never my intention. I just wanted Allie out."

"And so she will be." Cam hugged her. "Enjoy your ride. But remember, plenty of rest for tomorrows shoot."

"Oh no Cam, please, can I get out of this one?" Lilliana looked up into his deep blue eyes, so like his brothers.

He gently stroked her beautiful face. "No sweetheart, it should only take an hour or two, tops."

Damon stepped out of his office to find two people he loved dearly, standing very close and in a quiet conversation. He leaned against the door frame to watch them.

Cam dropped his hand and Lilliana jabbed his chest playfully. "I've heard that one before," she said, referring to her first photo shoot with him which was supposed to take an hour, but was closer to three.

Cam held up his hands, "I promise. Rest well. I'll come for you after breakfast."

Lilliana waved a hand as she took off outside. "I'll hold you to that," she called as she left heading towards the stables.

Cam turned to see his brother watching him. "Hello Brother." "Cameron," Damon responded.

"Feeling better?" Cam asked. He strolled over to where his brother stood.

Damon shrugged. "It's a good outcome. Allie is where she should be, and I don't appear to be dishing out favouritism this way."

"You should be thanking Lilliana, not punishing her," Cam said quietly.

"I haven't even begun to punish her," Damon said, sounding very unlike him.

Cam looked at him closely. "Perhaps you need to book yourself in to see Clair, or Hillary?"

Damon shook his head. "I'm kidding. Relax."

Cam sighed. "Has Johnson told you any news about your situation with Reid?"

"I'm heading up to see him now. Had a phone call earlier." Damon ran his hands through his hair.

"Good luck with that. And stop scaring Lilliana with your intimidating persona." Cam half joked.

Damon nodded to Cam and silently walked off.

Cam shook his head and went in search of George. He had a group to take out to the tennis courts for an hour before dinner.

He had been considering Lilliana's request which she had emailed him earlier about taking Scott out. He would chat to her about it tomorrow at the photo shoot.

He heard a commotion in the rear common room and took off towards it.

Never a dull moment. Just the way he liked it.

***

Lilliana had ridden Beauty hard for a good hour before dismounting and allowing her to graze.

Thomas had warned her not to take her past the stallions' stalls, or Beasts paddock, as it was mating season.

He had grown quite embarrassed to remind Lilliana that if she had her period to please avoid coming anywhere near the stallions.

Lilliana had to quietly remind him, that females, upon entering this establishment were injected to prevent periods, therefor pregnancies.

They had shared an uncomfortable moment before Thomas forced a brilliant smile, wished her a safe ride and quickly disappeared into the tack room.

Lilliana stroked Beauty's neck, leaning against her side, thinking back to Damon.

Her stomach tightened remembering his cold, handsome face staring at her.

She shook her head. She was desperate to have things right between them. Surely he could see that all she had wanted was the best for her friend. And being locked up was so not the answer

She let go Beauty's reins after tying them up to her saddle so she would not trip over them, as she grazed and frolicked nearby.

Lilliana walked over to a tall weeping willow and sat in a low hanging swing.

It was moments like these she felt so connected to herself.

Alone, with nature, away from everyone's thoughts and past demons.

She took a deep breath of the pure, cool air, enjoying the breeze ruffling her hair and the soft leaves attached to the long limbs giving her a curtain to hide behind.

Beauty snorted as she flung her mane, enjoying being out a much as Lilliana was.

Her mind wandered to the photo shoot tomorrow. She knew it could be fun. Anything with Cam, Tim and Fox, would be good to be a part of. But bloody Natalie!

She sighed; surely she could deal with Natalie.

She dealt with worse most days. Her mind drifted on its own accord, to the innocents who suffered daily out there in the world. No matter how many laws were put into place, decade after decade, bad people constantly doing bad things.

She thought of the poor victims who weren't as lucky as herself and thousands of others worldwide. If only there was something she could personally do for them.

A thought came to her. She couldn't believe she had never thought of it before, wondered if it was even a possibility? But if it could be, if she could actually make it happen? She leapt off the swing and walked over to Beauty. Pulling the reins down, she saddled up and kicked her into a soft canter.

It was so exhilarating to just escape. She promised herself if she could do some real good for those in need, and get her own personal safe houses launched, she would treat herself to outings like this with Beauty more often.

She finally reached the stables and asked Edward if he would take care of Beauty for her.

He smiled and said he would, as she went to the washstand quickly washing her hands and splashing some cold water on her face before heading towards the house.

A group with Lisa and a new male Team Leader were coming down the stairs as she was going up.

Lilliana could hear Lisa explaining that it was an hour to mealtime, and they were having a short tour of the H D.

Rupert would be pleased. He absolutely loved explaining all the benefits of having such an elaborate department with a fine team of scientists and willing hard workers.

Lilliana raced up to the bathroom and stripped off. Stepping into the shower she washed the dust off, followed by a deep conditioning treatment for her hair.

She sighed, leaning against the wall as the hot spray blanketed her.

She thought of how she would approach this meeting. Best do a proposal first.

After rinsing off she stepped under the drier and was dry and warm in seconds.

She wrapped a robe around herself and headed towards her room, passing Miranda and Haley, she said a quick hello.

Once in her room she pulled on one of her favourites, a comfortable black dress, and slipped on black boots. She brushed her hair until it shone and let it fall in a glossy wave down her back.

She popped on large silver hoop earrings, a spritz of perfume and twenty slim silver bracelets on her wrist that gave a merry jingle as she walked.

She arrived in her office in good time to quickly write up her proposal.

She wished she could address it to Cam, but she knew it would only be passed onto Damon anyway, and she did not want to appear gutless.

She was professional; surely she could have a business meeting with Damon and remain so.

She drafted a letter, re-read it, and after twenty minutes emailed a very well written proposal on what she would like to do with part of funds she earned through modelling from here on out.

She glanced at the time. Her stomach rumbled for food.

She shut down her computer and headed upstairs to one of the dining rooms.

There was happy chatter throughout the dining room that night. Lilliana sat, surrounded by friends, discussing what they'd been up to that day, and sharing in the excitement of Allie returning to them the following day. It felt like ages, since they'd all had a meal together.

Mostly everyone was excited by the arrival of Christmas in the coming fortnight.

Lilliana was listening to Jessica chat to Eric about one of the latest Given, who Eric was appointed to as Watcher.

Lilliana was smiling across at him as he answered Jessica. Who would have believed he would have such an important role here after all the hell he used to put her through when they were teenagers?

He caught her looking at him and smiled back at her. "What?"

She shook her head as if to say, 'Nothing,' before turning to someone behind her who had gently squeezed her shoulder.

Her smile froze on her face. Damon. Dressed in black. Tall, serious. He smelled incredible.

He bent down and said to her quietly. "Would you come to my office after dinner please?"

Lilliana nodded her head as she watched him calmly walk down the end of the table and sit.

She forced herself to look away and stabbing a piece of roast duck she dipped it into the orange sauce before popping it into her mouth.

Her gaze wandered back to Eric who was staring at her. She forced a smile, chewed and turned her attention to the conversation around her.

Her mistake was looking down the head of the table, to see Damon sitting back, watching her over his cup of soup.

She felt herself blush and glanced away.

What, was she sixteen again?

She couldn't eat anything and gently dropped down her cutlery.

She swallowed her cold tea, quickly told Jessica her plan on what she suggested this establishment could do with part of her modelling funds, and that she had written a proposal to Damon, which was why he wanted to see her.

Jessica nodded, saying she thought it was such a brilliant idea.

Lilliana leaned across to say goodnight to Orlando and quickly got up to leave the room.

She decided to wait outside Damon's office. She sat on the bench seat alongside the Koi pond, her fingers gently floating in the clear water, her thoughts far away and deep, were interrupted when a young voice yelled out "Hey Miss, wanna fuck?" It was sixteen-year-old Max.

New to main house, only two weeks out of the hospital after the general month's evaluations.

He yelped as a large hand slapped him hard on the back of his neck.

Max spun around to give the culprit a piece of his mind.

He paled when he saw it was the head of the establishment. "Um, so sorry Sir, I was only joking," he fumbled.

"Yes, well you will find it equally as amusing when you have a month straight on night detention, starting now. RICHARD!" Damon called out.

A few moments later Richard came out of the library. He had had an earlier dinner and had been setting up for his night detention class.

"Yes Sir," he addressed Damon, ever so politely in front of the newer Given.

"Max here is joining your night detention, starting now." Damon gently pushed the boy in Richard's direction.

"Yes Sir. Come Max." Richard led the ashamed faced boy, for the moment, into the library.

Lilliana could not take her eyes off Damon who had turned to watch Richard lead Max away.

She remembered days where his showing his authority would make her swoon. Funny, as a twenty-five-year old, he still had the same effect on her.

She watched him turn to face her, his eyes connecting with hers.

He slowly walked towards her, hands, back in his pockets.

He stopped near her, forcing her to lean her head back so she could look up into his eyes.

He looked down at her. She looked refreshed and a little nervous.

He held a hand out to her. "Come," he said quietly.

She reached up and placed her hand in his large, warm one.

He pulled her up, standing close to her. His thumb ran gently over her knuckles before turning away and dropping her hand, walked into his office.

She followed. The door closing them in.

"Tea?" he offered.

"Yes please."

He poured for them both and then sat down opposite the blazing fire that blanketed the room in warmth.

This was friendly. She thought to herself.

He had placed her tea on the coffee table, and sitting, she reached for it, wrapping her fingers around its heat.

"How was your ride?"

"Just what I needed." She took a small sip of tea.

He watched her closely. Watched her lips part as she took her tea. Watched them become moist, wet. Her eyes met his.

He took a mouthful of coffee, his eyes staring at her over the rim.

She looked away, then forced herself not to be a coward and stared right on back at him. Why was she so nervous?

"I have to say you have surprised me twice today. Although you shouldn't have. Ever since you were younger, I knew you would be an incredibly amazing woman. The suggested proposal you sent, is a wonderful idea. I hope you don't mind, but I did a quick edit and had Johnson approve it, before sending it off to the highest-ranking Official outside. He will then start setting up your organization. Hopefully this can be done after Christmas."

"Really? So soon?" Lilliana said, her voice catching. Her emotions high.

Damon nodded. "You will need a face for the campaign. I suggest you use yours. Give the kids out there some hope. I would suggest you use Dark Angel, for your campaign title, make it more personable for the public. You will have final say on every aspect for your safe houses. Training, hiring, advance programs, the buildings, fundraising. You will have the best help possible in all areas." Lilliana's head was reeling.

Her idea was to put half the funds earnt through extra modelling, as legal aid, to help any young girl or boy out there, who had nowhere safe to go in a crisis, or who didn't have family support, in any Official case.

Enabling them to seek council and be evaluated, in order for them to be able to have a placement here or at any other Given facility or stay at a safe house till they got their feet back on the ground.

She knew well enough, that not everyone that caused an offense, was pure evil. Unwanted images flooded her, along with an onslaught of hundreds of stories she had heard the past eight and a half years. She fought hard to keep all her emotions in check, with the thought she could really help, and possibly save some of the innocents in this world.

"I'm so proud of you Lilliana." Damon said softly, bringing her out of her thoughts.

Her eyes met his, tears filling them.

She placed her teacup down, nodding her head, before standing and quickly walked towards the door.

Her hand reached out to hit the switch to enable the door to slide open, but his hand got there before hers, stopping her.

She could feel Damon's stomach close to her back. She could feel his warmth; feel his hot breath on her neck.

"Hey," he whispered close to her ear. "Lilliana." he let her hand go and hoped she would turn around to face him.

She did and nearly fainted. He was so close, and he had warmth in his eyes.

The smell of him. He gently reached up and placed his palms against the door either sided of her head, trapping her.

She looked into his deep blue eyes; her fingers wrapped around his wrists.

"Thank you." she said softly, a tear escaping.

He bent, his lips brushing it away. Raising his head, she watched him lick her tear off his lips.

"You are so very welcome." he said, his voice deep, wanting.

Her fingers stroked over his warm skin.

"You're not angry with me anymore?" she sounded unsure.

He slowly shook his head, his body moved closer.

She stood on tip toes, and raised her lips, hoping he would claim them.

He did. His mouth swooped down, seeking her open mouth. His tongue plunged in to greet hers as his hands sank into her hair, pulling her away from the door and into him. His hands slid down her neck, along her back to firmly grab her hips, and pull her hard up against his groin.

She gasped at how very much he wanted her, her fingers buried into his hair.

She pulled back, breathing heavy. She shook her head.

"What's wrong?" he gently stroked her face.

"I struggled today, I thought you were so mad at me." She leaned her forehead against his jaw, her hands clinging to his back.

He sighed deeply, stroking her hair, wrapping his arms around her. "I was mad, but only for a short time. The fact is, you very clever girl, you helped me get out of a very uncomfortable situation." He kissed her hair before letting her go and walked over to the fireplace. Glancing into the flames.

"I didn't want Allie to suffer any more than you did. But I have responsibilities, obligations and expectations on how to act as Head Director of this establishment. Your petition and suggestion of a strike was brilliant. I had to release Allie, for the sake for all to function normally and one hundred percent here." He turned to face her.

"I was a little mad I hadn't thought of it myself." He smiled darkly.

Lilliana pushed her hair off her face and behind her shoulders.

"Well, that's what you have me here for." She crossed her arms and smiled at him.

"Yes, that is a fact. Do you forgive me?" he asked quietly.

Lilliana shook her head as she walked over to Damon. She stood before him.

"There is nothing to forgive Damon. I know how much you must do here. Your responsibilities are endless. I admire you like no man I have ever admired."

"Even your father?"

Lilliana's face darkened. The thought of her father and his betrayal to her mother sickened her. "He got what he deserved in the end." she said quietly.

He reached out and pulled her against him. "My dark beauty, so unforgiving."

"Only to those who deserve it." she murmured against his chest.

"You know you would be brilliant undercover." He kissed her hair. She looked up at him. "Only, and ever, if you were my partner."

He bent down, and this time his lips gently, sweetly, kissed her.

A knock at the door had them breaking apart.

They stepped aside as the door opened to reveal Josephine.

"Hello people." she smiled.

"All set Josephine?" Damon asked her.

"All set, with the promise to Cam that this will not be a particularly late night."

Josephine smiled at Lilliana.

"Thank you Jose." Damon turned to Lilliana. "Have a great night darling." he leaned down and kissed her, his hand stroking the back of her neck.

As she pulled back, she whispered near his ear. "I am so glad you are not angry with me. I couldn't bear that."

As she stepped away, he smiled down at her. "Never Love."

"Come on Lilly, the night's a wasting!" Josephine saluted Damon, grabbed Lilliana's wrist and pulled her out of the room.

Lilliana laughed at Josephine's mission like manner. It felt good to laugh when her heart felt lighter.

Josephine led Lilliana upstairs to her and Cam's apartments, and as the door opened, it revealed a happy gathering, who yelled out, "Surprise!" when Josephine gently shoved Lilliana into the room.

Lilliana looked around at fifty or more friendly faces and in the middle of them all was Christopher, his arm around a very smiley, healthy, happy looking Allie.

Lilliana squealed, and raced into the room and threw her arms around her friend and would have had them toppling to the ground if not for Christopher's large frame supporting them.

There was laughter all round, and a nice supply of champagne, which after many toasts, had Lilliana feeling happily dizzy, very quickly.

"Lilly. I will never be able to thank you. You saved my life" Allie said, tears in her eyes.

Lilliana smiled at her friend. "There's absolutely no need to thank me. My life isn't as smooth when you're not in it." She hugged her friend hard, before large hands slipped around her waist and held her up to the room.

"Everyone, hail to this beautiful woman who saved my girl's life!" Christopher said as he swayed a little, due to too much champagne. Lilliana laughed and said quietly, "Help," a smile on her face.

Cam reached up and pried Lilliana from Christopher's grip. "Don't ruin the goods man, she has a shoot tomorrow."

He placed Lilliana on her feet, and clapped Christopher on his shoulder. Fox placed another glass of bubbles into Lilliana's hand, as Rupert and Luke came up to say what a brilliant scheme her strike was. She assured them it was no scheme and would have insisted they all go on strike.

Luke thought that was the most hilarious thing he had ever heard, and was in fits of laughter as Leon came, to kiss her goodnight.

She smiled at Leon, as he and Dr Ryan, bid the others goodnight.

Allie and Jessica were deep in conversation with Orlando and Eric, when Cam called out to everyone it was 'good nighty-night' time.

There were a few groans, but all were happy to kiss Allie goodnight and wink at Lilliana as they left.

It wasn't long before all that remained was Fox, Lilliana, Allie, Jessica, and Josephine.

Christopher told Allie he would wait in his room for her.

Cam had gone to take a shower.

Orlando disappeared, after bidding all goodnight.

The girls sat quietly, enjoying the silence after such a high. Just staring at each other, occasionally laughing.

"Well, I say we do this again soon, minus everybody else," Josephine suggested.

"Absolutely," Lilliana nodded, yawning. So much had happened this day.

Jessica stood. "Want me to walk you to your room Lilly?"

"Yes please." She reached her hand up, for Jessica to pull her to her feet.

Once she stood, she waited a beat for the room to stop spinning, then smiled. "Right, ready."

She looked down at Allie. "Good night Allie Cat."

Allie smiled. "Good night Tiger Lilly."

"I'll see you on set," Fox called out, "go drink a gallon of water."

Lilliana waved her hand as she and Jessica took off downstairs to find their beds and sleep heavily after all the drama of a very emotional day.

CHAPTER 17

Two hours in, and about twenty different lingerie outfits later, Lilliana was grateful to find she was enjoying herself.

The fact that Fox was a buffer between herself and Natalie made it bearable.

The set was designed sensually in deep red and black velvet, with satin drapes hanging and billowing like ravens' wings.

From the ceiling hundreds of different shaped crystals hung like tear drops falling from the sky, with tiny white mistletoe here and there.

A large, old fashioned settee was placed in the centre of the set, the three girls spread out in separate poses individually, then all together.

"Okay," Tim called out, "Ladies, heels on, I need you all standing together up on the settee. Boys, I want you clustering around them, worshipping your goddesses"

"Shouldn't be a problem," Phoenix grinned.

"That's right." Fox smiled sexily down at him as she slipped on extremely high, pointed heels, and stood up on the seat.

Lilliana had not worked with the six male models for years.

Halo, Phoenix, Jeremy, David, Michael and Todd, all looked very different from the last time Lilliana had seen them.

Their usual blonde hair had been dyed pitch black.

They had long, fake nails which looked like sharp razor blades.

Pointed ears, sharp teeth, and pale pupil-less eye contacts, set them up very freakishly indeed.

All the girls' make-up was very dark and dramatic. Hair pulled up in high sweeping ponytails to show off their long-pointed ears also.

Natalie had been given a long chestnut brown hair extension.

Their contacts were opposite to the boys. Pure black.

Long, blood red painted nails, and 'to die for' lingerie.

Lilliana slipped her feet into her high heels and glanced over at Cam deep in conversation with Tim.

Fox reached down a hand to pull her up on the seat. "Steady friend, it is a bit difficult to balance up here."

"Don't worry Fox, if any of you fall, we will catch you," Halo bowed, before going down on one knee and getting himself set up for the next shot.

"You are a sweetheart Halo. If only you were a permanent here," Fox sighed.

Jeremy was trying to help Natalie up, without knocking the other two off.

Lilliana had to give Valerie and Nigel credit once more. They had done a brilliant job with Natalie. She looked lovely.

"Alright, let's get that smoke going, fans on, girls sexy, I want you sexy, seductive and smouldering." Cam clapped his hands, jumping as a pair of arms sliding around his waist startled him for a moment.

He felt a kiss being pressed onto his back.

"Hello Lover." His hands went on top of Josephine's smaller ones.

"Hello." She slid around his front so his lips could claim hers.

Once she pulled back, she turned around and leaned into his chest so she could view the set.

"Who keeps coming up with this stuff? It looks awesome! My god she is one beautiful woman."

"Which one?" Cam blew on the back of her neck.

"As if you need to ask. What say you Damon?" Josephine turned to face him as he walked up beside them.

Damon had come to catch Tim after the shoot, to talk to him about staying tonight, to do Lilliana's Dark Angel shoot the next day.

Now that he'd arrived his brain couldn't quite focus on a thing.

He shoved his hands into his jeans pockets, his stomach muscles clenched.

Lilliana looked like every man's wet dream. And he wanted her.

Now. His eyes darkened, full of lust just looking at her.

"That's a wrap everyone, well done!" Tim called out.

Lilliana laughed as Fox turned around and let herself fall backwards off the settee, knowing the men would catch her.

Shaking her head, her eyes looked up and across at Cam's, only for her gaze to slide right into Damon's smouldering eyes.

Her smile disappeared. All thoughts about her next few hours with Allie back in their office, faded.

Strong hands went about her waist and pulled her roughly down off the settee, her body slamming into Michael's as he placed her back on her feet.

Damon folded his arms across his chest not liking another man holding his woman.

But he was not a jealous insecure person, and knew no male would ever have her, touch her and love her like he did.

"Lilliana, did you want to do one more shoot?" Cam called over to her.

Josephine chuckled at Lilliana's dazed expression. "Lilly!" she called out.

Lilliana shook her head, dragging her gaze away from the extremely handsome man staring at her with lust in his eyes. She could not focus.

She gently pushed away from Michael.

"Sorry, what?" She forced herself to look at Cam.

He laughed, lightly punching Damon in the arm. "Oh no brother, you are not welcome on sets any longer if my little star can't focus. Go." Damon smiled across at Lilliana as he headed off to speak to Tim.

Cam strolled over to Lilliana and helped her off the set. "Did you want to do a shoot for the Birthday boy?"

"I would, but I have group with Allie, in like, well now actually." She started pulling off her fake nails as Cam reached out and snapped off her pointed ears. "Go see Nigel; he'll get you out of all this in a flash." He leaned down and kissed her cheek as Josephine pulled her arm through Lilliana's and they took off to the make-up tent for Lilliana to get cleaned up and ready for her workday.

***

Seven hours in, and Lilliana could not wipe the smile off her face.

To have Allie back, working their groups, hearing her voice and witty comments, her soothing advice and helpful direction.

They had ordered a Christmas trolley in, so all their patients and friends could relax and help themselves to the sweet pastries, fruit and savoury platters, and delicious freshly squeezed lemonade.

Because it was only a week until Christmas everyone seemed relaxed and in high spirits. It was quite a few of their Givens' first Christmas here. Some were unsure whether they ought to be happy or not, but all were extremely happy to have Allie back.

Lilliana was saying goodbye as the session ended and let them all know that even though sessions would close for a week that if anyone needed them at any time they would both be here for a one-on-one.

Once they were alone they turned to each other smiling. "That was a pretty good start to my homecoming," Allie said, pouring a drink and passing it to Lilliana.

"They are so happy and relaxed to have you back, as am I. I think if I had to have Richard here for one more session, one of us would not be breathing right now," Lilliana sighed as the cool, sweet drink slid down her throat.

"I've got Natalie coming along in a moment for her last one-on one."

"And that would be my mark to exit!" Lilliana drained her glass as her phone rang.

Allie winked at her as she headed over to her desk. "Lilliana speaking," she answered brightly.

"You are so desirable. I want you right now." Damon's voice was like black, silken sheets, smooth, sexy.

She flushed and sat on the side of her desk. "Well, hello to you to Mr Night."

"I could not take my eyes off you today."

"Oh." She almost sounded disappointed.

He chuckled deep in his throat. "Don't worry my angel, I can't take my eyes off you most days. Just, today. Well. Let's just say, I am desperate for some time alone with you."

"I know exactly how you feel." Her conversation was interrupted when Shelley raced into the office.

"Lilly, there's been an incident with Scott!" Shelley looked flustered and upset.

"Damon, I have to go." Lilliana half heard Damon's concerned voice as she hung up on him, and raced past Natalie as she followed Shelley down to Psych.

Shelley did the eye scan as quick as she could, and Lilliana signed in and followed her hurriedly down into a small room.

What she saw had her stomach falling into a pit of despair.

Scott lying on his side, fingers and toes curled up tightly on bent limbs. Expression blank, a flood of dribble flowing from the side of his mouth.

Lilliana pulled a tissue from her pocket as she quickly walked over and knelt beside Scott's face and wiped his wet lips.

She tucked the tissue back away and then slipped her fingers around Scott's.

"Scott, it's me. Lilliana. Can you hear me, baby?"

She stroked his hair, his green eyes staring into nothingness.

Lilliana stood and faced Shelley. In a low voice, she asked, "What the *hell* happened here, and who is responsible for his state?"

Shelley swallowed. Lilliana looked calm on the outside but was as mad as Shelley had ever seen her.

"Scott was being difficult. Again. He refused his bath and when Jaycee forced him in, he dragged her down and apparently tried to hold her under. Richard had security take Scott down to the reform room and issued shock treatment." She paled as she watched Lilliana's eyes widen and go very dark.

Lilliana turned her back on Shelley and bent over Scott.

Her breathing was heavy, even to her own ears. "Scott, it's going to be alright. I'm on this." She brushed her lips across his cheek, whispering close to his ear, "I'm sorry." Then turned on her heel and strode out of the room.

Shelley followed. "I'm sorry Lilliana."

"It's not your fault Shelley, but someone is going to pay for this."

She arrived at the front desk and addressed Mitch. "Where's Richard?" she snapped out shortly.

Mitch had never seen Lilliana angry. He had never known her to be rude. She was this close.

"He just went to see Damon." Mitch answered quickly.

Lilliana headed off at a pace Shelley thought impressive considering the height of her heels.

Within twenty minutes, Lilliana's temper had not receded, as she stormed into Damon's office.

He stood as soon as the door slid open revealing a wild vixen from hell.

He could almost see the steam rising from her. She was shaking with fury.

"Lilliana," he said calmly.

Richard too stood and turned to face her.

"You!" she all but spat out, "what the *hell* did you think you were doing, performing shock treatment on my brother? How dare you, you bastard!"

Damon walked around his desk towards her.

"No Damon." She stepped back. "He has gone too far this time." She glared around Damon to stare at Richard. "What have you got to say for yourself, tell me? I'd really like to know what's going to come out of that arrogant mouth of yours!" she practically screamed.

She wanted to slap him. Damon could see that clearly.

"The simple fact is, Miss Lilliana, your brother was a danger to our staff. That at least should concern you. I have told you before, he is uncooperative, doesn't eat or do as instructed. He is dangerous!"

"Oh please." Lilliana placed her hands on her hips. "You are the only one he doesn't listen to because he *hates* you You scare him, your bed manners are deplorable. Half the time I don't even know why you are still here?"

Damon ran a hand through his hair, keeping his eyes on her beautiful, furious face. He hoped he'd never see her turn those angry eyes on him. "Lilliana." he tried quietly.

Her eyes flashed to his. She was trying desperately not to cry in front of Richard, but she could feel the flood of angry tears rush up the back of her throat. She swallowed them down.

"Richard, leave us please. I want your report in one hour. Do not leave out a thing and include Jaycee's with it." Damon did not take his eyes off Lilliana as he addressed the other man in the room.

Richard left, casually, as if he was taking a stroll to a café and had all the time in the world.

Lilliana covered her face with her hands and let out a long, frustrated sigh once the door closed behind Richard, leaving them alone.

When she removed her hands, tears streaked down her face. She walked away from Damon and stood near the window, peering out towards the stables.

"Please, come and sit." Damon said, sinking down into his chair.

"No. Are you going to defend what he did?" She kept her back to him.

"No Baby, I just want you to come here."

She turned around; her arms folded tightly across her chest. "Please don't tell me he is going to get away with this? If you could see Scott right now, you would be disgusted. He has no right, *none*." She briskly wiped the tears from her face. She shook her head. "I want to protect him, help him and then, along comes Richard, and basically fries his brain."

Damon leaned back in his chair, watching her struggling with her emotions. Devastated and upset for her brother. Furious as all hell with Richard.

"Lilliana, please come here."

She pushed her hands through her hair and finally walked over to stand near him. He reached out and pulled her onto his lap and against his chest, tucking her head gently under his chin he began to stroke her hair.

"Listen, I have just told Richard he is not to go anywhere near Scott, that I am handing his case to you and Hillary. I rang Hillary just before you walked in, and she will be making sure Scott gets the best care for the next twenty-four hours, until he comes back to us. Vanessa is giving him therapeutic massage now. He will be alright Lilliana, I promise you."

She sighed against his chest, closing her eyes, tears just behind her lids.

"Today started off so well," she whispered.

His hands ran down her hair, down her back as he pulled back to kiss the top of her head.

"I know baby." He pushed her away from him gently, to cup her face, tilting her chin back, his lips came down on hers softly, offering her a moment of peace.

She kissed him back greedily; her hands crept up his chest to stroke his soft throat before reaching around his neck.

He pulled her tightly against him crushing her to his chest as he deepened the kiss.

She moaned, wanting to get as close to him as possible.

Her lips, still kissing his, she used the arms of the chair to push herself up and opening her legs, straddled him.

Her skirt rose higher, revealing firm, strong thighs, as her hand swept up underneath his shirt, the other swept down to massage his bulging erection pushing against his jeans.

"I want you right now Damon," she whispered against his mouth.

He reached around her and flicked a switch under his desk, locking all doors to his office.

He looked into her eyes, wild, weary and full of lust. Her breathing hitched, her hands reached up and she started popping buttons on her blouse and tossed it aside to reveal a pink bra that cupped her beautiful breasts like a dream. He sighed as he fell back against the chair, taking his time getting a good look.

He shook his head as her fingers went back to stroking him through his jeans.

"You are gorgeous."

She sank down and they ravished each other's mouths, wet and hungry.

His hand slipped around her back, while his other slid under her short skirt and his fingers slipped into her silk knickers.

He moaned into her mouth as he discovered how wet and ready she was. He slid a finger inside gently as his thumb started to glide over her bud, stimulating her over and over. She moved against his hand as she popped open his button, and slid down his zipper, reaching in to pull out his hot, throbbing shaft.

His tongue thrust into her mouth and she sucked it deeply, letting him know what she wanted to do to him.

She could feel the tide coming to take her, as his fingers worked their magic.

She quickly backed off him, leaving him panting, sitting there gloriously handsome.

"Lilliana?"

She sank to her knees and tugged his jeans down further. Her eyes smiled up into his, as she leant forward and her wet, sweet lips slid along and over his shaft, her hand holding him tightly.

Up and down, her tongue flicking his sensitive head.

He closed his eyes; head back against his chair, wanting to bury himself into her deeper and deeper.

His hands stroked her hair and she sucked him hard and deep.

He reached down and pulled her up before he came, he was this close.

"No you don't." He crushed her against him as he kissed her over and over.

His hand slid down and pulled her slick panties away. Gripping her hips, he moved her over him.

Her eyes widened as he slowly eased her down onto his throbbing erection, sighing as he filled her up. So tight, so wet.

His lips kissed her throat, his hands running down her back to undo her bra releasing her breasts. His lips sucked in a plump, perky nibble as she slid up, and down against him.

Her head dropped back as she rubbed herself against him, faster, harder, as the wave came close to crashing against her shore.

His hand replaced his lips, his thumb stroking her nipple, sending pulls all the way down to the pit of her stomach.

He pulled her mouth back to his, as he pumped hard, and feeling her climax, only then allowed himself to do the same.

He slipped his arms around her warm, beautiful body and continued to kiss her gently, as they both panted against the other.

Lilliana pulled back, first to kiss both of his cheeks, his lips again, then his nose, as she pushed herself off him, and tugged down her skirt.

She bent to retrieve her bra as she heard him stand and zip up his jeans.

"Where do you think you are going?" he asked.

She clipped her bra in place and turned to face him, smiling as he handed her the blouse.

"I am going to organize us to have a meal, and I would like us to eat it, peacefully, alone."

She slipped the blouse on and started to button it up as Damon reached for the phone.

"Allow me. Cook, Damon. Could you please send a tray for two to my office and a bottle of red? Thank you."

Lilliana slipped her heels off, and wandered over to the couch, she sat down tucking her legs under her as the fireplace burst into radiant flames sending a warm glow throughout the darkening room.

She felt so warm inside. A glow of happiness washed over her as she watched Damon make another call to Cam, letting him know he would be in his office with her the next few hours and could he hold off any emergencies till then.

He turned to her and was about to walk over to her when his phone rang.

He held up one finger and reached for it.

"Damon Night," he answered, then sat tapping on the glass keyboard.

She watched as he typed away, clicking on files and dealing with the situation of several more Given arriving the following day.

He must have released the door lock as it slid silently open, to allow one of the kitchen staff to roll a trolley in with covered trays and a bottle of wine, already opened to breathe.

Lilliana got up to pour as she thanked the young girl, bidding her a good night as she left.

She turned to Damon as he hung up the phone and passed him a glass.

"Cheers." She gently clicked her glass to his and took a sip.

He bent down and kissed her softly. "Cheers to you beautiful."

They sat down and had a delicious meal of spicy chicken and assorted roast vegetables with a small, warm pudding and vanilla cream.

They chatted quietly about the past few weeks, both not believing that it was only a week till Christmas.

"What do you want for Christmas Lilliana?" He finished his wine, got up taking her glass with him to the tray and poured them both another.

"That's easy. All I want is you." She smiled sweetly at him as he passed her the full glass.

He stroked her cheek. "That's already a given my darling." She shrugged and took a mouthful of the sweet, rich wine.

"What would you like?" She asked watching him, loving the way he looked so relaxed, sexy, sleepy. Just the two of them, no interruptions, a hot meal, hotter sex, and just being able to have her eyes filled with Damon.

She ran a hand through his hair and tangled her fingers in his silky, black locks.

"Just for you to answer one question."

"Oh, and what's that?"

"Finish your drink and I'll ask you," he smiled, taking her hand and kissing it.

She threw the contents back and an object hit her lips as the glass emptied.

Lilliana pulled the glass back and looked down into it.

Her breath escaped her. Her eyes landed on the most stunning, intricate ring she had ever seen.

The setting was elegant, holding a stunning emerald that wasn't too large that she would feel uncomfortable wearing it.

She tipped it out onto her palm as Damon took the glass from her.

He took the ring and wiped it on a cloth to clean any of the wine from it before holding it up between them.

"Lilliana, you are the woman of my dreams, the young girl I loved and wanted to protect, now, this incredible, stunning lady. Would you make me the happiest man alive and become my life partner? I will love, worship and protect you from all, if you will let me."

Her eyes could not move from his deep, intense blue ones.

She could feel the thrill of sublime happiness start to shake through her body.

Tears fell from her eyes before she knew they were even there.

She could not wipe the smile from her face as she launched herself into his arms.

"Yes! Yes, please!" she cried out, as his arms wrapped around her.

He laughed as she rained kisses all over his face, finally able to claim her lips with his own and ravish her with his.

"Okay then, can I please put this on you once and for all?" He took her hand as she nodded and slipped the ring over her finger. Her painted nails, looking even more elegant now with the beautiful ring on her finger.

He kissed her knuckles, collected their glasses and topped them up.

"To you my darling," he said.

"No, to us." She clinked her glass against his and drank happily.

He ran a finger across her smooth cheek and said quietly. "I will be forever sorry for the pain you suffered in the past Lilliana, but I am thankful to those evil bastards for sending you my way. Is that wrong of me?"

She shook her head. "Everything happens in life for a reason Damon. It was my path to you that I am forever grateful for." She leaned across and kissed him.

Then, as if thinking, a shadow passed over her features. She took a mouthful of wine.

"What is it Baby?" Concern filled his voice.

Lilliana sat back so she could look at him, holding her wine with two hands.

"Felicia," she said quietly.

He sighed. "What about Felicia?"

"Damon, I haven't wanted to ask you anything about your time undercover. I haven't wanted to upset you, but, I guess I have been curious about you and her."

He stood and walked over to the fireplace, setting his wine glass on the mantel. He turned to face her; his arms folded over his chest.

"What would you like to know? Ask away. Or shall I make this brief for us both?"

She nodded, not liking the way his face darkened when he spoke, his eyes looked like thunder clouds, his tone cold. She wanted to stop him right then and there, but she knew this was something that could come between them and she desperately wanted to hear this from him. For closure.

"Undercover is like nothing you'll ever know. It is dark, depressing, desperately hard work and often despicable. My time with that woman is something I still see Clair about, for two hours twice a week, to try to deal with. Whenever I had to touch her, be intimate with her, I was sick. But each minute, hour, week, month and year bought me closer and closer to the end of the mission. That's what it was all about for me." He ran a hand through his hair. "Leaving in the first place was imperative. I was trying to protect you, from me. The things I could have done to you Lilliana."

She didn't think his eyes could darken any more. They did as his mind wandered back to their first kiss, when he first put his hands on her young body.

"Don't," she sighed, leaning back into the couch, crossing her legs, "don't do that to yourself. If you recall correctly, I wanted you more than you wanted me. You did nothing wrong and I was not a child."

"Yes well, that's debatable. Let's just say, I left when I had to. The mission saved you from me and helped me save thousands. It was

what it was. Johnson let me know this morning, before I came to see you on set, that the Officials had finally annulled my marriage to that woman. I knew then, I had to put that ring on your finger ASAP."

She sipped her wine.

"Are we finished with this now?" His gaze not moving from her face.

She looked down into her glass. She didn't know if she could look him in the eyes and see the pain there when she asked her next question.

He knelt in front of her and gently pushed her chin up with a long, strong finger. "Lilliana?"

"The baby?" she whispered.

"Ah yes. The Baby," he said quietly. He was wondering when she was going to bring this one up. "What would you like to know?"

"Why did you have it aborted Damon." Her eyes met his.

"That's simple darling. Firstly, its mother was a drug user, and she had injected the drugs, that would have created a drug-blood baby. Its life would have been filled with pain. Secondly, it did have a blood line that was evil for over three generations and thirdly, I don't think I could have handled seeing it every day for the rest of its life, and not be reminded of my darkest time with its mother."

He pushed himself up and walked back to the fire to collect his wine.

He kept his back to her. "Disappointed?" He wouldn't blame her if she was. They were mostly selfish reasons.

"No," she said quietly behind him, wrapping her arms around his waist, kissing his back through his thin shirt, feeling his warmth as she laid her cheek against him. "I didn't want to upset you. I watched your files. I know it all, everything you went through. I'm proud of you and I love you. No matter what."

He turned around so he could look down at her. His strong arms coming around her as her head tipped back to look up at him. "You don't know it all my darling. You never will."

She felt hurt and went to pull back, but his arms stayed firmly about her as he watched the hurt flicker across her face.

"Not because I don't trust you, it's because you have been through so much, and I will never take you down that dark, disgusting path of memories. What I have just shared with you, knowing you watched my interrogation is hard enough for me. Do you understand?"

She nodded slowly. "Of course," she whispered, "Thank you for sharing that with me. I do know how hard it is to share certain information."

She smiled up at him as he gave a quiet laugh. Knowing full well what she meant, as she had never been good as a sharer of her thoughts and feelings when she had first started her group therapy as a new Given.

He kissed her nose as his phone started to ring, and let her go, to answer it.

She ran a hand through her hair, exhausted by the whirlwind of emotions this day had brought.

Once he had hung up the phone he asked her if she would be a darling and run down to the kitchen to get another bottle of wine.

"Sure, anything else?"

He smiled, as he shook his head, picking up the phone he waited for the door to close before he quickly made a few phone calls.

When Lilliana returned fifteen minutes later, after having a laugh with Christopher in the kitchen, Damon's office had a very serious looking Johnson and five of his men standing around it.

Lilliana spotted her heels over by Damon's desk, and he smiled at her, as he saw the embarrassment flood across her face.

He bent and scooped them up and walked across to her holding them out. She smiled and took them, surprised as he leaned down and kissed her softly in front of all the men.

She caught Johnson's smile out of the corner of her eye as she bent to pop her heels on.

"It looks like I am going to be caught up here for the rest of the night Lilliana. Sorry."

"No, that's fine. I'll see you in the morning?"

"Yes, Tim will be here around ten, so sleep well."

"Good night." she called to them all, as she headed out of the room.

A chorus of good nights followed her as she left, filled with peace and contentment, that all was how it should be.

CHAPTER 18

Lilliana headed up the stairs to her room carrying the bottle of wine she had collected from the kitchen, feeling afloat with happiness. Engaged. To Damon Night!

As she approached her room she found Fox, Jessica, Allie and Josephine leaning against the wall chatting quietly.

Lilliana laughed, so happy to see her friends. "My god it is so good to see you all! What are you doing here?"

"Thought we'd come for a visit honey," Fox said sounding sly.

Lilliana hugged them all and then flicked her switch for the door to open.

Stepping into her room she noticed how bare and fresh it was.

No sheets on the bed, only pillows, her photo frames were missing.

She stepped into her small walk-in robe. All her clothes were gone.

She turned around to face her friends.

"What the...?" Allie raised an eyebrow.

Josephine walked over to the window seat and picked up a note, her gaze scanned the contents before handing it over to Lilliana.

'My room.' was all it read, in Damon's handwriting.

All the girls read it over her shoulder. "Well, let's go then." Jessica turned and headed up the stairs, very excited as she had never been beyond the H.B.R. level.

All the girls, bar Josephine, were very curious about Damon's quarters.

Once they arrived at the top, Lilliana noticed Damon's security code pad was gone, in its place, was a security scanner, like the one Cam and Josephine had for their room. She stood in front of it, and the door immediately opened.

Stepping into the room, her breath caught in her throat at the sight before her.

The room was a flood of white and bright emerald roses in all sized vases on the floors, adorning the mantel of the fireplace, desk and bookcase.

On the coffee table in the centre of the lounge was a feast of assorted entrees, prawns and dipping sauces, sushi, and fruits, and a beautiful basket full of the finest chocolates.

Sweet champagne chilling in ice buckets.

"Well, this looks like fun girls." Fox strolled over to the champagne and began filling crystal glasses with the sparkling liquid, handing them to the others, as they walked in and got comfortable.

Jessica was having a good look around. She could not believe she was in Damon's domain. Now she knew how Lilliana had felt that time she had tried to describe her feelings after her first visit up here.

"This is cosy," Josephine said, popping a chocolate mini cake into her mouth. "What's the occasion I wonder?"

Lilliana sipped the sweet bubbles, as she walked over to the mantel, running her fingers gently over the rose petals.

Rupert and his team must have been very busy indeed getting all this together.

Her eyes rested on the mantels assorted pictures, and smiled, seeing her four photographs from her old room, sitting amongst Damon's.

The one of the very first picture she had taken when she had arrived at main house as a teenager. Her sixteenth birthday, sitting in the middle of a smiley young Jessica and Josephine.

Another one of her and Allie, proudly sitting on their beautiful horses.

She loved the one of herself and Josephine on set, wearing designer dresses, surrounded by fifty silver doves, both laughing their heads off.

And her favourite, of her and Damon, which Cam had gifted to her when Damon had left to go undercover.

She sighed happily. So many memories over the past nine years.

And now here she was, a ring on her finger from the man she wanted to be with forever. Surrounded by the most amazing friends a girl could ask for. How did she get so lucky?

She turned around to face her friends. They were all chatting happily about this, that and the other. Sipping champagne, nibbling on the treats left for them.

Josephine's eyes met Lilliana's. She smiled. "What's up girl?"

Lilliana simply held up her ring finger and laughed as Jessica squealed in excitement and launched herself over to hug her and snatch up her hand to inspect the ring.

"Oh my stars, it is the colour of your eyes! It is beautiful!" Jessica exclaimed.

Fox got up and strolled over. "Congratulations." She kissed Lillian's cheek.

"It's about time." Allie smiled.

Josephine hugged Lilliana. "Hello sister," she chuckled.

"Hello."

"This is cause for celebration, and thank Christ Damon had the good sense to supply plenty of alcohol!" Fox grabbed a bottle and topped them all up again.

"Here's to you Lilliana and that bloody sexy man of yours, Cheers!"

Lilliana laughed along with her friends as they clinked their glasses together and swallowed down the delicious liquid.

Lilliana's head was feeling nice and fuzzy as she had started on the wine earlier. She was grateful she didn't have too much of an early start with Tim.

Fox was strolling down the length of the room, inspecting Damon's views, furniture, and all his belongings in the bookcase. "Does this man have good taste or what? I want to check out the rest, do you mind

Lilly?"

"Go right ahead." She watched in amusement as Jessica scrambled up and followed Fox into the bedroom area.

Allie too, after winking cheekily, whispered, "Let's check out the devil's domain."

Josephine pulled Lilliana up off the couch and they followed the girls down the corridor and into the large bedroom area.

Fox was lying prettily on the bed stroking the covers. "It's a good work-out table!" She wiggled her eyebrows before sliding off and walked into the bathroom.

She spotted the deep spa and cried out in delight, "I want one, now. Can we please, Lilly?"

Lilliana laughed as she bent to flick the switch on. When did Fox ever plead?

The water gushed up through the jets, sending hot, therapeutic water to the top. She popped it on a high setting as she turned to watch Fox strip naked. Allie and Josephine doing the same.

Jessica shrugged and yanked off her jeans.

"I'll get more drinks," Fox said strolling out into the lounge, naked.

"And if Damon comes in?" Jessica called out.

Lilliana laughed. "I wouldn't know. Be happily surprised I guess." She too stripped off and stepped into the soothing water.

Fox returned with three bottles and stood gloriously naked her eyes on Jessica as she removed the last stitching of clothing.

"Oh my, but you are gorgeous." Fox stared openly. "Why have you never done a shoot before?"

Jessica smiled and stepped down into the water. "Who knows?"

"Mm." Fox raised her eyebrows and shook her head. "Have to do something about that." She placed the bottles on the floor where they could reach them easily, and stepped into the water, sitting between Lilliana and Allie.

Happy conversations and catch ups filled in an hour as the soothing waters flowed around them.

"What happened with Scott?" Allie asked.

Lilliana sighed, "Richard happened to Scott."

"That man just needs a good fuck in my opinion," Fox said draining her glass. "I mean he is not entirely bad looking."

Lilliana and Allie exchanged a look before they burst out laughing. "Oh please!" Lilliana said, choking on her champagne, "Would you volunteer for that service?"

Fox shrugged, "For the right price. I would do anything sugar."

Lilliana shuddered, "Unfortunately I do believe you."

"The man needs shock treatment himself," Allie said after Lilliana had filled them in on the sorry saga.

"Amen to that." Jessica agreed.

"I noticed you did very well ignoring Natalie this morning Lilliana," Fox smiled.

"It was either ignore her or deck her. After what she has put me through lately," she tapped her glass against Allie's, "I am very, very happy you are back in our office."

"As am I my friend. My god, but the day to day happenings the past few months. Unbelievable!"

"And Christmas next week." Jessica poured champagne. "Where has this year gone?"

"It's gone fast," Josephine said.

"I bet Christopher is happy to have his Allie Cat home" Fox said.

Allie smiled at Fox. "But of course."

"I saw Eric rushing downstairs earlier. He looked very serious." Jessica sighed leaning back into the jet so it could massage her back. "He has grown up into a hottie!" Josephine smiled appreciatively.

"That he has," Lilliana agreed. She let Fox describe in detail to Jessica and Allie, the set from this morning, and closed her eyes, happy to listen to the chatter around her as the champagne's bubbles put her into a sleepy haze.

***

It was eight the following morning, when Damon stood in his room, staring down at the three beautiful naked bodies in his bed.

He ran his hand through his hair; grateful he had a few hours sleep in his office, as it looked like joining Lilliana was out of the question.

She was in the middle of Fox and Josephine. The quilt tangled around the three of them, yet not helping hide an inch of what should have been hidden.

He reached down to the end of the bed and pulled the sheet right up to cover them all.

He walked into his bathroom, locking the door, shaking his head.

Naked women everywhere first thing in the morning!

He had already placed two mink blankets over Allie and Jessica who had greeted him with their nakedness as he had stepped into his rooms.

He knew for a fact; sweet young Jessica would have died of embarrassment with the thought of him seeing her so exposed.

After a five minute, extremely hot shower, he dressed, poured coffee and sat at his desk, ordering a breakfast trolley up for the girls, then made a few business calls, quietly so as not to wake the sleeping beauties on the couch.

He hung up the phone, sipping his coffee as he watched Jessica sit up and stretch her long, limber body awake.

She froze like a deer in the headlights as her eyes connected with his.

"Good morning Jessica. Sleep well?"

She blushed, looking down at the mink blanket she knew wasn't on her and Allie last night, or in fact, early this morning.

She pulled it up to her chin. "Yes, thank you Sir."

He smiled. "Why don't you go have a shower, breakfast will be here soon. Would you like Orlando to join us?"

"That would be lovely," she said standing, slightly mortified, pulling the mink around her tightly as she quickly walked towards the bathroom.

Damon chuckled to himself as he organized to have Orlando and Christopher join them. Cam was arriving soon, so a good start to the day.

Once all had arisen, showered, and said good morning, an hour later they were finishing up breakfast, laughing and talking about the night before, sharing their stories with the men.

Lilliana was tucked against Damon's side whilst they sat together sipping their hot tea and coffee.

Orlando was talking quietly to Jessica in the corner. They both looked relaxed and happy.

Lilliana thought Damon was so thoughtful inviting her friends' partners for breakfast, so they could all be together.

"Thanks for breakfast Damon," Orlando said, leaning down to kiss Lilliana's cheek. "Congratulations." He smiled into her eyes.

"Thank you Orlando." She watched as he left the room, to turn her attention to Christopher and Cam as they were laughing their heads off about one of the latest Chefs who set the kitchen ablaze.

Fox lazily got up, stretched, and smiled at Lilliana. "Do you need my assistance this morning with Tim?"

"I don't think so. It's going to be a quick shoot. Just a few natural close-ups, nice and simple." Lilliana thanked her.

"Nothing about your face is simple my dear. I'll see you later." She waved to them all as she left the room.

Jessica and Allie got up next, along with Christopher. "Time to get back to it."

"We have seven evaluations around eleven Lilly, do you think you'll be able to make it?"

"Absolutely, this shoot will only take an hour, I'll be there." Lilliana got up and walked them to the door.

Damon joined them. "I guess we can all go down, make a start."

He put his arm around Lilliana's waist and kissed her neck. "Come my darling."

They walked down the stairs to a very busy morning of Given bustling here and there. Quiet chatter and noisy laughter filled the hallways as most had finished breakfast and were making their way to classes, jogging groups, or work.

Lilliana was so happy to be a part of it.

***

Within forty minutes Tim had finished Lilliana's campaign shoot.

They were both very happy with the outcome.

Damon was leaning against the far wall of his office, hands in his pockets as he watched Tim show her a few of the shots he had taken, as he was explaining how he would put this new photograph in the back ground of the very first one which had made her famous in the outside world and had given her, her Dark Angel name.

Together, he said, would be a perfect ad. To give all the lost children a sign of hope.

"I love it, thank you, Tim."

"You are so welcome. Happy Damon?" He turned to the man; whose opinion meant the world to him.

"How could I not be, you are the best." He pushed off the wall to take Lilliana's face into his hands and bent to kiss her softly.

She smiled as he leaned back.

"Off you go to Allie. I'll sort out the campaign with Tim. It will be spectacular."

"Thank you Damon." She kissed him quickly, said bye to Tim and dashed out to make it on time to start evaluations with her friend.

***

Half an hour in and Lilliana felt as if her heart would break for a handful of new Given who had been brought in.

Three girls who had their vaginas sewn up, all thirteen years of age. One of them arrived with blood flowing from the sloppy stitches.

Rachael was furious and Dr Ryan had to take the gentle Nurse aside and calm her down.

"Bloody Bastards!" Rachael said quietly to Lilliana as she started to remove the stitches.

Lilliana agreed, staying calm, sending positive energy as she stroked the hair off the young girl's face, relieved she was unconscious thanks to the knock-out serum.

Leon walked in after finishing with the other girls.

"Lilliana," he said in way of greeting.

"Hi Leon."

"Allie needs you in room seventy-three."

"Okay. Call me if you need me Rachael." Lilliana left to find Allie, who was dealing with four young men aged sixteen to twenty-one.

They had to call for assistance and Lilliana was grateful Richard did not enter the room.

Hillary and two older male Given, who were in training to become

Watchers, came to assist.

It was good to have their strength and presence as Allie, Lilliana and Hillary, dealt with the angry difficult men.

It was an exhausting, emotionally draining few hours, and when Allie and Lilliana collapsed on their office couch, they both had sheens of sweat on their brows.

Lilliana got up and poured them cold water, handing one to Allie, she gulped hers down and poured another.

Allie shook her head. "There really are some sick fucks out there. It constantly blows me away. It shouldn't after what we see and hear day to day. But it still does."

"I know." Lilliana removed her white jacket covered in bits of blood and human matter and flung it down the wash chute, as she turned, Allie had removed hers and thrown it across to Lilliana who caught it and deposited it with hers.

Allie ran her fingers through her blue lengths of hair. "I need to do a bit of self-care and get Rupert to make me another of his natural concoctions. You know he makes my dye using blue petals. Interesting hey?"

"Anything Rupert mentions is interesting, and yes, you need to do something nice for you Allie. Why don't you head up to Fox, get a massage as well?"

"Sounds like a plan actually."

Lilliana checked the time and headed for the door. "I'm going to check on Scott."

"Okay, I'll see you later." Allie called after her.

Lilliana headed down the corridor, did the eye scan and signed in, noticing Mitch watch her.

"Sorry about yesterday Mitch." She had the decency to look embarrassed.

"Nah Lilliana, don't stress about it, I understand. Scott's been moved to room fifty-one. He's doing fine, I've been told."

"Good, good. Is Jaycee around today?" She was hoping to sort out the whole bath ordeal.

"Nope, she's coming in tonight."

"Okay, thanks Mitch."

"No problem." He watched her neat backside head off, wishing more of the staff down here had a backside like hers.

Lilliana entered Scott's room. It was the white room. Everything was thickly padded so he couldn't harm himself. The mirrored window was high enough that he couldn't smash himself against it, if that were his intention.

He sat, his back to her, sketching on a very small shelf attached to the wall.

"Hello Scott," she said quietly so as not to startle him.

He turned slowly to face her. She was shocked at the coolness in his eyes.

His fingertips covered in white chalk. "Lilliana."

She walked over toward him and sat close on the narrow cot.

She smiled a little. "How are you?"

"How do you think I am?" his green eyes held a flash of anger.

"I'm so sorry Scott," Lilliana shook her head; she ran a hand over the back of her neck, "Damon has ordered Richard not to come near you. I promise you; he will never hurt you again."

He ran the piece of chalk along his fingertips like someone would a coin. Back and forward.

"He zapped me Lilliana, like a poor, defenceless animal. Over and over. It hurt!" He slammed his hand down hard on the desk, smashing the chalk to dust, before dropping his head into his hands, close to tears.

Lilliana knelt slowly down in front of him, placing her hands on his knees. Tears clogged her own throat, but she swallowed them down.

"I'm sorry if you feel I've let you down, my darling, I truly am. I'm so furious that this happened."

He moved his hand to look down at her, dropping it down on top of hers, and squeezed lightly.

"I know you are," he said quietly, "I'm sorry if you feel like I'm blaming you. I just hate being here so much, I just want to die!"

"Don't talk like that. Listen, I am going to get you out of here. I will speak to Cam again today about you getting out tomorrow for some fresh air, and maybe I can appoint you a Watcher? If I can, and you aren't a danger to yourself or anyone around you, it will be easier for me to help you."

He nodded, his eyes staring into hers. "I hate that Doctor so much."

"It's alright. He's not coming anywhere near you. Scott, I just need to ask you one thing." She was hesitant, not wanting to hurt him further. "Did you try to drown Jaycee?"

He frowned and slowly leaned down, putting his handsome, angry face inches from hers, whispered heatedly, "No I bloody well did not." He leaned back.

She sighed. "Okay, I believe you." She stood and bent to kiss his cheek.

"I'm going to talk to Cam, and I will see you outside in the morning. Alright?"

He looked up at her as she rose. "Thank you."

"Don't thank me. Just eat, sleep and I will see you tomorrow."

"Until then," he said as he watched her walk out the door.

***

Lilliana found Eric, who seemed distracted and on his way back to a meeting he had been in with Damon for the past hour. She asked him if he had any spare slots available to have another Given under his watch. He said perhaps, if he and another Watcher, Alan, shared duties. She thought that was a good place to start for Scott, and thanked Eric before he hastily turned and strode hurriedly off. She hoped he was okay and went in search of Cam.

Thirty minutes later, she wandered out to the H.D, finding it more busy than usual, as a cargo plane was scheduled to come in first thing the next morning for a pickup. Crates were everywhere stacked high with colourful vegetables, fresh flowers, small trees and shrubs, compost and potting mix and many cartons full of seeds.

"Busy day?" Lilliana hugged Rupert as he stretched his arms out in greeting.

"Sure has been. Flat out and loving it. Are you looking for Jose?"

"No, Cam actually."

"He's in the coop." The H.D people referred to the poultry farm, as, the coop.

She glanced down at her heels. "Okay."

"Hang on a tick." He vanished behind the front door and came back holding a large pair of blue boots. "That should do the trick." He passed them to her.

"Fantastic, thank you." She slipped off her heels and popped her feet into the large boots. "Perfect, I'll see you soon." Carrying her heels, she left Rupert, who saluted her, before turning his attention to some of his precious cargo.

She enjoyed the walk around to the coop. It was such a balmy afternoon.

The scent of Rupert's amazing blooms filled her nostrils as she breathed in the fresh, perfumed air. She glanced across the field towards the stables as she could hear horses whinnying and galloping about their paddocks.

She smiled at the sight and lifted her face toward the sun as it was dropping lower in the sky. She loved this time of day.

She heard Cam before she saw him. Surrounded by fifty Given, explaining the extensions he wanted done within the coop.

"We want to expand the inner house and we are putting in three extra ponds and a separate environment for the turkeys." he smiled as he saw Lilliana, all prettied up in her sexy little blue dress and big gumboots.

"Excuse me." he headed across to her. "Hello darling, what can I do for you?"

"Cam, I really do need a huge favour. I am desperate to get Scott out first thing in the morning, he is in a bit of a state. He needs fresh air, exercise and a completely different environment. Please say we can get him out?"

He watched her eyes become soft as she pleaded for her brother. "My sweet soon-to-be sister. You never need to plead with me. Anything I can do, I will. That's a promise. If he is no risk to himself or anyone else, I can't see it being a problem."

She smiled up at him and touched his arm. "I suggested to Eric that maybe he could be his Watcher?"

"Shouldn't be a problem."

"Thank you Cam."

"You are welcome." He smiled. "Now, I must get back to these young things." He was about to turn away when young Haley came running towards them.

"Mr Night Sir, I have a message for you and Miss Lilliana. You are to go to Black Ops to see Johnson in an hour's time." She was out of breath.

"Thanks Haley, catch your breath, then get ready for dinner," Cam smiled kindly at her.

"I wonder what that's all about," Lilliana watched Haley walk off.

Cam walked backwards whilst watching her. "Guess we'll find out in an hour."

Lilliana headed off to return the gumboots and have a hot shower and a quick bite to eat before she had to find out. Hoping to the stars above it was nothing bad.

CHAPTER 19

Johnson's office was busy by the time Lilliana arrived.

Johnson, Cam, Brett and Damon were in quite a deep conversation as Lilliana took a seat up the back. She waved to Josephine who was sitting close to Cam. She waved back, her usual smile not reaching her eyes.

There were twenty people in the room, all talking quietly in hushed tones.

Brian, one of the kitchen staff, had been admitted into the Black Ops unit to serve light refreshments. Lilliana thanked him as he passed her a Mint and Lavender tea. Taking a mouthful, she glanced around the room noting who was here, and in on, this strange, out of the ordinary, meeting. There were plenty of faces she did not recognize.

Her eyes met Eric's; he was sitting up the front and seemed quite serious and forced a quick smile in her direction before turning his attention back to something Marcus was saying. Fox sat on his other side.

"Hey, you," Allie sat down next to Lilliana. "Do we know what this is all about?"

"I have no idea. But from the looks on their faces," she indicated to the men up the front, "I can't imagine it being happy news."

"Alright everyone," Johnson addressed the small assembly, "thank you for coming. We'll get this meeting started. Unfortunately, we have a situation involving Ex-Diplomat, Gregory Reid, that requires our immediate attention." Johnson reached behind him and picked up his coffee, nodding to Damon.

Damon stepped forward, clearing his throat. "We have an opportunity to put a team together that will help intercept Reid and infiltrate his organization. To do this convincingly we require the help of one man in particular."

Damon's eyes met Lilliana's across the room. She was sipping on her tea, looking wary and only a little interested in this speech. As yet, it had no impact on her. Unfortunately, it soon would.

Allie whispered to Lilliana. "The creep's father?" Lilliana nodded her eyes on Damon's face.

"We will be using David Reid for this operation." Damon paused as a gasp arose from a handful of people in the room, including Lilliana, who tried not to spit the tea out of her mouth as she choked.

"How can that be Damon," Clair called out, "he is a seriously damaged, dangerous man."

"Please, I just need everyone to keep an open mind in regard to what we are about to tell you." Damon folded his arms across his chest. "We have been working with an undercover unit that has affiliated with a few of Reid's people for two years now. These men have gathered useful Intel and have penetrated four locations of Reid's during that time, which of course has not shut him, or his illegal activities down, but has indeed damaged his inner circle of trust and bled him out of a few million.

Our goal is to make direct contact with Reid and shut him and his sector down for good. We believe the only one who can get us that close to him is his son, David Reid."

Johnson stepped forward taking over the next section. He nodded to eight men in the front row, along with Marcus and Eric.

Lilliana placed her empty cup under her chair and folded her arms, feeling a little uncomfortable seeing Eric up there with a group of strangers.

"You all know Eric and Marcus of course. Let me introduce you to our hardworking undercover team, Rocco, Max, Lincoln, Desmond, William, Ryder, Daniel and Rodney." Johnson indicated to each man as he spoke.

The men nodded to the group as they were introduced. All tall, well-built men, with serious expressions on their faces.

They looked like they would not put up with any bullshit whatsoever.

Allie whispered to Lilliana. "Cute for sure, but what has this to do with us?"

"God only knows," Lilliana whispered back nervously, as all the eight men's eyes were focused straight at her. "That Rocco looks like he could be Marcus's brother," Lilliana whispered to Allie.

"I was just about to say the same thing," her friend agreed.

Cam stepped forward as Johnson finished his introductions. "Gregory Reid has threatened chemical warfare on this establishment if we do not release his son, along with Lilliana."

Cam nodded to the men. "We have it on very good authority that this attack is planned for Christmas Eve. We are evacuating Lilliana, with her own security," Cam indicated to Marcus and Eric, "and will be taking David Reid with us to allow him to make contact, in order to prevent any such attack on this facility. We have a plan in order, and it will be executed in twenty-four hours."

Allie's arm went around Lilliana's shoulder as her friend was breathing quickly and shallowly, her face drained of blood.

Damon walked towards her, gently placing his hand on her neck before forcing her head down between her knees to hopefully prevent her from fainting.

She waited a handful of breaths before nodding her head. "I'm okay."

She sat up, taking a deep breath and looked up at Damon, Allie still rubbing her back.

He ran a hand over her hair before walking back up the front.

"Um, are we allowed to interrupt with, what the HELL?" Allie cried out.

"Yes you may," Cam nodded.

"Well, what the HELL? What, you're just going to take Lilliana and a psychopath out of here, and what then, what happens out there, and how do you intend to keep Lilliana safe?"

"I agree." Josephine stood, "If Lilliana goes, I go."

"Me too." Allie stood. "She is not leaving without a friend to help her through this."

"Ladies, please!" Damon held up his hands. "We will protect Lilliana, and she will not be without a friend. Your safety is important to us, and we are not letting you leave this facility. We are hoping that this case will take no longer than several weeks. Like I said our undercover team has been in play for quite some time now and we are at the end of it. You being out there with Lilliana will only make more work for our team and they will need all their focus on the mission itself."

Allie slowly sat back down, folding her arms unhappily.

"The fact is Lilliana has started her own campaign to assist the less fortunate children outside our walls. So, although it will appear to Reid senior that we are complying with his wishes, it will also be as if she is embarking in the next phase of her campaign. We have already sent that story out with our operatives." Damon ran a hand through his hair, his eyes returning to Lilliana's face. Her colour had still not returned, her green eyes standing out against her paleness.

Lilliana's mind was in complete disarray. She had a thousand questions, but no strength to ask them. What was Damon asking her to do?

Her eyes landed on Eric, then across to the eight undercover men.

"Lilliana. We don't have a lot of time, but you will be prepped on the jet out of here. In the meantime, put all your business in order, say your farewells as you will be leaving here in twenty-four hours." Johnson stated.

Lilliana could not even acknowledge him, simply sat, staring.

Johnson turned to address the men up the front, along with Marcus and Eric.

Damon walked over to Lilliana and held out his hand. She placed hers in his, comforted by his warmth. He tugged her up and led her from the room.

Cam and Josephine approached Allie and said a few words. Together, with Fox following, they left the room.

***

Once Lilliana and Damon stepped into his rooms he pulled her into his arms and held her close. His chin rested on top of her head. Her arms slowly went around his waist and she pushed her face into his chest blocking out everything but the warm scent of him.

A few minutes later a knock sounded, and Cam, Josephine, Allie, Fox, Jessica, Christopher and Orlando entered.

Everyone seated themselves around the large room. Damon lit the fire and soon flame shadows flickered everywhere, adding cheer to the cheerless atmosphere.

Josephine started making teas and coffees as two kitchen members carried in trays of sandwiches, biscuits and slice.

Cam quickly filled the others in, who had not been at the meeting, on all the to-do's. Jessica looking very unhappy.

"What are you thinking Tiger Lilly?" Cam asked, before taking a mouthful of slice.

Lilliana was watching her fingers, twined with Damon's, resting on his lap. His thumb gently stroking her wrist, back and forth, offering her that one small comfort.

"I think if I have to leave here for a while to protect our people, then I know it's something I need to do. Without question. As long as my people have full care here. And Scott," she looked across at Cam, "you promised me he would be out in the fresh air tomorrow."

"And so he shall be love, first thing, with you," he smiled kindly.

Josephine wrapped her arms around his waist. "Why can't Allie or I go with Lilly out there? We could pose as her make-up artists or something like that. She cannot go alone." She implored Cam, then Damon.

"She won't be," Fox said quietly, "I'm going with her. The world knows us both, so it will look like we are just doing extra modelling to benefit Lilliana's Dark Angel Campaign."

Jessica nodded, "But what about your safety?"

"That's where Marcus and Eric come into play. Both are trained martial artists and kick boxers and have also been training with the

Black Ops Marines unit. Thankfully it was something they were both contemplating for their advanced careers before this case came upon us, so they are both qualified. The fact that they both adore Lilliana made them want to take this case. She will not be alone." Damon kissed the top of Lilliana's head.

"Well, what about David Reid?" Lilliana pushed herself up off the couch and walked to the fireplace. Standing with her back to the flames, she faced her loved ones.

Damon bent forward, his elbows on his knees, looking Lilliana straight in the eye. "He will be no danger to you. Those men back there are the best at what they do. David will be watched every second of every minute he is out of this establishment. Plus, right at this moment, an explosive camera and audio are being implanted in his eye socket, thanks to the skilful hands of Dr Ryan and his team."

A knock sounded. Damon stood, glancing at the time. "Come in Richard."

Richard entered with a small silver tray in his hands. He walked to the coffee table and placed it down. He pulled a pair of clear rubber gloves out of his white lab coat and started snapping them on. "Who's first?" he asked Damon, peering over his horn-rimmed glasses.

"Fox." Damon smiled over at the tall red-haired beauty.

"What's this?" Fox strolled over to Richard, hands on hips.

"It's a small tracking device that will be injected under your skin so if you go off radar we can locate you," Cam supplied, stroking Josephine's back up and down. He knew how upset his wife was, not being able to help her friend.

But there was no way he was letting her anywhere near the danger that sweet Lilliana may possibly find herself in.

Richard picked up a long, slim needle and took Fox's wrist. Supporting her arm, he inserted the needle deep into her arm and injected the tiny tracking device.

"Christ!" Fox hissed in pain. "Shit! Sorry, that hurt."

"No need to apologize dear," Richard smiled at her. He always thought she was one sexy little minx.

She rubbed her arm, stepping back and went to sit near Jessica.

"So," Orlando started, "Can they be traced underground, underwater and the likes?"

"Hopefully. We've been told it is the most recent development in tracers. All our team has them inserted." Damon reached for his coffee.

Richard turned to Lilliana holding out his hand. She stepped toward him not able to meet his eyes, and was surprised when he gently took her arm, pulling her closer.

Her eyes met his as he swabbed her arm with the cool anaesthetic before sliding the needle deeply into her arm.

Her quick intake of breath indicated the pain she felt but said nothing.

"Good luck dear," he said quietly before stepping away. She nodded, placing her fingers where the tracking device had been injected. She rubbed it gently, her eyes searching for Damon. He stood and walked over to her, pulling her back into the safety of his arms.

She swallowed a lump of tears down and pushed her face into him.

To say she was frightened was an understatement. But, she would not be alone. She could do this. It was not forever. She took a deep breath and looked up at Damon, forcing a small smile. "All for the greater good," she whispered.

He bent and dropped a sweet kiss upon her lips. "Yes my darling. All for the greater good."

"I want to go." Allie stepped out of Christopher's arms. "I can do this and keep out of harm's way. I can help protect Lilliana. Hell, Fox doesn't even know any martial arts. Christopher has trained me fully in Wing Chun. I can take you two down in a second to prove it," she pointed to Cam, then Damon.

Damon chuckled. "We don't doubt you Allie. But the team will have quite enough to do with Reid and the girls here."

"I don't want you to come Allie. The thought of anything happening to you, any of you, just about kills me. Having Fox in harm's way is bad enough." Lilliana slipped out of Damon's arms and walked over to Allie taking her hands. "At least my mind will rest easy, knowing our patients have you, my brother, will have you."

"He'll have me and Jess too, Lilliana," Orlando said firmly. Jessica nodded in agreement.

Josephine and Allie shared a look. Cam sighed, shaking his head at Damon. They knew the girls would not let this go easily.

"Shall I get the others now?" Richard asked, collecting his tray.

"No Richard, please tell Johnson I'd like everybody assembled in the east garden at midnight. He knows who and why."

"Yes Sir." Richard quickly left.

"What's happening at midnight?" Allie asked.

"Well, as it's my birthday today, and we are all embarking on a challenging mission tomorrow, I am hoping that Lilliana will marry me this night." Damon looked across at Lilliana, who was still holding Allie's hands.

"Oh Damon, yes, of course I will!" She squeezed Allie's hands and quickly walked over to Damon, throwing herself into his open arms and kissing him solidly.

He kissed her back, stroking her length of silky hair.

"Well, it's nice to have some good news, finally!" Josephine sniffed back a tear.

Jessica wiped her eyes on a tissue Orlando handed her.

Allie leaned her face into Christopher's chest. Feeling a wave of emotions overwhelm her, and let her tears flow uninterrupted by any tissue or shirt.

"Alright then. If this is going to be a rushed ceremony Damon, I need you to leave. You also gentlemen!" Fox took command of the room.

"What can you possibly organize in two hours Foxy?" Cam wanted to know.

"Ah, you men know nothing of a woman's pleasure," Fox shook her head.

"I beg to differ," Josephine smiled up at Cam.

"Out so I can get the bride-to-be and her girls respectable." Fox sensed that Lilliana would need something a little special for a rushed ceremony.

Damon whispered into Lilliana's ear, "I know this is hard baby. But we will have a few hours after to talk. Okay?"

She tiptoed up and pushed her lips against his. Pouring her love into that one kiss. "It's alright," she whispered. "It's going to be alright." She may be feeling ridiculously overwhelmed, but she could fake a calm façade, to put Damon at ease. He deserved that much after everything he had done for others.

He smiled down at her and left the room, followed by Cam, Orlando and Christopher, all chatting quietly on their way out.

Fox turned to face the girls. "Right. Well. This may not be what we were all hoping for, for Damon and Lilliana's special moment, but I do believe in making the most out of any situation. So, let's get started."

In a matter of minutes Fox had put on some happy, relaxing music.

Rachael, Hillary, Shelley, Rupert, Luke and Lisa and Jaycee, were all asked to join them for drinks.

The extra people helped raise a merry atmosphere within the room.

Fox had returned from her room with armloads of dresses. She took Lilliana and Jessica into the bedroom.

Josephine passed Lilliana a glass of wine and kissed her cheek before going out to chat with the others.

"Thank you Fox," Lilliana said, taking a mouthful of wine.

"For what?" Fox had several dresses spread out along the bed, waiting for Lilliana to choose one.

Lilliana placed her wine down as Jessica gushed over a beautiful white gown, with a see-through silver silk over the top of it. "Stunning," she whispered.

"For this." She pointed to the dresses. "For coming with me on the outside. For always having my back."

Fox walked over to Lilliana and placed her hands on her shoulders. "It is completely my pleasure. We're family, aren't we? Hopefully we will make it back in one piece. But until then, let's make the most out of next few hours shall we."

Lilliana smiled and nodded before glancing over to what Jessica was making a fuss over.

The dress was simply beautiful. With thin straps and floating layers of silk falling to the ground. The front dipped elegantly, lined with intricate patterns that looked very similar, to the eternity symbol her friends, and herself wore on their bracelets. The white glowed softly through the silver layer of silk which floated along the top layers.

It looked like a dress a fairy queen would wear. Sexy, simple, stunning.

"That's the one," Lilliana nodded.

"Excellent, put it on love, then hair and makeup." Fox took the wine Lilliana had placed down and finished it in one gulp. "I needed that."

Twenty minutes later Lilliana entered the lounge room after Fox had styled her hair into soft waves falling down her back and her face made up naturally with simple shades that made her look stunningly elegant.

Everyone fell quiet when she stepped into the room, her high heels gently tapping against the floorboards.

"You look amazing Lilliana." Rupert's mouth was hanging open.

"Doesn't she always?" Luke smiled, shutting Rupert's mouth for him, making the others laugh.

Rachael walked over and handed Lilliana a glass of white wine. "Beautiful," she said quietly, before kissing her cheek.

"Thanks Rachael." Lilliana smiled around the room. Looking at these people who were such a special part of her day to day life, she could feel her throat clog with emotion, with the thought of not seeing them every day, let alone the unknown she was heading into. She forced the lump down, thinking of leaving Damon, and focused on the here and now.

"You are all here because I love you. I respect you and have enjoyed either working with you, or simply having you as part of my family. I know how blessed I have been in coming here and having all of you in my life. So, I say thank you. And wish you all nothing but the best." She raised her glass high with everyone in the room as they saluted each other.

Draining their glasses, Josephine and Rupert went around the room, topping everyone's up again.

A knock at the door an hour later had Fox opening it to a very dashing Cam, all dressed up in a dark suit of Steel blue. He smelled divine also.

"Hello poppets. I'm here to escort this beautiful lady downstairs to the garden. If the rest of you would like to find your partners and head off, we will see you shortly." He smiled around the room, winking at Josephine.

She walked over and kissed him. "See you down there my love." She turned to Lilliana and hugged her. "See you soon, sister."

"Thanks Josephine."

Everyone dropped a kiss on Lilliana's cheek as they disappeared out the door, leaving her alone with a glass of wine and Cam.

The door sliding shut as Cams' hands slid into his pockets. "How are you, Beautiful?"

Lilliana laughed, shakily. "Is that a trick question?"

"You're the expert, you figure it out." He walked over to her and placed a hand on her shoulder. "You look delectable. You have made Damon a very happy man."

She tipped her wine down her throat, placing the empty glass on the table. "Well, he makes me very happy. I almost don't see the point of this, if I'm going off-site tomorrow."

"The point is, you should have done this weeks ago, but circumstances wouldn't permit it. They do now, and life's too short. So, you will go down there, make your promises to each other. Love each other for a few special hours and then we will all put into play our actions in putting this evil bastard away. Together. Teamwork, okay?" He stroked her cheek.

"Well, when you say it like that," she tiptoed up and kissed his cheek. "Shall we?"

He offered her his arm and together walked down the stairs towards the man who Lilliana did not want to be parted from, ever.

CHAPTER 20

Cam kept a firm arm for Lilliana to keep a hold of as they walked towards the man of her dreams. Stepping out, and around the path to the east garden, Lilliana's breath caught in her throat.

The path had been lit with fairy lights, casting a glow on the sweet lily of the valley bushes that Josephine and Rupert's team grew so well.

The white flowers stood out prettily amongst the deep green leaves, scenting the air, with the wisteria that hung above them along the long archway leading toward the end of the path, where an arched pavilion stood surrounded by the sweet scent of roses. The night sky scattered with stars; the moon full.

Lilliana spotted Damon surrounded by two hundred of their close friends, and work colleagues, their family. The majority of Given, had been left to sleep this night away, undisturbed by the events of this night and the coming day.

When she saw the figure of her brother standing beside Damon, her heart beat happily.

Scott, tall and proud, smiling down towards his sister. He was dressed in a suit which fitted nicely, obviously one of Cams. He looked well despite his thinness.

Lilliana smiled up at Cam. "Scott's here."

"But of course Angel. He's your brother. Damon arranged it. He has his own Watcher and will be sleeping in main house tonight and from now on." Cam squeezed her arm gently.

Lilliana felt her love for Damon, double with Cam's words. The thought that he would do anything to make her happy. That he knew Scott's happiness, was her happiness.

Lilliana smiled at all her friends, as Cam placed her hands in Damon's before kissing her cheek and going to stand by Josephine.

They did not take their eyes off each other, as Johnson guided them through their promise of love and commitment, to respect and protect each other, from this day forward.

When Johnson finished, he stepped back and all applauded as they kissed. Holding each other with such love. Damon's hands swept over her neck as he pulled her closer, deepening the kiss as cheers and shouts of congratulations rang in their ears.

Once they drew apart to smile at each other, hands tugged them apart for kisses and best wishes.

Scott wrapped his arms around his sister, whispering over and over, "Thank you, thank you, thank you!"

She hugged him tightly and kissed his cheek. "Just eat, and stay out of trouble my brother, that is all the thanks I need."

"I promise," he nodded, as Josephine pulled her away from him, and together with Jessica, Allie and Fox, they had a group hug, filled with laughter.

And for the next four hours in the largest common room, they celebrated together, dancing, eating, and making the most of their time together, before Damon took Lilliana upstairs.

***

Once the door shut behind them Damon pulled off his jacket and unbuttoned his shirt. Tossing it on the couch, he turned around and swooping Lilliana up into his arms walked into the bathroom.

She laughed, running her hands down his sculptured chest. "You have plenty of energy for four in the morning."

He kissed her quickly before placing her on the ground, then bent to fill the tub.

"When a man has the most beautiful woman in the world for his bride, he has plenty of energy." He turned to face her. Gently reaching out, he slipped the gown from her shoulders, and then scooped it up, crossing over to toss it over a chair in the bedroom.

She stood there, in matching underwear and a very sexy garter belt.

"That's one thing I love about Fox," he said appreciatively as he returned to stroke a finger along her bra line on her soft, smooth breast, "her attention to detail."

The spa filled, and shut itself off, leaving a light mist to fill the room around them. With Lilliana's exhaustion, and emotional day, it made her feel like she was in a dream. And opposite her, running his fingers over her flesh, sending shivers along every inch of her skin, was a dark angel with deep blue, intense eyes, focusing on her and her alone.

She slowly pulled in a deep breath and stepped toward him so there was nothing between them. Her hands slid up his chest along his throat to stroke the back of his neck. Her fingers curled in his silky hair. Her heels giving her the extra height.

His fingers unzipped his suit pants and briefs. They dropped to the ground and he kicked them aside to disappear in the mist.

His fingers gently drew patterns on her back as he unclipped her bra. He tossed that to, in the direction of his pants.

Her breasts, jutting up, rubbed his chest, leaving them both breathless in anticipation. His arms pulled her slowly against his body as his head dipped to find her warm open mouth. The kiss jolted them both, and what he wanted to start slow and smooth, become hot and electrifying. Lilliana sank into him, her tongue searching for his, and finding it, did a mating ritual of its own.

Her hands slipped to his shoulders, and she leapt up, winding her firm legs around his hips.

He moaned into her mouth as he felt how wet and ready she was as her warm core rubbed against his stomach. He swung them around and headed into the bedroom. Dropping her down, he fell on top of her, his mouth connecting with hers as he ran his hands up and down her soft flesh.

She kissed him with everything she had, needing him right this second.

"Now Damon, I need you right now." she whispered frantically in his ear as his lips slid down her throat.

He tore the silk slip nestling between her legs, away. His fingers slid gently inside, rubbing her, making sure she was as ready as he was.

"Lilliana," he sighed her name, staring into her deep liquid green eyes, he slid inside her core.

Lilliana sighed, stroking his back, his neck, before pulling him down for a deep, long kiss. Their lips did not part as they sent each other on a journey of slippery strokes, silky glides, and intense orgasms which sent them reeling into euphoria.

They lay in each other's arms and tangled legs for a few minutes. Their breathing the only sound in the room. Damon leaned up on his elbows, his hands cradling Lilliana's head. He smiled down at her. "My wife." He sounded proud and in love.

Her hand slid along his smooth back. "My husband." She stretched her head up for a kiss, which he happily indulged in.

He pulled her up, and together they walked into the bathroom and sank into the hot water. Damon grabbed a sponge and herbal soap and started to wash Lilliana's back, as she did her face. Once they were clean and relaxed in the water, they dried off, slipped on robes and went to bed with tea and lemon.

A few minutes after Lilliana had finished her tea she lay across Damon's lap to look up into his face so they could talk about the coming hours.

He stroked her hair as he looked down at her face. "Talk to me baby. What's going on in that bright brain of yours?"

"Everything. Absolutely everything. Thank you so much for enabling Scott to be here in main house, and for having him at our wedding. He looked so happy and is so excited about joining in all the activities and classes."

"It's a big step. Hopefully he is ready for it. I've had a chat to him and together, with everyone's help, we can make this work for him." He ran a finger along her jaw line, before stroking her hair again.

"How safe is it going to be with David Reid?"

"Very. We have the best team that will be with you at all times. The microscopic microphone that's been inserted in his eye, will pick up any conversation he will have, along with the camera device that's been injected into his pupil. He can still see clearly out of that eye. And, so shall we. Everything he sees, the team will see. Along with the small explosive that can blow his head off if he steps out of line."

Lilliana nodded. "And so, Fox and I will carry on getting started on my publicity for my Dark Angel campaign. Of course, with the media, I assume Reid Senior will see that I am out of this facility?"

"We are making David initiate contact with his father and have a plan in place that will put you and he on friendly terms, thus eliminating any hostile forces with our team and his. Once contact has been made, and the location pinpointed, we will move in and shut him down." He bent his head down and dropped a kiss on her brow.

"It sounds so simple. Too simple." she reached up a hand to run along his jaw. Touching him while she could, was a priority.

"All plans need to sound simple in order to activate them. Complicated complicates."

Lilliana raised an eyebrow laughing softly. "Complicated complicates? Haven't heard that before."

"Yeah well, it was something our mother used to say to us." He shrugged a shoulder.

"No, I like it. I may have to use it," she smiled up at him.

"Please, go ahead."

"I'm worried about David. What if he tries something?"

"Like what?"

"Oh, I don't know, say, tries to kill Fox, me, anyone before you press the magic button that can blow his head off?"

"Lilliana, he is not going to get near you alone. Eric will be stuck on you like a burr. Trust me, both he and Marcus know what's at stake here. Eric was looking for undercover. When he heard about this mission he pleaded for it. He has phenomenal security tactics and has the highest-grade score Johnson has seen in fifteen years. Even Marcus blows us away with his skills. Do not fret love. You will never be unprotected or at risk."

Lilliana smiled. "Well, we both know that last one is a bit of a white lie. As soon as I leave this establishment Damon, I'm going to be at risk," she rushed on as she could see his upset features, "and I'm going to be fine. I'm simply saying anything can happen out there. Food poisoning, car accident, stray bullet."

"Are you trying to send me insane before you leave?" he asked drily.

"No my love, just pointing out some facts. You have done everything you can to ensure my safety. I'm just saying. If anything happens to me, I don't want you to feel guilty."

Damon pulled her up into his arms and buried his face into her soft neck. Arms wrapped tightly around her. "Don't talk like that. I can't think of anything happening to you without going insane. You'll come back to me Lilliana. You have to."

Her arms reached around his neck, as he pulled her back down to slip under the covers with him. He kissed her gently until she fell asleep, hoping to give her a handful of hours sleep before her jet came to take her away.

***

Scott and Lilliana were strolling in the garden. Scott's Watcher, Alan, was walking ten paces behind. Ever alert. A tall, blonde man. He was once one of the world's best UFC fighters.

The day was overcast with a slight breeze yet was muggy enough for Lilliana to have slipped on a cool, white cotton dress and flat sandals.

Scott came to a stop in front of a large water fountain, with fish swimming amongst the water flowers, colours of pinks and soft butter cup yellows.

Lilliana sank down on one of the stone seats, carved with horses on the sides.

She reached up and slipped her hand it into Scott's.

He turned his head down and smiled at her. "So, you should be back in less than a month?"

"I certainly hope so," she sighed, looking back at the fish. "I should be that busy, that time will fly. At least that's what I'm counting on."

"It's so good to be outside." He squeezed her hand before releasing it and strolled over to the other side of the fountain. Lilliana got up and followed him as they turned and walked back to the house.

"I'll miss you," he said quietly.

"And I you, but you'll be alright Scott. You've met all my friends and they will be here for you." She thought back to brunch. Damon had organized for a full breakfast to be served in their rooms and had the whole gang join them for Lilliana's last breakfast. It gave Scott a chance to meet Lilliana's friends, who would be here to support him while she was gone. He'd had a few laughs with Christopher and Orlando. And he and Jessica hit it off immediately with their love of drawing and art. Jessica had already made the decision that he would be the perfect partner for her art classes.

Damon too, after seeing Scott's drawings and recognising his talent, had decided that he would join the art team, in depicting a new Givens' story when they first entered this establishment.

"There you are," Damon looked down the steps where Lilliana and Scott were walking up. Lilliana smiled up at him as she quickly ran up the steps to take his hand and kiss his cheek.

He ran his free hand up and down her arm, lightly kissing her lips.

An aircraft could be heard approaching, in the distance.

"Not long now," she whispered to him, her stomach a frenzy of unhappy butterflies.

He leaned his forehead against hers, in constant wonder how she just cruised along and dealt with whatever situation was thrown her way. His brave Lilliana.

"Come along Scott, let's get you to your exercise class." Alan nodded to Damon.

"Sweet," Scott smiled. "Time to build these baby's back up!" He rubbed his biceps and grinned at Lilliana. "You won't recognize me when you get back sis, I'll be buff."

Lilliana reached up and ruffled his hair. "I'll look forward to seeing that!"

He winked at her and headed in beside Alan. "Bye Lilly."

"Bye Scott!" she called after him, looking up at Damon.

He put his arm around her waist and led her into his office.

It was full of the team that would be flying out with Lilliana, plus staff members who wanted to say farewell.

Jessica and Allie were sniffing into tissues. Josephine still looked unhappy that she was not allowed to go along with her friend.

Lilliana walked over to them and gave them each a big hug. "Don't cry," she whispered to them all, barely keeping it together herself. "I couldn't bear to leave with you crying. It's going to be hard enough getting on that plane."

"Yes, you're right, sorry Lilly, no more tears." Allie forced a beautiful smile.

Jessica hugged her hard, before stepping back. "If you see Stephan, send him my love."

"I am sure to Jessica. Fingers crossed." she looked at Josephine. "You take care my sister. It won't be long, and I'll be back." She forced a smile and swallowed the lump of tears which threatened to rise.

Josephine couldn't stop the tears that spilled. But she smiled through them. "I'll stay out of trouble till you return home to us."

"That's all I can hope for." They smiled at each other.

Lilliana turned to watch Eric, Marcus and Fox, say farewell to their nearest and dearest. She took a deep breath and went forward to say farewell to Leon, Rachael, Dr Ryan, Hillary and Clair. Among many other faces she had grown to love and respect over the years. It was a difficult few minutes with everyone forcing a cheer they did not completely feel. Understandably so.

Lilliana stepped into Damon's arms and buried her face into his chest, squeezing him firmly around his waist. She took the deepest breath she could. Breathing him in as if to take his scent with her.

"I love you," she said into his chest, her words muffled.

His hands came up to gently take her face. He smiled into her eyes. "I love you beautiful. You won't be out of my mind for a split second."

"Same," she smiled, and stretched up, with the room full of people, kissed him like there was no tomorrow. He happily returned her kisses.

"Time to go people!" Johnson called out. The room fell silent instantly.

Damon took Lilliana's hand and led her outside to the Hummer that waited at the bottom of the pavement. Their luggage had already been taken to the airstrip. Now the Hummer waited for its passengers to take them to the jet.

Cam, Lilliana and Damon, Fox, Marcus, Eric and Unit Eight, all stepped into the large vehicle after kisses of farewell were exchanged.

Lilliana kept her eyes on her friends' faces, her hand raised, until the Hummer sped away, removing their beloved faces from her view.

After five minutes the Hummer pulled up alongside the air strip. The jet was large and black, sleek looking in appearance, with red lettering that stated, *The Given*, on both sides.

Unit Eight stepped out, saluting Damon and Johnson farewell before boarding.

Cam and Damon exchanged a few words, shook hands, then hugged and Cam turned and jogged up the jet's steps.

Fox and Marcus said goodbye to Damon, after Fox promised she would look after Lilliana. He took her hands, kissed her goodbye and told her to look after herself.

Eric and Damon shook hands and Eric left to stand at the bottom of the boarding steps, waiting for Lilliana. It was his duty, from here on out, not to let her out of his sight. No matter what.

Alone, staring into each other's eyes, Lilliana could not help the one tear that escaped. Damon bent down slowly and kissed it off her soft cheek. "I'll miss you baby. Be safe, be smart and make the most of your campaign. I will be right here, waiting for your safe return." He pressed his lips to hers.

She wrapped her arms around his neck, kissing him back. "I'll be back before you know it. I love you. Look after my girls."

"Always. Goodbye my love."

"Goodbye Damon." She pressed her lips to his quickly, before spinning on her heel and ran towards the jet. Eric took her elbow and gently led her up the steps.

Once the door closed and Lilliana took her seat, she glanced down at Damon. Hands in his pockets, a serious look on his handsome face. He held up a hand in farewell. She returned it, allowing her tears to fall freely down her face thinking he couldn't see them from where he stood.

He could, and it nearly destroyed him as there was nothing he could do.

It took seconds for the jet to speed across the tarmac, and up into the sky. Seconds for the view of her loves face to disappear from her sight.

Lilliana felt betrayed by the loud sob that escaped her, and quickly took a deep breath trying to get a grip on her jagged emotions. Turning in her seat she took stock of her surroundings, wiping any stray tears away and found Eric's steady eyes watching her.

"Are you alright?"

"I will be," she said simply, leaning back into her seat, she glanced down at the beautiful ring Damon had gifted her with. She let her head fall back against the head rest, and with the picture of his loving face in her mind, closed her eyes and shut out the rest of the world for a few minutes to gather her thoughts on where the next few weeks may take her.

Away from her friends and the only home she had known for almost ten years, and away from the man who had been a part of her heart and soul.

She felt the seat next to hers get plonked in. She turned her eyes to Fox's.

"Hey you!" Fox stretched out, lifting her glass in a salute. "Here's to our next exciting episode."

Lilliana smiled. "I'm glad I have you here, I wouldn't feel as brave if you weren't here with me."

"Ditto love. Now close those pretty green eyes of yours. You look like a train wreck, and let's face it, there is going to be plenty of cameras snapping the famous Dark Angel, when we get off this thing. So, get your beauty rest darling."

"Thanks for your honesty, I can always count on you," Lilliana sighed and closed her eyes.

"Sure thing sugar." Fox smiled and slipped over to chat to Marcus and his brother Rocco.

With their quiet chatter, Lilliana sank back into her chair, feeling

Eric's eyes on her the entire time. Her mind drifted to Damon and how she would make him proud with all she would endeavour to do once they hit the ground in the outside world.

Cam sat down beside her and took her hand. He stroked her knuckles affectionately. "It's all going to work out Lilly. Go to sleep love. I'll wake you before we land." He let go her hand and settled back into his seat. He nodded to Eric, feeling relieved with the fact that they had a brilliant security team with them. In the coming hours they were going to need them.

"Thank you Cam," she said quietly. "It's so good to have you with us. I know how much you'll miss Josephine. You are a good man."

He smiled at her and watched as her eyes closed and she drifted off to a light sleep.

It would be the last decent handful of hours she would have in the months to come.

About the author

Mickey Martin feels blessed to live in the pretty seaside town of Frankston in Victoria, with the love of her life Jade, and their two gorgeous boys Jesse and Zane.

Mickey is a lover of animals and nature and believes in the healing power they bring to our souls. She relishes time spent in her garden with her birds and cats whilst conjuring up worlds full of colourful characters who have travelled and battled the darker paths, hopefully, to lighter days ahead.

Her writing is raw, emotional, compelling and can at times be confronting. She writes passionately about love and the world we live in today, because of it and to escape, and is currently writing the third book of The Given Trilogy, The Guardian.

Mickey Martin also writes Non-Fiction under her married name, Michelle Weitering, where she writes to make a difference. Through her writing, she becomes a voice for those living and dealing with issues such as anxiety, bullying, school refusal, and discrimination and invites the reader to question what more they can do to make our world a better place.

Michelle has raised funds for Ireland's INSPIRE, and Australia's HEADSPACE, and plans on doing more fundraising in the future, to continue raising awareness on Mental Health, and supporting those she can.

Her family memoir, Thirteen and Underwater, exposes the struggle of anxiety through her family's journey with this increasingly prevalent disorder that wreaks havoc on millions of individuals worldwide. Told with brutal honesty and a good dose of humour Thirteen and Underwater is being well received by many.

Mickey is a member of Peninsula Writers Club (PWC) and loves the camaraderie and support of fellow writers. Mickey has been featured in publications such as YMAG and MORNINGTON PENINSULA MAGAZINE.

Connect with Michelle on
Email: mickeyslba@hotmail.com
Instagram: www.instagram.com/mickeymartinbooks
Website: www.mickeymartinauthor

www.ingramcontent.com/pod-product-compliance
Lightning Source LLC
Chambersburg PA
CBHW020550120726
47903CB00001B/209